Love
IN THE
DARKNESS

RIAN MCMURTRY

Copyright © 2020 by Rian McMurtry.

All rights reserved. No part of this publication may be reproduced, distributed, or transmitted in any form or by any means, including photocopying, recording, or other electronic or mechanical methods, without the prior written permission of the copyright owner and the publisher, except in the case of brief quotations embodied in critical reviews and certain other noncommercial uses permitted by copyright law. For permission requests, write to the publisher, addressed "Attention: Permissions Coordinator," at the address below.

This is a work of fiction. Names, characters, places and incidents either are the product of the author's imagination or are used fictitiously, and any resemblance to any actual persons, living or dead, events, or locales is entirely coincidental.

ARPress
45 Dan Road Suite 5
Canton MA 02021

Hotline: 1(800) 220-7660
Fax: 1(855) 752-6001

Ordering Information:
Quantity sales. Special discounts are available on quantity purchases by corporations, associations, and others. For details, contact the publisher at the address above.

Printed in the United States of America.

ISBN-13:   Paperback   979-8-89676-216-4
                Hardcover   979-8-89676-217-1
                eBook   979-8-89676-218-8

Library of Congress Control Number: 2024925139

DEDICATION

For Angela and long cold nights with the ESL pups

Chapter

1

The auditorium was packed for the Junior Class Presidential Debate. Okay, Julian Kanekawa thought, they were required to be here. He smiled at his classmates, letting his gaze rest on his girlfriend, Jennifer O'Neill, in the front row. The slightly built redhead was an almost deliberate contrast to his own massive frame—he was well over six feet and heavily built, while she barely topped five; his Hawaiian heritage gave him dark skin and hair compared to her redhead's pale complexion—but they'd been going out since June. She was sitting with her friends, although she was the only one of them paying any attention to him. The other ten were debating something on their tablets, and doing it rapidly in some foreign language. He wasn't sure which one; they knew several, and had a liking for obscure ones. He thought they were debating in Nahuatl, the Aztec language, although it could just as easily be Gaelic or Phoenician. Maybe all three; he'd seen them do that before too, all of them speaking a different language but understanding each other perfectly well! He'd occasionally made his own comments in Hawaiian, but Jenny was the only other to have picked up much beyond 'aloha' and 'mahalo'.

He'd started to join their study groups last year, and had gotten to know them quite a bit better when he'd hooked up with Jennifer. They were brilliant, wrecking the curves in all their classes. Studying with them had produced immediate benefits to his own grade point average, even when they lapsed into an incomprehensible language. He was sure one of them would end up valedictorian, but which one was an open question. They might even decide it by an internal vote. Jennifer, he was proud to say, had a good shot at it.

He didn't actually mind that they were so absorbed, though. He was confident of their votes; Jennifer had told him they were sure ones. After two years of representing the class on student council, Patricia Guccione was his only opposition. Patti was loud, abrasive, hyper religious. No one much liked her, even the other Young Republicans; most of them thought she gave them a bad name. Why she seemed so confident of her victory he didn't know, since even her prayers at the flagpole were poorly attended. Most of the Christian students who wanted to do Christian religious stuff before school joined Jennifer's friend Teddy Pope in the outdoor auditorium. They quoted Teddy more than the bible. Teddy opened morning services by quoting a passage from Matthew that said not to pray in public, so he included a different verse and they discussed it.

While he was going over his notes again, Shevaun Lone Elk came up to him, her black hair in long braids down her back. She wore a jacket from the Standing Rock Reservation, where her family was from, and a t-shirt from her father's show that hardly disguised her hourglass figure. Her father was a popular actor on the sci-fi show "New Worlds", which filmed in the Bay Area. "Hey, Shevaun. You running for VP?"

"Yeah. I've got four opponents to your one, so we'll probably need a runoff. I figure veep'll look good on a college application."

"Yeah, that's what my grandmother keeps telling me."

Joy Ning came up to them. She'd dyed her hair yellow and purple—the school colors and wore a San Francisco Sirens azure and argent sweatshirt with her jeans. "Hey guys. Can I count on you? I'm going for treasurer." She was a clarinet player in the band and pretty popular.

"Sure, Joy, if I can count on yours," Shevaun said equably. She gestured at a group of students sitting together. "I've got the Round

Table sewn up, at least, or so they tell me. But I'm not really sure about anyone else."

"You do? Damn, I wish I did. They can swing a lot of the school. How much did they back you?" Joy said

"Just their votes. I've been studying with them quite a bit ever since freshman year, so we're friends."

"At least they're not backing you with celebrity endorsements and money!"

"I thought it'd be overkill for a student council election. I got out posters and a commercial on the school video channel. But I don't need them for celebrity endorsements. Dad volunteered to be in the commercial—in costume, filmed on the bridge set, no less!—and I didn't let him," Shevaun said.

"She has a point, though," Julian said. "I flew down to San Diego with Jenny and her parents just before school started so they could take a look at the promotional material for the Witches…"

"Why'd she go with "Witches"? I thought she got on well with the Wiccans," she said with a nod to a small group of kids.

"She does. She even has a local high priestess from the San Diego area as her team chaplain. As for picking the name, it was something about "strong women standing on their own as a team" being inspirational. She offered to change the name if the San Diego covens found it offensive, but they gave their blessing."

"Ah, okay. What were you saying?"

"She didn't quite offer to put the ad people to making the posters for this, but Seth and Bridget introduced me to the Valkyries and Unicorns when they faced each other at the Magic Bowl. They DID offer to help." Julian was still not sure how it had happened, but the Wizards of the Round Table, his fellow students, owned the California Women's Football League—however quiet they were about it to the public. The league's popularity was still exploding.

"Really? Cool," Joy said. "Did they ever tell you why named the championship 'the Magic Bowl'?"

"Not me," Julian replied. "I keep forgetting to ask."

"So do I," Shevaun said.

"Well, I'm curious. I guess I'll ask Dawn myself. 'Scuse me, I need to go get some more votes."

Joy smiled at them and walked over to Teddy Pope's Christian Student Ministry. They were looking a little lost with Teddy talking animatedly with the rest of the Round Table. For that matter—he'd never really noticed it before—the kids in the Round Table had more groups intersecting with them. The football players radiated off from Alex, Angela, and Dani; the cheerleaders were clustered with Karen. The swim team with Malcolm, the orchestra with Keisha. The Greens were near Bridget. The Goths gathered somewhere close to Seth. Astronomy club president Dawn presided over her group. Solly was near the Computer and Future Doctors clubs. Amazing how one group of friends could impact so much of the school. What were they arguing about, anyway?

"The elements are all wrong for a reliable biosphere, Alex. We need to adjust a few of them, and for that we need Angela," Bridget Sullivan said in Nahuatl, which Dani could at least follow. She tapped her pad to show the figures in a chart, relying on Alex Menendez's adjusted senses to read it properly. She was wearing an emerald green dress over a white T-shirt and a simple strand of seashells and dried nuts for jewelry, and as usual not a hint of make-up. The redhead's simple ponytail hung down her back without fuss.

"If you say so, Bridget," Alex replied. "We need to release a lot of nitrogen?" Alex Menendez was a big sixteen-year-old, already over six feet tall. He wore a purple and yellow Thunderbolts jersey over his blue jeans and a simple gold chain around his neck, a gift from his linebacker girlfriend Danielle. The big blonde, easily his equal in height, was running her hand over his black crew-cut—everyone knew he was headed to one of the military academies—as she chatted in English with the rest of the football team. She was the only player on the team with permission to tackle him during practice. The rest of the team was listening to their captain instruct them on a play she'd come up with.

"MAKE a lot of nitrogen. The atmosphere is over ninety-six percent carbon dioxide. That gives us a lot of carbon and oxygen, but we need more nitrogen for a solid biosphere," Dawn Takugawa said. She was a tall girl with her mother's red hair, currently in a French braid. Her bright yellow and red Hollywood Starlets t-shirt contrasted with her brown slacks. "If we do it, it'll take years and the atmosphere will be fighting us the whole way, even with us splitting the molecules. But if Angela's really involved, she can turn a lot of it into nitrogen."

"Me and Bridget. We want an Earth-normal atmosphere?"

"Probably higher carbon dioxide and water vapor content," Malcolm Muir said. His long hair was sun bleached and streaked with green from chlorine, as befitted the star of the swim team. "Not much higher, but it'll make the atmospheric changes a bit easier, I think."

"Maybe lower, actually," Bridget responded. "We'll be getting more intense sunlight from the closer orbit."

"Hey, I want to hear Emily and Hunter on the secretary vote," Keisha Johnson said. She was of medium height, an athletic five six, although her Afro added a couple inches. Her orange shirt from Zimbabwe—new this year—contrasted with her rich, deeply dark skin. She was toying with a magnifying glass pendant her boyfriend, Mike Wu, had given her for joining the school paper before his death. He wasn't dead anymore, but that fact was a secret. They hadn't let him leave Venus since.

"So listen to them. We're the only people who'd understand Nahuatl anyway," Angela Fujiwara said. Angela was five ten, heavily muscled, and played wide receiver on the football team. She'd cut her black hair to shoulder length this year. Well, cut wasn't the word—a shapeshifter didn't need to bother—but that's how she was wearing it. Her boyfriend, Dave Clebourne, was over with the rest of the football team listening to Dani since he couldn't understand the Nahuatl.

"I should cast in Swahili just to confuse you."

Angela had turned to her apprentice, Karen MacLeod. "Hadn't thought Keisha would object to spending time on Venus." Karen was wearing a sari in MacLeod tartan she'd gotten from her Indian cousins with her thick black hair in a braid.

"Lass, they're in love. That's something to celebrate, not give them crap about." She was a cheerleader whose features owed more to India than the Scottish ancestor who'd brought a bride back from Delhi.

"Giving them crap is so much more fun, though," Bridget said with a grin. "Wouldn't you agree, Seth?" She put her arm around the Goth boy sitting on the outside of the group, almost snuggling up to him, and gave him a squeeze. The two of them were in many ways as opposite as life and death, but they were very close. He shrugged.

"I've never been in their situation, so I wouldn't know which of you is correct," Seth Dupree answered her. He was tall and heavy, pale with black hair and eyeliner. Bridget poked him in the stomach. He twitched. "What's the next extinction you want me to reverse?"

"How about some of those Hawaiian birds?" Jennifer suggested, her eyes still fixed on Julian.

"Some of those might work," Solly Levison said. "I was reading that many are still in the "thought to be extinct" category, so Seth could bring them back and I'll get them breeding like crazy, as long as Bridget improves the environment for them."

"I'm a little more inclined to let the island extinctions be for now. There wasn't much habitat to begin with, there's a lot less left and the introduced species are still there. Resurrecting them might not really work."

"Back to Venus. We're going to need a lot of hydrogen too. And have you done the calculations to speed up the rotation?" Angela asked.

Julian had started his speech by now. Keisha and Jennifer paid attention to him, but no one else in the group was doing so. Julian was good at it, with a rich, deep, inspiring voice. He'd have made a great king, if he could actually take the throne.

"Yeah, we have. Check my numbers?" Alex said, clicking a send to everyone's tablet.

"You guys do know it's rude and irresponsible to ignore the campaign speeches?" Keisha said.

"No one in their right mind is voting for Patti," Malcolm said. "Julian doesn't mind as long as Jenny's paying attention."

"They are so into each other," Karen said happily.

"That's a problem," Solly said.

"Yeah, it is. We need to talk to her about it," Dawn said.

"Why?" Karen asked. "I think it's great."

"She's supposed to be keeping an eye on a possible wizard," Seth reminded her. "Julian's got just as much potential as any of the rest of us. Maybe we should go ahead and bring him and Shevaun into the fold?"

"Not yet," Alex said. "We discussed this in July. Karen fully trained first, then we bring them in. Shouldn't be too long. January, maybe. If we're going to have two people learning, we need the back up."

"A romance between two of us is a very bad idea, Karen. Breakups can be bad enough, but if someone broke, say, Seth's heart, there could literally be a body count, and only his restraint would keep it down," Bridget said. Karen drew back a bit from him. They'd never been involved, but Seth's crush on her wasn't a secret—and even though it would never be proven in court, he'd already killed a lot of people.

"Do you have to keep using me as the threat?"

"You're the one easiest to visualize," she replied in an innocent tone.

"After Alex's little thunderstorm last year?"

"Yeppers!" Bridget grinned at him. Karen caught the buzz of telepathic communication between them, a legacy of the bond from when he'd brought her back to life. Bridget chuckled, put a hand on his arm, and squeezed lightly. She winked at Karen.

"We can work on that later. I downloaded all their speeches and sent it to everyone last week," Solly said. "Didn't you get your copy, Keisha?"

"How'd you do that?" Karen asked. "Shevaun wrote her speech in Lit this morning! I know, I watched her!"

"We do have certain advantages. I read their minds and got what they were thinking about saying," he answered.

"You didn't read Patti's," Angela pointed out.

"Why bother? We heard it last year. And the year before. I haven't heard a new idea out of her in the last two years, half of what she wants to do is outright illegal—for someone who brings up the Constitution every other sentence, she obviously flunked Civics—and most of the rest are bad ideas. I mean, corporate sponsorship for school dances? Fuck that. If there's a money issue we'll step in."

"How's that any different?" Karen wanted to know.

"If we step up, we're not going to insist on splashing the league logos everywhere. We'll fix it with our own money, not the teams' funds."

"By the way, anything on the helmet front?"

"Solly, Dani, and I went by the factory. The pads and helmets are all up to our level of snuff. No concussions for our players," Alex said. "If you notice something substandard, here's the spell." The procedure appeared on their tablets.

"So that's why Dani has a new helmet."

"No, we do the school helmets every July. The bigger danger is someone bringing in their lucky helmet from home and us not realizing it."

"Someone will notice your girls not being hurt," Dani pointed out haltingly.

Teddy shrugged. "We know. But we have the power to prevent it; it would be reprehensible not to. So we credit the coaches and luck and don't tell the media the gear's enchanted to make concussions impossible. We started including as much of the county's gear as possible this July, too, and we've been working on how to do it for everyone who plays the game. Best bet right now is to introduce a better design with better materials and make it mandatory."

"What was that about it being reprehensible not to?" Karen asked.

Dawn sighed. "Ideally, the requirements would already be in place. We can force it. For our league, we do, on our responsibility. The vote on that was unanimous. We're a lot less united on what to do about everyone else. We could force the others. That's true. Where does our responsibility to act on our own end and respect for others take precedence? We're advocating better measures in Congress, the Legislature, before the Canadian Parliament…"

"Whether I go to West Point or Annapolis I'll try to push the academies. They, at least, have a vested interest in their graduates being fully healthy on graduation."

"L'obligation Divine?"

"Something like that."

A buzzer sounded, indicating Patti's time was up. She kept going until Ms. Lee came up and told her to sit down, loudly enough for the whole auditorium to hear. Laughter swept the assembled students, but Patti seemed immune to shame. She sat down with an imperious tilt to her head. The vice presidential candidates spoke next, and the Round Table quieted down.

The results stunned everyone. Patti Guccione had somehow won class president. Shevaun had won vice president, but Patti's friends Owen Ballard and Elizabeth Wang filled treasurer and secretary. Several recounts gave the same results. Keisha put it as a front-page story in the *Thunderbolt*. Alex called a meeting at the Temple for that night, and Mike sat in with them.

Chapter

2

It was a glorious Saturday in late August, the hills golden brown broken up by the deep green of oak trees. The creek ran along the main roadway and meandered up into the older housing, but down in the bed it was possible to ignore the houses and the unsettling results of that election. Angela remembered the bus crash that landed her, Seth, and Alex down here. It had been her initiation into the magical world when she'd died and Seth had decided not to let that stand.

"So how was the wizard's council?" Dave asked Angela as they hiked along Miller Creek. There wasn't much water in the creek, mostly rocks and the smells of vegetation.

"A little acrimonious. I have a vote now, Dave, but Hades argued that you dead would neatly solve the problems you pose. The master of necromancy still doesn't like you at all, and he does have support from the people who don't want anyone who's not one of us to know, although they'd settle for a mind wipe. They don't trust you. You might want to find an alternative way to describe us, because it increases their distrust."

"Any suggestions?"

"Nothing that indicates you know or suspect who or what we are," she responded. She briefly bit her lip. "Dave, I love you. The other wizards don't. And while only one of them hates you, most of the others don't particularly like you, either. It's not even that they trust his opinion of you more than mine. They just think he's more likely to see flaws and dangers you represent than I am. Since the defenses of the common areas were done by all of us, all of us need to agree before we bring someone to Mars."

"I thought you guys had a place on Venus, too."

"We do. But there's a secret stashed on Venus, beyond the mere base. If they don't trust you enough to let you know who they are—and they don't—they sure as hell aren't going to trust you with any other secrets."

"Oh, come on. I know they're…"

"Stop right there Dave," she put a finger to his lip. "Suspicion is one thing, knowledge is another. They'll live with suspicion. Boyfriends and girlfriends are going to suspect. Claiming knowledge triggers harsher measures to make sure we can't be betrayed, like putting in a geas to prevent you from ever mentioning it. Hades and Lucifer have the votes for that. I don't know I'd oppose them on that vote. But we have let a couple of people in. You, however, still need to prove yourself."

"How the hell am I supposed to prove myself to these guys when you won't even confirm who they are?" His frustration was palpable in his grumbling.

She smiled. "Simple. Assume we're watching you. We can be watching you whenever we wish."

"That's your idea of simple, is it? You're friends with Santa?" His eyes suddenly widened. "Are they watching now?"

"We are, yes." She grinned at his shocked expression. "You need to remember I'm one of 'them', sweetheart. Are any of the others observing us right now? No. They have better things to do."

"What happens if I do get let in?"

"Well, you'd be an associate. You'd know things but not be expected to do much more than offer your opinion."

"Not a member?"

"Dave, I can split atoms on my own. The guy who taught me has worked out how to bring about the zombie apocalypse. There's nothing hinting that you have comparable power. But we decide when, where and how to use our abilities. We make the distinction on power, and someone has to be equal to the rest of us to be a member. So even the two people we have brought in are associates. We know them, we like them, we listen to them, but unless what we're doing directly affects them, they don't get a vote. And even if someone loses a vote, we can't make them use their power if they don't want to or decline to use it."

They hiked along for a while before stopping for a brief rest. "Can you tell me how many votes I need to change?"

"You need a unanimous vote, sweetheart. I'm the only one who wants to bring you in. The ones willing to support doing that are mostly thinking about people they want to bring in." She dissolved a rock in her boot and healed the spot. "Bringing someone in exposes the secrets of the people who aren't your girlfriend. Everyone gets to decide who knows about her, so everyone gets a veto for bringing someone that far in. In fairness, you've got a tougher path than either of the two we've brought in, and both of them were special cases."

"Do you think it'll actually work?"

"Sweetheart, I was present at the final evaluation of one of them. One of the people strongly opposed to bringing her in did the evaluation. And he wasn't gentle."

"What sort of questions was he asking?"

She looked into his eyes. "You're not thinking, babe. We're not limited to asking questions. It's a mind probe, and he wouldn't even do that until she'd satisfied his verbal questions. You'll pass or fail based on what she finds there, with no possible way to lie. She doesn't like it, you're not let in. And the probe itself won't be any fun. He's not gentle in a living mind."

"There's no other way? What about how you were brought in? You've mentioned you weren't one of the original group."

"That's...not really a workable option, and you wouldn't like it anyway."

"What's that? I'll try it."

"Reverend Johnson targeted me for murder, and I had to be saved repeatedly. They eventually didn't have a choice but to act openly to rescue me. Other people died in my place," she said, breathing deeply. "Not something I'd recommend, even if…"

"Even if I didn't die," Dave finished. "What about the other special case? How'd they get brought in?"

"I'm not really free to talk about that. It's a secret, and you'd probably figure it out if I said anything."

"Really? Secrets? Does keeping secrets from your SO ever work out well?"

"Ask me a question about me, and I'll answer it. I'm not keeping my secrets from you. I'm keeping theirs."

"So I won't get mind wiped."

"Or something worse than that, actually," she smiled crookedly at his expression. "Hades really doesn't like you, and he's not someone who believes in forgiving and forgetting. He remembers it all. And… you know those dead eucalyptus trees on 80 towards Sacramento? He killed them when he lost his temper. He can kill you. Just. As. Easily."

Shevaun dropped into an open seat at the Round Table's joined lunch tables. "You guys wanted to know when Dad's newest movie was coming out?"

"Yeah. I thought "Apache Chief" comes out in November or December, catching the holiday crowd."

"It does. But "To Stand on My Wounded Knee" is out this weekend. He's staring as Russell Means. He's a little old for the role, but it's about the standoff there in 1973 and the elders and families wanted the role to go to a real Lakota. Since he's an established star, the studio offered it to him."

"There was a stand off there?" Dani asked

"Yeah. It got a lot of news coverage at the time. Dad brought home the old footage to help him prepare. Wanna see it?"

"We could put it up on our big screen sometime," Bridget offered.

"Cool, thanks," Dani replied.

"Sounds great Shevaun. Friday night? We'll be there."

"Thanks."

"Want us to class up the theater? Limos?" Keisha added at her blank look.

"I don't think that'll quite be necessary," she said with a laugh. "And Bridget and Seth can skip the horses, too!"

"Have you talked to Mr. Blanke or one of the other teachers? Might not be a bad idea."

"I don't think he'd go for it, not as an extra credit or something."

"History assignment? There's gotta be something you could do a report on for class," Seth put in. "Especially going beyond the movie."

"Didn't he tweak your last name so he wouldn't get type-cast?"

"Sort of. A secretary at SAG made the mistake. He decided to keep it professionally. It's one of the reasons he likes Captain Blackwolf so much. It never comes up. He's just the Captain. And then the person at the counter registering me for school recognized him and used it." She shrugged, got up, and then said, "Any of you interested in a walk-on extra's role?"

"What's it involved?" Keisha wanted to know.

"Not much. You put on a costume and walk around in the background of the shot. It can take a while, though."

"Sounds interesting. I'll give it a shot."

"We should carpool at least," Teddy said.

"I'll organize it," Keisha volunteered.

"Damn you guys are always looking for extra WORK," Catalina Zaragoza said as she passed by.

"It's not like it's hard," Solly replied. "Want to join us?"

"What?"

"It's a movie Shevaun's dad is in. You're welcome to come with us."

"I can't this weekend. But maybe some other time?"

"Sure."

Keisha's orange and bronze stretch—she had the longest of all of them, since she did more of the business end of things than anyone else—limo pulled up to the next stop. Dave started sweating and fidgeting even though he was in a normal t-shirt and jeans. His eyes were wide and he looked terrified. Angela took his hand and Karen could feel the restorative spell she was subvocalizing, but it wasn't easily countering whatever was wrong with Dave. Karen could feel the wards alerting him to their presence and Seth came out in black…was that a tuxedo?! With tails?! Yes, it was. The door opened for him and he looked in…and froze. There were two seats left, one next to Dave and the other next to her. Seth started to back up, and Karen could tell he was about to offer to get himself there.

"Oh, don't be silly, Seth! I won't bite. Sit next to me," she said, patting the seat.

"As you wish," he said after a couple of beats. Karen looked at him sharply. He sat, his face a mask.

"Unless he asks you to?" Dave said with a laugh. No one else seemed to find the comment funny. Seth's glare at Dave was quite unfriendly, and him putting on the sunglasses that would disguise his use of his power wasn't a good sign. Keisha grimaced. They rode quietly to pick up Solly. Seth said nothing, even as the rest of them talked about their research on the real events it was going to depict. She felt barriers going up around his emotions even stronger than he normally held them. Solly joined them and they headed for the theater. Dave turned to Seth.

"I haven't seen much of you this year. What are you taking?" Karen winced and ducked her head at the spike of pure hostility she felt through her link to him. He reached out a hand mumbling an apology in Bengali…quietly backed by his power to make her feel better. She could also tell he was strengthening his mental control to prevent it from happening again. Oddly enough, Angela hadn't reacted at all, and she'd strengthened her resurrection bond with him during her year as his apprentice. But he ignored Dave's question.

"Seth?" Keisha said.

He responded in Coptic. "Can I help you with something?" She answered in English. "You're being rude."

"I apologize to those who can understand me," he said, still in Coptic. "I will transport myself home."

"I'm bringing you, I'll get you home, Seth, don't worry about it."

"Don't bother."

"It kind of spoils the point of the evening if people go off by themselves," Keisha said.

"You knew what would happen when you chose to inflict that on me."

"What's going on?" Dave asked, unable to understand Seth.

"I dunno," Dani responded with a shrug. "I can't understand them either."

"It's nothing to do with you, sweetie," Angela said.

"Don't be so sure of that," Alex said in Nahuatl.

"You, too?" Keisha asked.

"I think she'd rather he not get mind-wiped, don't you? Seth will do that in a heartbeat if he learns something he's not cleared for. And before you answer, the English conversation is getting close to where he puts the line," Solly put in in Hebrew. Keisha frowned.

"What possessed you to put this car together?" Alex asked. "You're usually a lot more sensitive to social dynamics."

She looked around. "I was seeing what I wanted to see, and miscalculated where Seth was. I thought it would be a first step towards peace. I should have asked him explicitly."

"You might have mentioned it."

She inclined her head towards Seth. "He would have refused."

"Maybe that should have told you something?"

"Seth you're being ridiculous about this," Angela said

Keisha sighed and switched to Cushitic. "Actually he's not. I do know the history. Hasn't he ever mentioned it to you? I just thought that he'd been forgiving when he helped you get that date, but I see I was wrong. That was all about helping you get control back." She cocked her head at Karen. "What was the lesson from this little debacle?"

"Lesson? Oh, I don't know. Misunderstandings between us are dangerous, and not just to us." Angela had mentioned that.

"Precisely. But you should have used another language or telepathy." Dave's eyes had bugged out of his head at the word 'dangerous'.

A word in Coptic erased the memory from Dave's mind. He put his hand to his head in pain. Angela and Karen glared at Seth, as Angela put her own hand to his head and muttered something in Ainu to take away the pain. Dave's relief was obvious, as was his confusion. Angela didn't normally cast spells in company.

"You didn't have to do that," Karen said.

"Someone did. The people who don't care wouldn't do it. And you just ensured I'll do it again."

"I've got it, Seth," Keisha said. Her power had coalesced and been released as she spoke. Dave's eyes went blank for a moment but he didn't seem to experience pain. She cocked an eyebrow at Karen and continued in Cushitic. "You don't care if he knows. He, however, cares a lot—and specifically about *him* knowing. When we're keeping our magic secret, we've all got different levels of who we care about knowing about us."

"Yeah, yeah, I get you."

Angela joined in in Ainu. "Since my boyfriend's life kind of depends on it, I hope you do."

"And do you get your lesson?" Keisha asked Seth.

"That you're willing to gamble with someone's life to test my tolerance?" Karen's eyes went wide. Seth had been considering killing Dave? Really considering it?

"That even for people with our power there are situations best handled without resort to them!"

"My wards are set to keep him away, Keisha. They would have killed him if he'd gotten closer or spent much longer that close, even inside the protection of your vehicle."

"Well, here's the theater."

"That was fast," Dave said. A glance at Alex and Solly told her they'd sped up the car.

"Keisha," Angela said in Ainu as they got out, "That was a lot closer than I like." Seth had moved on ahead from where they were getting out, not waiting for any of the others

"I'm sorry, Angela. He hasn't come far at all, has he?"

"It was still an unnecessary risk."

"I didn't beat the crap out of Dave in third grade purely for kicks, Keisha," Bridget told her in Gaelic. Angela's eyebrows shot up. Dave had never mentioned that encounter to her, apparently.

"I'd call it a foolish one. What possibly made you think that would work?" Alex asked. She glanced at Karen for some reason, but didn't say anything. Dave looked confused, since they were still not speaking a language he could understand. Malcolm, Alex, and Solly shook their heads.

"The only new factor is him dating the Goddess of the Elements," Bridget said. "You know what his memory's like."

"Warn me before you do something like that next time. Warn *us* so we're prepared if we need to restrain him," Angela told Keisha. "We can't fix a death Seth causes, remember?"

The rest of the Round Table, plus Shevaun and Julian, joined them, but Seth had already presented his ticket and gone inside. Bridget glanced at them, shook her head, and caught up with him. They sat together for the movie...away from the rest of the group. She could catch the occasional snippet in Gaelic or Coptic before the movie. Seth didn't even give Keisha the chance to offer a ride home; Orcinus had appeared, invisibly, with full saddle and tack when they left the theater. It had not been a good night.

Chapter

3

Dawn pulled her Physics notebook out of the locker to find Seth waiting for her. "You got Dr. Pettigrew, too?" she asked.

"I did. She decided to assign lab partners," he grumbled—in Coptic.

"Let me guess—we're not together. You wouldn't be upset if we were. Do you know who I got?" she replied in Tsalagi. "And why are we speaking so no one can understand us?"

"No one else needs to hear this, do they? You got assigned someone named Charles Brown," he answered, still in Coptic, as they headed upstairs to the laboratory. "I think he just transferred in this year, but I haven't done any divinations on him to learn anything, just his name. I got saddled with Annette Hughes."

"Saddled? Come on, Seth. She's a perfectly nice, fairly bright girl with a solid B average. And since Dr. Pettigrew decided to assign partners, you could have done worse." Like Seth, she stayed in her casting language. He just looked at her. "And this is Honors physics. She wouldn't be in it if things were as bad as you're obviously thinking they are."

"I'm going to end up doing the labs all myself," he grumbled, unmollified. She swatted his shoulder lightly with a free hand.

"If you insist on keeping your notes in hieratic, you probably will. She won't be able to understand them."

"I kept my chemistry lab notes in English last year. Rachel needed to borrow them a few times."

"You weren't grumbling about her, but what about your class notes? I've seen your notebooks, you know. The only reason your notes aren't in hieroglyphics is that it would take too long."

"What are you two arguing about?" the brown-haired girl in jeans and a Sirens t-shirt was sitting near an overweight black boy in a button shirt, glasses, and shorts.

"Don't worry about it, Annette," Dawn said to her. "Seth likes to grumble. Although that t-shirt isn't winning you any points. The Valkyries are his team." A quick check of Annette's mind revealed she wasn't aware of their ownership. They tended to downplay their exact relationships with the league around outsiders. The boy—Charles—didn't know, either, but was finding her very attractive. Hmmmm...

"Like that really makes a difference," Seth said in Coptic.

"And he'd rather be partnered with you so you guys can flatten the curve and end the labs early," she replied wryly. She grinned at Seth's expression. "You DO have something of a reputation, Seth. You barely socialize with anyone who's not part of the Round Table. Dawn, this is Charles."

"Pleased to meet you, Charles."

"You don't look Japanese."

"Aren't you supposed to have a round head, Charlie Brown?"

He grimaced. "Walked into that one, didn't I? Sorry. What language were you speaking?"

"I was speaking Tsalagi—better known as Cherokee."

"Cool. I guess we'll give your friend a run for top of the class? Or is it boyfriend? You seem to know a lot about his sports preferences." He added that at her expression.

"Oh, we've been friends since around kindergarten, so he's a little more like a brother than someone I'd think of as boyfriend material. The Starlets are my team. As for the top of the class, it depends on how much he sabotages them. If he doesn't bother keeping his lab notes in English, it won't be hard."

"He speaks Cherokee, too?"

"Hai, but he keeps most of his notes in hieratic script—and the Coptic language. Unless Annette took a course I don't know about, she won't be able to make any sense out of them." She caught Annette's eye and winked at her. She liked Annette; needling Seth and making it a competition might get him to be her actual lab partner instead of a grudging one.

"I thought you were taking Spanish!" she said to Seth.

"I am. That doesn't stop me from being fluent in something else."

"If you're fluent in Cherokee and whatever Coptic is, why are you still taking Spanish?"

"Coptic is what Egyptian evolved into. The school district doesn't offer tests for any of the languages I speak."

"Languages? Plural? Just how many do you speak?"

He considered that for a bit. "Twelve, not counting English and Spanish."

"Seth," Dawn broke in, "are you showing off for the pretty girl?" She winked at Annette again, whose lips quivered.

"You can speak just as many. I was merely answering a question."

Annette chuckled. "It'd be spectacular if you did as much for my GPA as you did for Angela Fujiwara's last year."

"I didn't do it. She put in the work."

"Wow, you're actually giving the girl credit!"

"Why wouldn't I?" He seemed genuinely puzzled.

"I heard stories about your freshman year lab partner—Diana Ferguson? Never had a nice thing to say about her that I ever heard."

He snorted. "She's an idiot who spent more time on her nails and with her hair—or her phone!—than paying attention to what we were doing. I was so tempted to animate that frog..."

"Diana IS a fashion twit," Dawn interrupted before Seth could accidentally reveal too much. "I've rarely had a conversation with her that on anything of interest or substance. If it's not in a fashion magazine, she doesn't read it."

"How'd she scrape a passing grade, then?"

"Personal study time with Mr. Atherton," Annette said in an arch tone.

Seth cocked an eye at Dawn and switched to Coptic. "We didn't include that possibility in the curse, did we?"

"We were twelve when we cast it. Sex was still funny more than real; we were still joking around about being each other's prom dates! I'm not sure the possibility really entered our minds. Well, maybe Solly's, but the rest of us?" she replied in Tsalagi, shaking her head.

"Something to bring up next time. You want to put it on the agenda, or do you want me to?"

"Go ahead." She paused, cocked her head, and said, "Oh, and Seth? Not a word about magic to him, understood?"

"Why would I?"

"I'm going to date him."

Seth shrugged. "Enjoy. It's not like he's cleared for anything."

"I know. And I know he'll probably find out eventually. But I'd kind of like him to think I'm a normal girl for as long as possible."

"Do any of us still count as normal anymore?" She grinned and winked at him.

"It's amazing how you guys can do that," Charles said.

"Yeah it is. I've gotten so used to the Round Table doing it that sometimes I forget how weird it is," Annette added.

"Do what?" Seth asked.

"Hold a conversation in two different obscure languages at the same time and understanding each other. And their whole clique does it?" Charles shook his head.

"You think that's amazing. Wait until you see all of them together, each picking a different language. We think. No one else can understand them. But funny as anything when Mr. Cartwright demanded they 'speak a language a civilized person can understand'. They kind of looked at each other, each of them said something in a different language—and different from the one they'd been speaking—and Dani burst out laughing."

"What'd they say?"

"'We are civilized people. It's not our fault you're an uneducated barbarian.' In ten languages at once, none of them English," she said with a grin. "With Dawn speaking Klingon and Jenny speaking Elvish."

"How do you know what they said?"

"I was watching. I asked Angela later."

"And they said this to Mr. Cartwright's face?"

"It's not like he could understand what we said," Dawn replied with a shrug.

"Didn't he ask for a translation?"

"Of course. We all immediately translated into a third language he didn't understand. Finally I took pity on him and told him that it's not my fault he doesn't speak the languages we were using," Dawn said. She shrugged. "Close enough."

Annette and Charles laughed at that as Dr. Pettigrew stood up to begin the lab.

Chapter

4

The team room was packed with teenagers—mostly boys, but a few other girls had joined Angela and Dani on the team—as they listened to Coach Nguyen describe what Reagan High liked to do. Kristin Clebourne, Dave's little sister and now a freshman quarterback, leaned over to him and said, "This is pretty intense."

"Just wait till Alex and Angela take the field. That's when the magic happens."

"Dave, we haven't altered your memory because Angela assures us she's got it under control and you aren't going to say anything out of turn. Do we need to revisit that conversation?" Dave was looking around, shocked, as everyone else seemed to be completely ignoring Alex's sudden interjection. There was a purplish tinge to his vision.

"What..."

"Alex, it's not th..."

"Ange, be glad that I'm the one that caught this. You're disqualified, just as I would be if Dani spoke up. But we need to be able to tell everyone else it's been handled and won't be a recurring problem. The vote's still close. Dani, could you let me know if Coach Nguyen says anything important?"

"Sure, Alex." She and Alex maintained a formal separation during team functions.

"C'mon, Alex."

"Dave, Angela's the only one of us who fully trusts you with her secrets. The *only* one. I happen to consider you a friend, but that doesn't mean I'm going to tell you everything. At least one of us doesn't trust you at all. If he'd been here and heard you, he'd have taken steps immediately. No conversation, no delay, and no mercy. Do you understand me?"

"That's a little harsh, Alex."

"Ange, he wouldn't try to convince Dave to keep his mouth shut. He'd ensure that Dave couldn't say anything, and yes we can do that Dave. Angela could restore your ability, but that would just make things worse."

"What do you mean worse?"

Alex and Dani both shook their heads. "That's getting into areas we don't have permission to tell you about."

"That's bullshit."

"No, it's not," Angela said. "I still haven't told my parents who all is involved, because I get to tell my secrets but not someone else's. I don't really agree with Alex, here, but he knows the person better than I do, so I'll trust him on how he'd react."

"Who are we talking about, anyway?"

"No comment, Dave," Dani said.

"He hasn't agreed that you get to know that, so we aren't going to tell you. If he thinks you do know, him erasing it from your memory would be mild and merciful. And Dave? I will tell him if you start claiming you know."

"Alex, really? You'd do that to me?"

"Do we really need to spell it out for you? These guys are power personified," Dani interjected. "Even I know that, and I'm not one of them. They do a lot of things to keep from having arguments or fights between them, because they're smart enough to know a fight with their girlfriend wouldn't be as bad as a fight between *them*. I know not to make them keeping their secrets about each other and the magic about me. Do you?"

"Yes, I know not to make it about you," he said with a smile. "Not what she was asking, and you know it."

"Jesus, it was a joke!" He looked at them to see none of them, even Angela, was laughing. "Ok, yes, I know not to make it about me."

"Good. Then don't. We're already dealing with big egos that can actually back their talk up. You can't do that."

"This is really too much, Alex."

"You don't get what we're trying to do, do you?"

"Not a bit."

"Dave, we've got someone who's suggested we deal with the security risk you pose by executing you. Didn't Angela warn you about that?"

"Well, yeah, she told me."

"Then why aren't you listening to her?!" Dani asked with exasperation.

"But…I mean, who'd wanna kill ME?"

"We can't tell you that. Just keep in mind there's someone who's not acting solely out of respect for Angela. And he won't hesitate to do so if he thinks you're becoming a problem."

"Okay, okay."

"Hey Shevaun. I'm having some girls over for a movie marathon this weekend. Wanna come?" Bridget spun into a seat next to her at lunch.

"I've got a test on Monday. Mom probably won't go for it."

"No problem. The others are Dawn, Angela, Keisha, and Karen." Bridget's eyebrows rose with a grin.

"The Round Table? Everyone but Dani?"

"She's studying sex ed with Alex this weekend."

"Neither of them is *taking* sex…oh." She swallowed her laughter. "Gotcha. Let me check with Mom. I put it as a study session and she'll probably say yes."

"Fabulous! We start after the game on Friday at my place."

"Awesome. How do I get there?"

"Come to the game? You can get a ride with me."

"Cool thanks. I am a little surprised though." Bridget's brows rose. "Usually when you guys talk about the Round Table getting together, you don't exclude the boys."

"And they don't exclude the girls. It just worked out this weekend that way. They're scattered to the four winds this weekend on various college trips. Well, except Alex—he's already been to the academies. We aren't interested in the schools they're going to or have already been."

"They're really going to be going at it all weekend, and their parents are cool with it?"

"I wouldn't say 'cool with it'. I imagine they've come up with some excuse—he's been helping her study for the past two years—but neither of them mentioned what it was to me, and Alex's mom is more concerned about safety and responsibility than anything else. So they aren't expecting me to cover for them. As for at it all weekend…wanna be part of the bet?"

"You're betting on THAT?"

"Yeppers!" Bridget grinned at her. "Why not? If you want in, mention it to Keisha. She's won so many times she just keeps track of the bets now rather than participates."

"Oh, god, what'll they do to me if they find out?"

"Ask if you won. That's what Solly did last time, anyway. They know we're doing it. How else would we know who wins? Although there is one category with Solly we don't include for anyone else."

"I think I'm afraid to ask…"

"Gender."

"I was right, I didn't want to know." Bridget chuckled. "Betting among you guys? Owners of your own football league? I couldn't afford the ante, Bridget! Yeah Dad's an actor, but it's not like I'm making that sort of money!"

"We bet services—help on our projects. So don't worry about money. We won't ask you to do anything illegal or dangerous. We're mostly just setting whose project is next."

"Okay. I'll think on it. The bet, I mean. I'll check with Mom on the study session," she said.

Angela and Dave came into the courtyard at lunch to see a crowd gathered around one of the tables. She made her way over to Seth, who was rather disinterestedly eating his lunch with only a couple of other Goths—Ivan, Louisa, and Doug—nearby. "What's going on?" She asked him. He might not be watching, but he'd know.

"Joe bet Dani she couldn't bench-press Alex. She's about to prove him wrong, with Alex's enthusiastic cooperation." Joe was a chauvinistic idiot who didn't think girls could be strong enough to play on the football team. "It's not like they haven't practiced it before."

"How enthusiastic?" Dave asked. Seth ignored him. Dave repeated his question. Seth took a bite of his sandwich and ignored him again.

Angela sighed. Seth wasn't going to talk to Dave, who was getting upset about being ignored. She blocked his hand from poking at Seth, who would not take that well. "What's he doing?"

"He recruited the cheerleading squad to give her encouragement. You can probably hear them in a moment. I believe Miss MacLeod is leading them."

"And you're not over there watching her?" Angela asked.

"They know I'm here, if they need someone with first aid training." Then Angela caught how dark his eyes were and hid a smile she wouldn't be able to explain to Dave. Seth *was* watching; he was just being subtle about it. His normally dark eyes helped mask his use of his magic. Why deal with the crowd if he didn't have to?

"Okay. We're gonna get closer and cheer her on. See you later, Teach." He nodded back, saying something in Coptic. She gave him an exasperated look, but nodded in response.

"What was that?" Dave asked her as they moved through the crowd. "What was what?"

"I asked him a simple question and you grabbed my hand when I tried to get his attention after he didn't answer."

"I know him better than you do. He heard you. He was refusing to acknowledge you. He'd consider that an attack. You want the Lord of Vengeance coming after you? I'm sure everyone else on your teams and in your classes will be happy with that."

"I'm not worried."

"You should be. The cheerleading squad alone wouldn't be targeted by him, thanks to Karen's presence."

"We don't share any classes."

"That makes it more challenging for him, not impossible. After tutoring me for a year I'm in all Honors classes. You want him doing the same for some of the kids who are in your classes?" Actually that was more studying with the Round Table than Seth's tutoring in magic, but it might help encourage Dave not to seek a confrontation he wouldn't survive. "Or tampering with your cup of Sportyade? He can do that and still keep the squad's normal." Okay, neither was "normal" with Seth involved, but what he did to it was enhancement. He was just as capable of continuing to enhance the squad's drink and the team's drink and curse just Dave's.

"Anyway, what'd the little twit have to say? I know you understood him."

"If he'd wanted you to know he would have used English. He adjusts his responses to who's listening."

"You know what he said," Dave said accusingly.

"I do."

"Well?"

"Dave, we've had this conversation. It was Seth's decision not to include you even if I don't agree. I'm going to honor it. I know it frustrates you, but he and I are involved in things we don't discuss with outsiders. And that includes you, remember?"

"Well, what's this, then?"

"Call it League business if you want, or Round Table business, if you want. Either of those is a euphemism, but they haven't agreed you get to know what it really is. And until they do, that's the way it's going to stay. I'm not going to lie to you about it, but I'm not going to answer questions." When he started again, she said, "I'm not really interested in modifying your memory, babe, but an outsider knowing something they shouldn't is grounds for them…insisting." Actually, it was grounds for one of them taking matters into their own hands and just doing it.

"Didn't you say last May that you couldn't rely on fear to get me to keep the secrets?"

"I did. The people who told me that originally…are the ones backing altering your mind or executing you. They aren't going to rely on fear. They're going to take the steps they think they need to so you can't tell anyone. They're going to rely on force."

Bridget's place was huge, more of a ranch then a house—among coastal redwoods. Pulling up in the Arcata Unicorns green and white limo was an experience even for Shevaun, who'd gotten used to pulling into the homes of actors. Bridget's parents weren't actors. Her mom was a field biologist. Her dad owned the Wildlife casinos, but they liked Marin better. They were, in short, rich. Their idea of a "home theater" involved a movie theater screen—and Bridget had permission to appropriate it for the weekend.

"Holy fuck, Bridget."

"Thanks, Evangeline," she said to her chauffeur. "I shouldn't be needing the car before Monday."

"Thank you, ma'am."

"C'mon, kitchen's this way/"

"What, no snack bar?"

"Just wholesome, all-natural chocolate!"

"…Covered ants?" Bridget grinned at her. Bridget's taste for candied insects was notorious.

"Oh, no, not for you. Those're milk chocolate." She paused. "For you I've got dark chocolate covered scorpions!"

"Funny."

"Oh, don't worry. Not everything has an arthropod in it, and it's all been treated to be safe for you."

<Is it?> Angela asked.

<Not really. I adjusted her guts for the weekend. It seemed easier than maybe forgetting to treat something.>

<But does everything have an arthropod in it?>

<Of course not!>

<Maybe we should expand that to 'invertebrate'. We are talking to Bridget,> Jenny put in. Bridget chuckled.

"What's so funny?"

"I recognize their expressions. They think everything will have an invertebrate in it."

"Glad to know it won't"

"She didn't say that."

"There isn't an invertebrate in *everything*."

"Uh-huh," Dawn said skeptically.

"There won't! Honest!"

"Hi Mr. Sullivan!"

"Hi Dawn, Jennifer, Angela, Keisha, honey. You must be Shevaun. Welcome. Is there anything you need from me before you take over the theater?"

"US? Need something?" Bridget responded with a wink. Her father was clued in.

"Alright, then. Your dinner's in the oven. I'll be in the study if you care to include me in the shenanigans." He gave his daughter a hug, kiss, and wink before taking a narrow, curving flight of stairs.

"C'mon. The theater's got it's own kitchen."

"What are we starting with, anyway?"

"The Genre Wheel!" the others chorused.

"The *what*?" Shevaun asked.

"Bridget made a random movie generator. It's loaded onto the computer that her movies are on."

"Any movie?"

"Yep."

"Even your dad's porn?"

"No, just Mom's. Dad keeps his on the plane." Shevaun laughed. "Rom-Com!"

"How about this one?"

"What's it about?" She passed it around.

"Let's do something else," said Shevaun after glimpsing the cover.

"What? Why? Looks good to me," Keisha said.

"I don't need you giggling over how cute my dad is!" that got a burst of laughter.

"You're dad's in it?"

"I don't see him listed."

"As 'shirtless guy number two', yeah. He hadn't made much of a name yet. It's older than I am."

"Oh, well, then, we'll save it for later," she said with a wicked grin. "How about this one?"

"Sure."

"Really? Your Dad's in this one, too."

"So am I, actually. I was visiting him on set one day, and they had me add in as an extra. But he's playing a goofy sidekick, not the lead. So he keeps his clothes on."

"Bummer," Jenny said.

"Well, let's get it started and get the homework out of the way."

"Put of the way? You mean do it now?"

"Of course. Shouldn't take long."

"I'd usually put it off till Sunday."

"Really? I wanna be relaxing when the boys call to say they've finished."

"Oh, it's a contest?"

"Yeppers!"

"I can get behind that!"

Jenny and Karen were the only ones finished when Seth called, asking how far behind Jenny he was. Told he was second behind her, he congratulated Karen without being told who else had beaten him.

"What's next?" Jenny asked when they'd all finished their homework and spun the wheel again.

"Fantasy! Ooh, you have the extended Lord of the Rings?"

"Let's watch those tomorrow," Keisha said. "They'll take most of the day, and we do have some tests to study for."

"True. Something light then, that we can safely ignore. Hey, how about this one? 'Red Sonja'?"

"How is that outfit even practical?"

"It's not."

"Put some armor on, girl!"

"Push play and let's get to physics!" They spent a lot of time laughing at the movie. Shevaun didn't seem to think their laughing at how magic was working made much sense. They'd finished their notes for the tests by the end of the movie.

They watched movie after movie with plenty of popcorn and snacks. On Saturday, they were watching a prophecy horror movie when Shevaun noted, "Just because they see the signals the prophecy is coming true doesn't mean that's what's causing it. The fires may be lit when Gondor calls for aid, but they aren't the problem; they're the warning, the message. But in the movies they're always trying to stop the next indicator."

Late Sunday afternoon, after two all-night movie marathons, Keisha jerked upright when she heard Seth's call for help.

"Back in a minute," she hurried outside to teleport out of Shevaun's sight.

"Where'd she go?" Shevaun asked

"Dunno. If she needs help she'll call for it. How about one last spin? One last movie?"

"Sure."

"Thriller! Perfect!"

"Yeah!"

They were about ten minutes in, with Bridget getting more popcorn, when Keisha came back. "What was that?"

"Oh, sorry, needed to make a call I'd forgotten about." *<What was it really about? I know Seth's in Louisiana.>*

<He got caught in a riot or protest or something, initiated by some practitioners. He was about ready to kill them all to keep his Mom safe. My arrival let him take out just the trio responsible.>

"Take-out?"

"Delivery, Karen, unless you're volunteering to go get Ethiopian. Dinner before you guys go home?"

She switched to Bengali. "He killed people?"

Bridget answered in Gaelic. "We've had that discussion, Karen. Back when he did a mass killing rescuing you? Yes, he did. She kept it from being thousands. Our enemies died, the innocents lived, and the vulnerable were removed. He did something similar rescuing Angela freshman year."

"You make it sound like he's a hero or something," Karen accused.

"Chill, girls," Jenny said in Cornish. "Seth is our most terrible option, Karen. He knows it. We all know it. He's death incarnate. And he's on our side. He'll back us all the way, and the least we can do is be understanding. He's taken lives. So have I. So has Bridget." Karen looked at them in shock.

"What are you guys arguing about?" Shevaun asked in Lakota, unable to understand Bengali, Cornish, and Gaelic.

Keisha responded in Lakota. "It's nothing important. A boy. I think it's over for now."

"When the hell did you learn Lakota?"

"Last summer."

"You spoke it like an elder!"

"I'm good at languages," she said to dodge the question.

"I'm sorry, Bridget. I know that happens. And that I shouldn't judge too harshly when I didn't have to make the call. It's just…"

"You're a little conflicted when it comes to him and what he does— and has done."

"'What he has done?' What did he do to you, Karen?"

"Not now, Shevaun," Jennifer said.

"Yeah."

"Not a problem, Karen. We all have to come to grips with it. And you've never been comfortable with his crush." She tightened her lips, and then spoke in Cornish. "I know he'll do everything he in his power to keep it from happening, but you still might end up needing to take a life to save someone else's."

"It's fairly easy for one of us to say we'd die for someone, Karen. One of the others will bring us back. It's a lot harder on us to kill. When you have your necromancy lessons, you'll learn what I'm talking about," Bridget said in Gaelic.

"And that," Dawn said in English, "is about enough speaking in tongues! Sorry, Shevaun."

"You guys do it at school all the time."

"Yeah. But we could start teaching you some of it."

"You guys want your secrets, that's cool. Since you could obviously understand each other, you'd have used English if you weren't trying to make sure I didn't understand."

Jennifer grimaced. "I am sorry about that, Shevaun. We're not supposed to tell you yet why we're doing it."

"But you will anyway?" she said hopefully.

Keisha shook her head slowly. "There are limits to how far we can go right now. You'd figure out the rest, and the others haven't agreed to that. And the consequences would come down on you, not us. So I'd rather wait until it's time, if you don't mind."

Chapter

5

"Okay, everyone's here," Jennifer said as Seth took his seat. The Venusian racquet ball court had been converted into a conference room once Mike was marooned here. He and Dani were off catching up and running some drills; Alex had already created a magic football to practice with so they were using that. "I know it's disappointing that irritating brainless twit Patti's heading student council, but we've got other matters to deal with."

"You got that right," Malcolm said. "Starting with, who was that wizard who escaped from the slaver? Do we have anything more on it?"

"Her name is Maria Binay, Filipino, about ninety years old."

"She looked pretty well preserved," Karen said, remembering the woman. "I'd have guessed thirty, tops."

"Extending youth and lifespan isn't that hard," Bridget said. "And if you don't want the debilitating effects of age, I'm not surprised people use it for that. Immortality is something different. I don't think we've confronted a true immortal yet. Seth and I are still working on how to pull it off."

"You're right about that. Vampires are about as close as we've come."

"We need to be careful. My divinations have picked up indications of other practitioners coalescing against us. Taking out Reverend

36

Johnson was not a problem, but Binay is seeking out allies. I think we scared her, and that's what Seth faced in New Orleans."

"Not surprising considering," Teddy said. "She seemed pretty freaked when Alex and I confronted her, and I don't think it was the disguises. I don't think she was expecting quite so many wizard boarders. Facing two at a time is unusual."

"And, speaking as someone watching from the outside…you guys are capable of more than they were," Karen said. "By now, I'm capable of more than what I saw them do."

"Was one the apprentice of the other, maybe?"

"Maybe. I don't really think so. We'll need to do more research."

"Two wasn't the only problem. Experienced as they are…she's not really in our league in terms of outright power, Jennifer and I agree. The other one had some idea that Seth's necromantic power would be coming after them, and they prepared for it."

"What caused that?" Karen asked.

Keisha shrugged. "You know Seth went looking for you. They had to have gotten at least a hint of his power from that." Karen nodded at the reminder. Seth had sent his mind looking for her; she'd felt him searching for her, but he'd only been able to confirm she was alive. It had taken Keisha to pinpoint her location to let the rescue happen.

"And given how lethal he is, it scared them into preparing against him. If I had to pick one of us to ensure I was protected against, Seth would scare me the most," Alex put in. "There are mundane defenses to other attacks, but not to his."

"I think we're going to need to deal with her," Alex said.

Keisha answered him. "Give me a little time and I'll pinpoint her location for a strike. I expect it'll be a little more difficult than for a normal person. Alex, Teddy, I'll need your memories."

"Strike team?"

"We'll figure out who's available," Keisha said. "I don't know how long it will take me against her active countermeasures."

"Want some help?" Seth asked.

"You might trigger more warnings than anyone else, Seth. But I'll keep you in mind for the strike team. Are we interested in taking her alive?"

"If we can, that would be good. We need information."

"I can still get the information we want if she's dead," Seth put in. "That's not really a barrier anymore." Karen looked horrified. "But if you guys would rather take her alive, we can try that. So far they've never shown any desire to surrender. They either die or flee."

"Then let's remove the flight option," Alex said. "I'll put together something that would nullify her ability to teleport, or at least trace her."

"Sounds good."

"Terraforming's next on the agenda. Do we want to toss in Titan or one of the Galilean moons?" Dawn asked.

"We could *do* that. If our projections are accurate, we could terraform all four of the Galilean moons, even Io. But for now let's concentrate on Mars, Venus, and Luna," Malcolm said. A chorus of agreement with his sentiment sounded around the table as they shifted into the nuts and bolts of the planned grand gesture. Everyone involved gave a report, although Seth seemed to be getting restless as the discussion dragged on for a couple of hours. His role was more to support everyone else with his power than to handle the changes himself. Finally the discussion seemed to wind down.

"Anything else?" Seth asked.

"I don't think so," Keisha said. Seth nodded and vanished.

"I've got to go," Teddy said, and vanished himself.

"Dinner?" Keisha asked the remaining people. A word and gesture created an Ethiopian feast.

"Oh, I forgot to ask. What about bringing powerless people in?" Karen asked.

"Well," Jennifer said. "Unanimous consent is basically what's needed. You haven't put up your ward yet, but everyone else has. I could probably take each of them down, but it would be hard and dangerous work there's no real need to do. I know perfectly well that Seth's wards are designed to kill, and that Angela's and Dawn's are both deadly in their own right. They can take them down or give someone a pass through them easily enough; it's when it's someone ELSE trying to do it that problems arise."

"Okay, that makes sense."

"Did you want to bring someone up?" Alex asked.

"My little sister, Katie. She's got cancer, so I'd sort of like to show her something marvelous before...you know."

"Not a problem," Bridget said. "I took care of Mike's in a few moments. It won't take me that long to put her back to normal. Or do you want me to show you how to do it? Either way, she'll have a long, normal life."

"I've already suggested that. Mom and Dad want her to have a treatment they understand and not magic. They think I'm more likely to miss something."

Bridget shook her head. "Actually, the magic's more reliable than that. We're sure to get everything and prevent a recurrence. I can show you how to tweak her DNA to shut off the gene that caused the cancer."

"Still, though, it's Mom's call..."

"Not really. They can't actually stop you—or me!—from intervening. I get that they're your parents. But wouldn't a cured Katie be better than reviving her from death? She's all too likely to die in a hospital, in which case bringing her back means she's stuck here, the Castle, or the Shore."

"I hear you. It's just..."

"Considering what we can do, you'd think rebelling against parental authority would be easier," Angela put in.

"Yeah. At the moment we're still arguing about it."

"Do you know how sick she is?"

"We're told at least a year or two, depending on the treatment."

"Just to be on the safe side," Keisha said, "you might want to introduce her to Seth. He can tell you within the hour how long she has, at just a glance, or I can drop by."

"You dropping by would tell my parents what you are, though."

"Maybe. They both work, right?"

"Oh, right. I'll see if I can get them to bring her to practice. Then Seth can take a look too, and you guys can compare notes."

"Sounds like a plan."

"Hey, guys," Angela said, "what do you think of bringing Dave up?"

"I think what we think is irrelevant. Even if Teddy signs off on it and simply absents himself, Seth won't give him a pass," Bridget answered her.

"She's right, Ange," Solly said. "I doubt you'll be able to convince him. There's far too much antagonism. But feel free to give it a shot. Place your bets."

Angela watched with dismay as Karen was the only one to bet on her ability to convince Seth. They teleported back to Earth shortly afterward.

Chapter

6

"Hey lassie," Angela said to Karen early Monday morning as they walked from the parking lot into the school. Their bus pulled away and a different one came in. Patti's prayers at the flagpole had gotten a few new students, but they noticed Malcolm and Jasmine in a close embrace and felt his power cancelling the entrancing Patti added to her voice.

"What's up, lass?"

"I wanted to give you a heads up. Seth's going to be water boy for cheer squad this year, we've just confirmed."

"Inconceivable!" she said. They grinned at each other, recognizing the quote from the movie marathon. "What happened to Laura?"

"We got her into Drama. Romeo & Juliet, the big play. Don't worry about it. I'd be there myself, but I've got football practice. He's just there to deal with any accidental uses of magic."

"Wasn't anyone else available?" Seth? Did it have to be Seth?

"Not really, no. We could rotate people in to keep an eye on things, juggling schedules to be sure someone's there, or we can have someone already on the refreshment support squad handle it. Since half the reason he agreed to do it last year was to keep a teacher's eye on me, it made more sense to have him do it. Relax! At least you won't have to worry about anyone putting in roofies like they did to us last year before he took over."

"We didn't with Laura, either," she shot back.

"True. But, with all due respect for Laura, she doesn't have Seth's power. She doesn't have the ability to handle an accident. It's just for a year anyway; by next year you'll be fully in control and he won't need to be here."

"What about Keisha? She was doing it freshman year."

"She got assistant editor on the school paper last year and is editor this year. He's not going to hurt you, lassie. Embarrass you, maybe. But not hurt you."

"Well, if that's all he's there for…"

Angela grimaced. "I'm hoping it'll distract him from wanting Dave dead, too. Any chance you can hook him up with one of your teammates? Maybe if he had a girlfriend he'd be…"

"Less inclined to execute your boyfriend? Dunno if it'll help, but I'm on it, lass." They parted and went off to their classes.

The Round Table met up at lunch for a discussion on integrating the Las Vegas Gorgons into the league. That was fine, but Seth insisted on conducting the meeting in Nahuatl. Angela hadn't liked that, but Keisha and Teddy both pointed out that it was essentially a business meeting that should remain confidential. Which meant having it in a language few other people would be able to understand.

When they were fully enmeshed in their discussion, Dani quietly spoke to Dave. "Hey, I've got a question. Since they're distracted and you can't understand them anyway."

"What makes you think I can't?"

"I do understand them. They'd have picked a different language if you knew Nahuatl."

"Oh. What's the question, Dani?"

"Are you prepared to be second fiddle?" He looked blankly at her.

"I don't get it."

"Ange is enormously more powerful than you are. I've seen you in the gym, very impressive. But bench-pressing what you do is peanuts compared to what she's capable of if she puts her mind to it. You're dating a superhero. Love songs can call the subject a goddess. She's the closest thing to one you're likely to meet. She can turn you into a frog, melt wood, or juggle a few buildings. You are NOT her equal. Can you handle that?"

He sat back in the hard desk chair, evidently surprised at the question. He opened his mouth, and then closed it. He locked hard at Dani and then at Angela, who was still engrossed in her own discussion. He opened and closed his mouth again. "I've never asked myself that question," he admitted.

"You might want to think about it. You're Steve Trevor to her Wonder Woman. Can you deal with being her sidekick?"

"I guess. What are you getting at?"

"I love Alex. I'm there for him as much as I can be. At the same time…I can't do the things he can. If I try to join him in everything he does, I'll quickly be overwhelmed. I want to be at his side for all of it. But I know the limits of what I can do. Whatever he's enchanted my jewelry and clothing to do—and he's enchanted all of it—I'm the sidekick. Ange hasn't done that with yours," she said, tapping her sunglasses. "As much as we want to help, we have to know when we're more of a liability to them than we are a help. I know what Alex can do, what any of them can do. I'm not in their league and I know it. There are times when I can help him—them—best by being safely on the sidelines and out of harm's way…and listen to them when they tell me that it's too dangerous for me. If you really want to be with Ange, you're going to need to know it too."

"That makes sense, I guess. Angela told me about the meteor over Beijing."

"Then you know that sometimes their actions have side effects. You know Karen was there…briefly, because she's better than the rest of them at calculating things in her head. They sent her home first. Their defenses could handle it. She couldn't. So they—whoever they are—got her to safety first."

He nodded and changed the subject. "What language did you say they're using?"

"Nahuatl. The language of the Aztecs."

"What are they saying?"

"Sorry, Dave. I'm getting snippets; they're fluent, I'm not. Besides, using Nahuatl is a gesture of trust on their part since they know I'll understand at least some of it. But they're using it because they don't want outsiders to understand them…and that specifically includes you. Ange wanted to have it in English. Since they aren't speaking English, I'm not going to get myself banned from future meetings by telling you." She sipped her juice. "Ask Ange if you really want to know." Biting her lip, she leaned in towards him. "One thing Ange and Alex can do is alter or erase memories. I managed to avoid that, but you might not be so lucky."

"Are you sure you avoided it? You wouldn't remember if you didn't."

"Part of bringing me in was letting me know when and where Alex had stepped in. Yeah, he did it himself rather than leave it to someone else, who might not be as careful in my head."

"You think Angela would do that to me?"

She shrugged. "She might. She wouldn't want to, but if she does it you'll still have the rest of your memories. One of the others might not be that careful. Your call, Dave. Who would you rather be messing around in your head? Someone who loves you, or someone who doesn't?" She took a drink as he digested that.

Cheerleading practice was half done when the girls noticed that Seth was there for the squad's practice. Karen hid a smile at how quickly he'd gotten set up; he'd obviously used his magic. Barbara went over to confront him.

"What are you doing here?" she asked.

"My job," he answered, handing her a cup of Sportyade. It was purple.

"He's our new waterboy," Karen said, accepting her own cup. "Angela mentioned he'd been transferred from the football team."

"Which just coincidentally lets him watch cheerleading practice up close?" Stacey asked.

"That is a perk," he replied deadpan.

"Let's try again, Seth. How did you get this duty? I thought it was Laura's job."

"She's got a conflict." He blinked at her. "She landed the role of Juliet in this year's big play."

"You're here just to watch her, aren't you?" Marilyn asked, nodding at Karen.

"I'm here to make sure the cheerleading squad stays hydrated," he said… but he was blushing.

"Of course you are," Lucinda said archly. He handed her a cup too. "Your dream girl's presence has nothing to do with it."

"I'm here because there's no one else able, trained, and willing. I won't be doing it next year, and she'll still be on the squad."

"And you rearranged everyone's schedules?"

"No, I didn't."

Karen's brows were rising in disbelief when a thought came to her. Seth was certainly capable of rearranging schedules, even without using magic, but he wasn't the best at it—and someone else doing it would let him answer truthfully. Unfortunately, there was only one real way to get answers now without tipping off the rest of the squad. She inhaled deeply and reached out with her mind to touch his. *<Who did rearrange their schedules? Angela said you were here to keep a teacher's eye on me, so someone did.>*

<They did it themselves. Under compulsion from Alex or Jennifer if you must know, but as far as anyone other than us knows it was their own decision.> Right! Leave no tracks.

<Do you really think it's that much of a danger?>

<Me? No. You're further along in your training than Angela was last year at the same time of year. But having someone here to make sure there is no problem isn't a bad thing. Angela nearly killed someone in a game last year.>

<She told me about that.>

<So you know that she had no real desire to kill. She was about to anyway. I don't think you're likely to—not during cheerleading practice— but it's possible. I'll just be a safety net and enjoy the show.>

<You guys learned yourselves, without teachers. How'd you keep accidents from happening?>

<We watched each other. As many of us as we could get to go to a particular event. Why do you think we always came to the football games? We were keeping an eye on Alex.>

"Why are you two just staring at each other?" Anita asked.

"He likes staring at her, haven't you noticed?" Stacey answered the freshman. "He's in lurve with her." That got her a round of giggles. Seth flushed.

"Damn the blush really shows in the Goth pale," Christine said.

Another round of giggles.

"Doesn't he know she's not interested?"

"As I said, no one else was available to do this job properly," he said.

"He knows," Karen said. "We talked last year just after I got back from being on that ship."

"And he's still getting this job just to watch you? Damn. Isn't that called 'stalking'?"

"He's never done anything to me. I'm hoping he'll fixate on somebody else," she said arching an eyebrow him.

"Yes, Ma'am," he replied. "I'm looking."

"Yeah, at her."

"Don't make it worse, guys. We can laugh about it where he's not so likely to use the Sportyade for his chemistry experiments," Stacey said. "I've heard stories about him."

"Well don't believe half of what you hear," Seth said with a smile. "You're in no danger from me. Besides, I'm in physics this year, not chemistry."

"Well, that eases my worries," Karen said sarcastically. Alchemy was a different subject altogether; Dani'd mentioned him offering to turn her into a rabbit. He chuckled. "But I don't think he'll do anything to us. Not unless we ask him to."

"So you're saying he's harmless?" Stacey asked.

"Oh, no. He's certainly not harmless. You wouldn't believe how not harmless he is," she replied, almost shuddering with just how dangerous Seth really was. "But I have gotten to know him well enough to know he's not going to aim that harm at us, and that he's got pretty good target selection." *Let's just shut that down before the others decide to start adjusting minds,* she thought to herself. Then she grinned. "Think of him like one of those big black fluffy Canadian dogs."

"A Newfoundland?"

"Yeah. Gentle with us and a nasty handful for anyone wanting to hurt us." She grinned some more at Seth's less-than-flattered expression. "You want him, go for it, Stace. I'll be happy to set it up."

"C'mon, ladies," Coach Rice called as Stacey shot her a look. "Quit ogling the boy, you've seen one before, you'll see him again, and so get back to it!" As they dispersed back to the practice field, she sent him a thought.

<Just remember you're here to protect them, and we'll get along fine for this, Seth.>

<As you wish.> That stopped her. She shot a glance at him, but he just raised his eyebrows. After practice he gathered up the materials and left more quickly than she expected. She'd been expecting him to hang around and be friendly.

Chapter

7

They were down by a field goal when Alex took a hard hit in the helmet from Tiburon High's linebackers and Coach Nguyen pulled him out. The trainer looked him over, shined a light in his eyes, but said he should stay on the bench. Alex sat down next to Dave.

"C'mon. Cast a spell and win the game."

"No."

"Shut up, Dave," Dani said.

"Get in there! C'mon dude. I know you can."

"Coach pulled me out after that hit. He's worried about a concussion. He did the right thing."

"Oh, come on. You're fine."

"Sportyade, Alex?" Seth said. "Janice is covering for me for a minute. How are you feeling?"

"Thanks, Seth. I'll be fine."

"I know; you're tougher than you look. I've had enough of your blood on me to be sure of that. But the cheerleaders wanted a report on you."

"Isn't that sweet of them?" Dani mock growled. Seth shrugged. "Tell them he'll be fine, would you?"

"Naturally, Danielle, and all yours. See you later."

"Alex, we all know you guys fixed the helmets to eliminate concussions. Phil isn't bad, but he's not a magician like you are."

"Dave, not here," Angela had just come off the field while the offense concentrated on running plays.

"If not here, where?"

"When something more important than a football game's on the line, Dave. You need to shut it on the other stuff. I want to win as much as you do, but Alex and Ange aren't going to cheat to do it."

Alex muttered something in Nahuatl. "Sorry, Dave, I don't like doing that to you. But maybe now you'll realize we're serious."

"Don't be too harsh, Alex," Angela said.

"I'm not. I didn't even cast that on Dave."

"Mr. Cleburne, could you stay after for a few minutes?" Coach Nguyen said loudly.

"Uh, sure, Coach." He was off the team that afternoon, based on some minor discipline problems—like trying to convince someone with a concussion to go back in the game. He took off for a weekend of surfing when Angela told him she couldn't alter Alex's enchantment of the coach.

The football team was at Salerno's for the after game celebration of victory over Reagan High. The cheerleaders, the waterboys and girls, and most of the Round Table had come to join them; the big exception was Seth as Julian walked in with Jenny. She'd really put forth an effort, makeup and jewelry (stars and crescents in gold predominating) and a near formal blouse and skirt. His election defeat left a lot of time for being with her. Considering they were going to pizza with the football team, the effort didn't really make sense to him. When he asked her about it, she said it hadn't been any trouble at all.

"How not?"

"I'll let you know." She paused to sip. "One day."

"Hey Julian!" Eric Montoya called. "Want a slice while you're waiting?"

"No thanks. I'm not really into Hawaiian pizza."

"What's wrong with Hawaiian?" Angela asked.

"Everyone seems to think I like it at parties, so they order a big one. But I really prefer a simple pepperoni and sausage." He shrugged. "I'd rather have the pineapple raw."

"Oh, sorry, ah, Your Majesty!"

"First you guys started doing that, now half the school does!" Jenny chuckled and said something he couldn't understand. Angela responded in kind. "What was that?"

"Oh, I was just asking where Dave was. He went surfing after being dropped from the team."

"At night?" he asked.

"I guess so."

"I hope he knows what he's doing."

"Poseidon's friends are on it."

"That doesn't really make any sense, you know."

"One day it will. Do you need to study this weekend, or would you be available for an, ah, excursion?"

"Where to?"

"Bridget's mom needs some equipment that got left behind, so she's putting a group together to go out to the Farallones. We can study on the yacht."

"Cool. Let me check. Who else is going so I can tell her when she asks?"

"Well, I am," Jenny said.

"Studying is all you guys seem to do sometimes," Eric said.

"There's a lot to learn," Jenny replied. She suddenly cocked her head to the side, and let her green eyes go blank for a moment, as if she was seeing or hearing something only she could. Then she nodded. "But the team out on the islands will feed us before we head back in, so that's a bonus."

"Jules, is there anything you can do about Patti?"

"I'm not class president, Lance. I'm not even really involved in Student Council. I can talk to Shevaun. Why? What's she doing?"

"She's trying to move the Fall Formal to a church and cancel the camping trip."

"I'll see what I can do. I'll start putting petitions together to get as many students as possible opposing both and Principal Lee will nix them."

"Good idea," Jennifer said. "You'll have our full backing."

"Patti versus the Round Table?"

"Pretty much. We haven't really flexed ourselves, but it's time to show Patti just what the limits of Student Council President really are."

"Are we sure she didn't rig that election?" Julian asked.

"Not that the investigation committee found, anyway. Keisha had several students look into it for the paper, and I think Ms. Lee did too," Alex said.

"I'm amazed they haven't found anything." Alex shrugged.

"Angela, Miss MacLeod, Jennifer, sorry I'm late. Ms. Tegenfeldt kept us a bit long," Seth said as he came to join them for their study session. World civ would be…interesting with Seth involved. Over the summer he'd worked out how to get information out of a long dead corpse, even if he didn't speak the language. Then he'd gone out and used the new spell.

"Okay. Seth, I know you're just aching to tell us where the book's wrong, but let's start as usual with what Ms. Nalley's going to be expecting us to put on the test. You can supplement as we go along."

"I only got to the Middle East, India, and China, and I had to be fairly circumspect."

"So that's why there were those mass deaths."

"I only did some of that. And Bridget turned a bunch of those missing Chinese boaters into baiji river dolphins." With that comment they delved into the material, taking notes and quizzing each other. The study hall hour went by quickly, but fortunately Dave found them before it was time for the next class. Seth switched to Coptic as soon as Dave appeared and wouldn't drop it even when Angela and Karen asked him to. Dave wasn't in their Honors class, but Seth refused to even acknowledge his presence before everyone started getting up to go to class. His refusal clearly irritated Dave. She felt Jennifer shut him down before he could start in on Seth, and smiled gratefully at her.

"Hold up, Angela. I need to talk to you," Jennifer said.

"Sure." She kissed Dave and he went off to his own world civ class. "What's up, Jenny?"

Jennifer spoke in Cornish as she inclined her head in Dave's direction; he wasn't out of earshot yet. "He nearly took a poke at Seth before I took temporary control. I shouldn't have to tell you just how bad an idea that would be for him. He has no power, no talent, no defenses. If he gets into a direct conflict with Seth, he won't survive it."

"Are you saying you think he's going to come after him?" she replied in the same language.

"No, but he—Seth—does hold grudges, and they've never been friendly with each other. He's not going to tolerate anything physical, even as he ignores anything else. Dave's gotten a lot better since you two started dating again, not wanting to anger your friends. I don't think Seth sees that, though, and if Dave chooses to get physical Seth will treat it as an attack."

"Great. Any suggestions for reconciling them?"

"Nope. You may not be able to, not without changing Seth's mind."

"And he's got defenses up against that."

She sighed. "Magic's not the solution to everything, Ange. You're not going to like hearing this, but it's not like Seth doesn't have genuine reasons to dislike Dave. He might not be discussing them with you out of consideration for your feelings, but the rest of us know. If the two of you weren't dating he might have already done something permanent. You may have to accept that they're not going to reconcile."

"He seemed to get over it with Dani."

"That's Dani, not Dave. She'd pick fights with him, but she never crossed the line to getting physical with him, never made herself an enemy. I suspect that was Alex's influence, her not wanting to go too far against an old buddy of her boyfriend's. Plus a bit of boy-code psychology—he'd put up with something from a girl he wouldn't from another guy. Add it all together…"

"And he didn't let Dani in easy. I remember; I was there for that. She was scared witless when she learned what Seth was capable of doing."

"And she went out of her way to make peace with him after she did learn. Seth hasn't agreed Dave gets to know. But him trying to act like we're all old buddies is backfiring badly with Seth. Regardless, magic's not going to do it for you. Karen or Alex might be able to get through his defenses to influence him, but it's outside your concentration. Even if you were able to, do you really want to deal with his retaliation when he found out? He'd regard it as an attack."

"Fuck."

"Like I suggested, you may have to accept them not reconciling. Live and let live may be the best you can expect or get." Angela felt her mouth twist. She wanted more than that. Jennifer leaned in, raising her eyebrows. "'Live and let live' is better than 'live and let die', Ange. And we both know who would be living and who would be dying in that scenario. If you want to change his mind on the subject, you're going to have to actually convince him."

"How? His mind is completely closed on the subject."

"I wouldn't say completely. I'm not saying it's going to be easy, and I have no idea how. But I don't think he's being entirely serious about killing him…"

"You don't?" Angela said hopefully.

"No. I think it's a response to you refusing to accept his veto as the end of the discussion. He first vetoed it back in July, remember? I think you can change his veto, but it's going to take a long time, and Dave is going to need to step up. Challenge petty bullies around school. And absolutely positively not open the mummy's tomb. Make a positive contribution, redeem himself, be seen doing it, and not doing it just to impress Seth. He's not very good at reading minds, but he still can."

"And might do it if he suspects a show being put on for his benefit."

"If Dave suddenly develops a splitting headache, you should probably see if Seth probed his mind."

"Hey Karen. Did I hear you right that the squad needs another guy?" Dave slid his tray kitty corner from her. Stacey looked at him sort of goggle-eyed.

"Yeah…I did mention that. Why? You know someone?"

"Sure. Me. Whaddya say?"

She blinked several times. Stacey rescued her. "You don't know any of the routines, the moves, anything. About the only thing going for you is being tall and strong."

"I can learn."

"Can we take on someone who doesn't know anything at this point?" Valerie asked.'

"We can talk to Coach Rice," Lucinda said. "Speaking of which, I'll go see her now. Anyone wanna come with?"

Karen subtly encouraged Valerie and Stacey to, but said "Catch up with them" to Dave, and she put up a sphere. "Are you nuts, laddie?"

"What do you mean?"

"Have you talked about this brainstorm with Angela?"

"No, not yet. Why?"

"Seth's waterboy for the squad. I do not want him using our Sportyade as his chemical entertainment center. And you're an idiot if you think he can't do it," she said urgently.

"You and Ange can't pull strings and get him reassigned or canned?"

"We pulled strings to get him the position. He's there to keep an eye on me. So no, we're not going to do that." She shook her head when Dave opened his mouth. "No, you don't need to know the details."

"I can handle Seth. I handled him fine last year on the football team."

"No, you can't. He's the problem here, not you. The hostility's coming from him. I'll bet you never actually did anything with him. But at the same time it can't be about him." She paused and chewed on her lip for a moment. "You're going to be working your ass off. You aren't going to be having time to pick a fight with him."

"Sure thing."

She let him catch up with the others, then let her carefully blocked link to Seth open a little. He was in the library. Of course. She spotted Malcolm and sent him a telepathic message. He excused himself from Jasmine.

"Why do you need my help to talk to Seth?" he wanted to know.

"He's not going to be happy with what I have to tell him. I want someone there who can restrain him if necessary."

"Uh-oh. What's going on?" She told him. "Okay. This isn't that bad. It'll depend on how stupid Dave is."

"'I think it'll depend on how bloodthirsty Seth is," she countered.

"You know there's nothing we can do about it if Seth decided to kill him, right?"

"Yeah, so?"

"So does Seth." He cocked a sun-bleached eyebrow at her, and she slowly nodded. Certainly if she knew, the people who'd been at this for years before Angela started teaching it to her did. "There's history between them, and it's not pretty. Before you go blaming Seth for everything, you might want to look into why he has no patience or tolerance for Dave."

"But killing him?"

"He poses a problem with our safety. His death would solve that problem. I'm not surprised Seth proposed it. I'm not surprised he was voted down, either."

"With what we can do? How does he threaten us?"

"How many people did Seth kill for touching you against your will?"

"I…don't know."

"It's more than you think. He spent most of the summer hunting down and executing the people behind it." He grinned. "I think he likes you or something." She grimaced. "But the real point is more along the lines of what happens when we refuse to use our power for something. What happens if someone starts taking hostages? Or killing? Or some idiot celebrity too stupid to stay away from drugs overdoses? We can reverse death, and Seth's the ultimate authority on it. Dave's loose tongue doesn't really threaten us directly, although Seth suggested once that we'd probably have to leave Earth if it got out. It threatens everyone around us. And for all his willingness to kill, he doesn't like doing it."

"Well, Dave's gonna be on cheer squad. He'll just have to get used to it."

"No he won't. He can get him booted off easily enough. Any of us could, and I don't think he'd even bother bringing it to vote. Which means Ange wouldn't be in a position to oppose him until he'd taken action."

"I would!"

"And you might be able to overrule him. But this is precisely why we try to come to an agreement amongst ourselves."

"Regardless of its effect on someone else?"

"Play it out. What happens to Dave if we don't come to an agreement? Why did Alex kick him off the team in the first place?"

She considered that as they went into the library. "He pisses Seth off and dies. Seth's threshold is far too low."

"Is it? I mentioned the history, right?" A blue flash took them back in the stacks.

"What history?" Seth asked as they appeared at his hiding place.

Malcolm's teleportation spell had taken her by surprise.

"You and Ange's Dave."

"Why is my history with the idiot relevant?"

"You know Alex kicked him off the football team for not watching his mouth. He decided to join cheer squad."

"Well, that won't fly. Do one of you want to fix it, or shall I? I'm sure it'd just be a matter of getting Principal Lee to veto it on academic grounds."

"Doesn't really matter to me, but should we intervene at all? I know you don't like the guy, Seth, but too many weird things and even he'll start to suspect."

"Then…"

"Wait, Seth. The squad could use him. We've got a bunch of routines in the book that were designed with a fourth boy in mind."

"And? Why should any of you have to put up with him?"

"The squad's more worried about you using the Sportyade for an experiment than they're worried about him. C'mon, Seth. You'll have little interaction with him other than handing him a cup or something."

"That's more than I want to have." Malcolm had stepped back. "He's a security risk for Ange…and me. You'd be keeping the most skeptical and suspicious set of eyes in school on him." Seth frowned. She grimaced internally, but she could feel another objection coming. "Unless YOU want to join the squad? If you cheat I know you've got the strength and stamina for it." He shook his head. "Then stay out of internal squad matters, please. You're there to keep a teacher's eye on me, to make sure I don't accidentally hurt anyone. You're even better for that than Angela is. If Dave's presence is too much of a problem for you, by all means transfer your water boy duties back to one of the other teams and we'll get other people to make sure I don't hurt anyone. I'd rather have your experience keeping my friends safe from me, though."

He seemed about to respond and then changed his mind. "As you wish, Miss MacLeod. I will see you at practice."

They nodded to each other and she left with Malcolm. She let out a long breath as soon as they were away from him. "That was nicely handled, Karen."

"What?"

"Angela's told us you've been reluctant to challenge Seth. I'm not entirely sure why, not without probing your mind, but I know she's been concerned by it. You really need to get over whatever's inhibiting you."

"That was a test?"

"Oh, ah, no. We wouldn't have been able to set that up. That was a real problem. And you really solved it. Probably like no one else would have been able to."

She grimaced. 'Bridget and Jennifer told me something similar once. Any suggestions?"

"I don't know what the problem is. If you want my advice, I'm happy to give it, but you'll have to tell me why you don't want to confront him. It's not like I've seen you have any problem standing up to me, or even Angela."

"It's not something I'm comfortable talking about."

"I won't push. But not talking to each other is how we tend to get problems. Seth helped get Ange that first date in part because he figured she'd dump Dave after she really got to know him."

Chapter

8

*J*ulian still marveled at the fact that he and Jennifer were together. They'd been friendly before the accident that killed his parents and paternal grandparents back in June. He'd been very surprised when she sat down next to him on the first class Royal Hawaiian flight with a "Hey Jules. Mind some company?"

"Jenny? What are you doing here?" he'd asked.

"Going to Hawai'i," she'd replied, putting her hand on his and smiling sadly at him. "Solly and Bridget will be along tomorrow; they're holding a combine on Molokai." That was a lot more hands on than he expected out of them. "I know you've got family things to attend to, but just give me a ring. I'll be there as soon as I can get a boat or flight if necessary."

"Thanks, Jenno. But what about your finals? And how'd you end up on this flight?"

"I challenged the finals yesterday. I'm doing well enough the teachers let me. As for the flight, magic." She'd smiled at his expression. "I went online to book it—the Starlets' plane is needed here—and this happened to be the last seat left. I guess someone suddenly cancelled."

"Lucky for us."

She'd been as good as her word, only a phone call away. She'd had a lot of luck with inter-island transport, always arriving sooner than he'd expected. She'd supported him when he told his grandmother he wanted to finish high school in California. She'd somehow persuaded her even before Solly and Bridget arrived to help out, suggesting that he apply to college in Hawai'i.

He'd made it out to the combine, too, and spent most of it with Jennifer. Watching the players, conferring with her coaches, surfing on the north shore, the big luau they'd thrown the last night when the other league owners had come out—and announced the formation of the Las Vegas Gorgons. They didn't announce Angela Fujiwara as the team owner, but she was. They hadn't announced themselves as the owners; they had an official spokeswoman for making all the announcements and been using Bridget's father as their public contact. By the time the trip was over, they'd been a couple. He wasn't quite sure how she'd kept her complexion without burning. She'd told him 'magic' and hadn't explained further. But that memory had led to this Chinese restaurant in Terra Linda.

"Any chance of you guys putting a team in Hawai'i?"

"No reason not to. We're kind of selective about who we accept as owners, though. You want to start a team?"

"Beats playing fantasy football," he said with a smile.

"What do you think owning a team is? The Witches are mine, true, but I hardly get out on the field of play. I can bring you up as an owner, if you want. We've got game on Saturday, but I think you'd have the votes."

"You do? I thought the teams played in the spring… oh, your D&D game." She smiled at him. "How do you guys ever make kickoff?"

"Not a problem," she assured him.

He looked at her skeptically. "You didn't answer."

"No, I didn't," she smiled. "We don't have teams outside California—except the Gorgons, now, and Ange is just in Vegas—but we do have private jets. It'd be harder if we had to fly out to Honolulu, but we could manage it. And if it'd be too much problem, we can play with a video chat."

"Are you even looking to expand?"

"Somewhat. Karen's going to put a team in Santa Fe. It depends on whether or not we like and trust the potential owner. So you and Shevaun have good shots at it. That pack of investors from Salt Lake City, not so much."

"Kind of an odd business model, isn't it?"

"Yeah, but it's also a cover… Forget I said that," she smiled. His eyebrows rose. "What are you covering?"

She shook her head. "I'm sorry, Jules. But it's a private matter, and I don't have agreement from the others to tell you yet. Certainly not here."

"You know that just leaves me with more questions, right?"

"I'm sure it does. But I'm not going to answer those yet. From how often saying it turns out badly on TV I hate to say it, but you're going to have to trust me on this. I will tell you eventually, I promise. Just not yet."

"Why can't you tell me now?"

"You'll understand when I do. We're a little paranoid about security. We all need to agree to let someone know about us." She sipped. "I really am sorry. I don't like keeping you in the dark. Those who have boyfriends or girlfriends are either having the same conversation—and I know Alex had it with Dani once upon a time—or not mentioning anything."

Chapter 9

"What do you think you're doing setting my boyfriend up with Kathy?" Isabella Ward stormed up to Karen as she and Sarah were having lunch. Isabella did a lot of storming, a big blonde girl who was a star of the basketball team.

"You two broke up," Sarah said. "If you didn't want him, why are you surprised someone else did?"

"Kathy thinks Emmett's cute. He thinks she's cute," Karen said. "Neither was going to make a move as long as you and Emmett were dating—she likes him enough to not want to ruin his relationship—but he's free now."

"I oughta…" Isabella was clenching her fists.

"Chill and go eat your lunch," Dani said, taking a seat. "All for one, right, Karen?" Isabella deflated on seeing the linebacker step up. Dani might also be a big blonde girl, but that was where similarities ended. Athletic as she was, Isabella was still only about half Dani's size.

"And neither of us are full members. Where's…?"

"The Clubhouse. Something came up, League business I think. I can get a message to Alex if there's something we need them for, though. And there's someone even worse you could get a message to, isn't there?" She and Karen shared a tight smile.

"Buzz off Dani. This is none of your business. He is mine, Karen. I am not giving him up."

"Thanks, Dani, but I can handle this." She turned back to Isabella. "You already did, Izzie. Move on. I can set you up with someone, too, if you want."

"You have a problem with Karen, you've got one with me. And the rest of the Round Table," Dani said. Isabella took in the facts of Dani's taught muscles and larger frame. Dani led the school in sacks.

"Dani, it's okay. I'd probably be irritated too if my ex boyfriend found someone new before I did. I'll be happy to help you find someone, too, like I said."

"How about Seth?" Sarah suggested.

Karen shook her head. "If someone came to me wanting me to set her up with him, no problem. But…"

"You want him to start looking at someone else, right?" she said. "How does getting him a date with her not advance that?"

"Yeah, but I also don't want to put him with someone who's ambivalent about being with him. It wouldn't help anything if he's just there as a favor to me." She shot a loaded glance at Dani, who nodded.

"Well, I'm not even interested in the Deadboy. I want Emmett back."

"He's totally wrong for you, Izzie. Trust me. It's over, and it never had much of a chance to start with."

"What the hell are you talking about?"

"You wouldn't believe me. I know he is. He may be a great guy. But you're not right for each other. Larry Williamson is much more your speed, and he owes me a favor. Whaddya say?"

"Larry? You have got to be kidding!"

"You two would be great together. You've got a lot of shared interests. Give him a try. You two will definitely click."

"The class clown? You can't be serious. Like I would even touch him!"

"She knows more about matchmaking than you do," Dani put in. "You can take her advice or leave it. You do, it's your loss. I've never regretted taking it to accept Alex's invitation." Isabella stormed off in just as high dudgeon as when she stormed up.

"Glad she's gone," Dani said. "Let me know if she tries causing more problems."

"She wouldn't like the outcome if she did," Karen replied.

Dani nodded, and said in Nahuatl, "I know. I am a more…blatant… threat than you, despite your power."

"Alex been teaching you language?" Sarah asked. Dani grinned and nodded. "See you in class!" she said as Dani left.

10

Karen met up with Angela after school for a study session in the library. "Where's Dave?"

"Just Julian and Shevaun to start; he's running late, Jenny had a snafu come up with the Witches, and Bridget and Malcolm are in the Antarctic Ocean," she replied in Ainu. Julian and Shevaun were getting closer.

"And the others?"

"Alchemy lab with Seth and Mike at the Temple."

"I guess even Mike can only play so many video games, or is Seth just refusing to associate with Dave again?"

"Well, actually, he's avoiding *you*. Dave's not in the Honors classes. I didn't invite him until after Seth said he'd be on Venus."

"He doesn't socialize after practice much, and didn't even before Dave joined the squad. Is he mad at me?"

"I don't think so."

"Having someone who likes payback as much as he does pissed at me is bad enough. Add in how lethal he is, it's even worse."

"Yeah, it would be, but he's not, so nothing to worry about. He's just avoiding you. You're the matchmaker. You'll be better at figuring out what's going through his mind than I will." She grimaced. The connection to Seth was one she tried to not use as much as possible.

"Hey, Karen, when'd you join the incomprehensibles?" Shevaun asked as she took her seat.

"Last June, about the time the Chinese stopped that meteor." She continued in Bengali. "That's when I learned I could use magic too. We'll start teaching you two soon."

"What did you just say?" Julian asked.

"When you're ready to learn, you will," she returned to English. "You know, it was weird enough listening to the Round Table do that freshman year. Then Angela started doing it last year. You want me to start ending my sentences in Lakota and not explaining myself?"

"If that'd make you feel better. I don't promise that I won't understand you anyway, though. Did you still want me to set you up with Harry? You're perfect for each other."

"How about leaving the matchmaking for a couple hours and concentrate on physics?"

"I love seeing my friends happy with someone. Even better yet happy with each other. It's the best part of the matchmaking gig," she replied.

"Maybe find yourself someone?" Julian asked. "Why is it matchmakers—at least in the movies I've seen—never seem to have a love of their own? Seems pretty lonely to me."

"Especially when we all know there's someone who'd be over the moon if you dated him," Shevaun said with a wicked smile, gesturing at her Valkyries t-shirt.

"In the moon, maybe," she muttered.

"He could get over the moon," Angela answered in Ainu. "He's walked on it enough times."

"Okay, okay, sorry I brought it up," Shevaun said to Angela. "Can we keep this in a language we can all understand?"

"Sure."

"Why do you guys keep dropping into languages no one else can understand?" Shevaun asked.

"The answer to that can be found in what we were talking about. We're not ready to tell you yet."

"You know that's a really weird answer, right?" Julian asked.

"Yeah. We know. But for right now, it's the answer we can give," Angela told him.

"What are you? Superspies?"

"Superheroes," Karen's deadpan replied. Julian and Shevaun looked at her with raised eyebrows before deciding she was joking.

Chapter

11

"Ready?" Angela asked Karen. "This might be a little tricky."

"Aye, lass," Karen responded. She was actually a few months younger. She screwed her face up in concentration and opened her eyes, glowing pink in the bright history classroom Ms. Linehan let the Wizards of the Round Table use. After several moments, she said, "Angela, who uses gold?"

"Gold? Nobody. Dawn uses yellow, but no one uses gold. Why?"

"Because the ballot box is glowing gold in this sight, and I can't imagine Dawn enchanting the ballot box."

"Certainly not to elect Patti. Julian didn't need the help, but Dawn would never do that anyway. One sec." Angela briefly incanted in Ainu, and her eyes flashed from brown to teal. "Well, that's certainly not Dawn's work. Let's get Jennifer in here. Felarie, I beseech thine aid. Could you join Karen and I in the club room?"

"I thought that was the big meeting room out in the Headlands."

"That's the Clubhouse. There's a difference. And that place is a secret, remember?"

"Damn, sorry. I know that. But no one else is here."

"As far as you know. Have you checked for the invisible? Or someone scrying us? Neither of us put up a privacy spell, so what about listeners? Through the vents or at the door?"

"Oops. There's more to this secrecy stuff than I thought when magic gets added to the ways you can be observed."

Jennifer appeared in an indigo flash. "What's up?"

"Someone tampered with the ballot box. Tampered our way, Jenny." Jennifer looked at her in surprise, then spoke a few words in Cornish.

"Damn. This is Keisha's area. Kara, we need you, the ballot box was enchanted. I ducked into the girls' room, so I need to get going back to class."

"No idea who gold would be?" Karen asked

"Color doesn't really mean anything, you know. Fiat lux," she said, creating a ball of light that she sent through the entire visual spectrum and indulged in black, gold, copper, bronze, teal, maroon. Then she made it polka dotted, then striped, put it into rosettes and finally an ermine pattern. "Once you have real control over it, color's just a matter of preference."

"As she says," Keisha put in coming through the door. She said something in Cushitic. "You're right. We should probably discuss this tomorrow night."

"Agreed. I'll put it on the agenda."

"Right. I'm off to physics. Damn." Jennifer ducked out.

"So, that's how we ended up with Patti."

"It's only student council. How much harm can she do?" Karen asked. "Do you think she cheated herself, or did someone do it on her behalf?"

"I'm inclined to think she did it herself, since it's hard to imagine anyone wanting to fix a student council election for someone else. As for damage…if she's a practitioner? How much damage could one of us do?" Keisha responded. It was an unsettling thought. "Seriously. You do remember the meteor headed for Beijing, right? Angela took it out on her own and the rest of us were just shielding the ground from her fusion detonation."

"Oh, right." The full members could probably do that themselves—now that Angela had shown the way—but only Angela would be ready to play racquetball immediately afterwards.

"I'll see you ladies in class," Keisha said as she left.

"Later. We've got study hall. We'll look around for other clues."

Angela asked Seth to join her and Karen for lunch so she could get some guidance about magic teaching techniques. She'd actually managed to pin him down for it—over the summer she'd mostly had to ask questions telepathically—so the opportunity wasn't to be wasted. While they were talking—surrounded by a privacy bubble Karen put up—Dave sidled up and put his hand on Seth's shoulder. Seth's eyes went flat black and the shadow of a skull passed over his features.

"Hey guys," Dave said cheerily. "Is he bothering you, babe?" Angela's eyes went wide in sudden panic. Seth would interpret that as an attack.

"Dave, let go of him immediately." Karen backed her words with power and Dave obeyed.

"You can get rid of him or we can continue this in a way the fool won't understand," Seth said in Coptic.

"What'd he say?"

"Never mind, Dave. We're actually doing a bit of private studying. I'll be with you later," Angela told him. "Seth's not available much, and I need to pick his brain."

"Oh, cool. Coach said it was my grades that got me kicked off the team. Maybe I'll learn something."

"Not unless you can understand what he's saying, and he just said he's not switching back to English."

"He has more than enough trouble with that," Seth put in, again in Coptic.

"Insulting him isn't helping."

"He doesn't know Coptic anyway. Why not speak the truth about him?" Seth still wasn't returning to English.

"I do. Quit it," Angela said.

"You do what?"

"Know the language he's using to call you a fool," Angela responded. Dave bunched a fist. "Calm down, Dave." He looked down at his fist somewhat sheepishly and released it. "I don't suppose you'd be willing to conduct this in two languages?" she asked Seth.

"Not unless you two are going to shift to something else. He's not cleared to know anything."

"Now you're just being unreasonable," Karen said.

"As you wish." His eyes flicked back and forth between them. "Incidentally, Miss MacLeod, your barrier didn't work because it's got an exception for those in love reaching the object of it. You might want to correct that flaw." Seth gathered up his trash and left.

Karen shook her head. "Only he would consider that a flaw," Karen said.

Angela answered her in Ainu. "In what's supposed to be a defensive barrier, he's right. Much as he was enjoying spending time with you, the idea of a privacy bubble is to keep people out, and know who you're letting through ahead of time. I know you walked through one of his, but that one was designed to make people avoid us. Anyone with sufficient determination to come through the fear and nausea could have, and it would have repulsed Dave. If he'd been stopping people from reaching us, it would have been set to kill. And he's right about him not being cleared for anything. I don't mind, and you don't mind, but he does. I'd prefer it if we didn't give him an excuse to do a mind wipe."

"Or an execution, considering who we're talking about?" Karen replied in the same language.

"I don't think he'd get the votes for that, but he would for the mind wipe."

"Would he even put it to a vote? I mean, that's more of a courtesy to everyone else than something that we really need in order to do it."

"Now that you mention it, he might not. He can act on his own and do an execution. Great, something else to worry about."

"What was that, babe?"

"Sorry babe. If I'd wanted you to understand I would have used English. I had to pass a caution to Karen, and I needed for you not to understand. Speaking of which, I think we're done for now."

"You sure?"

"We can't exactly study with him when he's not here."

"I thought you could, you know, talk mind to mind," Dave said. "Everyone knows telepathy's impossible, Dave," she said, cocking an eyebrow at him. Hopefully he'd get the reminder not to discuss things like that in public.

"Enjoy what's left of lunch, guys," Karen said with a smile. She dismissed her privacy bubble, grabbed her things, and took off to spend the rest of lunch with some of her friends. Angela turned to Dave with an exasperated look in her eyes.

"Dave, are you looking for the Lord of Vengeance to start a vendetta against you? Because putting your hand on him wasn't a good idea."

"It was just a joke."

"Dave, he hates you. He didn't take it as a joke; he took it as a threat. Be glad he didn't take it as an attack and was willing to let Karen and I handle it. What if he can do the same things I can, Dave? Or worse, what if he wasn't tutoring me in math or English last year, but in magic? Did you think about that?"

"Oh, come on…"

"Dave, maybe I'm playing the what-if game because it's the closest I can come to directly warning you without breaking my promises to keep certain secrets. The "I-could-tell-you-but-then-I'd-have-to-kill-you" kind of secrets." She took his hands and stared directly into his eyes. "What if, Dave, he's the most lethal person on Earth, and he thinks you'd look great in a coffin six feet underground? What if he can kill you whenever he wants, and you'd have no warning whatsoever? What if whenever he wishes, you fall over dead? And what if the only thing keeping it from happening when you do something like that is that he likes me and doesn't want to pick a fight with me?"

"That's ridiculous. Seth?"

"Then how about you're on cheer squad now and he's cheer squad's waterboy? You want him taking up the challenge of whacking you one and leaving everyone else fine? Cause I'd bet he can do it." Dave grimaced.

"Hey guys. What are you up to this weekend?" Bridget joined Angela, Keisha, and Karen for lunch.

"Studying. I've got a history paper due."

"Me too. I've got an enchantment test with Alex a week from Saturday."

"Whaddya say to studying on a plane?"

"Where to?"

"London."

"London? England?"

"Yeppers!"

"Why London?"

"Dad's been approached about putting the Magic Bowl there in six years. And since we're the real placement committee…"

"We should check out the venue. Makes sense. But why this weekend? Why not everyone? There are only eleven of us, and with teleportation we can all arrange to be there with enough lead time."

"J.K. Rowling's doing a book signing."

"Oh, I love those books! I'm in."

"Me too."

"I'm not passing this up," Keisha said. "Should we invite the others?"

"Why not?"

"Seth's got that Linear A project this weekend," Bridget cautioned. The Minoan writing had never been translated. "I'm not sure who's working on it; I thought you were, Keish!"

"My part's done for now. We can still ask. Besides, this sort of opportunity is kind of rare."

"Can't you do it magically?"

"Sure. I've produced enchanted translations for him. But he wants to actually decipher the language." She shrugged. "It's a worthwhile project. He can hand the work off to a muggle at some point."

"A muggle?" Karen asked, giggling. Keisha just raised and lowered her eyebrows.

They found Seth having lunch with Malcolm and Jasmine. "Hey guys. You busy this weekend?"

"I am," Seth said. "You know that."

"Dad's been approached about playing the Magic Bowl in London six years from now. Since we'll be adults then he tossed the question to me. And since we just learned Rowling's doing a book signing, we were wondering if you'd be willing to put it off for a week."

"I've heard she's a very nice person, great with fans and everything, but Linear A is going to be tough to unravel. I think I'll keep at it." They'd already discussed the possibility of going to Crete to get information from the dead with his new technique, but Seth wasn't going to mention that in front of Jasmine. The main stumbling block was finding the corpse of a scribe or other literate person. As yet, they still needed the corpse to be reasonably intact for it to work, or Seth would have to resurrect someone.

"You guys using team jets again?"

"No, they're not cleared for international flights. Did you want to come, Jasmine?"

"Can I? I wouldn't be in the way? Malcolm is up to something with Solly this weekend, he will not say what."

"We've got a project." Mal's cocked eyebrow told the wizards it was Project Vaquita, reviving the recently extinct species on Venus and Luna. If Jasmine was still in the dark, then no she shouldn't be around for it.

"Sure Jas," Keisha glanced at the others.

"Oh, shit. Tickets to London are expensive. I don't think my parents will sign off on it."

"Maybe not, but as long as they're okay with you going I'll cover those," Malcolm said. "The Sirens are really popular in the City, and we get a cut of the merchandising. Have a great time, baby."

"Malcolm, don't…"

"I'm not worried about it. Go as my eyes and ears about the locations they're looking at. You're on the books as a consultant." She smiled and kissed him. Seth rolled his eyes.

"Oh, hell with it," he said. "Make it an official trip of the placement committee if you want. You have my vote to use the travel budget." Angela grinned. The travel budget was a cover, since the League owners routinely teleported wherever they needed to go or covered their own expenses. It mostly sat around collecting interest.

"Thanks, Seth, that's a good idea. I'll add my vote," Malcolm said. Alex and Dani came up and grabbed seats. "What's with the gathering?" he asked.

"We're going to London this weekend. Wanna come?"

"I can't," he replied. "I'm working on the Linear A translation with Seth and Teddy. Dani? Want to be on the books for a weekend?"

"If you guys don't mind me coming," she said.

"Of course not, Dani. Glad to have you," Angela said.

Jasmine looked back and forth at them. "It almost sounds like you had discussed that ahead of time." They smiled at her and Malcolm winked.

"How would that have been possible, Jas?" Karen asked innocently. Jasmine's tongue found the inside of her cheek. Angela could tell she wasn't about to claim knowledge; Malcolm had warned her about that.

"Oh, it would not, of course. But it certainly sounded like it! Almost a repeat of my conversation! The only difference was that Dani's not worried at the cost of the tickets!"

"Alex has me on the books as an occasional consultant for the Avengers, and he just offered to do it again."

"London and the placement committee? Mom mentioned someone approaching the trustees committee about some exhibition games played in foreign countries. Mexico, Cuba, England, Japan, Australia, South Africa, Brazil, Canada, Texas. Wasn't hard to put it together."

"Texas is a state."

"I know that. You know that. Everyone else knows that. They appear not to know that."

"With their policies, we might want to send Seth and Solly to check out any venues," Keisha suggested. Angela and Bridget shared a wicked grin at the idea. None of them suffered fools gladly, and Seth didn't suffer them at all, while Solly's defensive abilities were the best among them. Alex shook his head.

<Let's not. Seth confronted by a bunch of adults brandishing real guns is likely to kill them before they start shooting. He doesn't think anyone with peaceable intentions walks around armed to the teeth.>

"What about passports and stuff?"

"Won't be a problem," Malcolm said. "We'll go get yours this afternoon if you need to."

"It works that fast?"

"If you have someone who knows what they're doing." Dani's lips twitched at Malcolm's comment. No, it didn't work that fast. But magic could speed up even bureaucracy—and Jas apparently knew about Malcolm.

"Good to know that is in the sack," Jasmine said.

"Mine's already in order. My sack-toy likes to jet off places at a moment's notice."

"*Sack-toy?!!*"

"Dani's the best on the team in the sack," Alex said innocently.

Karen covered her eyes.

"You two are really a pair, aren't you?"

"Dani's the only linebacker to get me into a practice sack, you know." They grinned at her.

"Didn't Malcolm warn you, Jas? They can go on for hours about her sacking him. It's their favorite subject, at least while anyone else is around. Don't say the s-word around them. Please," Seth put in.

"They're talking about football, are they not?"

"No, they're talking about sex. They lost their virginity to each other May of freshman year," Solly said matter-of-factly. Their twin glares at him took away any doubt he was telling the truth.

"How do you…no, do not answer that, I don't want to know how you know that!" she said.

"Back to London…where will we stay?"

Bridget glanced at Angela and Keisha. Keisha spoke up. "I know a great place. It may be a little civilized for Bridget's taste, but it's completely fabulous, and I'll make the arrangements."

"Who all's going?"

"I've talked with Dawn and Jennifer. They're both in. Jenny invited Julian to come along but he's got a ceremonial commitment in Hawai'i. Shevaun's actually going to be in London with her Dad for the opening of "Apache Chief", but she'll hook up with us for what we're doing too."

"Any tickets available?"

"If we'd known about it early enough we could have gotten some," Kaisha said. "As is? Probably not."

Dawn's voice entered their heads, though from her expression not Jasmine's. <We could probably accomplish it, but I think this is a case of 'better not'. It would be hard to explain to Shevaun and Jasmine. We can go as a group next week. Malcolm, would you arrange the tickets?>

<Sure. Yes, Angela?>

<Can I get one for Dave?>

<Why I asked Malcolm and not Seth.> Dawn sounded amused. <Sure, Angela. Anyone else need an SO ticket?>

<Actually, I'd like one for Charles.> Dawn said.

<One for Catalina, please> Solly said.

<Catalina? Catalina Zaragoza? You guys getting serious?> Karen asked.

<I…maybe. I'll thank the rest of you not to scare her off!>

<Fair warning, Solly. I seem to frighten her every time I open my mouth in Lit.> Seth seemed amused by that.

<Only because you quote the book from memory.>

<You two are totally right for each other, Solly.> Karen said. <Let me know if I can help.>

<Thanks, Karen. I think I've got it, though.>

"Okay, cool. I'll see about getting on Shevaun's flight. No promises." Bridget raised an eyebrow.

"If anyone can swing it, Keish, it's you." Angela smiled.

"Sounds like a fun weekend." Keisha could easily arrange nine tickets on one plane; it would be only slightly more difficult to have them all sitting together, but they didn't need to be. She reached out telepathically to the rest of the round table and texted them. The telepathy came back first, but a minute or so later, after a series of chimes on her phone she said, "Okay. Travel budget approved." Teddy's father might still be a stickler about it, but the parents who were clued in would vote as directed by the unanimous decision of the owners. Her own parents had told her a decision that would come up after they'd assumed full control wasn't worth an argument with someone capable of controlling their minds.

"Angela, do you need a plane ticket for Dave? Or a hotel room?"

"He already told me he's got family stuff this weekend."

"His favorite euphemism for being grounded?" Seth asked.

"I didn't actually ask. Family stuff is family stuff. Are you dating anyone yet, Teach?"

"Of course not. No one's that masochistic. I'd need mind control to get a date."

"Is he being serious?" Jasmine asked.

"Still gloomy, so yeah, he is," Angela answered her.

"He's wrong, of course…" Karen said

"Says the only girl he's ever asked out," Bridget said. Karen felt her cheeks heat. Seth looked like he was on the verge of saying something but bit his lip instead. Bridget cocked her head at him, making Angela think he'd commented telepathically. "Sorry, Karen. I know that's something of a touchy subject for you." Karen gave Seth a look, but he kept his face still and his mental shields slick. Angela felt Karen's questioning probe bounce like a rubber ball.

<What were you trying to find out?>

<Never mind.>

<I know you're still a bit nervous about being one on one with him, but you could probably just ask. He spent a lot of effort improving his mental defenses after last year, but I think he'd tell you anything you wanted to know.>

<I can't ask it in front of Jasmine!>

<We do have ways of communicating she can't understand, you know. Like this one.> The bell announcing the end of lunch rang. *<And that doesn't stop you from using them.>* Karen grimaced at her. But she didn't pick up the buzz indicating Karen was talking to Seth.

The flight to London was long and boring. They enjoyed first class—though Bridget seemed to be wishing she'd teleported—and Shevaun was surprised to see them all somehow on her flight, but it was still mostly hours of sitting, reading, listening to music, talking. Catalina Zaragoza had been a last minute addition on Solly's word; even though she knew them all she was quiet. Keisha watched the inflight movie but the rest of them didn't bother. A little turbulence smoothed out easily enough under their influence. Since they were in the presence of outsiders, they stuck to telepathy when they wandered into secret subject.

There was one subject that they wondered about that had secret implications. Somewhere over the Atlantic, Shevaun asked Karen how her little sister was.

"Cancer. Twelve months, maybe. They're trying to get her a little stronger before the operation. But the chemotherapy to beat the cancer down is working against that."

"Oh, that's horrible," Jasmine said.

<*Still?*> Bridget asked her. <*Your parents know, right? Why haven't you done anything? Or asked me to?*>

"I've done some research on radical therapies for her," she said, arching an eyebrow at Bridget <*like magic*>, "Mom and Dad don't trust them, and don't want to risk it." <*I've already told them if she dies, I'm taking her to Venus and bringing her back minus the cancer.*>

<*Doing it that way is tricky,*> Jennifer cautioned her. <*You've never brought anyone back, let alone excised the cause of death like that. I suggest you have Seth standing by if you do it. It would be far easier—for any of us—to simply cure her now.*>

"Is there anything we can do?" Shevaun asked.

"Know any good authors she might not have read? She's been plowing through the library." <*Yeah, but...*>

<*But nothing. You decide when and where and how to use your power, your Mom doesn't.*> Keisha said firmly.

"A few," Shevaun said, and Jasmine and Catalina nodded as well. "I'll send a list. Dani?" Catalina was a little goggle eyed to be sitting just across the aisle from Shevaun's father.

"I don't know about authors, but…I've got some books she probably hasn't read I could loan her. If your parents don't mind."

"I can smuggle them in to her."

<You'll violate the approved reading list without a second thought, but not save her life?> Angela said incredulously.

<Getting past parental authority takes some getting used to, especially when it's about someone else,> Dawn said. *<I see what you mean, Karen, but it's your responsibility. You can't let someone else control your power like that. Have you asked Katie what she wants?>*

<Not yet. I've still been arguing with my parents.>

"So what do we want to see in London? Besides the book signing," Dani asked. "I know you guys need to check out the stadiums and stuff."

"I've heard a lot about the British Museum and Buckingham Palace," Shevaun started.

"We only have so long, Shevaun!" Jasmine said.

"And we have to be at the theater relatively early tomorrow," Mr. Lone Elk said. Shevaun started at the reminder he was even there.

"When does she have to be there?" Catalina asked. She'd pulled out her phone.

"Two on Friday."

"I already set my alarm, Dad!"

"We'll get her there in time," Bridget said. "A lot of us have that meeting at Wembley at that time."

"Thank you, Bridget."

"Look at you, being all business like and responsible! I thought that was Keisha's bag," Shevaun said.

"It is. But since my dad set up the meeting, I'm sort of the coordinating person," she shrugged.

Using their magic in subtle ways, they got themselves to their rooms with little fuss. Keisha's taste in accommodations was excellent. They spent Friday morning being tourists at Buckingham Palace, joking that they should have brought Julian along. Shevaun, Jasmine, and Catalina were always amazed at how lucky they got with the buses, and at how quickly they got places. Dani just accepted it as inevitable. She knew they were going to tweak things. "Are you sure we didn't just take the Knight Bus?" Catalina asked as they got back to their rooms so Shevaun could change for the premiere and the rest of them could get ready for Wembley. Jasmine and

"Yes, we are."

"Wembley Stadium now"

"That's impressive," Catalina said. "How big is it?" Dani rattled off its dimensions, while Keisha mentioned it's capacity and all the other events that had taken place in it. The stadium arranged a trio of escorts to show them around and discuss the advantages of holding a Magic Bowl in London.

At the stadium, they were taken on a tour, and they split into a few groups. Keisha, Angela, and Bridget went to the business section, Jennifer, Karen, and Dawn a second to tour the box and audience seating, and Dani, Jasmine, and Catalina to see the locker rooms and other team facilities. Dani tapped a crystal Alex had given her, and Angela recognized it an enchanted memory stone. For that matter… her lips quirked as she noticed…they were all wearing them. Malcolm and Solly would retrieve the information later.

It was a good thing they were wearing the memory stones, because the meetings were boring. She let Keisha and Bridget handle most of it, letting her mind's eye roam the stadium. She occasionally asked questions based on what she saw, and passed on questions from Dani or Jennifer.

Their tour ended with a promise to bring the matter to the full owners. They chatted about the venue while they waited for everyone else—they hadn't gone as far as the other two groups when they all sensed the magic in use…and it wasn't theirs. Eyes closed and seeing Dani from a far, they sent power to protect the three without appearing themselves. That would have been hard to explain to Jasmine and Catalina. The practitioner felt the sudden spark of an exposed power cable and suddenly started dancing around from rats that had fallen on him. It was enough to let Dani and the other two flee to a public area.

<What happened?> Jennifer asked.

<Practitioner attacked Jas, Dani, and Cat,> Bridget told them.

<We drove him off,> Keisha said.

<He lived?> Dawn asked.

<Yes. Once he was out of sight of the girls I turned him into a hedgehog and took his mind.>

<Let the others know.> Bridget nodded and told the others. They discussed it on Venus when Jasmine and Catalina were asleep. They didn't come to any conclusions, but Keisha put the data point into her divinations. The rest of the trip to London proved satisfyingly devoid of confrontations. They were, however, very pleased to meet their favorite author and get their books signed.

$\mathcal{B}$ridget dropped by Karen's to pick her up for Angela's birthday party. Her new car was purely electric, highly streamlined, and equipped with highly efficient solar cells. Angela opened the front door in the new Las Vegas Gorgons sweatshirt, the Medusa's head prominent on her chest, to let them in. Bridget was carrying two packages, not just one. She arched an eyebrow at her.

"Thantoris thought it better that he not come. Something about your dad waving a gun last year."

"He's not worried about getting shot, is he?"

"Death dying? No, he's more concerned that the bullet would hit someone else. He maintains more defensive enchantments than anyone but Bestarion. And he didn't see the need to antagonize anyone by being here."

"Oh, come on, Dad's not that dumb. He's clued in on what Thantoris can actually do, has been ever since he picked me up for the attack on the *Pelewan*." Maybe repeated use of the secret name would get him to actually show up. "And he knows he owes his daughter's life to him."

"Okay. That's what he told me, anyway. It's not like you can't give him a shout and ask him yourself. He's just doing homework at the

Temple and keeping the custodian company. It isn't like Keisha can bring Mike here, is it? Too many people here knew him."

"I'd have liked him being here, but I can see that. I'll see him next time we meet at the Temple."

"We could disappear up there after everyone else goes home."

"I can't bring Dave."

"If you're going to make that a prerequisite, you aren't going to be up there much. He'll be very disappointed that one of his closer friends is avoiding him."

"Seth's the one putting up the block. Complain to him."

Bridget switched to Gaelic. "I haven't given him a pass either, Ange. Nor have I agreed he gets to know about me. Other than Karen and Alex, who has agreed? In being pissed off at Seth, you might remember that you're wanting privileges for him that the rest of us have extended only to Dani. And she knew about Toranos for over a year before Thantoris even revealed himself to her to keep you from burning down Muir Woods."

"You're more reasonable than Seth."

"Have you asked Seth why?"

"He doesn't want to talk about it."

"You're going to need to find out if you want that veto dropped."

"Why, then?"

"I think this is something you need to work out with Seth, Ange."

"She's right," Dawn came up with a gift box of her own. "We can't speak for him. He was your tutor."

"He got me my first date with Dave! It makes no sense that he's got this implacable hatred of him!"

"It doesn't?" Dawn said. "If he won't talk to you, there's someone else he'll probably talk to about anything she wants to know." Dawn and Bridget both had slight smiles on their faces. Karen looked at them oddly before her eyes flew open.

"You're not serious!" she said.

"Completely. You have the connections to him, but we know him better than you do. If anyone can overcome his reluctance to speak on a topic, it's you."

"Don't worry, Karen. I'll get the info myself. Hey here come Jenny and Julian!"

"What's all this?" Julian asked seeing them all standing at the open door.

"Seth's not coming, and Angela was trying to figure out why."

"That's obvious. He doesn't want to put a damper on your birthday by being grumpy near Dave," Julian replied.

Angela had really gone all out in decorating for the party, Julian could tell. "How'd she *do* all this?" he asked Jennifer.

She shrugged. "She managed, that's what really matters."

"I guess so. Interesting crowd here. Hi Carmen."

"Hi Julian. How's Honolulu?" He'd just gotten back from another trip.

"Warm, windy."

"Girls in bikinis. The usual," Jennifer put in. Carmen grinned.

"Oh, right, you got to go this summer. Not that exciting?"

"Girls in bikinis don't exactly excite *me*. Julian, on the other hand, finds them very interesting."

"So do I," Carmen said with a smile. "By the way, Julian, I've got those petitions you were circulating with signatures."

"Great! Patti's never going to know what hit her."

"I should hope not. We're pretty sure she did rig the election."

"WHAT?" he and Carmen said at the same time.

"We've proven it to our satisfaction. We haven't managed to get our hands on the evidence we need to prove it to the principal, though."

"What DO you have?"

"Sorry, I shouldn't have mentioned it. How we got it is a problem. I think we're going to try to make her confess in public."

"That'll be entertaining!" Carmen said.

"How do you plan to do that?"

Jennifer smiled. "We're not saying. Scuse me, I need to talk to Hannah about history for a moment."

"How are you Carmen?" Angela asked coming up to them.

"Mmm. You know. Great party, Ange."

"Thanks. Mom's got the grill fired up out back."

"Hey Ange," Donovan O'Malley, a full back, said, "Is there any beer?"

"Nope. There are people here who really shouldn't drink, and I'm one of them. So no booze."

"Fuck."

"Besides, Coach hears about a boozed up party and I'm off the team."

"Can't have our star receiver off the team."

Julian circulated almost as much as Angela did. As he did, he became more and more convinced that Jennifer was right; Patti had somehow rigged that election. More and more people were coming up to him complaining about the agenda Patti and her cohorts were pushing, and while it might have all been rumors, Shevaun was still the vice president and confirmed all of it. She was usually outvoted three to one. Quentin Soltesz had already been circulating a recall petition for all three of them. He withdrew it without explanation after a week. Burgers and hot dogs formed lunch, until Dad brought out the (as he termed it) Angela Food Cake and chocolate fondue.

After the cake it was time for the presents. There was a lot of the usual footballs, gag gifts, and t-shirts from vacation spots. Dave got her chocolates. The Round Tablers' gifts seemed on the surface to follow that vein, too, but…Keisha's recording of classic Noh and Kyogen theater was marked to come from her and Mike, with Mike's name in ink only the Round Tablers could see. It was also enchanted in a way that she hadn't seen yet, but would have to wait until she could talk to Keisha about it. The other gifts from the Round Tablers were also enchanted. Finally, she got to the one gift that didn't have anyone present to account for. Seth's.

It wasn't large. It wasn't even in black wrapping paper; the paper was teal. "Who's that from?" Dave wanted to know.

"Seth. Bridget brought it with her."

"Not very big. Want me to open it for you?"

One glance told her that wouldn't be possible. Angela was the only person who could open the wrapping paper without triggering a deadly curse. "No, thanks, Sweetie. My gift, I get to open it!" The crowd chuckled.

Inside was a black jewelry box, and inside that were a pair of earrings in the shape of platinum-set gorinto. A quick divination showed her the gorinto were carved from sapphire, each level of the tower a different color—blue, purple, orange, pink, and yellow. They here also heavily enchanted with protective magic. She sat there looking at them, and reached out to Seth with her mind.

<Thank you, Teach.>

<You're welcome, Angela. Happy birthday.>

<Why aren't you here?>

<It's your birthday celebration. I freak your parents out, and you don't need me scaring your apprentice. You'll have a happier party if I'm not there. Besides, everyone else is down there so I'm keeping Mike company up here going over the monitor readings and simulations.>

<I thought you were doing homework!>

<I finished that two hours ago.>

<You're sure that's it?>

<I don't like one of your guests. It would really spoil your party if I gave in to temptation where he's concerned, don't you think?>

<You can't still be that mad at him.>

<Why not?>

<He soaked your clothes. Get over it.>

<Are you sure that's all that happened? Maybe you should do some research.>

<Get down here, Seth!>

<No. Miss MacLeod isn't comfortable in my presence and I do not wish to associate with your boyfriend. Not even for you.>

"What is that, Babe?"

"It's a gorinto. It's an elemental symbol in Japan, for earth, water, fire, air, and void."

"Cool."

The day after the party, Mom asked her to drive her to her dentist appointment, on the old "you need the driving practice" explanation, and they rolled down the windows since it was a nice day. Angela wondered if she should go ahead and enchant the old Honda Element. While she didn't really need to make it fly, and she could really just teleport the whole thing if she wanted to, she could make it harder to damage. She put up a simple privacy sphere—one that wouldn't let sound escape and would blur vision in—and asked Mom.

Mom started in surprise. "You can make the car fly?"

"Uh-hunh. Which way are we going?"

"Left. There are some legal issues with that, I'm pretty sure."

"Some of the wizards are talking about putting a garage on the moon, Mars, and Venus."

"How much control of the magic would you leave for Dad and I on the car?" Angela considered that for several moments. It wasn't like she'd be alone in driving it, but she hadn't really considered her parents.

"This is going to sound like an upside down idea, but whatever would be under your control, I'd want to be sure you both knew how to control it before I'd feel comfortable letting you use it whenever."

"You're right, that does seem unusual. But from what your magic can do, I can see why you want us to be safe in using it. We can't fix everything with a few words!" Angela nodded.

"I could leave quite a bit, though I think I'd lock down any sort of interplanetary teleport. You don't have the power to survive on your own interplanetary, and even an apprentice doesn't go out alone on the surface. And the bases are specifically warded to keep out outsiders. I can get you temporary permission to be there, but it covers a specific time before you'd be yanked back to Earth without agreement from the others."

"That's all that would happen to me?"

"The protections themselves are more robust; someone trying to penetrate them would be lucky to survive to escape. But, yeah, a temporary pass just expels you. Is this the exit?"

"Yes." A couple of stop lights on, a man came up to her window and demanded they get out of the car. He showed them a gun mostly concealed in his sleeve.

Angela glared at the guy holding a gun. "If you value your life, you'll put the cap gun away and run."

"Dear…" Mom was already unbuckling her seat belt to surrender the car.

"I'll handle this, Mom. This idiot has no idea what he's messing with. I've already died once. Death's a close, personal friend. He won't keep me this time either. I'll introduce them." She spoke a word in Ainu. He stiffened. "Take your little toy and confess to the first cop you come to," she ordered him. He walked away. The light turned green.

"Honey, you…"

"Took control of his mind, yes." She paid more attention to the road. "It seemed less destructive than killing him. No, I haven't done that to you."

"It's a little chilling to hear you casually say that killing him was one of your options."

"It was an option, Mom. But most of those options would leave strange evidence. Flash freezing, inexplicable burns, gamma radiation, that sort of thing. I haven't quite mastered Seth's 'whatever natural cause is most likely to kill him anyway' method, especially when my emotions are up."

"Honey…"

"Mom, Seth *would* have killed him. I needed to end that before he shot you. Which way?"

Chapter

13

The Fall Camping Trip up the coast once more featured the entire Round Table. That…wasn't really surprising any more to Karen as she scanned the list of names. The surprise was Dave.

"Hey, Ange! We getting a cabin again this year?"

"Yeppers. We only need to keep Shevaun from noticing anything, since Dani's along this year."

"The boys need two, right?"

"One. Dave's along."

"Ange. I like Dave, but we both know that'll never get past Seth. You're the only one that's going to back him against his opposition. Even for the camping trip."

"Well, let's ask." Karen shook her head. This wasn't going to go well. Despite everything, Angela still had rose colored glasses on.

They found Malcolm and Teddy having lunch out in the court yard and sat down.

"Ladies," Teddy said in his best formal tones. A word in Aramaic formed a privacy shield. "I presume this isn't a social call."

"Dave got on the approved list for the trip."

"Good for him," Teddy said.

"Do you guys mind if he bunks with you?"

"Does it matter?"

"What do you mean?"

"When we're filling up the cabin, we should go with people we can all get along with. So…Julian is number six. For seven and eight, we're looking at Erik Stevens and Eddie MacGregor. Dave…I know he's your boyfriend, Ange. But Seth wants absolutely nothing to do with him, and I'm willing to bet you that not even Karen can persuade him otherwise even if she offers to sleep with him. If he got assigned by random chance…he'll force a transfer. Ask him yourself." She got the impression Karen was blushing ferociously.

"Don't you dare!"

"I won't." Even as she said it, Teddy's eyes glazed over and returned to normal.

With a smile, he said, "I just asked him about the cabin. He suggested you take him into your own cabin instead."

"They're gender-specific. He'd only be eligible if he was trans."

"I mentioned that. He suggested you turn him into a girl, and then she can be in your cabin."

"We'd have to do a lot of mind altering! And that would put someone out, since Dani can go this year."

"You wouldn't like his solution of making Dave ineligible to go."

"No, I wouldn't, but you know they coordinate activities by cabin. I want to be doing things with Dave."

"We know, we know. What it comes down to, Ange, is that Seth will not share a cabin with Dave. If we insist, he won't go. I'm not going to do that to him. Having everyone get along is nice, but not everybody does," Teddy said.

"And why not?" Karen asked

"Have you asked Dave?" Malcolm said.

"He doesn't have a clue."

"Then maybe you should take off your glasses and see how he really is," Teddy replied. "I'm not sure you'll believe us if we tell you. You're going to need to learn the evil he's done for yourself, Angela. You might want to talk to Keisha about some of her better divination techniques."

"Hey, what are you guys plotting?" Dave came around the corner.

"I was trying to get you into their cabin for the camping trip."

"Oh, sorry, I didn't tell you. I got in with the team's cabin. Since Alex won't be there they had an opening."

"Well, that solves that," Malcolm said.

"Wait a minute," Angela said. "There's still…"

"Let's try this in a different language," Malcolm said in Phoenician. "We're much too close to secret subjects, and your boy isn't cleared for them."

"I think I see it, Ange," Karen said in Bengali. "This is better than cleaning his brain. As long as you're looking at someone with love, you're going to be suspicious of anyone telling you bad things about them, of what their motives are. If you learn yourself, with abilities you know to be true, or from him, you will have a better understanding of what's going on and why."

"Okay, I'll work at it."

With everything settled beforehand, the bus trip was a lot less chaotic than the last years'. Only one other girl on the football team had come—Dani—but Carmen was there, too. Carmen had a smirk.

"What's up?"

"If the idea of splitting us into boys and girls is to prevent us from having sex…"

"Why are they sending the lesbians to the girls' cabins and the gay guys to the boys' cabins?"

"Yep!"

"Maybe that's not the whole idea. What are you looking forward to?"

"We'll be doing more data collection as juniors. What about you?"

"Evening walks with Dave."

"Want us to provide cover for you?" Dani asked.

"Sure, but won't you need it yourself?" Angela asked her, then her brain caught up with her as Dani grinned. She switched to Nahuatl. "You just need to get out of sight, don't you?"

"Just as you do."

"Damn that's annoying."

"What?" Carmen asked.

"Dani and Alex already have plans to disappear," Bridget put in.

"A nice leafy bower of damp pine needles?" Dani grinned again.

Hardly. They'd sneak off out of sight and teleport somewhere more comfortable, like Alex's rooms on Venus—just like she wanted to do with Dave. Well, they could teleport off to the Seamount.

Karen nudged her and winked. Obviously she was picking up on her emotions. She'd been doing that recently…especially the amorous ones. She gave her a deadpan look that wasn't fooling either of them… or Bridget. Even Dani got it after a moment.

After a couple more hours they pulled into the camp.

"Think there's going to be a raid this year?"

"Not targeting us," Dani said. "That's already taken care of."

"Aw, it would have been fun," Carmen said.

Jennifer shrugged as she joined the conversation. "There's only one cabin that would be a challenge, and Dani and Shevaun can't do it safely. So why bother? We don't raid them, they don't raid us, and it's all good."

The first night they put Shevaun into a deep slumber before sneaking out; Angela and Jennifer making Dani invisible to facilitate things. They met their boyfriends in the burned out core of a redwood they'd spotted last year, and vanished as they got out of sight leaving Jennifer and Julian alone.

Julian found himself sitting by a small stream with a pair of binoculars watching some of the forest birds and taking pictures of them when the back of his neck tingled for no reason. He swung the binoculars down and caught flashes of colored light, but there was little sound. It was coming from the camp. He dropped his binoculars and ran towards camp. Something was smoking.

"Hey Jules. You okay?" Jennifer asked, matching his pace.

"I saw some weird things in my binoculars. I thought I'd better see what was happening."

"I didn't. I'm sure whatever it was has been handled."

"There's still smoke, Jenno."

"You have a way to make water?"

"Well, not quite WATER, but we can still help."

They got into the clearing holding the cabins to find…nothing amiss. Erik Stevens was lying on the ground being checked over by Seth.

"Erik! What happened?" he called.

"I don't know. I think I hit my head. A few minutes are missing. Thanks, Seth. Am I good to go?"

"You should get to the infirmary where someone can check you out, but as far as I can tell, you're fine."

"You're the one with first aid training. I'll take him," Karen said. "Come on, Erik." She and Seth seemed to lock eyes for a moment, then she nodded and escorted Erik away.

"Well, if he didn't know…do you?"

"He tripped and hit his head. He was out for a little bit. It shouldn't be a big thing, but head injuries and blacking out are nothing to take lightly."

Julian nodded, then…Seth was lying about something. He didn't know how he knew that, but he did. He didn't feel inclined to ask about it, though. "It's almost time to come back in anyway," he said.

"I suppose it is," Jennifer said checking her watch. She grabbed a seat on a section of log and crossed her legs.

"Any college visits planned, Seth?" he asked as they settled down to wait.

"A few. I'll probably go to Santa Cruz so I can keep an eye on the Valkyries. You're going to Hawaii, right?"

"Hey guys," Alex said as he and Dani arrived from their project. Then he said something in Nahuatl, and Seth answered him in the same language.

"Why do you guys use those languages?" Julian asked.

"Few enough up here speak them that we're unlikely to be understood," Alex responded.

"You're worried about keeping secrets from me? Do you really think that's necessary?"

"We're keeping secrets we haven't agreed anyone else gets to know yet," Jennifer responded.

"Maybe in January we'll explain it," Alex said. "I think you'll agree once we do bring you in."

"You sure about that?" Jennifer asked. Oddly enough, her voice cracked a little.

"Yes, I am."

"What about you, Alex? Decided where you're going after high school?"

"Mars." At Julian's surprise start, he laughed. "Annapolis. I can take both Navy and Marine courses. Dani's got applications out to a bunch of schools in DC, Maryland, and Virginia."

"We'll see if I get in," she said

"You will," Alex sounded absolutely confident.

"Not unless you…"

"You'll be in on your own merits, love."

"Easy for you to say," she muttered. Alex raised her chin and kissed her.

"Trust me."

"I do, I do."

"Trust him, then marry him," Jennifer said with a smile. They laughed. It was a good weekend…even if the Round Table seemed to know something they weren't sharing. It was a mystery where that hand Malcolm found came from that washed up on the beach, though.

Angela was having lunch with Karen and Bridget the Friday after the camping trip, discussing turning various people into animals. They'd been laughing a lot, as if it weren't a serious possibility, when Shevaun came charging into the cafeteria.

"Shevaun! What's wrong?"

"My grandmother…the hospital put her on hospice…"

"Oh, I'm sorry, Shevaun. Is there anything we can do? You fly out tonight?"

"Dad's on location in Australia. Mom's got a head stuffed so bad she can't fly. And there're no flights anywhere in reach to Sioux Falls or Pierre…"

"On it," Bridget said.

"Don't worry, Shevaun. We'll get you there. You have everything you need to fly out after school?" Angela asked her as Bridget pulled out her phone.

"Huh? What?"

"You just ran into two of the people here who can get you to South Dakota today," she said with a soft smile. "Bridget's on the phone with her pilot now. If you don't mind riding in a private jet, anyway."

"Private jet? Her pilot? I know her Dad's loaded and all…"

"Arcata Unicorns? She owns the team?"

"Oh, right."

"Let her know you're coming, while Bridget makes our travel arrangements. Well, there's one I should make," Angela said. As Karen distracted Shevaun with questions about her grandmother, Angela pulled out her phone, punched some random numbers, and subvocalized clear weather to the hospital. Bridget winked at her as she finished her real conversation.

"All set," Bridget said. "My car will pick us up and take us straight to the airport."

"Bridget, I hate to point this out, but it's cold in South Dakota at this time of year."

"I've got some cold weather gear in the car. We're not that different; you can borrow. Or we can swing by your place quickly and pick up Angela and Karen at her place." *<Or I will, as soon as I can duck out of here and create it.>*

"I expect Mom to be okay with it, but don't you guys need to check with your parents?"

<Can I help? I've never really done something like that.> Karen asked
<Sure.>

Bridget shrugged. "Mom's out in the Farallons and Dad's in… Taipei? Singapore? Sydney? Anyway, I own the plane, I pay the pilot, and they're perfectly confident in my ability to handle anything that comes up." Angela and Karen smiled at that. Their own parents objected less and less as their daughters' powers developed. "I'll let them know what's happening and that'll be that."

"I'll check with them," Angela said, "but I don't think it'll be a problem as long as I take my laptop and homework. Since it won't involve a weekend love nest with Dave, anyway."

"I'll be with Bridget, you, and Angela. My grades have improved dramatically since I started hanging out with the Round Table. They'll have no problem with it," Karen put in. "Where are we going to stay while we're there?" *<I mean the three of us could just pop in and out, but we'd need to come up with a place for Shevaun unless we tell her, and she'd figure out the truth if we did.>*

"I'll handle that, too," Bridget said. A few taps on her tablet seemed to get them reservations. "I hope you don't mind luxury suites," she commented

"Wow. You're a magician."

Bridget snorted. "This isn't magic. This is money, and I happen to have a lot of it. Remind me to show you the difference sometime." Karen and Angela started, but Shevaun wasn't really paying attention.

"Thanks a ton, guys."

"No problem, Shevaun. Let's get you to your grandmother."

"Not that I'm ungrateful, but…why? You're spending a lot just to get me out to see my sick grandmother."

"Money as such doesn't really matter much to me. If helping a friend out means I spend a little, so be it." Shevaun was still looking skeptical. "Shevaun, don't worry about it. Dad keeps funneling a share of what he invests in to me for tax purposes, and he's been doing it since before I was born. He's let a lot of what he's inherited pass through to me, too. I've got more than enough even without Keisha's investment advice. It's well within my trust fund's discretionary spending. Mom and Dad will want an accounting, sure. But that's as far as it will go. They'd have far more of a problem if I was buying clothes or video games or something like that. Getting you to see your sick grandmother will make them proud. But if it will put your mind at ease…" She pulled her phone back out and called her mother. Angela and Karen kept their faces straight as they sensed the mental communication she actually used. A few minutes of one-sided conversation and she smiled at Shevaun. "Done."

"Christopher? Yeah, it's Shevaun. Your cousin. Yes, the movie star's daughter. I'm flying in to see Grandmother at the hospital. Do you think you could pick us up from the airport today?"

"Do you think I should just order up a rental car? I've got Dad's info memorized," Bridget quietly asked the others.

"Maybe there are taxis? There should be taxis, right?" Karen said. "You'd think so."

"Chris, my friends are flying me in. I'm hoping you can at least give us a ride from the airport to the hospital."

"Shevaun, if it's a problem we'll get a taxi," Bridget said. "Don't worry about it."

"Bridget, you're flying us there on your private jet. You've already gotten us rooms, plus you've seen to your pilot. Let me do this at least! I don't even want to think about what I already owe you."

"Don't worry about it. I've got more money than I know what to do with." Angela and Karen rolled their eyes as Shevaun uncovered her phone. Like Bridget couldn't come up with ideas. How much land had she gotten her hands on, cleared of invasive species, and donated to nature preservation societies?

"Well, Christopher, sounds like we'll get a taxi…what flight? The Arcata Unicorns jet. I'm not sure what the call sign is…how did I score that? Well, the team owner's a friend of mine. She volunteered."

"This would have been so much easier if we just told her," Karen muttered in Bengali.

<True. She's not cleared yet, though, and if we revealed ourselves she'd put the rest together> Bridget answered her telepathically. *<The smarter the person, the quicker they figure it out if we're not taking steps, and Shevaun's grades are right up there with the rest of us. A lot of what preserves the secrecy is that everyone knows that what we do is impossible.>*

"By the way, Karen, Shevaun, we're looking to expand the league a little. California's kind of locked up, but you could put teams close by. Interested?"

"You're kidding, right?"

"Not at all. If money's an issue the League has a start up fund. Keisha's in charge of it, and it's grown to the point of being able to support three new teams."

"Who's the lucky third?"

"Julian. Which—since it's essentially decided he's going to the University of Hawai'i so he can do the ceremonials—puts his team in Honolulu."

"Why us? I mean, we're an economic burden on the rest of you just to get the teams up and running! Not that I'm ungrateful for the offer, and I simply dread having to go out to Hawai'i repeatedly, but..." Shevaun shook her head.

"We have our reasons," Angela said, doing her best to sound spooky and mysterious. Bridget spoiled the effect by laughing. "In a few years we may open it up more. But for right now we'd rather give our friends a hand to make a solid league than bring in a bunch of greedy outsiders. At least that's what they told ME when they started me up with the Gorgons."

Bridget shrugged. "There aren't a whole lot of people we can all agree on as owners, and the people rich enough on their own would want to be problems. You three, we agree on."

"I can't believe you guys have that sort of money to lend out."

"Keisha's investment abilities are kind of on the supernatural side," Angela told her. "She picks commodities that earn us enormous returns." Karen and Bridget smothered grins. Keisha's divinations made playing the commodities market just about a sure thing.

Jenny stopped the SUV at the Primates for Primates Aid shelter's loading bay half an inch from Teddy's foot. "I thought you were going to hit him," Julian said.

"I missed," she smiled at him.

"You've got the load?" Teddy asked.

"Canned goods, clothing, and blankets. Where do you want'em?"

"I don't know how she fit it all in. I was sure we'd be making another trip."

"She's the Tetris champion."

"I could have fit in more if I could have used the front seat…" Jenny mock glowered at Julian.

"I guess bringing along someone to carry this stuff will have to suffice," he replied.

"I could have carried it, or Teddy."

"Thanks, just when I was feeling useful for once."

"Wow," a woman only a few years older than them said. "You sure got it packed in here. What should I grab?"

"Miss Jennifer O'Neil and King Julian Kanekawa, Miss Jerusha Howell."

"Pleased to meet you, I'm 'Jerri'."

"Just Julian."

"What do you mean, King?"

"If you're going to insist on using his title, Teddy, you could make clear that that's what you're doing. There are enough people who use titles as names that it can get confusing. If it were still independent, Jerri, Julian would be the reigning King of Hawai'i."

"Oh!" She awkwardly attempted a curtsey. In jeans. It didn't go well.

"Thanks for the thought, but since I'm not actually on the throne we can forget about all the ceremonial nonsense." He easily lifted a couple pallets of canned vegetables. "Where does this go, oh Evil One?"

Jerri laughed. "Why do you call him that?"

"Back in what was it, third grade? Anyway, Teddy had memorized the Bible in Aramaic. He asked his minister a bunch of questions about it, calling him out on discrepancies between what the book said in English, what the Aramaic version said, and what he was preaching. The preacher, ah, didn't take it well," Jenny said with a smile. "He said only Satan would be coming up with what Teddy did. So, when we heard about it, "Evil One" became his nickname." Jerri laughed again.

"You can laugh. My posterior hurt for a week."

"Sounds like my parents," she said. "At least you get to go to school. I'm glad I escaped, but I'm lucky I can read. No one will recognize my parents' homeschool dipshitloma."

"God works in mysterious ways, Ms. Howell. If you want some studying help, I would be honored and pleased to assist you."

"Gee, thanks!" she said enthusiastically. "But only if you start calling me 'Jerri', got it?"

"Yes, ma'am. Jerri," he said. Julian chuckled.

Unloading the SUV went more quickly than Julian expected, mostly because Jennifer was stronger than he thought she was. She and Teddy joked with each other in Aramaic and Cornish, just grinning or flashing their eyebrows when asked for a translation. Jerri looked at the clock and said she had to go catch the bus to get to work on time.

"I can give you a ride," Teddy replied.

Her lip quirked.

"Ah, thanks, but I'll be okay."

"It wouldn't be a problem for us to drop you off either," Jenny said. "Thanks, but I already got the ticket."

"Blessed journey, then." Jennifer asked him a question in Cornish, and he answered quietly in Aramaic. Jerri hurried out.

"She seems nice. Where'd she come from?"

"Wisconsin, some small town. From what she told me, she hitchhiked her way as far west as she could. She said she has a job with a boutique studio—at least, that's what she put on the rental application." At Julian's questioning look, he said, "My parents own a bunch of seedy hotels and poorly maintained apartment buildings."

"Not all of them are that bad," Jennifer said, amused.

"Maybe not, but at some point they're going to be facing court orders to bring them up to code."

"Do you happen to know where Shevaun is? We were supposed to trade lit notes on Friday."

"Angela told me she's in South Dakota. Her grandmother took a bad turn."

"Oh, okay. I'll see her when she gets back."

"I'll probably talk to Bridget before then; want me to have Shevaun call you?"

"Oh, they're together? Sure, if she's up to it."

"You might say they're together. They took the Unicorns jet." Jenny paused and then said something to Teddy in Aramaic.

"Thank you, Jennifer," Teddy said in a disappointed tone "What was that?"

"Teddy asked me to check something out for him. It wasn't quite what he was hoping for. Sorry, Teddy."

"It was a bit much to hope for. Still, my parents would be horrified if I brought her home, so that's worth pursuing."

"Horrified? What on earth would they think is wrong with her?" Julian asked.

Teddy shrugged. "She's a few years older than he is, an actual legal adult. They have some weird notion that it would make a difference; I'm not really sure why," Jenny said. Julian again got the strange feeling she wasn't being accurate. There was some other reason that the older girl would horrify Teddy's parents. He'd been getting that impression a lot lately when they discussed the Round Table and it's activities. All of them but Teddy actually, although Dawn simply didn't tell everything. He shook his head and got back in the car as Jennifer got in to drive.

The Bismarck hospital was a dreary place, brightly lit, antiseptic, dull. Angela and Bridget practiced Bengali with Karen quietly in a waiting room before Angela got up to use the restroom. As she came out, an elderly woman said something to her. "I'm sorry, I don't speak that language." Her earring would have translated it for her, but she'd taken them out on the plane.

"It is Tsehesenestsestotse. You would say Cheyenne in English. What I was saying was that you have great power for such a young girl."

"I don't know what you're talking about." A stranger saying this? She brought defensive measures to the front of her mind, and the air started to get distinctly warmer.

The elderly woman spread her hands. "I mean no intrusion. The difference between what I'm seeing in you and what I'm capable of is so great that I'm not foolish enough to argue with you about it, even if I think you know exactly what I'm talking about." She inclined her head towards Angela. "I am Marilyn Carpenter, should you wish to find me again."

"Okay. Why are you telling me?"

Marilyn paused, as if very carefully weighing what she was about to say. When she spoke, it was with a cautious deliberation. "There are rumors, among those like me, who can do little things, of a rising group of VERY powerful young people, powerful enough to mold the world like clay. The whispers also speak of some who can do little things rising in opposition to the youngsters and being destroyed. I would not wish those young people to think me a threat, or in opposition to them. If I am wrong, no harm done. If I am right, I may have delivered my message to someone I want to hear it, before she goes hunting." She weighed her words more. "I would be overwhelmed quickly by too many people without the knowledge to reach beyond themselves for power, and what I can do I can't sustain more than a minute or so. What I'm seeing in you is the difference between a candle and the rising sun."

They looked in at Shevaun just holding her grandmother's hand. The elderly lady was unmoving and unresponsive, and had been for several hours. But they all felt Shevaun's untrained power keeping her alive.

<Bridget, should we offer to cure her?> Karen asked

<Why?>

<It's cure or kill at this point, or we lose Shevaun. What happens when we bring her in, let her know we could have saved her grandmother, and didn't, just to preserve secrecy?>

Bridget's lips twisted. <You're right. Who wants to make the offer?>

<You're best at healing> Karen said.

Bridget smiled a bit. <You need the practice.>

<Best compromise between healing her and secrecy would be me, since Marilyn Carpenter already identified me as having power. I'll do it. Karen, you be prepared to adjust their memories.>

<Okay.>

"Shevaun."

"She hasn't opened her eyes for a while."

"It's Sunday."

"And you guys need to get back, I get it. I'll call Dad about a ticket back in a few days."

She put her hand on Shevaun's shoulder. "Don't worry about it. If I could save your grandmother, would you be able to keep that a secret? Or would you prefer to lose the memory of how and why she was saved?"

"Ange, you're speaking nonsense."

"No, I'm not. I'm a wizard, Shevaun. Bridget and Karen already know. I can cure her. But I'd rather not have it get out." She felt Bridget and Karen isolating the room. "Fiat lux." The teal light came into being. Shevaun's eyes were wide.

"What…how…?"

"Does it matter?"

"No, not really, I suppose. Go for it."

"Let's find out if it's what she wants, though. If she wants to die, I'm not going to force her to live." She extended her hand. "I'll bring you with me."

A few words in Ainu connected them, and she took Shevaun's grandmother's hand. It bizarrely only occurred to her than that she should have asked the elderly woman's name; Shevaun had mentioned it at some point, hadn't she? Oh, well.

"Grandma! Grandma!"

"I can hear you just fine, Shevie. What's going on? Who's your friend?"

"Ma'am, my name is Angela Fujiwara. You are currently in a coma that will prove fatal within a week. I can cure you, if you wish me to."

"You can? I was ready to die. The doctors have given up hope. How long can you give me?"

"I don't know. Life and death are other people's talents, not mine. At least a couple of years, and it would remove your pain. You would live to see Shevaun graduate high school, but I don't know if you'd see her graduate college."

"What do you ask in return?"

"Only that you do not reveal my role in your healing. Shevaun's a friend. It will take a few days to accomplish—I'm not the best person in a living body—but you will be cured."

"Whom should I attribute it to?"

"You can attribute it to whomever you like, as long as you leave us out of it. We're not ready to publicly announce ourselves yet."

"I will." She drew them back out of contact and began the tricky work. Bridget grabbed Shevaun's arm.

"Not now. Let her do this, without disturbing her. It's tricky for her."

"You knew?"

Bridget nodded. "I keep the secrets I'm entrusted with."

"It's gonna be hard not talking about this."

Angela finished. "I can adjust your memory."

"I'd rather you didn't. I'll be good!"

"Fine by me."

"At least she didn't die while we were here. That would have been messy," Karen said.

"Why?"

"I can bring back the dead, too. But…should I is always another question, and I couldn't have asked her. I can't get answers from the dead if they never considered the question in life."

"Oh, I see that." It wasn't until they were on the plane heading back that she asked the next question. "You couldn't. Get answers from the dead if they never considered the question while they were alive, I mean. Does that mean…is there someone who *could*?"

"That's a question I won't answer right now."

"I understand."

"Ask me in January."

"January? Why January?"

"Because I should be fr…er, able to answer it then."

Chapter

14

Study hall was a generally quiet period. Today it was mostly being used to research for reports. Karen noted Seth's presence, his nose buried in a book and a pad of paper he was using for notes. Carmen Burns sat down next to her with a pained expression on her face.

"What's wrong, Carmen?" she asked quietly as she drew up a privacy sphere around them. Carmen didn't need to know about the sphere, so she made it light and designed to shunt people away.

"I don't want to talk about it."

"Okay. You look like you want to. Something's wrong." She was contemplating reading her mind when she spoke up.

"I was raped. I don't remember it, and he used a condom."

Fury rose up in Karen and she demanded, "What? Did you report it? Did you…" she looked up to see the boy in black pull up a chair.

"What's wrong, Miss MacLeod?" Seth asked grimly.

"Hey! Girls only private conversation!" Carmen protested. Seth ignored her and kept looking at Karen.

"I appreciate the concern, Seth, but none of your business."

"Miss MacLeod, I just picked up a wave of murderous fury from you. What is wrong?"

"Seth…" Carmen started.

Karen stretched out with her mind to touch his. Sure enough, he was being serious and deadly concerned. "Again, thank you, Seth," being polite to him was simply a good idea, "but I'll handle it."

"Miss MacLeod. You're ready to start blowing someone away." He closed his eyes. "You've never killed anyone. I would spare you that if I can. How can I help?" The girls looked at each other and then away from him. He sighed. "Okay, Carmen. I'll open the chest. I'm a wizard. Specifically I'm a necromancer. The Goth look isn't pure affectation. I'm one of the ten people who boarded the *Pelewan* and took you and your fellow captives back." At Carmen's disbelieving expression, he asked, "Which one was I, Miss MacLeod?" He kept his eyes locked with Carmen's. Karen grimaced. But if Seth was going to put aside his secrecy...

"He was the bony one in black with a scythe. Death in person."

"What?!!"

"Miss MacLeod identified me before she got on the radio to the navy, and we fogged your minds a bit to disguise our presence. As you may recall, I went after her when you two were dragged away. I have something of a connection to her; how we have it she can tell you. I can sense the murderous fury coming off her in response to something you told her. I'm not trying to interfere in your privacy. I'm trying to keep her from killing somebody."

"That's kinda..."

His eyes locked with hers. "Have you ever been in direct contact with a mind as the person slips away into death? Heard the terrified shriek of anguish as you extinguished a life? Felt a pulse die to nothing under your fingertips? Held someone in your arms to watch the light leave their eyes?"

"No. I haven't. But you have, haven't you? Sorry Seth," Karen said. She shuddered and turned to Carmen, her lips tight. "He can help, if you're willing to trust him. I owe him my life, and he's never asked for anything in return. And...I'm just an apprentice wizard. He's one of my teachers."

Carmen's eyes widened and she blinked ferociously. "I'm going to put that aside for a moment. What did he mean by a connection?"

"I was murdered. Seth refused to accept that—you may have noticed he's fallen for me rather hard—and brought me back. That act created a bond. We can talk to each other telepathically, and he can apparently pick up emotional surges from me."

"You could probably pick them up from me. I have some additional help—and experience—keeping them contained," he said. "If mine were getting loose, people would be dying around me."

"Okay, Seth. I was raped at a party. I didn't report it."

"Do you know by whom?"

"No! I barely remember the party!"

"Okay," he paused, considering something. "Have you ever seen 'Star Trek'?"

"Which series?"

"Any of them, as long as a Vulcan did a mind meld."

"Yeah, why?"

"I'd like to try something like that with you."

"What?"

"It's possible the memories are still there, blocked by chemicals or something. I may be able to access them."

"Shouldn't we wait for…" Karen began. She stopped when Seth put up a hand and shook his head.

"That would be her decision, and as yet she's neither identified herself to Carmen nor agreed to act at all. Both of those decisions are properly and solely *hers*, and I will not even try to make them for her."

"You identified me."

"Check your memory. I confirmed we rescued you and you knew which one I was. She might have gotten a hint, but I never said you were one of us. You were the first to specifically say that." Damn, he was right.

"I thought you'd told her trying to impress her into dating you."

"She's not interested, but that's not how she knows."

Listening to the exchange seemed to settle Carmen. "What do you need to do, Seth? Touch my face?"

"I don't need to touch you at all. But this is easiest with skin-to-skin contact. What I'd like to do is clasp hands to provide it. Fair warning, though—I'm not the best or most gentle person in a living mind. This will be painful."

"Okay." She seemed to steel herself, then took his hands. "Do it." He spoke a phrase in Coptic and they locked gazes, sitting unmoving except for facial tics and their heavy breathing. Seth started sweating, the drops rolling down his face and weighing down his shirt.

"What's going on?" Teddy asked sotto voce. Karen hadn't noticed him come up.

"Carmen was raped and can't remember. Seth's trying to get the name," she responded quietly. He nodded and leaned against a bookcase while scribbling down his math homework. Carmen winced several times, and tightened her lips in a grimace.

Bridget came by a moment later, getting the story from Teddy in quiet Aramaic. She grabbed a seat of her own and pulled a juice box out of her backpack, setting it next to Seth. After what seemed an eternity, Seth let go of Carmen's hands and closed his eyes. "Drink," Bridget commanded. "I know that's strenuous for you. Why didn't you ask me to do it?"

"I was trying to stop something," he replied after finishing the box.

"I was feeling murderous when Carmen told me what happened," Karen admitted.

"And Seth picked up on it," Bridget said, squeezing his shoulder. "He's going to be able to do that, so if you don't want him getting involved you'll need to work on your mental control. What'd you get?" she asked him.

"Peter Danglume." Peter was a senior, apparently popular and well liked by his classmates.

"The question is how do we prove it. Seth's method isn't going to work in court, and I'm guessing there's no physical evidence?" Teddy turned a questioning look at Carmen, who shook her head. "Then we need a confession, and I don't think we can give the cops enough for them to get one."

"So that was for nothing?" Carmen said plaintively.

Teddy grinned evilly. "Not at all. We just need to get…creative."

"I know that look, Teddy. Spill," Bridget said.

"We need to talk to some people but I bet we can present something that gets him to admit what he did."

"How?" Carmen asked skeptically.

"His only shot at mercy."

"But…"

"Compulsion if we have to. But with good enough stage management, convincing enough illusion, he'll volunteer. I'll be prosecutor. Seth, will you sit as judge?

"What are you talking about?" Karen asked.

"In the older Hebrew texts I've been reading, Satan is God's prosecutor. We manage it properly, guilt or innocence won't be the question. Only the punishment—at least as far as he knows."

"I have a question," Bridget interjected. "I hate to be the one to bring this up, but could he have made a mistake? Thought you were agreeing? Not that I doubt you, Carmen, but we need to be sure before we do something drastic, and Seth taking direct action is about as drastic as it gets."

"Bridget, I'm a lesbian. I told him that."

"Oh."

"No mistake, Bridget. I got the whole memory. She couldn't fight—she'd been drugged—but he knew perfectly well she didn't want to. She'd turned him down four separate times that evening and was in no shape to say much by the time it happened," Seth said.

"We know who. We'll probe his mind and get his memories too."

"Wait, you're wizards too?

"I outed myself," Seth said. Teddy and Bridget looked at each other.

"We weren't being very circumspect," Bridget said.

"Yes, Carmen. It's not something we make known. I hope we can trust you to keep quiet about it and not tell anyone," Teddy said. "Especially since for this to work, you'll be finding out about all of us,"

"What to work, Teddy?"

"You executing him does have a certain appeal, Seth. But I think it's inappropriate. It gets vengeance for Carmen, not justice. We present it as him coming before Death deciding where to send his soul for eternity, and we can disorient him by having it in the Castle. Bringing the Steward of the Temple will help. We get him to confess, on camera."

"Executing? Wait a minute. I'm grateful for the help and support, guys, and I really didn't think anyone was going to believe me or that there would be no way to get proof, but I don't want you getting in trouble over this."

"Seth is capable…"

"Miss MacLeod."

"Sorry." Eagerness to reassure Carmen had gotten the better of her, but Seth's secrets were his to reveal.

"It may interest you to know, Carmen, that although none of the kidnappers or crew of the *Pelewan* survived, oddly enough each autopsy gave a different natural cause," Bridget said. "Some of them had a variety of infectious diseases. Some had strokes, allergic reactions, heart attacks, accidents. But they're all dead. All but the wizard who fled. One hell of a lot of coincidences."

"You did that?" she asked Seth.

"The autopsies said natural causes or accidental deaths. And I have no intention of arguing with them," he replied with a slight smile. It put her in mind of a grinning skull.

"That's another part of my wanting to extract a confession and hand him over to the police. Carmen, there's no appeal from Seth executing someone, no override, no last minute phone call. He decides to do it, and Peter will fall over dead, and regardless of what he's doing at the time—even if they're nowhere near each other. I kill someone, Seth can bring him back. He brought Karen back. I could have done that, too. But we, the rest of us I mean, can't bring back someone Seth executes, only he can. The ship, White Hill, and that place he was taken… there's at least the argument that it needed to be done, that other people's lives were immediately in danger if he didn't eliminate the opposition. Here we're talking about a single deliberate killing. There's no battle, no innocents to rescue. It's just punishment," Teddy said. "And I don't really like the effect I've seen on Seth. He's gotten a lot colder since June. Let's put the burden of punishing Peter in the hands of the cops and the courts."

Carmen wiped her eyes. "I didn't think anyone would believe me."

"The cops and school still might not. That's why we're going to make him confess, if that's what you want. Seth has already offered his help. If you give the word, Peter dies."

"I hate to say it, but it's not simply a matter of knowing you and him. We know—know, to an absolute certainty, that you're telling us the truth. We'd know even if Seth hadn't gone into your head to look at your memories."

"I think we're going to need compulsion anyway, Teddy." Teddy looked at Seth for an explanation. "Mom's a lawyer. Even videotaped, that confession might not be admissible. Compelling him to confess to the cops AFTER they read him his rights might be needed."

"That's fairly easy," Teddy responded.

"Couldn't that get thrown out too?"

"From what Mom told me, no. As far as the courts will be able to tell, it will be completely voluntary on his part, so none of the arguments that it was coerced by the government will apply."

"Okay," Carmen said. "What do I need to do?"

"If you want to denounce him in front of the whole school, we'll back you all the away," Seth said. "From what Teddy's saying, he's got a plan that actually sends him to prison, and from the cop shows Mom likes, he's probably done it to others who haven't come forward. What do you want to do, Carmen?"

"Let's get him." They nodded.

Chapter

15

"*A*ren't you ready yet?" Seth's voice came through the door. "He's close to waking up."

"Almost. Just gotta do makeup." Karen replied.

"As you wish, but you hardly need it."

"You never quit, do you? I want to look my best, even if I'm in costume."

"Not what I meant," he said floating ghostlike through the wall. "Do you mind?"

"You said you were almost ready to start." He spoke a word in Coptic and touched his face. She was surprised to see it take on a golden color highlighted with dark blue, a living death mask from an Egyptian mummy. It was an odd sight over the open black robe. "You're a wizard; you can achieve the same effect with magic. Hasn't Angela covered this sort of micro-transformation?"

"No. Neither has Bridget, but neither of them wears much makeup."

"Bridget mentioned she's got a philosophical objection when Keisha explained the process to us; she only wears it to formal occasions. It never came up with Angela. It's just a targeted transformation, really. Get a picture in your mind of what you want the effect to look like.

She suggested using a mirror, putting what you wanted on the mirror image, and then transferring it to your own face."

"And you just happen to have that memorized?" She followed his advice and that was a lot quicker. "How do I look?"

He shrugged. "You look great to me, but I'm biased; you may remember calling me out on it a few times. So my question is, is that the look you wanted to achieve?"

She checked the mirror. "Aye. Let's…" Seth had pulled the hood of his robe up, and his features melted away to reveal the grinning skull. "Take our places."

Peter woke to the tolling of a bell. Sitting up, he found himself in a hard iron chair, painted a deep, dark red. The chains binding him to it were a flat, dead black; he wasn't wearing the underwear he'd gone to bed in but a black suit and white shirt. The bell continued to toll its' deep, foreboding tones. He looked around to see a grinning skeleton draped in black presiding over the room, and the Devil himself sitting at the other table.

"Ah," the Devil spoke in an ominously deep voice. "The guilty soul is with us. State your full name."

"What the hell?"

"You can state your name or I will do it for you, Guilty One. Cooperation and honesty are your only possible hope for clemency. We already know you are Peter Philip Danglume. Admitting your name is simply demonstrating your compliance."

"Well fuck you!"

The Devil smiled at him. "You misunderstand. This trial does not serve to determine guilt or innocence. You are guilty. The only question is whether or not you will take responsibility for your sins."

Peter suddenly started trembling. He pinched himself. He couldn't seem to wake up from this nightmare. Then he recognized the warrior angel standing by the bench. Mike Wu looked straight ahead, seeming to ignore his former classmate, wings beating gently to keep him aloft. It was really happening!

"Do you wish to begin taking responsibility for your own actions, Guilty One? Or will you force us to determine your punishment for rape."

"But the Bible says that I owe the virgin's father…"

"Do you have any shekels of silver? No? I did not think so. So defiling a virgin…"

"She wasn't a virgin! I defiled no virgins! They were sluts! Whores! I have committed no wrong!"

"The law says otherwise. As do the girls praying for your just punishment," said Death from the bench. He started naming them. Each name resounded in the hall, and the chains tightened.

Then the Devil took over again, repeating the names and describing the encounters in full. He went over each sin in detail. Finally Peter couldn't take it any more and made a weeping confession to each one, describing how he had spiked drinks and taken the girls…many of whom had thought of him as their friend. He passed out before Death could pronounce sentence.

He woke up in his own bed, the sheets drenched in sweat.

The video was all over school. Peter's confession—apparently freely given, broadcast on the school's closed circuit—resulted in the cops arresting him in history class. Whispered stories told of other girls he'd raped, almost identical to Carmen's. Teddy arranged to be at the hearing; Peter didn't get released, even though Teddy was just there as a student journalist and didn't influence the judge at all.

Carmen was eating lunch with Karen, Angela, and Bridget when he reported that to her. "Thanks, Teddy."

"Of course, Carmen. While I was down there, some other people came forward, and he's facing more charges. He didn't get released until trial, but don't hesitate to call on us if someone decides to get revenge or something for him. The names you heard in the trial will get our attention."

"Get your attention? How? You won't be anywhere near me!"

He shook his head. "Near you or not. Speak my name and you'll have my attention."

"That goes for all eleven of us, Carmen," Angela said.

"We just conducted an interrogation on Mars," Bridget pointed out to her skeptical expression. "We can do what we decide to do at least on this scale, unless one of the others objects. Speak our names, and you'll not only have our attention, you'll have back up. We can get you support immediately if necessary."

Carmen opened and shut her mouth, then tried again. "Thanks. I guess no one will mess with you guys."

"Well, they might. You're one of three people not one of us who knows the truth," Teddy said seriously. "Since they don't…"

"Three? Damn that's an exclusive club."

"Three. Some of our parents know more than others. Teddy's the most secretive of us. His parents don't know, and he keeps it that way," Bridget said firmly.

"Don't fuck with the people who can alter memories," Carmen said with a little laugh.

"If we both wanna do it, fuck with one of us all you want," Bridget said with amusement. "We might take you off world first."

"Oh, and thanks for letting me talk to Mike. That's really him?"

"Yeppers. He's stuck on Mars and Venus, though, unless he's with Keisha. If you pay attention, you'll occasionally hear us discussing him. We try to remember to speak of him in the past tense unless we're speaking one of the other languages." She glanced at her watch— now that Carmen knew what to look for, she could tell that it was enchanted—and started gathering her things.

"Bridget, can I ask you something?"

"Sure, Carmen. Whaddya need?"

"It's kinda personal," Carmen replied glancing around at the others. "Carmen, I don't really have any secrets from the rest of the Round Table. Misunderstandings between us are dangerous. They might not have all the details, but it's better to keep them apprised so we don't end up working at cross-purposes. I'm probably going to tell them about it at some point anyway. So out with it before I read your mind and find out that way."

"Would you be interested in going on a date? With me? As a date-date?"

Eyebrows rose all around. Bridget colored and smiled. "Sure, Carmen. Sounds like fun."

"Good for you," Teddy said. "And apologies in advance for what some of my groupies are going to be saying." Carmen looked oddly at him. "Who you date is none of my business unless you're dating me. I hope you make each other very happy. I'll work on my groupies more on this angle than I have been."

"Hearing you like this is still weird," Carmen told him. "You're being supportive of...of..."

"You're just not used to hearing me, and not the act I put on."

"You don't even sound like you think much of the people at morning services."

"I don't. Listen to some of them in class sometime. I do try to educate them and treat them with kindness, though. Excuse me, I need to go put the mask back on."

"Wait, Teddy, you forgot your book...what language is that?"

"Aramaic," Bridget said. "It's just some version or other of the bible. I wouldn't know which one. I'll get it back to him." She took it, spoke a word in Gaelic, and the book vanished.

"Some version or other?"

"Didn't you know? Different churches use different versions. Different groups of translators had different agendas. Different conferences put in different books. Stuff got added later. Just as an example, the older Greek refers to Mary with a word that means "young woman". It got translated as 'virgin', but by the standards of the people who spoke the language at the time, the same word applies to me or Dani, and we are most definitely not virgins."

"How do you know about someone else?"

"Solly burst out laughing when she tried to pretend she and Alex weren't having sex," she shrugged. "Most of us have something we can tell about."

"So he'd be able to tell if you and I...?"

"Probably. Look, I'm not worried about it. He can tell. So can I, which is how I know they've always done it on Mars, Venus, or the moon. So what? You just heard Teddy's attitude. The rest of us have a similar one. Yes, Angela, even him. He's not disputing you dating or sleeping with whoever you want. He's just refusing to trust Dave with his secrets."

"I seem to have walked into an argument."

Angela nodded. "Yeah. It's frustrating…but 'tell no one' does include Dave. I'd rather not have S…er, him mind wipe him. Or, even worse, execute him, and yeah he can and might do that."

"Catching Peter meant you've gotten further in than anyone but Dani and Mike. But everyone still has their own secrets, and I'm only free to share mine," Bridget said. "Angela, may I fill her in?"

"Sure."

"So…"

"There are two sides, Carmen. He hasn't agreed yet, and while I don't think he'd have a problem with you knowing, he can be touchy about it. I'd ask him telepathically, but he's concentrating on something. Incidentally, you remember his disguise? It's that way for a reason. So I'll get permission and fill you in on our date. Where are we going, anyway?"

"How about ice cream? This is a relief. I wasn't sure you were gay."

"I'm bi, actually. But there's the bell, and ice cream sounds great. See you after school?"

Chapter

16

Angela was just getting out of English when Seth spoke in her head. *<Do you really want to keep your pet idiot alive?>*

<Do you really have to ask?>

<Then why is he wandering around off the leash?> His tone was very annoyed.

<On my way.> She didn't want Seth dealing with Dave his way. At least he'd asked her to handle it. She ducked into a girls' room and teleported to the one nearest them. As she did, she sent a thought to Seth. *<I doubt he'd bother you at all if he knew what you're capable of doing, Seth. You're too fucking scary. So why don't you let him into the outer circle and get him to leave you alone?>*

<You know perfectly well why.>

She muttered darkly as she headed down the hallway. *<No, I don't. No one's talking about it. All I know is that you've vetoed him five times in the last three months, and I'm no closer to figuring out how to get you to drop your veto than I was in June.>*

As she arrived on the scene, Dave and several guys on the o-line were blocking Seth from leaving them behind…unless he used his power, which Dave would recognize. It sounded like they were trying to be friendly and Seth wasn't having any of it. But she could also tell that Seth was getting angrier by the second as they kept blocking him.

118

"Hey Teach. Coach Rice wanted to see you about first aid supplies," she said. If there were any missing. She suspected he kept those magically stocked.

"Thank you, Angela." He slipped between them and headed for the locker room, where he could find the cheerleading coach. He tossed a mental question to her, and she replied that it could wait for practice.

Dave spread his arms and got a big goofy grin on his face. "Ange! I was just making friends with Seth, like you want me to!" Oh, boy, was Dave reading him wrong.

"Dave, leave him alone. Your attempts to socialize with him are just ticking him off, and sooner or later he's going to do something we'll both regret."

"I know all about him, and he's not that dangerous. Uncomfortable, maybe."

"No Dave. He's not that dangerous. He's far more dangerous than that."

"What do you mean? I know he goes on vengeance kicks…"

"That'll do. He's not going after you yet because he doesn't want to pick a fight with *me*. He's not your friend. Quit trying to pretend that he is. He's taking your attempts as outright insults."

"Really, Ange, relax. I've known him for years…"

"No, Dave. You haven't. He's been avoiding you for years or getting himself payback. Intervening back when we started dating the first time was a favor to me, not to you. If you don't leave him alone I'm going to have to do something I really don't want to."

"Like what?"

"I can do a lot of things. In this case, apply a geas to you that makes you stay away from him. I'd rather you just listened to me and stayed away from him on your own because you realize it's a good idea."

"And if I don't?"

"You don't want to find out and I'm not permitted to tell you." It was time to remind him of what she could do, so she switched to telepathy. *<I got a telepathic message referring to you as my pet idiot running around without a leash, Dave. Yes, I want you two to be friends, but I think you're pushing too hard. You haven't been friends and he's suspicious of you.>* Suspicious was probably the wrong word, but it would do.

"That's ridiculous."

"If you were dying, he would let you. Don't make the mistake of assuming he's okay with you."

"Okay, okay." He obviously wanted to stop the argument. "Any chance for an off world trip?"

"I'll see what I can do. There's a meeting on terraforming Venus on Saturday."

The meeting on Venusian terraforming had already lasted several hours when the discussion came to a close; Karen had long since grabbed a bed in her new suite. They were almost ready to give the planet a push to speed up its' rotation. "Anything else?" Jennifer asked, glancing around. Everyone at the table was tired when Malcolm asked for a temporary pass for Jasmine.

Jennifer glanced around and Teddy spoke up. "A temporary for Jasmine is doable. Let me know when it is; I need to be checking out bible schools to keep my parents happy, so I'll just do it that weekend."

"Good idea, Teddy. I'm sure Mike will enjoy some time with me in the Caribbean," Keisha said. "No one would recognize him there."

"Ange? Was there something?" Jennifer asked.

Angela bit her lip as Mike and Dani poked their heads back in; they'd taken a gate to Mars and enjoyed playing racquetball in the lighter gravity. "I'd like to bring Dave in fully."

All the other heads swung over to Seth and Teddy. "Veto." Seth said it marginally ahead of Teddy.

"Well, then, anything else?" Jennifer repeated.

"Wait, now, we haven't even discussed this yet," Angela protested.

"But with Teddy and Seth both vetoing it, there's nothing to discuss, Ange. Their vetoes trump any discussion. We can talk about it as much as you like, but until you've convinced them it's pointless," Jennifer said reasonably.

"And until Seth gives him a pass through that death ward, you're not bringing him up here anyway," Bridget said equably. "So let's break and head home. We can come back to it some other time."

"Death…ward?" Dani asked hesitantly.

"We all put up defenses for the communal areas. There are several of them that will most likely kill any intruder getting in. Mine happens to be of the instant death variety. We agreed that you two get to be here, so you don't have any worries. You guys have passes. You can't bring someone with you—some ill-intentioned person who tried that would bounce or die while you passed through—but you're fine," Seth said. "As for Dave, I put up with him enough at school."

"What?!" Angela responded. "You have no classes with him, refuse to talk to him, and you only interact with him at practice or when you come over to talk to ME!"

"And that's plenty for me," he answered with an angry tone.

"What the fuck, Seth? What is your problem? I want to be able to be completely open and honest with my boyfriend for once," she responded angrily. "Is that really so much to ask?"

"You trust him. You like him. Okay, you love him. I sure as death don't. I neither like nor trust the idiot. You're asking ME to trust him with MY secrets. And the answer is no."

"Seth! Referring to her boyfriend as an 'idiot' isn't helping anything," Keisha said sharply.

"He is an idiot. A proud C moron. And he only maintains that with difficulty so he can play sports. I refuse to let him know my secrets. He dies first." Angela blanched, the blood draining from her face. Seth had never made his opposition an outright threat before.

"Well what about a temporary pass for him up here or the Castle?"

"Fine by me," Teddy said.

"Veto," Seth said implacably.

"Come on, Seth," Keisha said. "It's a reasonable compromise. You don't have to be here. It'll only be people comfortable with him knowing about them. He won't be able to go anywhere he doesn't have permission to go. So give him a pass."

"After your movie debacle I thought you'd have more sense. No." Keisha's nostrils flared.

"Seth, you're being ridiculous."

"No. I will not let him pass through my wards. He dies first."

"You're argument has gotten really loud, guys," Karen came in, yawning. "What's going on?"

"We'll have your word that you won't unilaterally kill Dave, Seth. If he becomes an actual threat we'll reconsider," Keisha said.

Angela felt the darkness of Seth's power coalesce "You have it." He vanished. The rest of them looked around somewhat uncomfortably.

"Dave's safe," Angela said in relief.

"At least he agreed," Mike said, nodding.

"That's just it, Mike. We didn't come to an agreement. We extracted a promise from him…and unless I miss my guess, he struck back at the same time," Bridget responded. "When Keisha wanted to bring you back, Seth blocked it—you died spectacularly, in public and on camera. That felt very similar."

Alex nodded. "Seth's not going to kill Dave. But now—I think Bridget's right. If he dies now, Angela can't bring him back. We didn't come an agreement. We pissed him off. Dave isn't safe."

"But…he didn't say anything in Coptic!" Dani protested.

"The casting languages aren't required, Dani. We use them to give us a little more time to consider. We just pissed Seth off enough to not care," Jennifer said.

"Maybe someone should go talk to him?" Dani said.

"We can't. He went to the Mausoleum," Karen said. She tapped her forehead at Dani's questioning look. "I'm fairly sure he invoked his defenses. And Angela gave back the talisman to get through."

"Well, we can talk to him at school," Angela said.

"You think so?" Bridget shook her head. "Karen, how pissed off is he? Is he in any danger of losing control?"

"Um… How do I tell?"

"You've got the connection to him, I don't. I'm not entirely sure how that bond works," Bridget responded.

"He's fine," Angela said dismissively.

"No, he's not. I can get that much. So could you if you were paying attention," Karen told her.

"He's blocking me, so no I can't. Are you sure you're not just getting feedback from your own views?"

"I'm not. I think it's great that you and Dave have each other. The hostility to Dave is open, intense, and is coming entirely from him. I don't think he'd have done anything to him before this, but if he makes himself a threat he's going to push for execution. A mind wipe isn't going to satisfy him after this. We've got a fucking problem here, Ange, and dismissing it really isn't helping."

"Karen's the emotional specialist, and given that Seth's still in love with her, I don't doubt she's in closer contact with him through that bond than you are, Ange. If she says he's that pissed, I'm sure she's right," Jennifer said. "Seth's history with Dave is ugly, as we know. You and Seth are going to need to work this out, Ange. The rest of us owe him an apology."

"For keeping him from killing my boyfriend?" Angela bristled.

"For telling him what to do with his power," she responded grimly.

"We broke the agreement, he didn't."

"You'd better not tell Dave about this. If he gets stupid enough to try bullying Seth again he'll do something permanent."

"But he just promised…"

"He can still take an action that will inevitably result in death. You want him turning Dave into a fish on dry land, or an adult mayfly, that will naturally die in a day? He can do that and let nature take its course. Transformative spells aren't that hard for him. So he can keep his word and still cause Dave's death, if he really wants to." Angela blanched at Bridget's analysis. "He could also leave him alive as, say, a seed or a mouse. Extracting that promise didn't make Dave any safer."

Dani paled in horror. "It just made him get creative."

Alex shook his head. "It didn't even do that, really. We have no way of making him keep that promise if he chooses not to."

"Which is why agreements are better," Teddy said. "I trust Seth. But if Dave does something really stupid like try to bully him again, he might be angry enough to kill him anyway."

Looking around, everyone else seemed to have their grim faces on. Angela considered what they'd been saying. "Oh, fuck. I just fucked up big time." She swallowed audibly.

Chapter

17

"You wanted to talk to me, Mother Elaine?" Angela asked, pausing in the door of the pastor's office at St. George's. She still hadn't had a chance to speak with Seth. Now he was actively avoiding her, and he'd sealed his mind from her.

"Angela, come in. This is a private conversation, so…"

She caught the hint and drew up a privacy sphere. "What's up?"

"Your Mom says you were almost carjacked."

"He confessed to the first cop he came to, but it wasn't really that close. She was in more danger than I was. I had to end it quickly to keep her safe."

The pastor sat back for a moment. "What she was really concerned about was how ready and willing you were to kill him."

"She's upset about me recognizing my options and choosing to spare the guy's life?"

"That's not the way I'd put it. It certainly wasn't the way she put it."

"I was tutored in magic by a necromancer. Immediate death is what he does, so I know how to do instant death too, but that's not *my* forte. I…my first inclination would leave someone flash frozen or with extremely incongruous plasma burns."

"That's…"

"Not what you meant," she interrupted. "The last time someone pointed a gun at me was on board the *Pelewan*. I melted a lot of those. The time before that was… Karen's murder."

"What you and your fellow wizards do puts you in danger to protect others?"

She waggled her hand. "We've protected ourselves pretty thoroughly. Just because I'm wearing paisley blouse and skirt doesn't mean it wouldn't be easier to hurt someone in a tank than me. But our ability to defend those we love depends heavily on what we reach for first. My first inclination carries some additional risks, so I try to think of alternatives. My tutor… rarely does. I've seen and felt some of what those killings cost him, though."

"You have? How?"

"I had to rescue him, last year. I took control of his body. I was still in his mind when he killed the people responsible, and their minions. Believe me, Mother Elaine, I know it costs him, if not exactly what it costs him. I'd really rather not pay those prices if I don't have to." Mother Elaine closed her eyes in sympathy at the horror in her tone.

"Have you ever killed anyone yourself?"

"I…don't know, honestly. Probably. What I do has a very violent side. He stopped me from killing someone on the football field last year. I could have killed some of those people on the *Pelewan*. I know that. He clouded that question by ensuring all of them died."

"I'd be willing to talk to him about it. I suspect from our past conversations that you're not going to name him, and that he wouldn't talk to me, though."

"He wouldn't. In fact, if he thought you knew about him, he'd wipe your memory. I'm sure he'll wipe Dave's if Dave claims he knows something. Wipe it…or worse."

Mother Elaine considered that for a moment. "How do you feel about what he's done?"

"I understand it. I don't know that I agree with how ruthless he is, but I understand it, at least when I draw back. Some of it was justice, some vengeance, some ensuring they wouldn't get away, some keeping us hidden. I suspect, on the ship, there was a lot of making sure no one who'd touched Karen against her will survived."

'But..."

"None of us like killing people. We've probably got the power to take most of them alive. It's just... then what do we do with them? We're not cops. We can't arrest them and put them in jail. Our lairs aren't set up to hold people. How we get the information we use would never make it in court, even if we were prepared to drop the disguises and testify in public. It's kill them or take a page from Circe's book and transform them. One of my friends does that to poachers.

"At the same time, we usually go ourselves when it would be difficult or impossible for...I know it's Rowling's word, but it's so perfect... *muggles*. A vampire kidnapped me. A wizard—or several—had to be involved in taking him; there's no other explanation for them being able to block his abilities. The *Pelewan* was under the control of a pair of wizards. If we'd just tipped off the Navy, they'd have gone in blind—or not at all if we told them what they were facing, because they wouldn't believe us. It would have been a massacre of innocents instead of guilties," she said.

"I'm not sure what advice to give."

"Thank you, Mother Elaine. You may not have any advice, but talking to you has given me an idea." Angela toyed with a zipper. "I'm wondering if you could advise me on something else."

"Of course, Angela."

"My tutor hates my boyfriend. I get why. My boyfriend was a bully towards him. I think he's changed quite a bit. But the truth of the situation is that my tutor has all the power; he's been hiding it so Dave doesn't really know. I want my boyfriend protected, which means bringing him in. My tutor keeps vetoing it."

"Why does your tutor get a veto?"

"First rule of the magic society—we decide who gets to know about us. It's why I've never named him to you. Bringing someone in means those secrets get exposed to a new person. We've got two muggles fully inside. Both are significant others of someone on the inside. One of them is someone we've all known for years. The other died on camera, was brought back, and is currently at one of our off world bases. Bringing in my boyfriend…"

"Means he would learn who everyone is, and your tutor doesn't want that."

"That and more. I thought by getting my tutor to promise not to kill him, I'd at least be protecting him from that. But…we're wizards, and this is his domain. He doesn't need to instantly kill him to do something fairly permanent. The only upside is that we could reverse whatever he did, assuming it didn't kill Dave in the meantime."

"I'm not sure why you added that. You died and were brought back; why not your boyfriend, too?"

"Each of us has something we're particularly good at, and no two of us have the same thing. My tutor's area of expertise is necromancy. Death magic. He brings something back to life, that life will end again at some point. It's the nature of life. But if he kills something, that something stays dead. We could clone it, but a clone is a twin; it would take a different spell to make it an adult twin. Without his agreement, we can't bring back the same person."

"Not even with CPR?"

"CPR, electroshock, whatever. It won't work if he's opposing it." Mother Elaine considered that for several moments as Angela's agitation increased. "Do you think he'll act on it? Do something to Dave?"

"I don't know. He was mad enough to leave for his safe house and seal the door shut behind him."

"Sounds very mature," Mother Elaine said with a laugh.

"He was angry. He wasn't throwing a temper tantrum. He's still in control of himself."

"What makes you say that?"

"No one's dead," Angela said grimly. "He loses control and he can wipe out life around him. Do you remember when those eucalyptus trees died all of a sudden? That was him losing it with something. He's never told me what." The blood visibly drained from Mother Elaine's face.

"Would his safe house have the means to contain that?"

"You know, it might. I hadn't thought about that. Mine doesn't. But…I don't have his focus, and mine is a lot more isolated. Mine may have a design flaw; it's not really built to contain my fury."

"Does it need to?"

"A furious word from me can fuse or fission matter at a the atomic level, and the other wizards might be able to contain me long enough to calm me down. Sort of like my tutor. What do you think?"

Chapter

18

$\mathcal{A}$ngela brought Karen along to Inferno to meet with Teddy on her new project. The place had a hellish motif; it was decorated in reds, blacks, and bronzes, with illusions of leaping flames providing light. It looked like stone and metal, but the chairs were sinfully comfortable. When that adjective occurred to her, she cocked an eyebrow at their host, who grinned at her. Teddy had been eating lunch with Dawn as they discussed a problem with Martian terraforming. "Knock, knock, Teddy."

"Girls. Welcome. What's up?"

"I was thinking. Let's build Hell."

"Excuse me?" He sat up.

"We were thinking that a place to put the nasties might be better than killing them."

"It might, at that. But you do know that Seth's still likely to go ahead and kill them, and Bridget regards them as raw materials," Teddy cautioned them.

"I know; it's easy for him. But we don't have a place to just confine them, and I think that would be easier on us. Them too. Killing, transforming or mind-wiping them are our only options at the moment. I was thinking of a shielded chamber, deep within the Earth."

"For how long?"

"What do you mean?"

"Confine them for how long, in this prison of ours? Life? Release them?" Angela and Karen looked at each other.

"Life, I guess," Karen said. "Maybe less if there's a reason to."

"I think that would be an exception," Teddy said. "More of Tartarus than a prison."

"Yeah, but killing them wears at us, even when it's us or them or someone else or them. Let's give ourselves another option."

"We're still probably not going to have an option against other practitioners," Dawn said. "I like the imprisonment option, but unless we strip them of their abilities they could probably escape eventually."

"I think we'll need to create food and water."

"Nice and bland," Teddy said. "Automatically created in precise amounts. Use the shit and piss?"

"Makes sense."

"Oh, and the spell that transports them just takes them. Nothing else. They arrive naked," Karen added.

"Finger food and water fountains."

"Make it warm enough to be uncomfortable, but not dangerous."

"Medical care?"

"None. They can be kept healthy magically."

"Sounds like hell so far."

"That could lead to problems, though. From our perspective, we'd be removing dangerous, even evil, people from society. But we'd be kidnapping people and holding them prisoner until they died. We have the power, but should we?" Dawn wanted to know. "Who are we to do this?"

"Something to talk about together?" Karen suggested.

Angela deflated. "I was hoping to find an alternative to killing or transforming them."

"It is one. But…we're not gods, whatever we call ourselves as a joke. Locking them up sounds better than simply executing them. On the other hand, not all of us will see it that way."

"Why would it make a difference if we were gods?" Teddy asked. "Why should a god be held to a different moral standard? Might makes right? I don't think so. But here's another question for you. Is Seth's direct execution worse than Bridget's Poacher Plague, or Hurricane Malcolm forming right over the tuna and whaling fleets? What about Keisha's targeting of criminal gangs? Half the gangs and tongs in the world are hemorrhaging members, from death, imprisonment, or flight due to her actions."

"Let's not forget your crusade against the holy terrors," Dawn put in. "You've got religious fanatics the world over massacring each other, and others going down for fraud and pedophilia."

"I know. Biggest obstacles to peace and harmony and saving the world."

"Be that as it may," Angela colored, "my pastor was saying that killings are hard on the person who does them."

"And we shouldn't be asking Seth to do all the killings. We need to take responsibility for them, too, when we're the ones in the fight."

"I see that," Teddy said. His eyes flicked to Karen for a moment and he gave an obscure smile. "My attacks tend to be something that confuses them into harming themselves, overtly doing something, or betraying their allies."

"But, yeah, let's do it. How big do you think we should make it?" Karen asked. Teddy's proposed list of inmates was appallingly high. The vote on doing it was acrimonious on other matters, but everyone agreed. Seth's suggestion of putting Dave in it as one of the first inmates was voted down by everyone else. Building the prison in the mantle didn't take long. They started putting inmates in quickly…those who had believed no one would ever stop them. Inmates who went to bed in comfortable surroundings and woke up in Hell. Teddy in full costume explained their crimes to them…and laughed at their complaints.

Chapter

*H*er necromancy lesson was coming up fast, and she was still extremely nervous about spending that much time alone with Seth. She could bring someone else—Jennifer, for example—but Angela kept insisting that she needed to learn to deal with Seth on her own. Then she spotted Keisha.

"Keisha, would you mind coming with me for this?" Karen asked her. She'd have asked Angela, but… there was no need to bring that dispute into this. Angela and Seth hadn't spoken to each other more than necessary in meetings ever since he'd said he wouldn't kill Dave, and a lot of it was sniping at each other.

"Of course not. What do you need?"

"I want to ask Seth a fairly personal question, and I need someone he'll respect backing me up."

"I'll come if you want, but you don't truly need anyone. I know he's a bit scary, but he's not going to hurt you."

"Angela keeps telling me that. I can't quite make myself believe it. But I've got my big necromancy lesson this weekend, so I want to clear this up before that. And I don't want his argument with Ange clouding things."

Keisha shook her head. "Karen, if he didn't respect you he wouldn't have fallen so hard for you. His attitude towards most people is that they're idiots, and he's not going to waste his time on them. A lot of what made that situation with the football team so dangerous was that outside of Alex—and later Angela—he doesn't respect them at all.

Sending them home with the flu instead of to the morgue was his idea of being merciful. To a bunch of people who didn't deserve his mercy." They walked into the library and up the stairs to the darkened corner where Seth liked to hang out, Karen feeling his presence through the resurrection bond. Keisha walked along texting someone on her phone…undoubtedly Mike. At least she's relaxed enough to seek a distraction, Karen thought.

"Keisha, Miss MacLeod. Greetings. What's your question, Miss MacLeod?"

"Why do you keep calling me that? I have a first name, I know you know it, and it makes me think you're holding a grudge," she replied.

"It's nothing for you to actually worry about."

"My 'pretty little head' is plenty worried that the most lethal person I know won't call me by my first name, when I know I've dashed your dreams, Seth. What is with the formality?"

"Miss MacLeod, I said nothing about your head or your physical attractiveness. I'm using the formality to keep my emotions in check where you're concerned. There's no reason for you to worry at all."

"That doesn't make me feel better or safer, Seth."

"Why not? What emotions do you think I'm keeping in check?"

"Bitterness. Anger. Hatred…"

"No," he said, shaking his head. "I feel none of those towards you, Miss MacLeod."

"Then what is it?"

"Miss…"

"Please call me 'Karen', or at least 'Calyrine', at least for this, Thantoris," she insisted.

"As you wish." She twitched. He spoke a word in Coptic to draw a privacy shield around them, and Keisha reinforced it with a word in

Cushitic. "What we do is dangerous. What I do involves the single most debilitating and lethal focus we've found," he began.

"I know that, which is why you freak me out more than just a little." He sat back, considering what she'd said. Then he held his hand out to her. "I'm sorry I scare you. My feelings towards you haven't changed, but I don't believe words are going to convince you. So…I believe you were present last year when Angela entered my mind?"

"I was in her room…"

"Then take my hand, and enter for yourself. Kara, will you ensure that she is able to return to herself and that I do nothing to harm her?"

"Sure, Seth. Mike says hi." Keisha didn't look up from her phone.

"Are you going to pay attention?" Karen asked her.

'Of course," she replied, not looking up. "I just think you're concerned about nothing. I'm far more worried about what Thantoris would do to a guy who broke your heart than I am about what he might do to you. But I can certainly keep an eye on you and text with Mike at the same time." She spoke a few words in Cushitic, her eyes flashed orange, and Karen felt her power coalesce. A third, bright orange eye, appeared in the middle her forehead. "Satisfied?"

Karen breathed deeply, but Seth's hand remained outstretched. It was an offer and a challenge. Did she have the courage?

She reached out and took his hand, speaking a few words in Bengali. Seth's mind was dark and forbidding. It wasn't quite the black pyramid fortress Angela had described to her, but it was definitely not someplace welcoming. Where Angela had described something sealed tight, the gates were open. Seth had lowered his defenses. She could enter without risking her life, at least.

She was surprised when Seth gave her free reign to wander where she wished in his mind. He didn't give her control, as he had Angela, but the labyrinthine interior of the pyramid was open to her. She wandered through his memories, learned his passions and agonies, his hopes, dreams, fears, and nightmares. She'd never had the opportunity to probe someone's mind like this. Angela had once told her Seth had shielded her from the death and darkness in his magic, and she noticed those shields in place here. But he wasn't stopping her from touching those places. She touched one of the dark places, and felt his rescue of Angela from White Hill. Ange had described, way back, an almost casual killing of the vampire's living minions, but from Seth's mind there was nothing "casual" about it. He'd felt each and every one of those deaths. She finally understood what Angela had been talking about, the death and darkness, and from there she withdrew herself from Seth's mind. She wasn't surprised to find herself feeling exhausted and sweating, but she released Seth's hands.

He looked at her, eyebrows slightly raised. "Do you believe me now?" In response, she hugged him. "Yes. But justice, vengeance… these are mine to deliver, Seth, when I'm the one harmed. You don't need to protect me. I can and will protect myself."

"I know. Those are the impulses I'm controlling with formality. But as I've said, that's MY problem. It's not, and shouldn't be, YOURS. I'm sorry that my difficulties in letting go of what I know is and was an impossible dream have worried you. That was never my intent."

She smiled at him. "I get it. It's a desire to protect someone you care about, not a doubt of my capability or a desire to control me…and you are still deeply in love with me."

He nodded. "Unless you ask me for help, it's none of my business."

"Hey. If you see some danger I'm not recognizing, let me know about it, just like you would for someone else, so I can deal with it. You were my hero on the ship. But I don't need you to stand between me and danger. Got it?"

"Aye." She lightly punched his shoulder as she stood to leave. Seth spoke a word in Coptic to gather up his own books to fit in his black satchel. The three of them walked out together.

"Told you it was nothing to worry about," Keisha said, dismissing her third eye as she continued texting with Mike.

"I was expecting you to say "as you wish" again."

"Either works," he shrugged. "Means the same thing." She cocked her head at him.

"What do you mean?"

"You announced something I have no quarrel with. Why? What did you think I meant?"

Keisha barely smothered laughter. "He's never seen it."

"What are you talking about?"

"You've never seen "The Princess Bride"?" Karen stopped short, staring at him.

"No, I haven't," he responded, puzzled. "Last time Bridget keyed it up on their big screen I was in Juvie. I never got around to reading the book, either."

"Oh, God," Karen said with her hand over her eyes. "Sorry, 'as you wish' is a line from the movie that means something completely different, and I thought you were saying it to me every time. Sorry."

"Okaay," he said as they got to the library doors.

"Anyone for the Temple this weekend? He's hoping to have some company, and I've got a lot to put together down here," Keisha said suddenly.

"As long as Seth doesn't mind doing the necromancy lesson up there, sure," Karen said. Seth shook his head when she glanced at him. "I've been meaning to get up there. I want to do a search for a lair."

"I hope you like football," Keisha said. "He'll probably be watching that. Angela's not going up as long as she can't bring Dave…"

"Which will not be happening," Seth interjected. "Sorry for the interruption."

Keisha nodded her acceptance of his apology, "…and Alex and Dani have something special planned this weekend. Solly's doing a private session with Catalina. Malcolm and Jasmine are surfing in Santa Cruz. Teddy's counseling Rebecca on her relationship with Jesus."

"Football's fun; I see plenty of it from the sidelines as a cheerleader. I don't see the problem with Ange bringing Dave up, though. He and Mike were friends before Mike died."

"He's dead if she does," Keisha reminded her, "And he'll stay that way, since she can't reverse a death spell from Seth. But everyone's got something going on with their SO but us three and you two don't have one."

"Isn't that kind of a nasty thing to do to Angela?" she said to Seth.

"I'm not doing anything to Angela. She has fair warning. If she really needs to get the dumbbell out of it, the Seamount is always available."

"He's got a point, Karen. The defenses of the Castle, Temple, and Clubhouse were erected by all of us, and it takes unanimous agreement to lower them for any particular person. It took Alex over a year to get agreement to bring in Dani, and that was only after she passed a mind probe from Seth. Lazarus," they'd passed into the hallways, so Mike got the code name, "came up dead, and he's been confined there—or the Castle—ever since, unless I was with him. Seth did have a slight advantage in that he can override the death of someone he brought in, but that was before Angela put in a ward to rip atoms apart."

"Give me some of their dead tissue—hair, baby tooth, blood, whatever—and I still can."

"Damn." She cocked an eyebrow at Seth. "So what'll it take to get you to let Dave in?"

"He doesn't come in." Seth's voice was flat. Seth and Angela's argument may have cooled off, but the dispute was still there, and Seth wasn't sounding like he was at all interested in resolving things to Angela's satisfaction. Hell, she knew that from her exploration of his mind.

"Sooner or later you're going to want to bring someone in, Seth. Do you want Angela blocking that?"

"Irrelevant inquiry. That presupposes that there's someone who'd want to be brought in by me, and there is no such person. My friends are already involved."

"Don't be so sure, my gloomy friend. I'm matchmaking for everyone else. I'm good at it. I will find someone for you."

"Don't bother. Love is for the living." He turned towards his history class.

She reached out to stop him, stood on her toes and lightly kissed his cheek. "That includes you."

Chapter 20

Rain had come to school today, which meant the lunchroom was pretty crowded. As Angela and Dave came in, he nudged her. "Someone's happy." They saw a bizarre sight…Seth holding court over a table full of the cheerleading squad and some of their closest girlfriends. With the enhancement to her hearing it was obviously a tutoring session in a variety of topics. Karen had stepped out to work on the long-abandoned church in the high desert she was adapting into a base. They called it "The Chapel"; it was near Las Vegas.

"He's just helping them out with homework."

"Really? Awesome! There's a couple of seats nearby."

"There are some over there. I'll make sure we can hear everything, but there's no need to antagonize anyone."

"I get along fine…oh. Are you sure about that?"

"Dave, if you get hurt at practice or a game, he'll do his job. But he'd really rather not. Stay away from him, you'll both be a lot happier."

"Okay." Listening in on Seth's session with the cheerleaders shocked Dave. Seth was giving detailed, complete answers that might be in the books, as well as references to track down the information themselves. Angela had seen him do just this sort of thing when he was tutoring her in magic and wasn't surprised. Seth knew *a lot.*

"Are you sure we can't move closer? I've got some questions."

"He'll ignore you, just like he did when Alex was bench pressing Dani."

"But…"

"You can try asking Jennifer. I'm not sure which of them knows more, but she's at least willing to talk to you." She took a few more bites. "What are you up to this weekend?"

"Studying my ass off, according to Mom. I've got a paper due Monday. Why? You got something better?"

"Whaddya say we study at my place? You write your paper there?"

"My parents would get twitchy about me doing it at your house."

"Not at my house. At my place. The Seamount? We'll be completely isolated and able to focus all our attention on the homework."

"They'll call BS on that, you know." She shrugged.

"You do better on your papers when you study with me."

"Let me run it past them."

"Salutations, Angela!"

"What's up, Keisha?"

"Are you available to help with the book drive next weekend?"

"Getting people while they're trapped inside?" she smiled, rolling her eyes up in thought. "Sure."

"Wonderful, thanks."

"I should be available, too," Dave said.

"I'll have to juggle the schedule a bit, but thanks, Dave. You two seem a bit distracted."

"We're listening in on the lecture," Dave replied.

"Don't get caught. Everyone else is about to vanish off to other rooms for lunchtime socializing." Just as Keisha predicted, soon few other people remained in the room—them, some scattered students, and Seth's question and answer session. They stayed in the room quietly talking about the weekend plans and the game on Friday night, but were still paying attention. Angela marveled at how Seth hadn't broken his act once; it was a trick the other wizards were still a lot better at than she was.

Karen was getting out of her last class when she ran into Bridget in the rain. "Hey, can I get a ride? Mom needs to take Katie to the hospital."

"Sure. My car's just pulling in." Karen looked out in the parking lot to see the green and silver limousine of the Arcata Unicorns pull up. Bridget's chauffeur, Liana, got out and opened the door for them. "Gotta go into the City for a bit; we can drop you at your place or you can come if you want. It's just some league snafu one of us needs to deal with, and it's my week for it."

"I wanted to ask you something anyway, so I might as well come."

"Well, ask away. Nice cover, by the way. You could have just slipped away somewhere and teleported."

"So could you. Bridget, what's the origin of the no dating each other rule? Precisely what spawned it always gets glossed over."

"Thinking about someone in particular? In...black, perhaps?" Karen felt her cheeks heat. "Just trying to understand it better, lass!" Bridget laughed. "We've been giving him crap about you for years.

The opportunity to tease you, too, was too good to pass up."

"Now that the comedy routine is over?"

"Jennifer's older sister—Debbie—got involved with a guy, Bill Devine. First love and all that. He was...a couple years older than she was back then. He had a car..."

"Oh, what kind?"

"A convertible. Other than that I'm not sure. It's not like I pay much attention to cars. I need the formality of the limo today, since I'm representing the owners' committee. But anyway, Debbie's like five, six years older than Jenny. But they broke up when Bill graduated...or at least that's what Debbie thought. He was close enough to come back, though, and he did. They started getting in fights. Big, noisy fights, and they hit each other. I'm not sure which of them started that. But it ended with Jenny launching him through their plate glass window. He's still convinced she's a black belt."

"Oh, wow. But one bad relationship?"

"Not quite. Malcolm's got a half-brother a few years older than he is, and around the same time he broke up with his girlfriend. She threw things. Malcolm didn't have to step in, fortunately, but...it scared us. Dawn was already learning to throw fire and electricity around, and so could Jennifer. Teddy could obscure what was really there so well he could get people to walk into walls they knew about. And let's not talk about the frog incident."

"Frog incident? I haven't heard about that one!"

Bridget plainly didn't want to continue, but she switched to Gaelic. "We were headed into the hills from Keisha's when her mom insisted we take her older cousin Jeremy along. He was visiting, seventeen or so. He made himself a pain in the ass, "don't go there" sort of thing. Places we'd already been plenty of times. So I turned him into a frog."

"A frog? Why?"

"First thing that popped into my head from a fairy tale." Karen was barely containing her laughter. "I was twelve!"

That stopped the laughing. "TWELVE?!"

"Yeppers. Twelve. I turned him back and we wiped his memory, but…we could do a lot of harm to each other, to everyone and every thing around us if we got really pissed at each other. Around then is also when Seth lost it with someone—he's never said who—and wiped out that whole stand of eucalyptus trees. We need to keep our heads when we're dealing with each other. You've heard about the gang wars all over the bay area? Repercussions from those idiots putting roofies in the Sportyade last year—Alex losing control. It wasn't just the storm."

"Ouch. How do we get him to bring peace?"

"It's…complicated. Keisha's not so sure that having the gangs eliminate each other wouldn't be a good thing. There're reasons the fighting's resulted in so many deaths, maimings, and arrests with long prison terms. Alex hasn't tried forcing peace on them yet, so it's still playing out. And there's always Seth's peace option."

"Kill them all and let God sort them out?"

"Kill them all, anyway. Tacitus's "make a desert and call it peace". Angela—and maybe you—'s the only believer among us, and she's wavering. Solly went through his bar mitzvah and hasn't been back to synagogue since. He's even regrown his foreskin." Karen blinked in surprise, but it wasn't exactly relevant.

"What about Teddy?"

"He's putting on a show for his parents. We've been too many places that are supposed to be holy, seen too many supposedly holy people, and found nothing special about them. Tossing every divination we can think of at them, and getting nothing at all. If you think of something new, don't hesitate to speak up, but we're running out of places and people to check." She looked out the window and darkened the separation. A word in Gaelic turned her clothes from the t-shirt and jeans she'd been wearing to a green business coat and skirt with a seafoam blouse. Her shoes had gone from tennis shoes to heels. "She'll hear some sounds of changing. Thank you, Teddy."

"That's still all-natural, isn't it?"

"Yeppers! And sustainable. Dad was doing that even before I started learning magic. He really makes the effort in the gift shops and such. Not to mention the contracts for the linens and everything."

"I was wondering why so much of your jewelry tends to be of the hippie nut string variety. Same thing with your shells and pearls?"" she asked, referring to the strands that had appeared around her neck. The pearls were all different sizes and of various colors.

"Sustainable and renewable. And the oysters were very tasty." She smiled. "And as a bonus, the products of living things are pretty much under my control."

They went into the offices and took the owners' elevator. "Oh, could you explain something else to me? Everyone still seems somewhat down on Keisha's peace promotion efforts between Seth and Ange."

"Well...it's not really between Seth and Ange. It's between Seth and Dave. And Keisha occasionally goes on a wildly optimistic tangent. She did it here, too. She knows the history and didn't bother to talk to Seth before setting it up."

"I know they don't like each other. I know Dave used to pick on Seth. But that hostility was just..."

"The last incident was last year," she replied grimly. "As far as Seth's concerned, it's not over, and there's absolutely no reason to forgive and forget. Dave is still the person who's been picking on him for years. If you really want all the details, talk to Seth. He remembers."

"He's not over it?"

"I was shocked he was willing to be in Dave's presence long enough to get Angela that date. He must not have been able to think of anything else to get her back on track."

"But, still, he did it…"

Bridget sighed. "Karen, you're making the same mistake the school did, the same mistake Angela is in trying to bring them together, the same mistake Keisha did for that movie back in October. You're doing your best to minimize what Dave was doing to him, focusing on what Seth might do and not why he'd be doing it. This could have been headed off years ago but nobody did anything. Dave is *not* an innocent in this. Your presence was the only thing that kept the situation in the limo contained long enough to get to the theater. Otherwise, Seth wouldn't have been in the car in the first place, or if Keisha had gotten him first, he would have teleported away after wiping Dave's memory of his presence. It's a perfect example of how dangerous it is for us not to talk to each other."

She was pretty grim. "He hasn't really been interested in discussing it so far. I know Angela's tried."

"That's Ange, not *you*. It's an effect of you being goddess of love; we're pretty much all willing to talk to you. I'm not saying it would be easy, and I still don't know everything. If he's willing to discuss it with anyone, he'll talk to you."

"This doesn't seem like the most exciting role for me to play."

"Yeah, well. Solly's more suited to creating barriers. Teddy crafts illusions. They're not quite as suited to going toe to toe with the bad guys either. It's an individual thing."

"Any suggestions?"

"It's really not my expertise. It's yours. You might want to probe Dave's memories. Or have a long, heart to heart with Seth. Yeah, I know. You don't consider either a pleasant prospect. But he's going to keep vetoing any suggestion that Dave be given a pass, much less that he be brought into the outer circle."

The Fortress was Alex's lair, and the meeting room was decorated as he liked it. The walls were adorned with weapons from many ages and every continent except Antarctica, as well as a lot of the islands of the Pacific and Indian Oceans. Shields and suits of armor fit between them. He had other rooms decorated with uniforms. He'd rebuilt a lot of them from fragmentary remains.

"Okay, you two. This has gone on long enough. Let's at least bring the feud to an end before it gets serious." Alex looked at either end of the table, where Seth and Angela sat. The big meeting table of solid oak was elaborately carved and stained a deep purple. Keisha sat across from him. Dani was off doing homework.

"That's simple…" Angela began.

"Ange…Seth gets a veto. So does Teddy, and they're the only ones that can rescind them. We can't override. If you want those vetoes rescinded—and no one else to cast one—you're going to need to convince them. This is a peace conference. The best way to peace between you is to get you to accept that and go for some sort of live and let live agreement."

"But you can't enforce it!"

"No, we can't," said Alex. "We can only rely on Seth to keep his word not to kill Dave. I'm not suggesting we can or will solve this here and now. But can you guys get back to working together? Talking, at least?"

"Hmmph."

"And?" Seth asked. Alex sighed and nodded at Keisha.

"And, Angela, you owe Seth something. He's made a promise, and you've given him nothing to seal the bargain. What is it you want, Seth?" Keisha asked.

"He gets something for not killing my boyfriend?"

"For agreeing not to use his power," Keisha said. "I never should have insisted that he promise not to. I can't hold him to it. If you want him to hold himself to it, you need to bargain." Angela looked away stonily. Keisha shrugged. "It just so happens that his power primarily focuses on death."

"What I want shouldn't be hard. Keep him away from me."

"He's on the cheer squad! You're waterboy for the squad!"

"Your point? He only joined it this year when he got kicked off the football team. It would be easy enough to get him kicked off the squad."

"And when he asks why? I can tell him the truth?"

"About Seth? No. He still gets to decide who knows the truth about him," Keisha said. "Seth, forgetfulness and not execution? Can you live with that?"

"As long as he doesn't become a threat. He's…I don't think he's going to keep Angela's secrets. I do not trust him to keep mine. I'm not particularly eager to rush into the consequences of my power being publicly known."

"I've been trying to do that anyway."

"I think you're going to need to try harder, even using magical compulsion if necessary," Keisha said. "I think incidental encounters are one thing, we do all go to the same school and live in the same town. I think Seth seeking you out when he happens to be with you wouldn't violate the agreement. And the squad is neutral territory."

"Agreed," Seth said. The three of them looked at her. "Okay. Sounds like the best I can get," Angela grumbled. "Ange…"

She held her hand up, fingers splayed. "Yeah, yeah."

"I…" Seth started. Alex kicked him.

"Good," Keisha said. A wave of her hand and a word in Cushitic summoned a quartet of root beers. "Compromises don't give anyone everything they want. We're powerful enough that we don't really have to compromise much, except with each other. But compromises everyone can work with are a basic part of civilized life, guys. Good enough to be going forward with.

"I'm going to need a little time to talk to him."

"Compulsion doesn't take any," Seth replied.

"I really don't want to do that, Seth!"

"Tell you what, Ange. Take a week. I'll keep him away from Seth that long," Alex said. "That okay by you, Seth?"

"As long as he stays away from me."

"You'd see things differently if you had a girlfriend."

"That was uncalled for Ange. You've got your bargain that Seth won't unilaterally use his power to execute Dave if you keep Dave away from him. Maybe instead of sniping at Seth you should concentrate on what you've got."

Chapter

21

The study session with Seth was a lot easier now that she wasn't worried about him. He conducted the lesson with a clarity that had been missing with the others, undoubtedly a legacy of teaching Angela. Even with that, though, Necromancy was a bit uncomfortable—and it wasn't just being in the deserted morgue with Seth after midnight.

"Calyrine, what's wrong? You're getting the healing easily enough. Animation and extracting information hasn't been all that hard for anyone. Is there some other problem?"

"This is kind of disgusting, Thantoris. Sorry, I know you've gotten used to it, but… these are people." The secret names kept things formal enough without him constantly using "Miss".

"Were people, Calyrine. There's almost no point to extracting information from a cow's brain. But from a human brain, there's useful information to extract. Try to get how they died." He paused, then spoke a few words to summon an animal brain to his hand. "Would this be easier for you to practice on?"

"What was it?"

"It was a road kill victim. Identifying what species it belonged to would be good practice."

"Okay..." She concentrated and delved into the rain of the animal on the table. Lightly touching it. "Speaking of cow brains." He laughed in response.

"Good."

"You could have gotten more."

He nodded. "The cow saw herself in mirrored surfaces enough for me to be able to get her tag number, remember her home barn, and quite a bit more."

"I'm going to go for some of that." She concentrated, determined what she wanted, and tried again. She didn't get much more than a picture of the barn and the other cows. It was very tiring when Seth broke the connection.

"Careful," he said. "Necromancy tends to be hard on stamina for other people; it's one of the reasons that even though they can, even Jennifer tends to leave it to me. Let's take a break and get some food." Wooden platters came flying out to the table, loading up with a steaming lunch of soup and grilled cheese. He ate faster than she did as they talked about tricks of necromancy and he fed his parakeets. She wasn't sure why he'd brought them along.

"I'd like to try reviving that cow. You said it was roadkill?"

He nodded. "It's a lot easier to revive something recently dead and still intact. All we've got here is the brain."

"Still, I'd like to try. Do you mind?"

"Not at all." He handed her a bone pin. "This will let me monitor you more easily...and not accidentally inflict pain."

"Thanks." She put it on and started her spell to bring back the cow. She felt the sweat pouring off her despite the chill. She thought she heard him distantly, but the spell coalesced and soon she saw a blinding pink light. A cow had appeared...but it looked almost nothing like the Guernsey she remembered from her probing the cow's brain. The cow started to panic when she saw Seth. A word from Seth sent the cow to sleep. He spoke a few words in Coptic.

"What happened?"

"Your penchant for randomness and lucky strikes," he replied. "I know Angela said you got control of it over the summer…but you seem to have adjusted the cow on a genetic level."

"WHAT?!"

"That's an aurochs."

"Oops."

"Chiomara, I beseech thine aid." Bridget appeared after a few moments. With her present Seth dissolved the sleeping spell.

"An oops?"

"Got it the first time."

"Well, okay. C'mon, big girl. Time to take you to Bavaria." Karen laughed. "I'm glad nothing like that happened when I was training with Dawn!"

Seth smiled. "Why don't we break for the day and try something relatively intact? Say a week from today?"

"It's the Fall Formal, remember?"

"Oh, is it? I haven't been paying much attention."

"Why not? It's plastered all over school!"

"It would be worth paying attention to if I were going."

"Oh. You went to the winter formal last year, right? Why not the fall?"

"Why bother? It's a couples date night. I'm neither dating nor part of a couple."

She heaved a sigh. "I told you I'd find someone for you, and I will."

"Thank you, Miss Macleod. You really don't need to bother. It's unimportant. Especially in comparison to you getting your magic under your control."

"Need to bother and want to are different things. And you're trying to convince yourself that what you're saying is accurate." But she could tell through the link they shared he didn't see any reason to be optimistic.

Fall Formal was big and spectacular as usual. Angela knew that Karen had stepped in to help cover Keisha's use of magic to get some of the decorating done, but the basketball court had been polished to magical perfection and the hoops taken up. They pulled up in her new Gorgons limo just in time to see Solly hand out Catalina Zaragoza. He grinned at them.

"You guys color coordinated?" Catalina asked. Hers was a light aqua and sea green.

"She insisted I match the car," Dave said deadpan. Catalina chuckled.

"You two must be cold in those gowns," Dave said.

"I'm fine, actually," Angela said. Someone capable of her control over states of matter had no particular difficulty staying perfectly comfortable.

"I'm cold," Catalina said. "Shall we, Solly?"

"Of course."

As they presented their tickets and went in, they saw Keisha performing as master of ceremonies. The stunning gown in shades of orange really complimented her.

"Hey, Tiger Lady. Good to see you," Dave said.

"Dave. You're over at table five, Ange."

"Not a Round Table tonight?"

"No, Ms. Hughes wanted to split up the cliques a bit." She answered in Ainu. "Is that safe?"

Keisha responded in Cushitic. "With one exception we're all *here*, so probably not. And only the suicidal will go after him, so we should be fine." She switched back to English. "Solly, you guys are at table three."

"Is he in any danger?" Solly asked in Hebrew. "Just because it would be suicidal doesn't mean whoever won't try."

"Not according to my divinations," she answered, again in Cushitic. "But be watchful. There was an indication of an attack somewhere. They've got a bunch of minor practitioners cooperating." He and Angela nodded.

As they took their seats, Dave asked he what she and the others had talked about. Her lips twisted. "Never mind what we talked about. If I should tell you to take cover, do it and stay there until I say you can come out. If there's a problem, Alex, Karen and I may be getting support from afar, and the person behind it would consider you acceptable collateral damage."

"Oh, it's like that? Really?"

"It's been done before." She saw Karen take a seat next to her date, Todd Giannini. She reached out telepathically and got an affirmative response. They were all prepared if something happened.

The dance, though, was scheduled to go on for several hours, so they kept watch in shifts…with those with clued in dates taking a few more. Keisha, overseeing the event, didn't do much of the shifts since her attention would keep going back to something mundane.

It also meant that they nearly missed the spiking of the punch bowl; they'd shifted to drinking water. It wasn't until people started not feeling well and little Natasha Howe fell over that they realized something was deadly wrong. Examining her, Bridget and Jennifer determined that the poison was magical in origin. Bridget, Solly, Keisha, and Malcolm stayed with the crowd while the rest of them magically tracked the person who did it. A few other spells kept their dates in the room and tending to the stricken under Dani's direction. They spit into pairs, Dawn and Teddy, Alex and Angela, Jennifer and Karen.

"Damn," Alex said. "We could have really used Seth down here tonight. He senses dying."

"He didn't want to come. Really, Alex, he doesn't go to dances. And if he could have told, why didn't he tell us?"

"Because Keisha told him to take the night off if he wasn't going to come. Part of apologizing for sticking him in that car with your boyfriend." At her look, Alex continued, "It's not like this is anything one of us can't handle." A spell traced the minor practitioner's path. He had jumped to Berkeley.

The minor practioner looked at them in panic as their own teleport spell dropped them right behind him. A blast of lightning from Alex had him sparking uncontrollably as his muscles spasmed.

"Thantoris, I beseech thine aid. This idiot died too quickly." Seth appeared in the black shirt and dockers he usually wore.

"What, I can't take one dance completely off?"

"There was an attack, Seth. This guy decided to poison the punch, and I hit him with a jolt. If we're going to get anything out of him, we need you."

"I'll give it a shot…" He concentrated. "He's Greek. Named Georgos Yspalantes, or that's about as good as I can get it. He was recruited to help by Binay. They're afraid of us. He used an alchemical potion on the punch…relaying it to Bridget and Jennifer now to help in healing… okay. Did you want the body for something?"

"Not really."

"Deep sea scavengers it is." He teleported the body out to sea and prepared to teleport himself.

"Wait a minute, Seth," she said. "Why don't you join us for the rest of the dance?"

"There's no reason to."

"Yes, there is," Alex corrected him. "There are several ladies who asked me where you were."

"I bet I can name them, too."

"I bet you can't," Angela responded. "Keish, Bridget, Jenny, Karen, Dawn, and I all knew where you were."

He shrugged, spoke a word in Coptic, and vanished. "What was that about?" Angela asked Alex.

"There are two ways to interpret what I told him. He…chose the pessimistic option that the girls asking wanted to make sure they could avoid him and not need to worry about him being present. I'm not really surprised that's how he took it."

"It's ridiculous!"

"Is it? Why do you think he deliberately set out to cultivate a reputation as the Lord of Vengeance? It wasn't because he expected to be Mr. Popular." She nodded in agreement.

Keisha came up to Karen in the library as she was researching a history paper. "Did Ange and Alex have it right that you need another extracurricular for your college applications?"

"Yeah. Cheerleading, writing for the paper, and swimming aren't really it, according to my parents. Especially since I can't count magic tutoring."

"How'd you like to be on the dance planning committee? Mitch got convicted last week for theft and vandalism. He'll be spending the rest of the year and two more in Juvie."

"Okay. Sure. You want me to take over his stuff??"

"Yeah, precisely.

"I'm glad we just had one. I've got some ideas for the Valentine's Ball." She smiled. "Also known as my birthday party." Keisha grinned at that.

"You're the right person for it." She pursed her lips. "I'd also like you to see about getting Seth to the dance for once. I know he had a good time at that one he went to last year."

"I'll give it a shot…but he'd turn even me down now."

"He would?" Keisha asked with surprise.

"Yeah, too painful."

"We need to be doing some more things as a group. We're starting to lose some cohesion. I don't suppose you have any ideas on healing the breach?"

"Not yet. I don't know enough about what caused the problem. I was avoiding Seth up until a few weeks ago. And besides, Angela hasn't graduated me to full use of my powers."

"It's not something that's going to be solved by power. Angela's protecting Dave and Seth's reinforced his defenses. With Angela worried sick about Seth taking unilateral action on Dave…they need an outsider, and all of them will listen to you. You can do this, Karen, and quite possibly you're the only one who can. How's that for a graduation present?"

"I'd have preferred chocolates." They laughed, and Keisha left her to it.

Chapter

22

"Hey Dave. Whaddya think of my car's new features?" The minibar hadn't been ready for the dance. They were standing in the parking lot of the high school. Freshman eyes were bulging out at the parade of limousines "Gorgons limo? Sweet. Not sure the color scheme is one I would have gone with, but you're matching the uniforms' teal and bronze."

"Yep. The other owners do it, too. Oh, this is my driver, Felicia. My boyfriend, Dave."

"Nice to meet you. Thanks for getting me out of the oldsters' clutches. You used magic, right? And why are you wearing a business suit?"

"I did. First there's an owner's meeting at the San Rafael office, then we've got a team dinner up in Santa Rosa I wanted to take a look at. But," she inhaled deeply, I also need to talk to you."

"What about, Sweetness?"

"You need to stay away from Seth."

"I thought you wanted me to make nice with him."

She paused, looking at him. "One of the others doesn't want you near him, and I agreed to make that happen."

"Why?"

"It was a bargain for something else."

"Oh." He shrugged. "I'll try for you for a week."

"Dave…I really hate to put it like this. I'm not making a request. If you don't, I'm going to have to make it a compulsion."

He looked at her, stunned. She'd never threatened to use her magic to force him to do something. "No you won't. I'll…"

"Dave you don't control what I do with my magic. If I need to do the compulsion, I can also make sure you don't know I did it. I don't want to do it, but I will if I have to."

"How am I supposed to stay away from him at the League offices? Or cheer practice?"

"We all have offices. You can stay in mine. Here's your visitor badge. As for cheer practice, that's a neutral event. You've been mostly keeping away from him there anyway at Karen's insistence."

"This reminds me of my parents taking me to work when I was little."

She smiled wearily. "Sorry. Manipulating time isn't something I'm very good at, and I needed to talk to you before Alex's compulsion wore off."

"Alex compulsed me?"

She nodded. "He put a time limit on it for me so I could talk to you about it first. The compulsion he used will wear off tomorrow."

"Are you serious?" She just gave him an exasperated look. "I guess you are. Okay, okay. I'll stay away from him. Should you turn around and drop me back at home?"

"We've still got a date after the meeting," she reminded him. "I could, of course, fetch you directly here when I'm done, or send you out. It makes more sense to leave direct from the meeting, though. Your parents would be surprised if you were back in your room."

"Okay, yeah, alright."

Angela subtly increased their speed to get them to the offices faster. They took the elevator; she pressed a recessed "Owner's Key" that shot them up impossibly fast. "That key only works for one of us."

"You guys made all these alterations just since you…Oh. It just took you a few seconds, didn't it?"

She smiled. "Once we figured out what we wanted done, yeah." They walked down the corridor to a door with the Gorgon's charge on it. He saw doors with the Avengers charge, three blank ones, and one with the Sphinxes' device.

"I thought your office would be by Seth's."

"It was, originally. We swapped some offices around in June."

"I thought you didn't get your team until the middle of summer!"

"Seth told me they voted on it when I was his guest at a Valkyries-Sphinxes game in the spring. They voted to let me use the start-up funds. I have to pay it back, but not only is Keisha amazing at working the commodities market, I've got plenty of time. And I'm quietly feeding certain minerals into the markets."

"Like what?"

"Rare earths, mostly. They're very valuable in cell phones and things like that."

"Where are you getting this stuff?"

"I go out beyond Pluto's orbit, pluck some of the smaller rocks, and transmute them. As long as I don't flood the market, it's making me rich. I'll have the start-up loan repaid by July."

"You…you can *do* that?"

She opened the door to let him in. "Dave, you have a very limited idea of what one of us can do, which is mostly my fault because I don't do a lot in front of you. We can do almost anything we want to do, and the only exceptions come in when we're doing something one of the others doesn't want done or it's too strenuous. We can still do it if we work out an arrangement with the other person—or if it's in our dominant area of power.

"It's easier to not tell you about what we're doing in the first place than to keep telling you I can't elaborate on things because no one else has agreed you get to know what we're doing and who's involved." She grimaced. "I do the same thing to my parents, actually. Before I go, is there anything you need?"

"Are you sure I can't come to the meeting. I'll be quiet in the back."

"Nope. First, it's a lot easier to hold this part of the meeting in English. It's a private business meeting. Only the owners and the two people who have the votes to be future owners will be present, not our significant others. Second, you just agreed to stay away from Seth, and he still owns the Valkyries."

"I hear you. I'll be good. Are we still…skipping that. You can make it anywhere you want in seconds." She smiled, kissed him, and went off to verify everything was on track on Venus and Mars. Football? They'd done that at lunch.

Julian grabbed a seat at the public student council meeting. Patti had a clear majority on the council—she'd gotten her people elected to the senior and sophomore seats and two of the freshman seats. The nature of the topics being discussed—the school dances, instituting prayers over the public address system, and removing books from the library—had prompted a lot of students to come to the meeting to hear the plans…and from the muttering, to loudly protest them. Julian had brought his recall petition, and it concealed a bombshell.

"First order of business…the Grace Christian Church has graciously offered to host our Winter Formal. All in favor?"

"Have you forgotten, you pathetic little twit, that not all of us belong to your cult?" Grace Minh piped up immediately from the audience. "That our school includes Buddhists, Jews, Muslims, Sikhs, Hindus, Wiccans, Druids, Pastafarians, Satanists, and atheists, many of whom recall the historical persecution by you Christians?" A wide muttering spread.

Catalina Zaragoza spoke up. "This is supposed to be a school dance. It should be on school property."

Seth actually joined in. "We will not be providing funding for an event at a church. The vote was unanimous." His statement seemed to alarm some of the other members of the student council.

"You can't back out now!"

"On the contrary. We have not committed to funding any school dance. The vote was nine to one, and the one doesn't have control over his finances."

"But it's already agreed!"

"Even if it were, our trustees technically have the power to void any contracts we make at the moment. They would void them on our behalf if it were necessary."

"If you want to have a dance at a church," Erik Stevens said, "go for it. But don't try to hijack our school dances. I don't want to be in a church, mate."

"Patti," Clint Boulos, the senior treasurer, "we don't have the money to put on the dance if the someone doesn't fund it. And especially since it's a fundraiser for later events. We've been counting on it to fund other things."

"Call the vote," she said in disgust. They voted it down.

"Next order of business. Inspirational prayers over…"

Elaine Sutherland spoke up. She was the spokesperson of the Wiccan Student Circle. "That is unconstitutional."

"If you get equal time?"

"It's about the principle of the thing, not access. Dad's on the bench. The law is clear. The school would lose the lawsuit."

"And there WOULD be a lawsuit," Jasmine Alassad said. The council, even with that warning, voted to go ahead with it anyway. It prompted a lot of shouting from the audience.

"Finally, remo…"

The Round Tablers stood up wearing shirts proudly claiming they read banned books. The students council took a lot of abuse, but with few voting objections voted to remove their "horrid" books from the library.

Finally Julian signaled Shevaun.

"I believe we have a petition with three times the needed number of signatures.

"Yes," Julian said. "I move that the entire Student Council be disbanded for voting fraud. I have already presented copies of the evidence to Ms. Lee." The room dissolved into pandemonium.

Chapter

23

For three weeks, into December, the whole school was on edge after Julian dropped his bombshell about cheating in the election. Shevaun had immediately backed his proposal in the council, and resigned her seat to run again. Patti seemed entirely unconcerned, and unsurprised when Ms. Lee cleared her.

Karen noted that Ms. Lee was showing evidence of enchantment. Her relations with Seth had gotten oh so much better, but when he casually asked if they should kill Patti, the others took the idea seriously, especially Teddy. "I hardly that is appropriate for rigging a high school election!" she said at the meeting on Mars. Martian terraforming was the main subject on the agenda when they got sidetracked.

"I don't think so either," Dawn said. "Exposure would work better."

"We just DID expose her," Bridget pointed out.

"*Julian* exposed her. She took control of Ms. Lee's mind to stay Junior Class President. We all know it," Jennifer put in. "If WE get involved, her minor magician's skills will be up against us, and she's not strong enough to counter any of us."

"Is it time for us to move against Patti and her little group?"

"She has no more than ten or twelve hangers on with any sort of power," Keisha said. "And they're even weaker than she is."

"So what do we do?"

"James Bennett is her boyfriend and one of the people who has some power. I strip him of it as a warning to her."

"If we're going to strip someone of their power, Jenny, shouldn't it be Patti herself? James has been supporting her, but he hasn't gone out and used his power much himself," Dawn said. "Targeting him seems… an over reaction, almost as much of one as killing her."

"He doesn't have much," Angela agreed. "What about removing her control of Principal Lee and resubmitting the evidence of her rigging the election? And putting our own magics on Principal Lee to prevent her from doing that? Or maybe less us and more Solly and Alex?" That vote passed unanimously, and on Monday they put the plan into action.

On Friday, Julian disappeared.

Julian started awake to the touch on his shoulder. His eyes lit on Angela, who was oddly glowing teal in the darkness as she crouched over him. "Your Majesty," she said. "Do you want to deal with the cuffs or do you want me to?" She continued in an ordinary speaking voice, not bothering to keep it down at all. "Jenny's making sure Patti and her minions don't interfere."

"Just the two of you?" he asked, working a bit at the cuffs. "If you've got the keys…"

She grinned. "We split into pairs, with Karen coordinating. That's normally Alex or Jennifer, but we need him in the field this time and there was no way she was staying back when you were taken. I'm along just in case more than anything else. Jennifer's pissed. Usually it's just Seth that goes all the way and deliberately kills the bad guys, but she might take a few of them down. He and the others are on the way as soon as they can slip into a hidden spot. Patti was smart enough to hide you, and not smart enough to leave you alone entirely." She paused, cocking her head as if listening to something. "We should get moving. Jennifer says the minions are stirring. Patti's either ignorant or not too bright."

"I can't seem to get the cuffs. Since you've got the keys…"

"Well not the keys. Hold tight it's going to be a little warm." She took the cuffs' metal between her fingers, said something incomprehensible, and the metal glowed and ran liquid to the ground. She repeated the process on the leg cuffs.

"What did you DO?"

"I melted them. I'm not hearing screams of pain from liquefied steel, so I don't think I burned you, right?" she replied.

"With your fingers. You melted steel with your fingers."

"Yes, Majesty. It's actually a little easier for me than unlocking them. C'mon, exit's this way." She sounded completely matter of fact about doing the impossible.

"Um, Angela, not to delay us or anything…"

She shook her head. "Ask Jenny. She's the one who gets to fill you in. At least you like her."

"Huh?"

She grinned at him. "I got told to talk to Seth, whom you might remember I wasn't exactly speaking to two years ago." She paused, putting her hand on the wall. "Let's go."

"Won't they be expecting that? Isn't there some other way we can go?'

"We can go any way you want, including straight through the ceiling. Jenny's waiting for us with Karen, though, and Patti's already made teleporting you out of here dangerous to you, so that would take energy I might need to protect you."

"Don't you mean us?"

"Nope. You. You're the one she wants. You don't know enough to defend yourself. I do, and Patti really doesn't want to take me on. And the interdict she put on this place only covers you. Jennifer or I can shred it without difficulty, but she wants to get you safely out first."

He followed her. The security door was melted into a puddle, and there was a guard loudly snoring at a desk. "What was that about Seth?" he asked softly so as not to wake the guard.

"You'll have to ask him, Majesty," she said in a normal voice. "Talking about me is my choice. Talking about someone else isn't. If Jenny hadn't asked for permission to let you in, I wouldn't have mentioned his name."

"Won't he get in trouble? I mean, killings get investigated. And, shhh!"

She glanced at him. "That guy won't wake up for at least twenty-four hours. No autopsy would find anything. Well, not nothing, but a death by natural causes. Yeah."

"You mean as far as the cops are concerned, there were no killings?"

"Precisely."

"How'd he manage that?"

"Again, ask him."

They walked cautiously forward, coming to the stairs. "How come you came after me?"

"If it comes down to a fight, Jenny is more… flexible, I guess you'd say, than I am. I'm more likely to go nuclear."

"I thought that was Seth," Julian protested.

"Take me literally." He drew back, shocked, and then realized she didn't mean it that way.

"Where are my brains? 'Take you literally.' No comma. You mean…?"

"Exactly. It's not a figure of speech for me. My talents are in matter manipulation, including fission and fusion. I'm more likely than she is to cause massive collateral damage, and we don't need that. So she keeps an eye out, I pull you out, and Patti doesn't get her atoms ripped apart."

"So that's why you're kicking ass in physics. Wait, you'd kill her?"

"There's some difference. I'd take an action that would inevitably cause her death. But I'm not the person who makes someone dead by wishing it so."

"Kind of a thin distinction, isn't it?"

"It feels a LOT different, Julian."

"Okay, okay. Sorry I said anything," he said placatingly.

"I'm not about to blow you away or anything," she said with a smile. "I learned from him last year, so I've tried it. I was aiming at a mosquito when I simply killed it, versus turning some nitrogen to plasma. A "boom, you're dead" means you link with what you're killing. It's a horrible feeling."

"I thought you and Seth weren't getting along again."

"We're having an argument, but we've come to a truce. I want to bring Dave in. Seth prefers Dave die."

"Dave's bullying ways have finally run into someone who's not going to put up with it, and has the power to make doing it a really, really bad idea?"

"WHAT?"

"Dave's been a bully for years, Angela. He's never tried picking on me—there are benefits to being as big as I am—but until he got taken on that ship he wasn't very nice to boys smaller than him, or outsiders like Seth. From your reaction, I assume you didn't know that."

"No, I…didn't. Are you sure about this?"

"Ange, I remember helping Seth to the nurse's office in first grade after Dave beat him up. He was a bloody mess. I think Bridget caught Dave alone a few days later. He didn't want to admit a girl beat him that badly. But that didn't mean he let up on Seth, he just didn't go that far."

"And Seth remembers all of it."

"I don't know about that…but I wouldn't be surprised."

"You agree with Seth I should dump Dave?"

"Dave's been a lot less like that since he came back from the ship. Does he know you guys had something to do with it?

"He knows I did. He doesn't KNOW about most of the others, as only two have revealed themselves to him…"

"Karen and Alex, I'm presuming. It's not that hard to guess when I know the people involved. Wizards of the Round Table? Hiding in plain sight and Patti's an idiot for taking on Merlin's personal students alone."

"With the exceptions of me and Karen, we don't have a teacher. But yeah, kind of. She's got some minions who'd be terrified if they saw what I did freshman year, let alone what I'm capable of doing to them now."

"Didn't Alex and the football team…"

"Nope. The team would have had a very hard time handling zombies or a vampire."

"But Seth wouldn't. He's the one that saved you."

"Yeah," she said softly. Had she been being too hard on Seth? The tunnel wasn't that deep, so they emerged to find Jenny waiting for them. He picked Jenny up for a kiss

"Careful, Julian. She can pick you up, too." He laughed as the rest of the Round Table showed up. Jennifer turned back to the tunnel and spoke a word in Cornish. She cocked her head, nodded, and turned to the rest of them. Solly said something in Hebrew.

"Anything else?"

"Not right now," Alex replied. "But I think our plans for the Magic Ball just got accelerated." The others murmured agreement.

"Magic Ball?" Julian asked.

"Oh, sorry, Julian. We decided to throw our own dance while we were looking for you. Patti will be in attendance."

"Can I help? If you'd like to conceal what you're up to, you can borrow my title. "The King's Hawaiian New Year's Ball" has a nice ring to it."

"Yes it does. Thank you, Julian."

Chapter

24

With Julian taking the public face of the ball, the rented room in San Francisco had taken on a very Hawaiian theme. The dinner was a luau, the punch bowl filled with pog, and the decorative palm trees covered the live band. Julian himself was shocked by how quickly the Round Table could put everything together on such short notice right at Christmas. Jennifer shrugged.

"Magic," was all she said. Having seen Angela in action, Julian had decided to wait for Jenny to tell him the rest on her own schedule, despite his curiosity. She seemed in no particular hurry…in fact, she seemed to be resisting the very idea of answering his questions, as if something terrible would happen once he knew the answers. Which was ridiculous…wasn't it?

A lot of the class had made it down to the ball. He even noticed Seth, who was usually perched off to one side watching the dancing rather than participating. Jennifer had mentioned him providing security. Patti hadn't shown up yet. In between his duties as host he got several dances with Jennifer. The evening played on, and still no sign of Patti, so he started to subtly encourage the remaining unknowing guests to depart, and before long only the Round Tablers and a few people he suspected knew the truth about them were remaining.

164

"She's just arrived," Jennifer whispered to him as they danced. "Get ready, Patti's a fool." He didn't quite understand what she was saying, but Patti and her eleven cohorts went straight to the middle of the dance floor. Their eyes were fixed on Jennifer and Julian.

"Jennifer! If you keep your moronic friends out of this, it will just be you and me. I will spare them."

Jennifer whispered a word to him. "Now." Her cohorts screamed and collapsed, writhing on the floor.

"Keep my friends out of it and you'll spare them, Patricia?" Jennifer looked at her quizzically and waved her hand. "Your little minions have no power. Not any more." She gave Patti a tight smile. "If you really want to challenge someone else, I can't promise you'll survive the experience."

Dancers swirled about them, Julian noticed. He stood behind her with his arms around Jennifer's waist, leaving her arms free. It looked protective, but really left her free to defend them. Seth and Bridget, Teddy and Dawn, Angela and Alex, Keisha and Solly, Karen and Dani, Malcolm and Shevaun. Shevaun spun away from Malcolm as Karen pulled Dani out of the circle, and Julian suddenly noticed Jennifer's friends had surrounded them. Shevaun grabbed his hand as she spun, pulling him with her as Jennifer spun to join Malcolm.

Now they were surrounding Patti, standing alone in the middle of the floor. Jennifer said something quietly and lines appeared. Glowing lines, and Julian felt sure they formed a five pointed star in a circle, with the girls as the points if the star.

Karen was awed by the subtle strategy Alex had devised for dealing with Patti and her minions. A dance well known to the student body that Patti wasn't invited to. Making use of Julian's unknowing, untrained power to convince the innocents to get out of the room and safely away.

"That was sloppy, Patti. Walking right into a binding circle?" Jennifer said. "You now have three choices. To be bound and banished, to be stripped of your power, or to die."

"Your problem, Patti, isn't that we don't know what you can do. It's that we do know…and each of us is more powerful than you are," Alex said.

"If we had wanted to kill you, any of us could have easily done so," Seth said.

"Before you decide to resist, if you leave this room with your power you will be dead within three days," Jennifer went on. "It has already been pronounced."

"A slight correction, Jennifer. If she leaves this room with her power, she will be dead in sixty six hours, six minutes, and two seconds," Seth said. She looked skeptically at him. "By all means, you bigoted cretin. Test my pronouncement. It will do nothing to me."

"Not if I kill you first." The ten laughed at her, and Karen joined them. She'd sensed Patti's castings, and she was far more powerful than the class president. So were Shevaun and Julian, and they hadn't learned how yet.

"Don't be ridiculous, Patti. Do you have no ability to measure relative power? We do."

Patti looked out around at them with her eyes glowing gold and steadily widening. She seemed to be starting to panic. She turned to stare directly at Seth. Seth, in line with the plan, contacted Karen telepathically to let her know what his senses told her about Patti, adding to what Jennifer had sent her earlier.

"Yes. He will kill you without a moment's hesitation, but he doesn't need to. In pushing to make yourself more powerful, you cracked something, you broke a barrier. You're cannibalizing your own body reserves. What power you have is eating away at you as we speak. We know how to counter it. The consequence is that you will lose your power completely. Or you can wait until Seth's pronouncement of your fate is realized. He raised me from death. I'm fairly certain he won't do it for you. You've made yourself his enemy," she told Patti. "Saving your life will remove your power. In the end, though, the decision is yours.

Patti looked at them in horror, taking note of their glowing eyes. Black, green, yellow, indigo, and purple. Teal, pink, blood red, blue, orange, and brown. Of the people looking at her, only Dani, Shevaun,

Julian, and Keisha's date Michael weren't obviously powerful and ready to use that power. Karen noticed the probe she tried of the binding circle; it didn't fare well at all.

Bridget advised Patti to do a self-check. While she did that, Julian sidled over to where Dani and Shevaun stood with Michael, getting the explanation for what was happening from Dani. Patti eventually glared at Seth. "Blaming the messenger, Patricia, won't help you. If you didn't have this problem I might very well have simply executed you already. Should you desire to continue living, you will take option number three."

"You could fix this."

"Why would we want to do that? You're a cancer," Keisha responded. "We don't have to do anything to help you. What we're willing to do… strips you of your power. You'll have only your personality and the reasonableness of your position to convince other people to do what you want."

"Alright. Do it. Just so I can get away from you." Jennifer spoke in Cornish. Patti's power vanished into the night, and they opened the circle to let her flee as fast as she could. Patti left the people who'd followed her into the ballroom in pain on the floor.

They were back out in the clubhouse after stripping Patti of her power and dropping off Julian, Dani, Mike, and Shevaun at home. Angela stood up. "Ladies and gentlemen, I present Karen Indira MacLeod as fully trained and ready to take her place among us. Her name is Calyrine."

"Congratulations, Calyrine. Welcome to our number." That was Seth. There was a chorus of congratulatory remarks and raised mugs of root beer.

"With that," Alex began, "it is time. Both Shevaun and Julian have learned a little bit about our world now. Were there any negative signs anyone noticed?"

"No. They've both tapped into their power at various points. I don't think either of them is particularly suited for combat in their abilities," Angela said.

"Who's going to have the conversations with them?" Alex wanted to know.

"Dawn and Jennifer were keeping their eyes on them," Malcolm said. "They'd make the most sense. Karen?"

She was shaking her head. "Dawn and Shevaun, no problem. But Jennifer and Julian are in love. It should be somebody else. It needs to be Julian's decision, and even Jennifer's presence could affect that. He's going to want to talk to her, but someone he's not in love with needs to break the news to him And he needs to know about the no-dating-each-other rule at the outset. I'm sorry, Jenny."

Jennifer closed her eyes and leaned forward. "I know you're right. It still hurts to know that either we're going to strip him of his power or break up."

"He knows about things like arranged marriages and divorces for reasons that have nothing to do with the real desires of the people involved. Much as it pains him, he'll understand."

"I know," she whispered. "I know." Seth was the first person to put his arms around her in sympathy.

Chapter 25

"Hey, Shevaun. You wanted to know one of those places we disappear to at lunch where only another of us can find us?" Dawn asked her their first day back at school after New Year's.

"Absolutely. Where is it?"

"It's time to bring you there."

"But where is it?"

Dawn leaned in close. "Mars." A word in Tsalagi put them in a large, panoramic room looking out onto a red-tinged sky and a short horizon.

"Hi Shevaun," Angela said from an easy chair where she was reading a book.

Shevaun was shocked to be looking out from the observation room onto the imposing bulk of Olympus Mons. The light gravity amazed her even more as Dawn came up beside her. "Trippy. *Mars*. We're on *Mars*."

"Hai. But we're not actually alone. Ange and I didn't do all this ourselves. The others are watching us."

"So why are we here? You never said."

"So that we have privacy. Because we have a question for you. Do you want to learn magic?"

"Me?!"

"You," she replied with a smile. "We've had an eye on you since last year. You've definitely got the potential. I know you did something accidentally, which is why we're stepping forward to offer you training now. We think most people who have the abilities we do, either just never develop them—get what they think of as serendipity—or accidentally kill themselves. Another option would be to take the power from you so you don't accidentally hurt yourself or someone else."

"If you took it, and I changed my mind later, could I learn then?"

"No. We don't have any idea how to give it back, which is why we just stripped the power from Patti. You don't have to accept now, of course. You can turn it down and not learn. Learning to control your abilities is just the safer course for you and everyone around you."

"Who is 'we', Dawn? Besides you and Ange."

"There are eleven of us now. And you just saw us in action at the dance. We're talking to two people today about joining us. I volunteered to check you out since we did girl scouts together. We're all involved in teaching a new person, but you can make up your own mind who you want as primary instructor."

"Who's the other person? Something's wrong, obviously. Your face is scrunched up like it was that time at camp."

"We don't date each other, and he's become someone's boyfriend is the problem he presents. Which is why two of us are having the talk with him."

"Oh, hell. It's Julian, isn't it? That was kind of spectacular at the dance," she said. Dawn didn't say anything. "What can you do with it? I've read enough fantasy novels to know what can be done varies widely."

"We're not sure what the limits are. Everything takes a bit of effort. Some things come easier for some people than other things. We'll have to figure out what you're best at by trial and error, I'm afraid. We've had exactly one contact with an older, more experienced practioner that didn't end in a fight. Most of the time, it also ends up with the other person dead sooner or later. We haven't quite figured out why they're so hostile, but they are."

Shevaun considered. She looked out the window. She bounded across the room to look out before returning to Dawn. "Let's do this."

"Good. We don't have much time for this, though. Come on, the den's this way."

Keisha and Solomon sat down at the lunch table across from Julian, and Keisha said something incomprehensible. They set down their bags and pulled out their sandwiches as Julian felt a tingle in the chill January air around them. "What's up guys?" No one else was around.

"We got picked to have this conversation with you. We've already had it with Jennifer," Solly replied. He seemed fairly serious. "We've been warning her about it all year. Now it's here."

"At the dance, Julian, you tapped into power. We already knew that you've got as much potential as any of us. And that leaves us with a problem," Keisha said.

Solly picked it back up as Keisha ate a few bites. "Put simply, we don't want to have to deal with a bad break up. And we all know it can happen."

"Now come on, guys, we're not headed for a break up."

"Jennifer was supposed to be keeping an eye on you, Julian, not fall in love with you. But she did," Solly said.

"You guys are sounding a lot like parents."

"We decided that with sort of power we've got, we needed to grow up fast or we'd accidentally do a lot of damage. I can bring civilization tumbling down if I want to, Julian," Keisha said.

"The rest of us are looking at the problem a step removed," Solly replied. "Whether or not you're headed for one, we need to think of what might happen if it DID happen and none of us like to think about it if two of us ever got into that sort of argument. We don't date each other."

"What about Seth and Angela? They certainly act like they're a broken up couple!"

"Former teacher and student, actually," Keisha replied. "And a more perfect example of why I can't come up with. You do not want them furious with each other. You saw both in action at the dance. Seth holds death in his hands; he can kill—a person, a population, even a species—with a word. Those die offs of boars, starlings, ice plant, and eucalyptus trees are his doing. And while most of her focus is on states of matter, Angela's the only one of us who's ever whipped up a nuclear detonation purely by will."

"Nuclear detonation?" he asked, stunned. Then his brain caught up with him. "The meteor over Beijing? Going nuclear really wasn't just hyperbole on her part?"

Solomon nodded soberly. "Yep. That was Angela, not the Chinese. The rest of us were shielding the city, and she had enough left over to help with that. And, Julian, it wasn't reported in the press, but that explosion was fusion, by the way."

"We don't want to interfere with your lives. We really don't. We'd be more than happy to simply cheer the two of you on. But, think, for a moment, about what the two of them could do, not just to each other but to everyone and everything around them. We don't know what your particular bent is when it comes to this. What we do know is that you're going to continue accessing it."

"What makes you think that?"

"Because you're doing it now, trying to influence us to do things your way. We're just protected from mental intrusions; if you were doing it consciously you'd already know that. Seth and Jennifer have a hypothesis that most people with the ability never fully develop it or accidentally destroy themselves," Keisha said

"We can either…"

"Oh, come on!" Jennifer appeared as if from under a blanket, then sighed at his expression. She took Julian's hand in her much smaller ones. "Jules, you've got two options here. If you want to develop your power, we'll help you. But you and I can't be together, and it needs to be your decision.

"I don't have an inclination. It takes me a little more effort but I can do everything everyone else can do, and nothing's likely to put me in a coma. And I mean everything. It'll exhaust me more quickly, but I can cause the zombie apocalypse like Seth, trigger World War Three like Alex, or start the final plague like Bridget. I'm the versatile one."

He felt his lips twitch at 'zombie apocalypse', but then he realized she was being entirely serious.

"And with that versatility, she's the single most powerful of us."

"If that's not what you want, if you want to 'just be Julian', I can take your power from you." Solly and Keisha put their hands on Jennifer's shoulders and squeezed as she spoke. But their solemn expressions didn't waver.

"What aren't you saying here, Jenno?" he asked softly. Jenny's eyes flicked to either side, but didn't speak. No one spoke into the silence, until finally Keisha sighed.

"She can take the power. Or we can. It's what we did to Patti. That part doesn't matter so much. Pretty much we can all do anything the rest of us can, although the strenuousness varies and some things can put us in a coma. The end result we expect to be the same."

"You think that no matter what, I'll be resentful." He grinned. "Petty. Jealous. Bitter."

"Displaying your "A" in English vocabulary doesn't help, Julian," Solly replied. "I can do the same thing in Hebrew or Aramaic. You have no idea how many languages Jenny can do it in. None of which changes the decision you need to make. And I'm afraid you're going to have to make it here and now."

Julian blinked furiously at them, but Solomon's face was impassive. Keisha's was expressionless. And Jennifer's… was full of regret. But she was in agreement with her friends. He could tell that much. She might not like what they were saying, but she didn't think they were wrong.

"Julian, as far as we know, once we take the power, we can't give it back. Patti will never again be able to do anything out of the ordinary. We know we can't give it to someone who never had it in the first place."

"I tried to give Mike power when Seth pronounced that he wouldn't survive the year. It didn't work."

"What did Seth do to Mike?"

"Nothing. He's particularly attuned to death. He knows how much longer someone has to live, if he wants to. He warned me when he noticed Mike's time drawing short, although that was due to cancer. It gave me time to cure him."

Jennifer cut in. "Seth could have cured Mike's death. Any of us could have, although Seth would have had the easiest time. Angela died in that bus crash two years ago, and Karen was murdered in Golden Gate Park. Seth healed both their deaths and no one knew the difference. But Mike died on camera at a Sphinxes-Valkyries game, with thousands watching. We weren't—and still aren't—ready to announce ourselves by publicly doing the impossible.

"Or," she continued, "even by doing the impossible where it will be publicly learned. Angela died on a bus, in a ravine, with only Alex and Seth knowing she'd died at all, and they didn't tell her. Neither did the rest of us. If Johnson hadn't tried to murder her the rest of the year, she may never have realized. Karen was killed behind a wall of trees with only Angela knowing it had happened. The guy who shot her…never woke up." Julian's eyes went wide.

"I never knew. But that makes sense knowing who's involved."

"That was part of the idea. Even Alex only told Dani with permission. Now you know."

"I've gotten so used to Angela hanging with you guys I almost forgot she didn't always do that."

"She'll be crushed. But more to the point, what's your decision?"

He took a deep breath. "You know, I've been a prince in exile my whole life. There's no chance of me ever really ascending the throne, whatever ceremonies we hold. And a large part of me was grateful, that what I was would never impact who I was. That I would never have to deal with an arranged marriage. That I'd never have to choose between love and duty.

"But here I am, facing that choice. I've picked up enough to know you are out to save the world, however ruthless you can be. You're bringing back extinct species and restoring endangered populations. Those storms that sunk the whaling fleets with no survivors—simultaneously!—were caused by you guys, I can see that now. That new climate treaty is your doing. There are sudden breakthroughs in fusion and solar energy, renewed commitment to space. Casualties are going up so high in those little wars around the world that sustaining those conflicts will be impossible. Repressive governments are falling.

How many police abuses have been exposed, this past year? And those truly sensational stories about torture, not to mention those fighting dogs. All of that was your doing."

"There were survivors. We just turned them into whales. The rights and bowheads really needed the population boost." Julian's eyes widened at Jenny's off-hand comment.

"I was planning to go into politics. I've got an internship lined up in Washington this summer, and the idea of the president being the current heir to the Hawaiian throne amuses me. I'm finding the call to public service is difficult to fight for me, and I can do even more to help as a wizard. I'm sorry, Jenno. Breaking up is the last thing I want to do." Tears were streaming down both their faces.

Keisha's voice was husky. "We've got about fifteen minutes before lunch is over. Let's get this finalized. Dawn's with Shevaun at the Castle, and Solly just let everyone know. They'll meet us there." Jennifer spoke a word in Cornish as Solly put his hand on Julian's shoulder and said something in Hebrew. Keisha followed a moment later.

Julian was surprised by how light on his feet he felt. "Where are we?"

"Quick rundown, guys. This is the Castle; it's on Mars. The Temple's on Venus, the Clubhouse is hidden at Battery Wallace in the Marin Headlands. The Shore's on the moon. We've got our own little scattered places on Earth. We'll send that list on an eyes-only text to your phones. We know there are other wizards on Earth, and the ones we've encountered have been rather nasty," Alex said.

"Like Patti?" he said with a grin.

"Patti's fairly nice comparatively," Karen said. "Two of them were on the *Pelewan*, and one fled rather than face Toranos and Angoral. Thantoris killed the one threatening me. This Christmas, he and Felarie tracked down the other one and stripped her of her power. She aged to death in a few seconds."

Bridget picked up the intro. "Fawedea and Calyrine," nodding to Angela and Karen, "joined us last year. We've all got secret names that we're attuned to. Sorry this is going so fast; we can stretch time some, but it's nobody's focus. They were both resurrected by Thantoris and have something of a bond…"

Seth interjected, "Not relevant at the moment, Chiomara. We can go over the history later. The point being that they got to select their primary tutor. With the caveat that Felarie and Julian need to be apart, we think it's best if you do that too." Jennifer's face twisted. Karen's arm went around her.

Shevaun spoke first. "Julian, would you object to me asking Dawn to tutor me? She's my oldest friend here."

He shook his head. "I don't want to cause Jennifer any more pain, so I was going to ask Malcolm. I know him best from swim team."

'Sure," Dawn said while Malcolm let out a sonar click of agreement. "With that," Solly said, "We need to get back. Kara?"

"Bathrooms are clear." Seth vanished first, then the other old hands, leaving Shevaun and Julian with their new tutors.

"We'll meet up on Venus after school," Malcolm said.

"Okay, call this lesson one, and we'll get back. Imagination, knowledge, and will are the three elements. We're about to disobey the laws of physics. Image the bathroom in your mind, and we'll go THERE," Dawn said.

"Julian, Shevaun. Good to see you again. Welcome to Venus."

"Holy shit! Mike? *Mike Wu?*"

"But… you died! It was all over the news! I even saw the unedited version online!"

"I did die. I, however, have a totally awesome girlfriend in Keisha and she didn't like that. Since these guys have the power to do something about death, she asked Seth to bring me back, and he did."

"Mike, Dawn, and Malcolm can fill you two in later," Alex said, taking his chair.

"You guys have color coded chairs?"

Malcolm muttered in Phoenician and a new pair of chairs—maroon and gray—appeared. The maroon chair was next to Malcolm's blue, while the gray was next to Dawn's yellow. "Yeah, we do. Each of us enchanted our chair to our maximum comfiness standard. We first did this summer after freshman year, when our teleportation ability enabled us to go interplanetary."

"Okay," Alex said. We're all here. We weren't able to earlier, but why don't you two ask any questions you've got?" The next four hours were a question and answer pizza party. When Shevaun mentioned her problem with milk, Bridget offered to—and did—reactivate her lactase-production. But by the end of it Julian and Shevaun knew everyone's special skill, except their own. That would take time to develop.

"So we are thirteen."

"Yep."

"Any chance of something symbolizing all of us?"

"What, like a circle of stars on white?"

"That would do. Whose flag it is…alters the color of the star at the top?

"I like it," Alex said. "Maybe add our personal symbol in the middle of the circle."

A quick vote, and it was agreed. The next day the flags had appeared on their lockers.

Chapter

26

"Any idea when you'll be able to take me to see your place on Mars?"

"No time soon. Dave, we need to talk."

"About?"

"Something Julian told me." She paused.

"What'd he tell you?"

"That before you were taken on that ship, you were a bully. That Seth was one of your victims. That it's the reason he hates your guts and would be perfectly happy to see you dead."

"I joked around with him a bit. He can't still be mad about those little things."

"Have you ever been in a literature or reading class with Seth? Have you ever listened to him exactly quote the book from memory? He's been doing that for years. He remembers all of it. And he was never having fun where you were involved."

Dave looked uncomfortable for a minute. "What does this have to do with Mars?"

"It's a history that makes the others very wary of trusting you. If they aren't willing to extend that sort of trust to you, they aren't going to give you a pass through to the base. If Alex or Karen are willing to act as control, I can take you up to the surface."

"You need their help? Okay. I didn't think you did, sorry."

"I don't. I've walked on the surface of Venus all on my own. I'll be fine. The backup is there to make sure you survive.

"Maybe after I've built a little place of my own there that, like the Seamount, is MY place, I'll be able to bring you up. I'm not sure if they've put wards around the entire planet."

"Guess I can't really do anything about that."

"Not really. But getting back to my conversation with Julian when we pulled him out of that prison Patti had him in. What are you going to do?"

"I…don't know." She sighed. She didn't really have an idea on how to fix it either. Not when Seth didn't want Dave anywhere near him.

"Ready for the party at Lucinda's?"

He grimaced. "I've got work at the pizza place tonight."

"Work? Pizza place? Since when?"

"I got the job earlier this week. Mopping floors, clearing tables, that sort of thing."

"Ah. Well, Karen and I are going."

"Have a great time."

Angela picked her up in the new prototype car she'd gotten from Keisha's developing car company, the Evolutionary Motor Company 2 Shiseirei. When asked about the 2 in the company name, Keisha suggested abbreviating it and smiled. Angela had groaned and tossed a bottle cap at her. It was based on an old Aston Martin Atom.

The door was open, so they walked straight in…to see people on top of each other on the floor. Fortunately it was mostly carpeted, but they were paying no attention to anything or anyone else.

"Ange, this is an orgy," Karen said as they looked around at the intertwined bodies. A lot of them hadn't taken off their shirts in their eagerness. Isabella Ward and Larry Williamson had ripped each other's clothes off in theirs. Karen smirked seeing them together. "A very intense orgy, not that I've seen many."

"You're right. Helen and Conrad despise each other, and they're going at it like long lost lovers. Damn, that's powerful. Only Solly. We need Bridget." They both winced as a wave of lust passed over them. Like everyone else in the Round Table, they had adequate defenses for something like this…but those defenses were weaker than others. Oddly enough they were aimed primarily at physical damage or mental intrusion, not…lust.

"For?"

"We need to get Solly back in control of himself," Angela said urgently. "And as soon as possible."

"You know, those two don't really hate each other. That's a pose on both sides. No one here is really doing anything against his or her will. They've just lost all inhibitions when it comes to sex; they're doing it against their *judgment*. They may not be doing it with the person they most want to, but they do want it—and the person or people," they spotted a few threesomes, "they're doing it with. Quickest method is to get the alcohol out of Solly's system, and he'll have defenses up to that sort of meddling."

"Oh right. Not aimed at us or the alcohol, but ANY manipulation of his body chemistry by an outside agent. For that, she's strongest."

"Maybe we can get him to get control of himself. It's not like he can't purge the alcohol if he knows he needs to."

"You know, that's a good idea. First let's end the orgy itself. You're better at that than I am."

"Just make them sleep?"

"Might as well."

"Mid-fuck?"

"Sure, why not? We're still going to have to figure out what to do about the fertilizations."

"Oh, god. Under Solly's influence? Every girl here but us is going to be pregnant, isn't she?"

"As Bridget would say, yeppers. But it's a bit beyond that. Solly uncontrolled…I didn't make my birth control as strong as I could have. It's aimed more at normal sex than a fertility god's indirect influence. Since he's not aiming it at us and we're powerful enough to keep it at bay…"

"…strong as it is it's not going to overwhelm us, but even our defenses aren't really prepared with this in mind." Karen looked around. "Even Grace and Mary?" Karen incanted the sleep spell.

"Even the lesbians, yep. Magic at work," Angela said as the sounds dwindled to snores. Then they dimly heard Solomon's protest at Catalina suddenly falling asleep.

"Hey, Catalina, what gives? You okay?"

"Solly," Angela shouted at him. "Before you wake her up, purge yourself of the alcohol spiking the punch!"

"Huh? What?"

"You're drunk, Solly. And out of control. You're leaking power all over the place. We came to a party to find you causing an orgy."

He looked around at the naked and semi-naked people all around him, sleeping mid-coitus. "As Grandpa says, "oy!" He concentrated and spoke several words in Hebrew, the effects of the alcohol visibly leaving his face as he did so. "I take it you know you're the only females here who aren't pregnant?" He still wasn't bothering to put anything on, though.

"Yeah," Angela said as Karen focused on a word.

"*Females?*"

"Yeah. Including the spayed cat, the isolated goldfish…and the adult humans. Welcome to my power," he said a little ruefully. "I think we're going to need the tanks on Venus. One or two accidental pregnancies would be normal enough—no big deal unless Grace or Mary was involved—but this many?" He shook his head. "I think project Elf is about to get an infusion."

"You've mentioned Project Elf before, Solly. What's going on with it?" Karen asked.

"Oh, sorry. Project Elf is a new subspecific race of people. With pointy ears and enormous lifespans. I've been harvesting unwanted embryos from in vitro clinics all over the world, ones that will normally be destroyed for whatever reason. We can just add these in a special section."

The girls looked at each other. "What do you mean special section? I wasn't aware there was more than one."

"I'll hold them until I know they won't be needed here. If someone wants a kid later, it'll be easier to provide one of these. I'll take the kittens, too. It's impossible for that cat to be pregnant."

"Oh. I don't think Grace and Mary would be bad parents," Karen said.

"Neither do I, but do a genetic scan of those pregnancies."

"What?...Oh, my." He nodded. "What?" Angela asked

"Their zygotes are both female. And each of them shares half her genes with Grace and half with Mary. They fertilized *each other*. You want evidence that something supernatural happened? They're it."

"I guess it was a good thing Dave had to work."

"This time. You do know Seth got him the job, right? I suspect it was to keep him busy and away from him. He doesn't like that pizza place."

"Is he mellowing?" she asked hopefully.

"I doubt it. It means you're freer to do other things. It offers multiple possibilities."

"I like the fact that Dave has a job. I'm not so thrilled about ulterior motives on Seth's part being responsible for him getting it." Solly shrugged.

"Let's start getting them dressed and waking them up."

"You know, we might want to do an adjustment to our digestive systems. If we broke down alcohol and other things like it in our stomachs, this wouldn't happen again."

"Good idea, Karen. I'm just glad this didn't happen to Angela or Dawn. That would have been bad, especially given Dawn's predilection for playing with black holes," Solly said, and Angela murmured agreement.

"I'll bring it up on Tuesday."

Chapter

27

$\mathcal{A}$ngela looked at the wards Karen had set up around her home with an appreciative eye. They were much more designed to keep people away without hurting them than her own were. Dave came up the walk as she sent Karen a telepathic message that she was here. The birthday girl opened the door and came out to meet her.

"Angela! So glad you're here," Karen said. She was wearing pink jeans and a white sweater with a big pink heart on the chest and more hearts on the cuffs and neck. "The rest?"

"They'll be along. They're discussing Bridget's latest project, and I didn't have a whole lot to contribute. So I volunteered to come tell you what was going on once I picked up Dave."

"Oh, hi, Dave. I didn't notice you back there. Is…?"

"He's coming. He wouldn't miss being invited to your party even if he had to get up out of his coffin."

"And…?"

"And I will stay away from Seth." He spread his hands to her. "Good."

"I know you don't need that kind of dispute at your party."

"Most of the people currently here are on the squad, so you should know them."

183

"What's Bridget's project, Ange?"

"A secret she doesn't really want shared with you," Karen responded. "Sorry to be mysterious like that, but if you're not involved with it, you'll have to ask her what it's about. Hey, Stacey!" she said as another guest came up the driveway.

"Happy birthday! Why's everyone standing out front?"

"You'll have to ask Ange," who looked at her before heading on in. "Katie's wrapped herself in a blanket and scarf and hidden herself in the den with a Disney movie marathon. She doesn't really have the energy for a big party, so she can nap in there when she feels the need."

"We'll leave her alone, then," Dave said.

She stayed by the door letting people in. The Round Table arrived from Venus en masse, with Mike disguised as a blue-eyed blond. He made her snort in amusement. Watching him get introduced as "Mike Thorsen" to people he'd known before he died and was resurrected prompted smiles and chuckles from the people who knew the truth. People were standing or sitting, flirting, and every other thing they thought they could get away with in public. Dad was baking. Mom was out getting the pizzas. As she moved around, subtly prompting good matches towards each other, she suddenly realized she'd lost track of Seth. At least he hadn't run into Dave, but she opened her connection to him and went looking. She also felt his power in operation.

She followed the link to where Seth talking to Caitlin in the den. She was telling him all about her cancer from her nest on the sofa, while he sat in an easy chair. It was hard to tell what Seth was thinking of her story without touching his mind, and she didn't want to do that if she didn't have to. Besides, a vocal interruption was something Katie could hear, too, just in case.

"Caitlin, are you bothering him?" she asked in her best 'big sister' tones.

"I think I'm bothering her far more than she's bothering me," Seth said. "I was looking for a place to sit and she very kindly offered to let me sit and watch her movie with her."

"You're sure?"

"Very. She's a little young compared to the hospice residents, but this is kind of what I do after school."

"Okay. We're going to be doing some dancing a little later. Please join us." <I'm not sure Katie knows what 'hospice care' means, Seth. We're trying to keep her spirits up.> Sometimes passing a message secretly couldn't be avoided.

<You mean you haven't told her. One of you should, you know, but I agree that it shouldn't be someone she's never met before.>

<No. But thank you for talking to her. I think she was feeling a little lonely and left out with everyone focusing on me.>

<Not a problem.>

"You seem a little livelier, Katie. Do you think you'll be up to joining us for the dancing? Or at least listening to the music?"

"I hope so," Katie replied as Seth telepathically informed her that she would have the energy for dancing—at least a little—even if she had to get it from him. Karen gratefully put her hand on his shoulder.

"We'll be doing food, then presents, then dancing. Starting in about five minutes."

"I'm not supposed to have pizza," Katie said.

"I know. Dad's making something special for you that you can keep down."

"Oh boy, boiled rice, enriched with vitamins, and some chicken that's about as tasty."

"Unfortunately, probably yeah."

<You could spice it up for her.> Karen felt her head fall. She hadn't even considered that.

"I'll see what I can do, but Mom, Dad, and Jimmy don't need to know if I do, okay?"

"What? You're going to…OOO! Thank you! I didn't know you could do that!" Katie jumped up and hugged her, then staggered She heard a car pull up.

"The food for the rest of us is here. Can you make it to the table after that?"

"I'll help her," Seth said. As he stood up, he offered Katie his arm. "Lean on me," he said. He managed to guide her without much difficulty as she leaned on him to compensate for her weakness.

Barbara noticed them coming in and pulled a chair out for Katie as Karen made her own way around to the head position. The pizza was pretty good, so was the strawberry cake, and Katie winked at her.

She'd made boiled brown rice and chicken taste like pizza. An impish sense of humor made it taste like chocolate. Katie was very good at the aggrieved, long-suffering little sister look...but she didn't say anything where Mom and Dad could hear.

Presents were something different. The most unexpected one, that provoked the most comment, was from Seth. Mom and Dad had been making a game of presents for years requiring them to guess the giver, but she as fairly confident of which one Seth had given her so she'd saved it for last.

"Thank you, Seth."

"How'd you know?"

"Well...the fact that there aren't any more? Or that no one else used paper from Halloween?" Katie said. Seth gave a small smile.

When she got the paper off, it proved to be a black jewelry box. Dave apparently couldn't help himself. "Looks like you got a proposal."

"It's too big for a ring. It's obviously a necklace. You apparently don't give Angela much jewelry," Alex said. Dani was wearing rings, necklaces, bracelets, earrings...Alex had good taste. Karen could tell he was heading Dave off from picking a quarrel with Seth.

It was a necklace, a silvery chain leading to a pink stone heart and a tiny light that made it appear to glow...and as the Round Tablers' eyes widened, she saw it had been enchanted.

"Looks like a gift for a girlfriend," Dave said. Angela elbowed him sharply.

"He obviously hasn't paid any attention to your sweater. You are the love, you are the pink, you are Heartgirl!" Seth looked at her with amusement.

"This is a memory stone, Miss MacLeod. I've noticed you like hearts, so that's why it's in that shape, and that is the only reason it is in that shape. Most of them are simply crystal and the light."

"You crafted it yourself, didn't you? You didn't buy it. You can't buy one of these."

He nodded.

"Thank you, Seth." She put it on; a memory stone worked best if it was present at whatever she wished to remember.

"Now that that's over with, shall we move out to the dance floor?"

"You have a private dance floor?" Seth asked as he offered to help Katie to her feet.

Karen answered as she took his other arm. "Mom converted the garage ten years ago. We never park anything in there and the gardening tools are in a shed out back." She switched to Coptic. "Thank you for the necklace, Seth. If I wear it in class I'll get everything that happens, right?"

"Yes, precisely. Or anything else, unless you deactivate it," he answered in the same language.

"Can you show me how to make them?"

"Of course. When do you want to learn?"

"Next week?"

"I am at your disposal."

"Thank you."

"Are we sure they're not hiding something?" Dave said loudly to some of the other cheerleaders on the side of the room.

Angela came up to them, having left Dave for a moment. They watched Alex and Dani tell him to give it a rest. "Karen, Seth, I apologize for Dave's behavior. I've had babysitting jobs where the two and three year olds were better behaved." She said it in English. Dave winced, since her voice carried to the entire room.

"Thank you, Angela," Seth said. Karen nodded to her.

"But it's time for dancing," so she took off her sweater. Her t-shirt read 'I heart Edinburgh'.

"I see it's better than new," Seth commented on noticing the enchantments she and Angela had applied to it. "The Genie Queen's work, if I'm not mistaken."

"Yes, it is," Karen replied. "If you don't mind, I'm going to start the dancing. Oh, Julian! I need a royal favor…" He laughed and started the dance with her. After a few dances she saw Seth leading Katie onto the floor, and she smiled to see her sister enjoying herself. And when she caught the buzz from Seth's telepathy to the other male members of the Round Table, she noticed that at various points they all had a dance or two with Katie—and more to the point, they selected modern waltzes to dance with her so they could be sure to keep at least one hand on her supporting her in her weakened condition. Seth had the Victorian rule of three dances with Katie, and when she grabbed him herself he admitted that's what he was doing.

As the clock chimed midnight, the party was over. Katie was still up and chattering away with Angela and Shevaun. When everyone left, Karen joined her parents cleaning up. Mom commented on her new jewelry.

"You really like that pendant, Karen?"

"It's nice. Why do you ask?"

"You've been wearing that ever since you opened it, dear." She nodded. "Aye."

"I'm a little surprised you're so taken with it. It's a light and piece of rose quartz."

"It's a bit more than that, really."

"Okay," Mom said. "A heart-shaped piece of rose quartz. And a flashlight."

"What did he call it? A memory stone?"

"Aye."

"What did he mean by that?"

"I can't say."

"Honey!"

"George, I think we may be getting into secrets she's obliged to keep. She said the boy saved her life once, which is why she invited him. They had some sort of discussion about her shirt being good as new, and spent more time talking in a language I couldn't even identify. I think the lad might be more than he appears. If he is one of the other magicians, who knows precisely what that pendant is capable of doing?" Her father stilled suddenly.

"Is the stone enchanted, honey?"

"She can't say, dear. That would confirm he's a wizard."

"That nice guy is a wizard like you?" Caitlin spun into the room, excited.

"No he's not a wizard like me. I manipulate probabilities, he doesn't. Why?" Strictly speaking that was true. Seth was a lot more easy-going about people other than Dave knowing about him than she'd thought, but it was still something to be careful of.

"You have a lot of energy," Mom said. "Are you feeling well?"

"I feel a lot better!" she shouted. "Ever since I danced with him. I don't know what he was muttering, it was pure gibberish, but I really feel lots better!" Their parents looked at each other, while Karen said a few words in Bengali.

"The tumor's gone."

"I thought…"

"I mean outright GONE, Mom. The cancer cells have been killed and the remnants sent back into her bloodstream to be reabsorbed by her body. Nothing left but healthy tissue." She paused to try to come up with a way to explain it. "Hades fell hard for me. He's left me alone—he's definitely taken 'no' for an answer—but he often leaves early when I'm there. So he missed the no magic cure directive, and I forgot to tell him later."

"I thought the really powerful healer was a girl."

"She is, but that doesn't mean he can't do it. He's one of the original nine."

"What's he good at?"

"He's the one who resurrected me." Caitlin's smile was blinding. Karen continued with raised eyebrows for emphasis. "He's also the one who executed every guard and crewman on that ship, and all the people holding Angela when she was taken freshman year, and all the people who took him last year. We're all dangerous, and he's the most lethal of us. He's good at death, kiddo." Noting the panic on her parents' faces, she shook her head and said, "I've been in his mind. He's not going to hurt her, or me. Keep in mind he's my age before you start the hero worship." But then her sister's emotions hit her. "Uh-oh."

"What?" Mom wanted to know.

"Too late. Excuse me." *<Seth.>*

<What can I do for you, Miss MacLeod?> Oh, good, he was awake.

<You cured my sister.>

<Yes. She only had a week if I didn't. In fact, she was right on the cusp of needing Bridget.> That shocked her, but when Seth predicted death, he was right.

<Okay, lad. She was scheduled for surgery, and the doctors were telling us months, so thank you, but that's not why I called. They figured out what you did. You were the only one who spent much time with her, and they do know about me.>

<Do I need to take steps?>

<Steps? No, they'll keep the secret. But she's got a serious case of hero worship where you're concerned.>

She caught the mental snort. *<Okay. First time for everything. Forewarned, I guess.>*

"What did he say?"

"Two things. He wanted to know if he needed to take steps to safeguard his secrets, Katie. I told him he didn't. He doesn't, does he?"

"No. I wanna tell my friends, but he just did something really spectacular for me. No more chemo. No more surgery. If he doesn't want anyone to know about it, I'll keep my mouth shut." Their parents nodded in agreement.

"Good to hear." She hugged her sister and caught her mother's eye. "The other thing he said was that she only had a week if he hadn't acted."

"The doctors said…"

"I called him 'Hades' for a reason. I'm not sure how he does it, but he knows, just like I know when people are right for each other. When he predicts death, it's going to happen unless someone intervenes."

"Well, done is done, Katie. But I don't want you near someone that dangerous."

"Daddy..." She was clearly rebellious over that parental ruling. Maybe she could help.

"Katie, it's going to be a while before he sees you as anyone but my little sister. He's not 'dangerous' like some bad boy in black leather with a great ass who's oh-so-sexy. He's dangerous as in him telling someone to 'drop dead' means that person will die immediately. I've been in his mind. I know how he thinks, even though he'd never met you before today. He's still not quite let go of the fantasy of him and me even if he does know it's not happening and is looking around. If someone came after you he'd protect you. But if you really decide you want to be with him, let yourself grow up a bit first. Okay?" She felt Mom and Dad relaxing a bit.

"I have to agree with your father, Katie. He's too dangerous..."

"Mom." Karen interrupted. "When you get right down to the base of it, I'm just as dangerous as he is. He's just a little quicker to reach for a lethal option. There's nothing he can do that I can't. In some ways, my talents make me more dangerous. I'm far more likely to make someone else do something. And there are a couple beneficial aspect to this. Seth finds big brains attractive."

"So if she wants his attention, she'll need to get her grades up?"

"Uh-huh." She smiled. "And the other thing is that she will come home alive if she's with him."

Katie hadn't been listening. "Nothing? Even..." She had clearly gone there.

"I can take male form, Katie, and he can take female form, so nothing, even that. Switching the hormones running around in our blood is uncomfortable and distracting, so we don't do it much."

"Oh." Katie pondered for a moment. "So you could make him..."

"Could doesn't mean going to, Katie. Hypothetically, yes, I could—maybe. Like all of us he's taken steps to ensure that sort of thing doesn't happen. There are thirteen of us now, and a conflict between us would not be pretty."

"But..."

"No, Katie. I'm not going to make him do anything. There's no reason to intervene, even if doing so was a good idea. And it's not. I'm not saying you're wrong for each other. You're just not ready, and neither is he."

"C'mon, Karen, he'd never even know!"

"There's no guarantee of that, Katie. Someone else would notice and bring it to his attention, even if he didn't. Gaia, for example, is very close to him. He's been friends with the rest of the original nine for years."

"Karen!"

"He could have controlled me. At a time when he could have made me, and made me be happy with the compulsion, he didn't. No, Katie."

"Okay, how about just a little push."

"Katie, it's a very bad idea. If you really want to be with someone, forcing him—or her—to be with you is never the right call. You met Alex and Dani. They're inseparable because she wants to be with him and he wants to be with her. Give it time," she said. "Even if he didn't vastly increase his mental defenses after he got taken last year. Even if trying to control his mind wasn't the sort of thing he'd treat as an attack, and respond to with lethal power. It's wrong, Katie."

Chapter

28

"Oh, come on, Jake! I'm too old to attend these things at the kid's table, and Dad's up for Best Actor this year! I need a date! It's the Oscars! Who else is going to invite you to the Oscars?" She listened for a few moments. "Oh. Hospital? I'll…"

<You're not up to curing him yet, and wanting a date is no reason for us to intervene. There are other guys.> Dawn's warning reverberated inside Shevaun's skull. It stunned her momentarily

"…um, uh, come visit you. Which one?" She hung up before joining Dawn, Angela, and Karen. "Why shouldn't we heal him?"

"Because it's not necessary; he'll heal up just fine under the doctors' care. And it would be inexplicable."

"You and Alex heal the team all the time," she accused Angela, who nodded.

"We do…if we get there before the trainers and the coaches are able to evaluate. But we also don't go all the way. Something happened, they're still hurt—god forbid an actual injury to Dani!—it's just not as bad as feared."

"But the key point is that the trainers haven't had a chance to do a full evaluation. Seth's been using that on the squad all year."

"Oh, he finally got training?" Angela said

193

"While in Juvie; it was part of his rehabilitation. He's kept it up, too. It's needed for his waterboy position. He was doing it last year for the team, too."

"Anyway, enough about him. What am I going to do about the Oscars? I could ask…"

Dawn gave her a slight smile. "I'd thought that was obvious. We were just discussing your best solution."

"What?"

"Take Seth," Angela said.

"SETH?"

"Of course. You're not looking for a boyfriend. You want some arm candy for a night. Put him in his tux and he cleans up nicely, if you'll remember when Bridget dragged him to a dance last year. Neither of you is famous enough for the red carpet, so he'll stay out of the way if your dad wants you with him for it."

"He's one of us, so it's no strings attached. This is the sort of favor we do for each other all the time. He actually owns a tuxedo, so getting him properly dressed on short notice isn't a problem. He can teleport home, so he won't need a room. It's not like he's got a girlfriend to get jealous, so no problems there…"

"Jealousy issues? Seriously?"

Karen shrugged. "Jasmine's a little possessive."

"Compared to Dani, I guess "a little possessive" is accurate."

Karen shook her head. "Dani's fully clued in, where Jasmine knows about Malcolm but not the rest of us. And her relationship with Alex is far stronger and more stable than Jas and Malcolm's. That possessive streak is almost entirely a pose—Alex has a lot of admirers, and it keeps them from being more than pests since no girl in her right mind wants to get physical with her. She'd be able to handle Alex doing you a favor."

"But more important than that," Dawn said, "Seth's skills are better for something like this."

"What, it's an awards show, not a killing field!"

"He taught Angela, he helped teach me. He knows what to watch for if you accidentally draw upon your power. Most simply, he's best suited to helping you keep control on a night where your emotions are going to be running high—or quashing an accidental power release."

"So it's a practical suggestion…" A sudden suspicion gripped her. "He didn't have anything to do with Jake's illness, did he?"

"Of course not. We'd have done something else to keep things contained if Jake hadn't gotten sick. It wouldn't have been that difficult for us to secretly get in and stay hidden; we've been places with real security, guards and dogs and cameras and stuff. This is just easiest."

"Ok, it makes sense. I'll take him."

"Now you just have one problem," Karen said.

"What's that?" Angela asked her, puzzled.

She smiled beatifically. "Asking him."

"Oh, shit," Dawn said, her eyes flicking back and forth in thought. "He *can* get into a snit about that, can't he?"

"I'm lost," Shevaun said. "If taking him's such a good idea…"

"I think it's a good idea. Karen and Angela think it's a good idea. You just agreed. But we haven't discussed it with him yet, and he gets sort of upset if someone makes plans for him without talking to him about them first. Upset as in refusing to go along with it, not upset as in randomly killing living things around him. Don't worry, it's on me not you."

"That doesn't sound good."

"Don't worry about it, but if you've got the free time let's go poke the mummy."

"Why not the bear?"

"She's in class." They headed for the locker room. Seth was cutting up oranges, alone in the room. When he saw them he said a word in Coptic to finish the task.

"What's up?"

Dawn poked her. "I need to ask a favor."

"Sure, Shevaun, what do you need?"

"Dad's up for an Oscar this year, so I need to go to the ceremony. But Jake's sick in the hospital."

"I assume Dawn's already told you you're not ready to cure someone, she won't do it, and neither Angela nor Miss MacLeod will, either. I agree with them. Angela was barely able to heal herself at the same point. Miss MacLeod was a little better at it, but healing herself was still about where she was. Jake's sick, but I assure you he'll recover just fine. Unless he's near death, there's no reason to intervene."

She blinked. Seth obviously had no real idea of why they'd come to talk to him. He thought she wanted reassurance that Jake wouldn't die. "Yeah, I get that, but I wasn't asking you to cure him. What she suggested was that I take, um, you."

"And this takes all four of you?" She stood there embarrassed. "When is it?"

"It's the Oscars, Seth…" her brows rose at his ignorance.

"Yes, you said that. I don't pay that much attention to award shows, though. I've usually never seen what's being nominated."

"Oh. It's this weekend. Is that a problem?"

"Not at all. How do we get there? Or should I just meet you at your hotel?"

She blinked again. He wasn't being a problem? "I don't even know what…oh, right, you can just find me mentally and teleport, can't you? This takes some getting used to."

"Are your parents clued in?"

"Wait a minute. You won't let me bring Dave in fully, but you're blasé about her parents?"

"I get to decide who knows about me, Angela…"

"Not the time you two," Dawn interrupted firmly. "Shevaun, what do your parents know?"

"I was invited to join the Round Table study group. They have no idea that means studying magic."

Seth nodded. "Good enough. I'll meet you there." Angela stayed as the others left. "Seth…"

"Angela."

"I don't get you. I really don't."

"Death is patient, Angela. Dave is an idiot. He's going to piss you off into coming to your senses and dumping him sooner or later. That will put him outside completely, and we'll be considering steps to protect your secrets. So why reveal anything to the moron?"

Angela quickly stepped on her anger at his "come on, be reasonable" tone. But she was sure he wasn't being entirely sincere, even though she still couldn't read his emotions any more. His reasons for opposing Dave had nothing to do with a potential break-up. He was reaching for an argument that might convince her—and doing a lousy job of it.

"That's bullshit and you know it. You want me and Dave to break up. Not happening, Seth!"

"I wouldn't be heartbroken by you realizing he's not worthy of you. You already broke up once. But you're missing the point. I've told you before. I don't like Dave. I don't trust Dave. I don't want anything to do with him. Do whatever you want with him, except betray the secrets of the rest of us. I only promised not to kill him. A persistent vegetative state will work just fine. It's a little more difficult, but I can just kill his brain cells. You probably wouldn't be able to tell the difference, since he's already a walking vegetable." He paused, and then said in a poisonous tone, "Would you like to know his natural date of death?"

Angela felt her eyes fly open. Was Dave in danger from something she didn't know about? Or was Seth just tormenting her? She couldn't dismiss either possibility, but given Seth's attitude towards Dave she'd better check him out herself.

"You think I won't check?"

He shrugged. "Whether you do or not is up to you. There's enough supernaturality associated with any of us that my perceptions where we're concerned are clouded. I can still tell you about a mere mortal like Dave, though. I don't think you'll be able to prevent it."

"Mere mortal? Getting arrogant in your old age, are you?"

"I can't die, Angela. The Immortality Project is in full swing. Bridget and I are using ourselves as the test subjects. We WILL regenerate from whatever's left, and we've both put fail safes in the box room at the Temple. Would you care for some nectar and ambrosia?" He gestured, and a peach nectar and bowl of fruit salad with small marshmallows appeared.

"What? That will…"

He nodded. "That will work. At the moment, the formula only works on people with the genetic ability to do what we can. It won't do anything for Dani or Mike, which is why we haven't brought it out in the Temple yet. We may have to do something specific for them."

"Maybe after you've got it perfected. See you in class, Teach."

Shevaun and her parents were just finishing getting dressed when her phone rang. "Hi Seth."

"Should I just meet you down here?"

"Let me check." She turned to Dad. "He wants to know if he should wait down there."

"He's already here? It'll be a few more minutes. I want to go over my presentation lines a few more times. Besides, we'll be taking the VIP elevator down to the car. Why doesn't he come up?"

"He could still probably intercept us, but okay. Did you hear that Seth? We're in the Marilyn Monroe Suite."

"I know. See you soon."

She'd just gotten her silver and gray gown on when they heard the knock at the door. Seth let her know telepathically he'd arrived, so she opened the door; he was wearing a black tuxedo with bone buttons. "Hi Seth. Any problems?"

"It was easy enough, but thank you."

"Glad you could make it, Seth," Connor Lone Elk said. Dad was wearing a tux too, but he'd altered it slightly to replace the bow tie with a choker and a quillwork enhanced cummerbund. Dad cocked his head. "How'd she get you into this?"

Seth shrugged. "Thank you, Mr. Lone Elk. She said she needed a date on short notice who could be appropriately dressed for the show, and I was free to be arm candy. So here I am. I expect to be going over physics with her."

"Study study study? That's admirable dedication, but this is something of a party. You can probably leave off for the night," Mom said.

Seth eyed her. "You can explain that to Dawn if you want."

She groaned. "No, better to get the studying out of the way before the party. I won't be able to get much done there."

"Can I run a joke by you...:

"Dad!"

"What movie is it referencing? I don't see that many."

"Oh, it's the 'Citizen Kane' remake."

"I didn't see it. Sorry."

"Since I can't try out my comedy on you without embarrassing my daughter, I'm ready to go."

"I'll call down for the car," Mom said.

The trip to the Oscars was crowded, and Seth told Dad he was planning on staying in the background. "I expect all their attention will be on you anyway."

"Some of the people with microphones like to talk to just about anyone walking the red carpet, Seth. Especially if one of their rivals has managed to corral a nominee and they're left high and dry. And since you're obviously with us…"

"I'll be polite." He'd also just drawn on his power, probably to keep reporters from talking to him. That was a neat trick; she just had the thought that she was looking forward to learning it when Seth started telepathically telling her how. She had a bit of trouble suppressing her smile. <Someone who knows what to watch for will still notice what you're doing; this just keeps your parents from noticing.>

When they got to the red carpet, Dad and Mom walked it first. She and Seth came along behind them. A reporter from the network covering the show got to Dad first, and they talked a bit about his projects. Dolores Bedno, a reporter from an entertainment show, caught up to her and Seth. "Miss Lone Elk, good to see you! My how you've grown. You look stunning, by the way. Who are you wearing?"

"This is a Janice Wyeth original, she's local to me, but just fabulous. And a delightful person, really. And the jewelry is made by Liana Gutshall. She did a marvelous job, too."

"Any anticipation about tonight?'"

"I'm rooting for Dad, of course, but it's not like I can affect the outcome!" She glanced sidelong at Seth, who'd backed up to let her do the interview. He shook his head slightly. He probably COULD affect the outcome still, but wasn't going to. There were a couple more typical questions. Finally, the reporter seemed to notice Seth.

"And who are you, young man."

"No one important," he replied.

"Seth…" she said reproachfully. He shrugged.

"I know I've seen you before somewhere, ah, Seth, is it? Santa Cruz, maybe? I seem to remember your face from a story last year about a death at a Valkyries game…"

"For some reason, society reporters make it clear that a woman alone at an event like this is doing something profoundly wrong, so she asked me to be a an accessory this evening. I'm arm candy. You can—and should—ignore me. Shevaun is a straight A student, plays three instruments, won the state science fair, and placed sixth nationwide. I'm not that interesting. Why don't you interview her some more, and actually ask a single substantive question?" His little speech seemed to nonplus Ms. Bedno, who asked about her science experiment investigating perceptions of time. As they left her she squeezed Seth's hand.

"Thanks, but I really didn't need the attention."

"None of us do, but that was particularly inane. 'Who are you wearing?' Do you have on a corpse I didn't notice? You'd think I'd have noticed. I keep an eye out for zombie material." She covered her mouth as she giggled.

"It is a kind of macabre way to ask who the designer of my dress is, isn't it?

"Just a little," he replied.

"As amusing as that was, please don't go scaring the reporters."

"Scaring the reporters?" Dad asked.

"Seth just tore a strip off of Dolores Bedno for asking me fashion questions and trying to ask him about Mike Wu's death. He, ah, didn't want to talk about it." Mom and Dad laughed.

"Oh, you were there…silly me, of course you were. You're the owner of the Valkyries, aren't you?" Dad asked. When Seth nodded, Dad went on, "That must have been hard to witness."

"It was worse for Keisha." He glanced at his ticket. "We're on the upper section, I see."

"Yeah, we'll see you after the show."

As they took their seats, she asked Seth in Lakota, "If Dad wins, can we get backstage?"

He replied in the same language. "Easily. The question is if we should. We'll see them soon enough, but are people from up here normally allowed backstage? If they're not, it makes more sense to not go but simply to meet up with them afterwards."

"I'm pretty sure I can. They'll let family in."

"Do you want to? We can go back there if you want."

"I'm not so sure they'll…you already have an option."

"I can turn myself into something on your flower pin—whatever it's called—and keep an eye on you that way."

"Okay. Are you going to stick around for the after party?"

"Did Angela and Miss MacLeod tell you about the party they found Solly at? With the spiked punch?"

She giggled. "Yeah. Orgy time."

"That's Solly losing control, and fertility is his focus. He causes an orgy, and impossible pregnancies."

"Your focus is death. You'd cause a tragedy."

"And we don't know what yours is, so it's harder to predict what you'll do."

"Should I skip it then? Tell Dad I have a headache?"

"Mostly it's a matter of being careful what you ingest. Have they had the opportunity to adjust your digestive system for alcohol?"

"Yeah, they have. Other things that might get slipped to us, not so much."

"I can tag along if you think that would let you enjoy the party."

"You don't mind?"

"It'll be fine. I wasn't sure how long this would take, so no one's expecting me home before tomorrow. I told my parents I'd sleep at the Temple, since I want to talk to Mike."

"Oh, they're starting!

They sat watching for a while, and then Seth asked her, *<Do you want to know the answer?>*

<What? You took a peek?>

<If you do…>

<I want to wait. It won't be long.>

The ceremony took its usual long hours. Dad was funny as a presenter for Best Supporting Actress, and then he won Best Actor. Seth was prepared and kept her from leaking her power. All she did was scream in delight and hug the people around him. Fortunately Seth seemed to have anticipated that reaction too, and didn't let it break his concentration

When she asked Dad if Seth could come along to the after party, he said sure. They met him outside and made their way to the home of the movie's producer, who was throwing the party. Seth maintained a mental connection with her the whole night, and they frequently drifted back towards each other. She corrected several of the young stars and the kids dragged along by their star parents that thought he was her boyfriend. She was amused when Seth turned down beers by letting them know he was underage. It took a while before he found the recovering alcoholics bar and got water; he then kept his cup filled magically. She'd have done the same thing but it was a lot harder for her.

Around two in the morning she found the latest teen singing sensation lying unconscious in a red dress on the floor of the bathroom with an actress about the same age in a black one, who'd starred with her dad years ago. They'd been featured in a lot of tabloids as a pair of bad girls. She sent out a telepathic call to Seth. He appeared quickly. Just as quickly he knelt down beside them. "Keep the other people out of here, would you? No one needs to know I'm doing this. Wait, check that, start CPR on her."

"What do you mean?"

"They've been poisoned. They're dead."

"But…Oh, right."

He started 'CPR' on the girl in the red dress and she felt him draw on his power. She felt an immediate breath in and called for someone to call an ambulance. The girls were taken away, they gave statements, and that was that. Seth managed to subtly emphasize Shevaun's role rather than his, and "luck" was a common word in his description. They took the limo back to the hotel and Seth bid them good night. As Mom and Dad went upstairs, Shevaun asked Seth to stick around for a minute.

"I'm surprised you revived them, but thank you."

"It was a few things. They were poisoned…something in their drinks. I put in the EMTs' minds what the poison was. And…it was a big night for your dad. He shouldn't have to remember it as a night one of his former co-stars died."

"Oh my god. I wasn't even thinking about that. Thank you."

"By next year you should be able to handle it yourself. The killer was hoping it would be passed off as a pair of overdoses, not hard with the number of needle marks between their toes."

"Are you going to…"

"I'm going to see what the mortal justice system can do. But I did eliminate their addictions, and give them a profound distaste for alcohol. They should be fine."

She chuckled. "You like them." It wasn't a question. He gave her the ghost of a smile and nodded to her. They went into the stairwell. Seth vanished for Venus. A few moments later she returned to the lobby and rode the elevator up to the suite. What a wild weekend.

29

Karen and Katie grabbed a small table at the Copper Club so they could celebrate Katie's clean bill of health from the flabbergasted, disbelieving doctors. The thirteen-year-old had managed to act surprised—a little bit, anyway—when they told her, but she'd been grinning in the car the whole way back. The teen hangout wasn't very crowded, and half the people seemed to be doing something on their laptops or tablets instead of dancing. The big screen game consoles were popular, though, and the music was at an appropriate level. The manager wore earplugs.

"Wow, is that Rachel?" Karen turned to look on hearing the comment as Katie headed over to the bar for another Coke. Rachel was a blond girl who preferred t-shirts three sizes too big for her with jeans and sneakers that she wore until they fell apart. Not tonight, though. Her deep red top had spaghetti straps, the short skirt was the same color, and her shoes had three-inch heels. Some spiteful girls had speculated she didn't own a dress. Brian Gorman came straight over to her.

"Damn, Rachel! You should come out of your clothes more often! You look good enough to eat!"

Rachel smiled at him, "You too," she said, pulling his head down. His eyes went wide and his arms waved around before stopping—not around Rachel, but limp at his sides.

Rachel raised her head from Brian's neck, flush with blood for the first time in weeks. Brian fell over, a little blood dribbling from the twin punctures. and she looked for her next meal. Her eyes lit on Katie.

"Go, Katie! Run! I've got this!" Her little sister stood frozen at the sight of Rachel dribbling blood down her chin. Karen short-ported beside her. "Don't make me do this, Rachel." A word in Bengali unfroze Katie and she fled for the door screaming for Seth. Why, Karen hadn't a clue; it wasn't as if he were anywhere around.

Rachel tried chasing after her and Karen's binding spell trapped her feet. "You really have no clue what I am, Rachel. Stop this before I stop you." Rachel snarled at her and bared her fangs, then slipped out the bindings by shifting to mist. She flung herself at Karen, who spoke a word in Bengali, vastly increasing her strength, as she backhanded Rachel into the wall. As Rachel hit and twisted like a cat to stay on her feet, she glared at Karen. "Stay down, Rachel, and I'll cure you."

"Cure me? *Cure me*? You think there's something wrong with ME? I'm strong. I'm powerful. I'm…"

"A parasite," Karen shook her head. "I can cure your vampirism, Rachel. Let me help you." In response Rachel tore a brass railing out of the floor and threw it at her. A word put it under her control and she let it fall to the ground. Rachel grabbed a stupefied player and used him as a shield to rush her. Karen dodged and sent a wave of force into Rachel, tearing her away from Henry and knocking her back.

Then Katie came back into the room with Seth at her heels. Karen nodded to him. Rachel seemed to sense something, though; she spun, her mouth agape, fangs dripping, to face the entrance, she brightened at Katie's return. Catching sight of Seth, though, brought a look of utter defeat to her face. She went to her knees before him with a wail of despair and bowed her head.

"What am I here for?" he asked. "You seemed to have everything in hand. Why'd Caitlin call me? And how'd she know how?"

"Had she overheard your name? I suppose I might have used it where she could hear me accidentally."

He pondered for a moment. "No," he said slowly. "She called out to me as Seth."

"That's all I need to reach you, and you saved her life from cancer. Would that have given you enough of a connection?"

"I don't think so. I've done other heals and cures and it didn't feel like this did. Previous connections have been with people I've brought back from the dead. I'll put it on the agenda for the next meeting."

"Good idea. I'm going to suggest bringing Katie. I think examining her might be a good idea. I'll put it on the agenda so Angela doesn't get her nose bent out of shape. You two really need to reconcile."

"Tell her that." He reached into a pocket and pulled out his phone. "Time for one of the magic apps, though. Memories need to be fuzzed." The wave of magic emanating from his phone was black, but the four of them weren't affected—and anything recording the scene experienced a short.

"Where were you?" she asked him. "If you were close enough…"

"I was doing homework in the Temple. The lovebirds said to say hi."

"Then you certainly weren't close enough to hear her in any normal way."

"Why not?" Katie asked.

"The Temple's not on Earth," Karen answered her.

He nodded. "In the meantime, we need to decide what to do with Rachel. The last vampire I found I ripped apart."

"Please don't destroy me, Lord."

"You beat the crap out of her, but she's terrified of *me*. I didn't even touch her. That's bizarre."

"'Lord' is it?" Katie asked with a giggle. She quieted at a glare from Karen.

Rachel appeared frozen in her posture of submission. "Hate to break it to you, my would-be lover, but your abilities are pretty scary. If she's figured out that death is your domain, she knows her dead vampire body is subject to your control."

"COOOL," Katie said. At a look from the two older kids, she subsided again with a smile on her lips.

"You offered to cure her vampirism?"

"She didn't want me to."

He sighed. "Someone did this to her. Johnson did it to himself, but he had at least a measure of power. He botched the transformation. Rachel...doesn't have any power, not the way we use the word, just the abilities that came with her transformation. But she needs to consume blood to...continue, is the best I can come. I'm not willing to let her run around free in these circumstances."

"Imprisonment?"

"Hell? Could work, I suppose, but it's not set up for a vampire. I expect she'd end up snacking on all the other inmates. Temple's out for a similar reason, we don't have facilities at the Castle, Shore, or Clubhouse."

"Maybe you and, ah, Artemis could work something out? Something that would maintain her? I don't like the idea that destroying or imprisoning her are our only options, Seth."

"They're only our only options if we choose to follow her desire not to be cured," he pointed out. "I'd prefer to simply cure her and send her home. Or finish what was started."

"She could still go home if you and Artemis can work something out."

"Aren't you going to ask her? I mean, she's right here..."

Karen nodded. "She is. But we're contemplating finishing the job of killing her, Katie." Her sister knocked over a glass of Coke in shock. She put her arm around Katie's shoulders. "The power is ours, and we're the ones who need to decide how to use it."

Seth nodded. His eyes went distant, and Karen could tell he was reaching out mentally to Bridget. "She's putting on a disguise and on her way."

"If you're going to kill her, why does she need... oh. I'd recognize her without one, right?"

"If we accomplish the transformation, Rachel doesn't need to know me, either," Bridget said, appearing in a swirl of green and the scent of wildflowers. She'd turned her hair black and curly, tanned her skin, altered her features, and put on a dress of leaves. Her voice had dropped an octave or two. She and Seth switched to Coptic for their discussion while Karen kept an eye on Rachel. Then they approached the vampire, joined hands, and started a long chant.

"What are they saying?" Katie whispered to her.

"They're reviving her bone marrow, intestines, and heart. She'll produce blood on her own, but she'll need nutrients to do it. They're not undoing the rest of the magic. They're also extracting the identity of the person who did this to her."

"He really is the god of death, isn't he? Which means she's the goddess of nature from her dress."

"That's just a joke, kiddo. Someone's little sister misheard "Goth", which does apply to Seth." The process took most of an hour. When it was over, Bridget took herself back to wherever she'd been. Rachel sat up, passing her tongue over her teeth.

Karen crouched down next to her. "We will be watching. If you start going after other people to satiate your thirst, we will finish what we started. We love you too much to simply destroy you," she said. Rachel locked eyes with her and nodded. She still flinched away from Seth.

"You can go home, Rachel. You might want to put on some sunscreen," he said. Rachel stood slowly and retreated from Copper Club. He turned to Karen. "Do you want to go after the one who infected Rachel while I get Caitlin home? Or do you want me to go after the vampire?"

"Hey! I'm coming after the vampire, too!"

"No, Katie. Mom and Dad are going to want you safe at home, not hunting a vampire." Katie tried sending an appealing look to Seth.

"I didn't get the impression that you'd had any training. TV shows like to show untrained people surprising the hell out of the bad guys. But I didn't cure your cancer so you could end up as something's snack. Johnson had a bunch of minions. This one does too, from what Rachel remembered. Until you've had some training, you're a liability in a fight and not an asset. Let's get you behind your sister's wards." Katie pouted a bit.

"And don't even think about trying to follow us."

"What does it matter if she thinks about it?" Seth put in. "She won't be able to follow us when we teleport anyway."

"You'd be better about going after the vampire—no question. But why don't we get my sister to safety and go after the bad guy together? Having some back up's never a bad thing."

He smiled. "You're getting more comfortable with me. Sounds like a plan. But first…" he turned to Brian's body and spoke a word. He breathed in suddenly and sat up.

"That was casual."

"He wasn't quite dead," Seth replied with a shrug. She felt him begin gathering his power.

"What are you doing?"

"Preparing to teleport as soon as you're ready."

She gave him a crooked smile. "We got here by car, Seth. I'll be happy to give you a lift, but I need to take it back and Katie's still too young."

"Oh. I haven't bothered to get a license."

Katie looked at him in bewilderment as they left the building. She'd been chattering non-stop on the way to the appointment about it not being fair that she couldn't drive yet. "Why not?"

"Why bother? I can teleport anywhere I want to go."

"You can fit more stuff…" Even Karen had to smile at that. "How much stuff do you think I have in my purse, Katie?" she said as she pulled out the key and opened the door.

"I haven't been in there recently, so I have no idea," she replied with a sniff.

"Ange and I worked on it last summer. The space enlargement spells are really spectacular in what they can accomplish."

"You didn't put a blind on it?" Seth asked from the back seat.

"I decided not to. If Katie fell in, I wanted to be able to see her." She looked back at Seth and winked.

"What do you mean a blind?"

"It would only let an unauthorized person see what they'd expect to see in a purse, like wallet, keys, pens, whatever. I've got one on my book bag. Of course, I don't have a little sister wanting to go pawing through my book bag looking for something."

"You really have no clue what goes in a purse, do you?" Katie asked him.

"I don't carry one," he shrugged.

"Hmmph." She sat back with her arms crossed. "What're you going to do to the vampire, Karen? Kill him? Put a stake through his heart?"

"I probably won't. Rachel was far more afraid of Seth than she was of me, so he'll probably kill it."

"A stake's not needed. Vampires are kept going by a badly cast immortality spell, even ones like Rachel who can pass it on as a disease. Undo the magic and they fall apart." He smiled. "Resurrect one and it also ceases to be a vampire. It's just a person. If they didn't screw up the immortality part too much—or are a fairly young vampire—they don't die immediately." The rest of the ride was made in silence. When they got back, Karen and Katie insisted Seth come inside.

"Look, I already told you my parents have figured out what you did. It's not a problem. I need to let them know where we're going now that Katie's here and safe, and grab my armored coat."

"Alright." He got out. "Have you talked to Pan about that detergent of his?"

"The one that armors everything? Yeah. I haven't gotten around to using it much, though, and if my parents do the laundry they're a little skittish about magic still. I don't think they've used the armoring detergent."

They walked up to the door and Karen called out as she went in. "Brought Katie back, but we're headed out again."

"It's late on a school night... Hello, Seth, isn't it?"

"Yes. There's something we need to do as soon as possible."

"I understand we owe our daughters' lives to you. Thank you."

"What is it you're doing?"

"Dropping Caitlin off. This will be easier if we don't have to protect her."

"Looked easy enough for you at the club," Katie interrupted as Karen disappeared to her room.

"We can't count on the other one being that terrified," he shrugged. "Reverend Johnson certainly wasn't."

"Your parents don't have a problem with you being out this late on a school night?" Mom asked as Dad said, "Other what being that terrified?"

He smiled. "I'm told you figured out about me. They don't particularly like it, but they also acknowledge that there are things only we can do…and that trying to stop me from doing something is beyond them."

"What is it you need to do?"

"Stop a vampire," Karen said as she came back in wearing a long pink coat. "Rachel Strauss was already turned. No more of our classmates will suffer this. We already alerted the cavalry?" she asked him.

"They were alerted when Caitlin's cry for help reached me," he reminded her. "And again when we called in Artemis to help with Rachel. They're checking the surrounding area while we concentrate locally."

"YOU called him for help?" her father asked. His disapproving gaze tightened on Katie.

"She did. We're going to need to examine her at some point, though, Dad. She shouldn't have been able to reach him. We don't know how she did it." She turned to Seth. "Any idea where we need to go?"

"We can check from the Clubhouse to narrow it down." She nodded, then cocked her head.

"Don't you have more accurate divinatory stuff for this at the Mausoleum?" she asked.

"I do, but the Clubhouse's facilities should be adequate."

"Then let's go to your place." Katie's eyebrows rose.

He nodded and extended his hand. "Getting past my wards will be easier if I bring you." She took his hand and felt him gather his power.

"Where's the Mausoleum?" Katie wanted to know.

"In the middle of a graveyard," Karen answered as Seth's magic swirled around them.

They arrived in the marble-clad room without any fuss, Seth activating the lights by vocal command. The cold flames provided a flickering light, but no warmth. She shivered a bit. At a cocked eyebrow, he brought the temperature up. "Cold doesn't bother me," he said. "Can I get you something? Coffee, tea, cocoa?"

"No, I'm good, thanks." Seth had put in a couple of black easy chairs to watch a wall-sized TV screen, and he summoned up a map of the county with necromantic hotspots scattered all over it. A brief command removed the ones solely pertaining to him.

"What about the ones the rest of us do?" she asked him.

"Most of you avoid using necromancy, but…" another word of command removed the uses of necromancy by the other wizards. There weren't a lot left.

"I'm not really sure what your map can do. Can you remove any that Patti and her minions did?"

"She didn't do much. It's one of the reasons she started panicking when she realized what my focus is." But more dots vanished. "And these are the ones involving a walking copse."

"Don't forget to exclude Rachel."

"Actually…one of Rachel's may be important. Where she was turned. But the board isn't that sensitive. Let's start focusing in." She nodded.

"Mind if I bring up a sensitive subject?"

He glanced at her through the corner of his eye. "I get the impression you're going to do that whether I mind or not."

"I'm trying to be polite, at least. I know it's a problem, and I'm not sure the two of you are going to be able to resolve it without someone stepping in. So I'm electing myself to do the stepping in."

"Since you're going to bring it up anyway, just go ahead. I assume you're talking about Angela and her pet vibrator?" She winced at his choice of term.

"That's not helpful."

"A zombie has more in the way of intelligence."

"You're being a dick about this, Seth."

"I said I wouldn't kill the asshole."

She winced at the venom in his tone. "Wow. This is going to be harder than I thought."

"That's all the mercy he gets."

"It's not very much."

"And?"

"You're not talking to either of us. The other eight keep referring me to one of you. Dave's memory is nothing like yours, and he honestly can't seem to figure out where your hostility is coming from."

"Have you tried divination?"

"Not yet. It's hard to get anything from any of us with divination, and you're more closed off than most of the rest of us. Besides, what I need to know your motivations, not the actions, and motives aren't exactly something that comes through divining into the past like that. I learned that when I had my divination lesson from Keisha! All she wants is her boyfriend safe, Seth."

"No, it's not. She wants him admitted to knowledge. Alex had to intervene to get him to keep his mouth shut. Twice. He won't keep the secrets she's entrusted him with. He doesn't get to know mine."

"He's kept mine. I know you don't have anyone you want to bring in, but Angela does, and you're being really unfair to her to not even consider bringing Dave in. There's no discussion. You just veto it.

"Then perhaps, Miss MacLeod, you can explain to me why HER wishes are paramount in this instance. I'm not stopping her from dating Brainless. I'm not stopping her from doing anything with him."

"You are keeping him from the full protection of the Round Table, Seth."

"If Angela wants to work out defense arrangements for him with other people, I'm not stopping her from doing that, either. That doesn't mean I have any interest in keeping him from collecting his Darwin Award or protecting him in any other way." Karen drew in a deep breath before he said, "There's the vampire. Shall we?"

They arrived in a small cul-de-sac to see a man in a suit heading up a driveway. He turned at their arrival and his eyes flared. Taking in Seth he ran.

"Stop," Seth commanded him. He froze in mid-step and fell to the ground. "Don't move."

"Why am I here?" Karen asked.

"You're better at interrogation than I am."

She turned to the vampire. "Why did you attack Rachel?"

"You may move your jaw to answer her questions."

"I was told to take someone from your school."

"Who told you?"

"The Seadog. I don't know his name! He's a wizard, says he's from England but doesn't sound English."

"The English accent is a relatively new development, she tells me," Seth commented. He flashed a picture of Keisha to her mind. She nodded.

"And what do we call you?"

"The Texan."

"The dead vampire," Seth answered. On the word vampire, the one in front of them collapsed and rotted away. "Thank you, Miss MacLeod. I've got his memories in the stone, and I'll have a summary a week from Saturday."

"So I was just a distraction for the vampire?"

"Sort of. He might have had something that let him be more resistant. He was coming to get Rachel back, after all. But answering your questions made his mind work, so it was harder for him to resist."

"What?" Seth motioned to one of the houses. Sure enough, Rachel's. Then she caught his emotions. He'd liked spending the time with her. What he'd said had been true as far as it went, but he still thought it would have disturbed her if he'd said it out loud.

"Seth…I know. You really don't have to hide what you're feeling about me from me. I already know. Fixing you and Angela is going to be harder than I thought."

"I don't have a problem with Angela."

Chapter

30

"*Katie*, are you ready for this?" They'd gotten everything set up to examine her and Dani and Mike were at the Shore for the day playing video games.

"I guess." She was wearing her best outfit; it was new, black and red. She and Mom had gone shopping after the diagnosis of 'cancer free'. Karen's lips quirked.

"Trying to impress someone?" she teased. Katie glared at her. "Relax, lass. I'll be there with you the whole time. No one is going to hurt you, but you won't remember what happens. I will, though, and I think we'll give you back your memories before too long."

"I don't really like that part. What if I do something embarrassing?"

"You'll be conscious and aware. So you will." She grinned at her little sister. "Here, put this on." She passed over a smoky quartz crystal on a silver chain. "This is a memory stone. It will record what happens, so we can be sure to get your memories back to you."

"Like yours?"

"I've adjusted mine a bit, but aye, same idea."

"Cool. Who…you're not going to tell me who made it are you?"

"Oh, that I can do. Seth did the enchanting. He developed the process and makes most of them for his hospice work. This is the one he made while he was showing me how to do it," she said.

"Thanks. How does it work?"

"Magic." She grinned at the dirty look she gave her. "That's about the best technical explanation I can give. You remember when I explained magic to you?"

"Yeah."

"We're going out!" she called to Mom and Dad.

"You're taking the car?" Jimmy asked.

"No, it's free for you." A few steps out the door—but not the atrium—and she took them to her room on Venus.

"Wow, it's a lot cleaner than your room at home. Does Mom know?"

"No, she doesn't. It lowers her expectations if she thinks this room is just as bad as that one. Besides, I can use my magic freely here. This way."

As they came into the conference room, she saw that not everyone was present, but Seth had already reconfigured the room for the examination. A softly glowing platform floated in mid-air about three feet off the ground, and there were glowing gems on small tables. Their chairs were moved back to the wall.

"Caitlin, you can sit or lie down here, whichever is easier for you," Bridget said. She was dressed like she had when she appeared to adjust Rachel.

Then the Gregorian chanting began and a flaming crack seemed to open in the floor. Rising up came Teddy in full Devil regalia. Katie screamed in terror and threw her arms around Seth, burying her face in his chest.

"Really?" he asked Teddy.

"What are you complaining about?"

"She has a piercing scream, and she was right next to my ear."

"Oh, sorry."

"Not yet you aren't."

"Could we get back to why we're here, you two?" Keisha asked.

"Sure. I can wait," Seth said. He helped Katie to the platform. "Are you comfortable? This may take a while." She nodded and smiled shyly. The examination DID take quite a bit of time. Seth teleported to Mars and Katie tried to contact him…and succeeded. He teleported out to Triton, and still heard her loud and clear. With Dawn's help, he teleported to Alpha Centauri…and could still hear Katie just fine. Katie was a lot more loquacious with Seth out of the room, asking questions about what they were doing and trying to figure out what was happening.

When Karen tried that herself, she could only hear Katie when she called her Calyrine. The others kept close watch with all the detection spells they could, and they varied the spells among them. Solly even borrowed some instruments from his parents' clinic and attached them to her. After a few hours of additional scans—including some suggestions from Shevaun and Julian that scanned Seth, Angela, and Karen—they took Katie's memories and sent her home.

With Katie gone, the others dropped their disguises. "What was with the pyrotechnics, Teddy?" she wanted to know. "You scared the shit out of her."

"Just being dramatic, actually. I wasn't expecting her to react by trying to crush Seth."

"In any event," Angela said, "did we learn anything?"

"We confirmed that distance isn't a problem for her reaching him. Or us, if the secret names are used. We never really tested that on an interstellar level before. We've got better information on the link between you and Seth and between Karen and Seth. Karen and Seth's is stronger than the one between you and him, which is odd."

"By the way, guys, did you notice any useful planets while you were out there?" Malcolm wanted to know. They shook their heads.

"From the perspective of immediate use, no. From the perspective of "We can make anything habitable with magic", yes."

"So not much, and for that we gave her a pass to Venus."

Jennifer cocked her head at her. "Has Dave demonstrated any unusual ability? No one gave Katie the ability to contact Seth with just his real name. We're still looking at the information we got. We still don't know how it happened. If Dave is suddenly doing something, we'll examine him, too. If it's just a matter of having sex on Venus, there's no need for a pass."

"And if there's not," Keisha said, "You need to actually persuade the people saying no and not just complain about it. As infuriating as I'm sure you find it, they get to say no."

Angela scowled.

Chapter

31

Shevaun walked into the school lounge after most of her classes to see Keisha being confronted by Janie Lindquist and Graham Cho over an article in the school paper. Dawn and Malcolm were sitting together on the old brown couch with a bag of popcorn, watching.

"What's with that?" Shevaun asked as she dipped her hand into the popcorn. It was fairly obviously the wizardly version; Keisha and Bridget had bred the color variants from other flint corn back into their popcorn varieties.

"What's with what?" Dawn replied, passing the bag back to Malcolm.

"The way you guys sort of show up and sit down to watch when there's a confrontation with someone else. You're not even going over to see if Keisha needs help."

"Ah. Well, Keisha *doesn't* need our help. She might appreciate it—or, more likely, tell us off for interfering in something we know nothing about—but she's perfectly capable of handling it all on her own. Even if she hadn't seen us sit down, we didn't need to say anything out loud to let her know we're here," he said, subtly tapping his forehead. "What we're doing really, is keeping the situation contained. No one wants or needs this getting dangerous for anyone."

"I don't get it."

"Do you remember last year when the football team all came down with the flu at once?"

"Yeah. Really bad luck right before a big game."

"Luck had nothing to do with it. That was Seth's idea of a calm, rational, restrained response to some ignorant idiots deciding to bully him. They had no idea they were playing Russian roulette in picking on him, no clue just how close they came to dying on the spot. We started doing it this way when he let them recover. It lets Keisha—here—know she's not alone, and tells the people she's having a confrontation with that they've got a problem with the whole Round Table if they push it too far," Dawn said. "Which means the people causing her a problem are likely to find themselves isolated and ostracized if we get involved. Or, at the very least, that there will be witnesses."

"He'd have really killed them?"

Dawn nodded imperceptibly. "Yeah. He was actively contemplating it, even if he hadn't reached for his power yet. His first inclination to deal with something like that is to kill it. While he likes Alex and Angela, he doesn't really like the rest of the team. And unlike those stories you hear about school shooters, Seth's target selection is perfect, undetectable by someone who doesn't know what he did, and completely lethal if he's going for a kill. In a fury, he would not leave survivors of his wrath. But it would publicly be a tragedy, not a massacre."

"So we stepped in to keep it from escalating. Keisha's a lot less prone to reach for deadly options, of course," Malcolm said with massive understatement, "and she doesn't have those sorts of problems with Janie and Graham, but we're here if she wants us."

"And until then, we just enjoy the show," Dawn said. "We're waiting until Jasmine gets here and has done her afternoon prayer before starting the study session."

"Cool. This is good popcorn."

"You've never had it with real butter, have you?"

"Not until Bridget adjusted my guts, no. Lactose intolerance is really irritating to deal with sometimes. But if I suddenly start in on dairy it's going to weird Mom out something awful."

"You haven't told her?"

"Not yet. I haven't found the right time to let her in on such a big secret. And telling Dad is a little difficult. I'd rather do it in person than over the phone or email."

"We'd prefer you not use email, too. Someone might intercept it."

"Ooo, popcorn!" Jasmine's hand sneaked over Malcolm's shoulder. "Don't let me bother you, guys." She smiled at them.

"We won't," said Dawn in Lakota.

"That is a new one," Jasmine said.

Malcolm's cocked eyebrow told them he hadn't understood either. Dawn reached over to thump Malcolm on the head. Shevaun heard the muttered word in Tsalagi that she used to transfer Lakota. "Ah," he said in Lakota. "Shevaun's casting language? I like it."

"What did you say?" Jasmine asked him.

"Can't tell you." She nodded her understanding of what he hadn't included.

"That was rude," Betsy said. "Where'd you get the popcorn, Jas?"

"From my wonderful boyfriend. And he is not being rude. He told me upfront there were things he wouldn't be able to tell me, especially when he was saying it in a language I didn't understand."

"Sounds like he decided to give himself a ready made cover, and you're letting him."

"Just because you keep falling for tomcats doesn't mean I did. He isn't going to tell me—or you—one way or the other. I would rather have him just tell me the truth that he has promised to keep a secret than to lie to me about it. Besides, from what he has told me, I have a fairly good idea of why he is not speaking, and it makes sense. And I will not revealing what should be concealed either."

"Okay, okay. Where'd he get the popcorn?"

"I did not ask," she said with a smile. "If YOU want to ask him, you can. I do not think he will tell you, though."

"I brought a bag from home and used the microwave." Something seemed off about that explanation to Shevaun; she noticed the microwave was unplugged. Dawn answered her in Lakota.

"He used his power both times, teleporting the bag to him and heating it up the same way. It's simpler, especially since we make popcorn anyway. But they don't need to know that, do they?"

"That they don't. How do you do that?"

She and Dawn continued talking in Lakota on the theory and practice of bringing something to her by teleportation, or making it on the spot. Jasmine talked with Malcolm before excusing herself to conduct the ritual purifications. She got back just in time for her cell phone rang with the call to prayer for the Asr salah. She did her duty to her faith while the others were generally quiet. Malcolm helped her back up, and the study session commenced now that Janie and Graham were gone. History class wasn't quite the bore it used to be; she'd been with Seth a few times when he disturbed the dead for answers. He'd always returned them to their graves...but he was bothering them.

32

The moon was full and high when Karen floated through the door to the main office. It was locked, of course, but that couldn't really stop a wizard of her power. Seth was still reticent to talk about the origins of his problems with Dave and Dave couldn't think of any reason for Seth to hate him. Divinations suggested that Dave had hurt Seth many times…maybe not too seriously, but he'd done it a lot. Beatings, theft, tauntings. Why hadn't anyone stepped in? The doors to the files were also closed and locked, and they were no more difficult than the front door.

A detection spell found her the files she was looking for—one for each of them. She cast another spell to simply duplicate them and put the originals back away. She looked harder; they'd already been accessed magically. That was an unexpected development. But she had what she came for and teleported home to study the files. Katie was downstairs enjoying the lifting of her dietary restrictions. She hoped she wouldn't have to dissolve her little sister's crush.

Karen walked in to her mother's home office and laid the first folder down. She kept the second one. Mom looked up from the spreadsheet she was examining. "What's this?"

"It's Dave Clebourne's permanent file. I think I need some advice. I haven't been able to make much headway."

"Dave…Angela's boyfriend?" She nodded. "And that one?"

"It's Seth's. I'd hand it to you, too, but since you're not authorized to see it, the spells he put on it won't let you remember anything in it. I could undo them—it's not like his necromancy—but it would take a lot of effort and he put in some magic traps. The traps are nothing to me—they bounced off my defenses—but they wouldn't be nice to you."

"Why are you reading their permanent records?"

"The others have told me there's a lot of ugly history between them. And having read the files, they're not kidding. Shevaun and Julian both met Seth after Dave and his cronies beat him up. Using some of the divination techniques I've got, there were a lot of instances of bullying that were reported that didn't stick to Dave. Some of his other friends beat up Dave in retaliation. I could really use your advice."

"Let me read Dave's, then."

After several minutes, Mom looked up. "Angela picked quite a catch."

"What'd I miss?"

"Seth stopped reporting the bullying after third grade. Before then he was about the only person who wasn't intimidated, and there are a lot of reports from him. Dave wasn't always the primary person he named, but incidents with his buddies are common. Including several notations where they believe he was lying to protect them. They obviously never became friends."

"That's about when Seth started getting a reputation for revenge. He stopped thinking the school would help him and went about helping himself. His file puts a lot of "suspected" things happening to people who picked on him but…no witnesses. No evidence. No proof he did any of it. And his mom's a lawyer."

"Dave's got lectures and notes home. A couple of suspensions and discussions with his parents, but that's about it. Is something happening now?"

"Did I miss anything on his more recent behavior?"

"No reports, nothing, this year or late last year. Why?"

"Angela thinks he's cleaned up his act since the ship."

"That's possible. There's no evidence he's fallen back into his older ways according to his file. But the first incidents were reported twelve years ago, and there are incidents with other students all the way up to late last year. There aren't any notes from preschool. If Seth was being hurt and Dave was getting off that lightly I'm not surprised he quit reporting. Nothing was happening. The school failed him."

"Ouch. So if we're going to get peace…"

"Dave is going to really need to publicly and visibly change. I'd suggest he see what he can do about supporting Seth in any fresh confrontations, but considering what Seth is capable of doing…"

"Yeah, Seth's power throws a pretty big wrench in getting him to the peace conference."

"Will Angela accept a peace conference, though?"

She cocked her head at her mother. "What do you mean?"

"A peace conference ends the war. From what I've seen in this file and what you've told me, Seth doesn't trust Dave and has excellent reason not to. Ending the war…is about as far as you can probably get him to go, and that's with you advocating it. To use the diplomacy analogy a bit further, Angela wants Dave brought into the alliance. You've mentioned a couple of people like that. But unless something changes, that's not something Seth is going to agree to."

She thought about that for a moment, and did a quick divination. Mom was right. It was going to be very hard for Dave to persuade Seth. Seth didn't just hate Dave, he didn't trust him. He'd be looking for an ulterior motive to anything Dave did. The best she could do was to get things started.

"Hi Dave. You have a moment?"

"What's up, Karen? Surprise party for Angela?"

"I think what I have in mind would please her no end, but it's not a party. We need to heal the rift between her and her tutor—and unfortunately, you're in the middle of it."

"Hey, this is NOT MY FAULT!"

"Chill, lad. I read your permanent file. You need to understand. This problem is dangerous, and we need to get it fixed. And unfortunately your actions are the root of the problem. The kid you used to bully is still holding a grudge, and he's on one side of the argument about you. If it weren't for your earlier actions, the discussions would revolve around whether or not you were trustworthy. As it is, we're not really talking about it at all, because he keeps shutting the discussion down. So this rift is, at base, your fault."

"It won't be a problem."

"It already IS a problem, Dave. Angela's pushing to have you admitted to the outer circle. He vetoes it. He proposes killing you to resolve the matter. He doesn't get the votes. It's regular as clockwork. We're ending every meeting with the same bloody argument. Either she needs to quit pushing—and she's worried as hell that you're exposed by being outside the circle—or he needs to accept you. Or you need to go away. You don't want to go away, she's not going to stop until you're protected, and that leaves his solution of you dying."

"Well, then I'll just..." Dave flexed his arms a bit and grinned.

She stared at him in stunned disbelief. "You can't be this stupid. You know, or at least have some idea, what Angela's capable of doing. What I'm capable of doing. What do you think he was tutoring her in, baking cupcakes? His specialty is death magic, reviving and killing. What the fuck do you think you can do to him before he kills you? He won't be fighting you if you push it, Dave. He'll simply execute you. Why do you think Angela's so worried? You're alive now because he's been merciful and doesn't particularly want to pick a fight with Angela. Make yourself look like a threat, keep bothering him, and he will demonstrate why he's known as the God of Death. This isn't a threat, Dave. It's not even a promise. It's a simple statement of fact, and you can check it with Angela if you want." She thought about telling him that he would live if he stayed away from Seth, but...that was a secret too.

He stood up, looming over her. "Sit back down before I make you." He remained standing. She spoke a word in Bengali that made him fall back into his chair. "The only one of us that you can take anywhere is Angela on a date, Dave, and that's only because she wants you to.

So drop the macho bullshit and engage your brain. That's the only way to solve this. Or at least the only way that leaves you breathing. If you weren't dating Angela, he might have already done something permanent to you." He looked at her in stunned disbelief.

"Him? S…"

"No names, Dave. We both know who we're talking about. But I'm obligated to keep the secrets, too. I'm not going to confirm or deny his—or anyone else's—identity. If I did I would have to alter your memory.

"You have no defenses of your own against one of us, Dave. If we don't mind pissing off your girlfriend, we can do whatever we want to you. Execute you. Turn you into a frog. Make you impotent. Whatever. The practitioners we've faced—on ship and elsewhere—are what make her worried about your exposure. You don't have any protection against them either. Dani doesn't have any more defenses than you do—although I suspect Alex has enchanted every piece of jewelry he's ever given her—but we all know who she is, she's been admitted, and we'll step up to protect her if necessary. That's what she wants for you, what being brought into the circle means for someone who's not one of us. It also means we trust you enough to know our secrets and not talk about them. Right now, you're her problem."

"Shit." He sat there for several minutes, visibly calming down after she made him sit back down. "You have a plan, I'd guess?"

"If you want to be part of Angela's life—really be a part of it, be a part of this world we've come to live in—you need to change. She's going to be standing into danger, big time. She's not quite as lethal as he is, but she is more destructive when she decides to be. He has no reason to change his veto of your inclusion. None at all. He can—and will—refuse to change his veto of bringing you in if you keep on."

"Why the fuck does he get a say in who she dates anyway?"

"He doesn't. He's not claiming one, either. He's asserting his prerogatives on deciding who gets to know about his secrets and who he socializes with, and in bullying him you crossed the line to 'enemy' as far as he's concerned. And you crossed it a long time ago."

"So you're finally getting together with him?"

She sighed. "No. Dave, I'm on the side of love. I want you and Angela to succeed. Whether that means you're fully informed and involved or you both accept you never will be."

"That's not fair. What about Alex and Dani?"

"Whining about other people doesn't change the problem of what to do about you. And you're not really in a position to protest about fairness. It wasn't exactly fair to bully him then, was it? Now your actions are coming back on you, and you don't like it. You might want to remember that he could have killed you whenever he wanted over the past few years and still can. He sees not doing that as having been more than fair to you."

Dave was digesting that as Angela grabbed a seat of her own next to him. "What are you two conspiring about?"

"Trying to explain some of the facts of our world to him before he does something suicidally stupid."

Angela gave her a long look. "Thanks." She turned her gaze to Dave. "What'd she tell you?"

"Something about everything being on me if I want to be a real part of your life."

Her eyes flickered shut for a moment. "Probably true. I tried to get a promise from him and it just made things worse."

He drew back a little. "What do you mean, worse?"

"Die and you're not coming back."

"Well, DUH."

Angela and Karen exchanged a pained smile before Karen showed off her charm bracelet. "The bullet that killed me in Golden Gate Park. He brought me back." His eyes went wide and searched Angela's face.

"You've asked me before what I owe him. I mentioned him saving my life. What I didn't say, because it comes close to revealing the secrets we've promised to keep, is that there were only two people who survived that bus crash freshman year, and I wasn't one of them." Dave looked confused, then his eyes widened. She nodded. "He didn't just save my life. I lost my life, and he gave it back to me. But if you died... hypothetically I could bring you back myself. I know how, and I've brought back animals," she smiled crookedly at his expression. "But you're a different story, and it all has to do with your relations with him. Are you familiar with the myth of Orpheus?"

"Never heard of it."

"I didn't know it before I started learning magic. Orpheus loses the love of his life and goes into the underworld to beg for her release. Hades agrees, on condition he doesn't look back, he does and she has to stay in the underworld. The point being, Hades can say no to letting you live again."

"Really? How?"

She shrugged. "I'm not entirely sure, but each of us is… supreme in our specialty, I guess you could say. We haven't exactly tested it, but we think that I can stop a critical mass from melt down, even if one of the others is trying for it. Artemis would be able to clone another from a live cell—life is her supremacy, so that wouldn't be a problem—but it wouldn't bring back the same person. That's one of the reasons she has him doing the resurrections on extinct species. She does it and she's just going to get a baby. Forget the bad sci-fi that produces a copy of an adult; she can force it to adulthood but it would still have the knowledge of a baby. He's blocked a resurrection before until a compromise on secrecy was worked out. Since he doesn't like you…"

"Before we think he would have grumbled but not opposed Angela bringing you back herself without good reason, like you dying in public. Now, we think he's saying no."

"You think? You're not sure?"

"There's really only one way to be sure. You don't want to risk it, and neither do I," Angela said equably. Dave blanched. Angela nodded. "He hasn't blocked me resurrecting anything else. But you…"

"I think it's finally getting through to him."

"Do you really think I'm in danger?"

"Yeah, I do. I think the danger from Hades can be managed, but we've been seeing more and more minor wizards appear. We don't know if they're complete newbies or people attracted to what we're doing. You can't protect yourself against them, either; what they try might not work, but that's a limit on their abilities rather than any defense you have. I've mentioned I've enchanted the stuff I've given you, but you don't wear it very often. The safest thing would be to bring you into the outer circle, but with your history and the actions I just took that's not happening any time soon."

"Okay. I've heard you guys talk about inner and outer circles before. What's the difference?"

"Dave, I am capable of hitting every city on Earth with a thermonuclear detonation. Simultaneously. Karen can control the emotions of everyone on Earth. Alex can bring about World War III. That's the sort of thing we mean by "inner circle." Those who can or have the potential to wield power on that sort of scale. The "outer circle" is people who don't have that sort of power but whom we like and trust."

"Okay, okay, I get it, picking on him is really fucking stupid. How do we fix this?"

The girls looked at each other. "We can advise you, but in the end it's got to be you and him," Angela said.

"How can it be me and him if I can't even approach him?"

"Carefully. Respectfully."

Karen nodded. "You're going to be facing—sooner or later—a mind probe. From him, probably. We wouldn't be doing it; you don't have to convince US. We can advise but we can't coach. Coaching would be pointless. If you're not genuine, he won't change his veto." She gathered up her things. "Well, I'll leave you to it, then!" She gave them a cheery smile and walked off.

"Is she serious?"

"Yep. Dave," she said, taking his hands in hers and looking him in the eye, "This isn't about me. It's about you. You're bigger than he is. You can certainly bench press more than he can—unless he cheats. He cheats he can throw an aircraft carrier at you. There really isn't much we can't do if we cheat, and most of the "can't" has more to do with someone else's opposition than anything else. You need to remember that all the power's on his side, not yours; that he doesn't like you, and that you want something from him that he doesn't want to give and doesn't have to. You can hit a punching bag harder than he can. He can kill you by wishing it so."

"So what does that leave?"

"You'll have to earn it. In a game where you don't know the rules and he can change them whenever he likes, and you need to stay away from him."

"Sounds like I can't win."

She shook her head. "He's fair. Ruthless. Harsh. But fair. I wouldn't be encouraging you to try if I thought you had no chance. Start by publicly being the good guy I know you are around school. If you happen to run into him, be polite, and leave him the fuck alone. You've already had penalties assessed against you and you're on your own one yard line." He grimaced but nodded.

Dave's birthday came along, and Angela's present to him was a trip anywhere he could go. His sister thought that was a very strange way to put it. But Angela just smiled. Dave nodded his understanding; if he named one of the off-world bases, or one of the personal lairs, she wouldn't be taking him He selected Singapore.

She took him there the next day, teleporting in. She also took the time to learn the local languages. They wandered the city all day, and went into places his parents would never have let him go. Angela's parents had gotten a lot more blasé about where she went since the new year. Someone who was more concerned about concealing how she'd dealt with danger than in what the danger might be could take care of herself.

As they were coming to the end of the night, they were taking a short cut down an alley when a small gang surrounded them, demanding the wallets of the foolish American teenagers walking where they had no business being... Dave, unfortunately, immediately got his macho on and plunged into them with the souvenir knife he'd bought earlier. Angela had been about to deal with them all when he did that. She changed tactics and spells to make them all sleep. Then she woke Dave up and teleported to the Seamount, leaving the gang members snoring in the alley.

Angela said, "Dave, I get that you want to protect me. It's adorable. I love you. But sweetie...it's harder to shield you from whatever I'm going to do when you're that close to them. You're getting in my way more than you're helping."

"Sorry, Ange. Thank you," he said, chastised.

"I've never killed anyone with my power. But I could. I know that. I don't want to. But there's someone else who can and will. Leave the real rough stuff to me and stay close to me if something like that happens again, okay?

"Yes, ma'am." She smiled and kissed him.

Chapter

33

"Hey, Ange. What's up?" Bridget was high in the wild coastal mountains amid the dead remnants of a marijuana grow. Coastal redwoods towered overhead. Raccoons squabbled over the contents of a cooler. Turkey vultures perched on the corpses of the growers, pecking at them.

"Nature red in tooth and claw indeed. What happened?"

"I'm scouting locations for grizzly bears. They decided to shoot at me, so their carotid arteries burst. I was just about to handle the trash." Angela nodded. Bridget's plans to restore the California Grizzly weren't a common topic, but they all knew about it. "I'd have turned them into bears, but they pissed me off."

"Let me." She broke down the molecules of the plastic and metal garbage strewn in the clearing, including the guns. Bridget nodded her thanks and the plants destroyed by the growers revived. The vultures and raccoons paid no attention, trusting in her presence.

"Now that we've dealt with that, what's on your mind?"

"What do we have to do to set up an extraterrestrial environment?"

"Self contained, I assume." She considered for a minute. "It'll take some work. We're more powerful now than we were when we set up the

Castle and Temple, but it also involved nine of us working together. Do you know where you want to put it?"

"Not really."

"Why do you want to build a place of your own off planet?"

"I want to prove some of what I've been saying."

"You want a temporary pass for your parents, that's easily doable. I think most of us who've clued our parents in have brought them up at one time or another. For that matter, Karen's been approaching people about bringing hers up."

"Not who I was thinking of," she admitted.

"Oh. You're getting around Seth and Teddy vetoing Dave."

"Yeah. I wouldn't bother you about it but you're the biosphere expert. So about the self contained environment?"

"Gravity. An Earth-normal atmosphere. Food. Water. Space. I suggest you include a full garden; you can keep it clean magically if you want to, but it's a better environment with plants, and we can set whatever temp you want. You prefer tropical, too-warm-to-wear-anything or chilly, let's-snuggle-under-the-blankets?"

"Will you help me set it up?"

"Sure. You still need to figure out where, though. Oh, and you'll also need to conceal it."

"If I pick far enough away…"

"Even then. We're trying not to be noticed, and satellites might still pick up something. Ask Teddy," she replied.

"I was hoping to do it all with people who are supportive."

"Of you? That'd be all of us. Don't confuse opposition to Dave learning our secrets to not being willing to help you on a project. Besides, if you're off Earth, having someone available for rescues is a good idea."

"And? I can tell there's an 'and' coming up."

"And Seth is most likely to be available in an emergency. He has least of us going on."

"He's also the most likely to let Dave die."

"I know." She breathed in deeply. "He's still the best emergency contact for availability. He makes sure you stay alive, you save Dave."

"Are you going to be okay?" she asked, gesturing at the bodies. She grimaced. "I should be. I may spend another night in the Mausoleum talking to Seth about it."

"Another..." Bridget had never mentioned killing someone before.

"I came across a bunch of poachers in Africa. I gave them highly accelerated cases of Ebola. It was the first time I'd ever deliberately killed anyone. Talking to Seth helped, a lot. It's not as if we can talk to a shrink about it, you know. A psychiatrist would label us delusional unless we were willing to prove it then and there. But he knows what it's like."

"Wow. I never knew."

Bridget gave her a wry smile. "I don't do it that way much any more. I transform them into an endangered species now, and turn a bunch of them female since there are a lot more men in their ranks than women. If they get killed by a human...they turn back and it becomes murder. While they're transformed, they contribute to a new generation of the species." She paused. "You know, you could also talk to Alex. I helped him set up some off-planet love nests for him and Dani. He could either give you the process or loan you one if you're interested."

"I think I'm going to regret asking..."

Bridget smiled. "You know about Solly and his kids. Seth borrowed his mom's account and found out that the age of consent for sex in California's eighteen. So they avoid the whole thing by leaving the jurisdiction, just like Keish and Mike or me and Carmen. I just haven't bothered to set up private spaces other than my rooms."

"And when our parents ask it's a nice off hand reminder of our power." She paused for a second when the words hit her. "Wait a minute. What's Carmen doing coming up to the off-world bases?"

"Getting stuck in my rooms. She can't go anywhere else. I don't know whether or not the wards would let Dave through just to your rooms, but if they do, he really would have to STAY there." She paused at Angela's outraged expression. "Oh, I see. I expanded my rooms outward behind a wall and door; the section she stays in isn't technically part of the base itself. There's an obvious demarcation between where she can't go and where she can be."

Chapter

34

Spring Break was an wonderful bit of freedom from school. Angela invited Karen along to her home opener, the Gorgons against the Starlets. Five minutes in she left Angela and Dave alone. She'd have been willing to bet that Dave had told his parents he was at the park, but didn't need to; he'd volunteered that tidbit almost immediately. Fortunately Jennifer was alone in her box. "Hi Jenny. Mind some company?"

"Hey Karen. Something up, or just giving those two some privacy?"

"They're certainly acting like they want to be alone, although I don't think she wants to test Seth's wards on the Temple, Castle, or Shore. But I'm trying to figure something out. I'm trying to get him and Angela to come to an actual peace, but…Why is everyone so focused on not pissing Seth off rather than getting him not to kill? Seems like we're blaming the victims for being killed."

"Well, in one sense we are." She smiled wryly at Karen's expression. "Seth's a pretty restrained person, Karen, and he gets a lot of crap. Look at freshman year; he called in Dawn and Alex to deal with the football team instead of killing them. Most of us would have already taken action by that point. He knows what he's capable of doing by accident, and it's not like he goes out looking for someone to kill," she pointed out. "The last time I really saw him do that was when we were taking the *Pelewan*."

"Yeah, but shouldn't we be focusing on Seth more than on other people? He's the one killing people."

"Really? Seth's power has been what it is for years. He hasn't moved on Dave yet. Why's he doing it? Why's he killing anyone?"

"Does it matter?"

"I think so. You might not. But you also didn't answer the question."

"Cause he's pissed at them."

"You know better than that. If he was killing the people who pissed him off we'd have a higher class death rate than they did on "Buffy". He does it reflexively and easily. And you'd have been the only person who could do anything about it." She grinned at her.

Karen grimaced. "Do you have to keep bringing that up?"

"No. I don't have to. Needling you on it's a bit more fun than needling him, though, because that got boring years ago. And I'm still waiting."

"Because…they did something to him. Or to someone he cares about. Like…" she grimaced at herself, "on the ship when he killed them all for touching me."

"Bingo. He kills in reaction to someone else doing something. And what can we do about it if he's decided someone needs to die?"

"We can restrain him," she replied confidently. Jennifer shook her head.

"Long enough to calm him down, yes. But if he's determined that someone needs to die, that person will die. We can't keep those sorts of restraints up indefinitely, not against someone's specialty. We could restrain you from making someone fall in love with someone, but if you really wanted it to happen sooner or later it would. So the best way to keep him from killing someone is to keep that person from provoking him."

"Can't you take his power from him?"

"Maybe, but we all have defenses up. Taking his power would be as hard as you making him fall out of love with you, and he'd respond with his own power." She locked eyes with Karen and nodded grimly.

"It would depend on whether he killed me first. Neither one of us really wants to do that sort of thing to the other, though. You're probably the only one of us who would be able to prevent a killing he'd decided on, and that wouldn't have a lot to do with your magic."

Karen sat there blinking, but Jennifer was making sense. However frustrating Seth's crush on her was, there was no denying her ability to influence him just by talking to him.

"There're other reasons not to, you know."

"Which are?"

"He thinks about life and death differently than anyone else. He can reverse death at any time for any one. It's only as permanent as he wants it to be. If someone can convince him to resurrect someone, he can easily enough. He's really worried about the sort of pressure that would be brought to bear on him if we went public with what we can do."

"I can see that. But it still seems like we're giving him a lot of authority over who lives and who dies."

She shrugged. "He's going to have that. Dave hasn't really done anything to make him think that he's improving. There's no reason for Seth to think otherwise, and Dave has done nothing to make Seth think he's turned his life around. So why should he bother?"

She thought about it. Dave had never picked on her. But… divinations had shown what he did to Seth. She couldn't really blame Seth for not wanting anything to do with Dave, and she suspected Angela hadn't really looked into it herself. His actions were going to make this hard. Still, she was probably the best person to handle getting them to drop the feud. Reconcile wasn't the word. They never had been friends in the first place.

Chapter

"*H*ey Ange. I'm outside. Come on out." She came out to see Dave leaning against a red and black motorcycle. The seat held plenty of room for a passenger. "Cool bike, Dave."

"Thanks. Wanna go for a ride?"

"Back in a moment." She dashed inside for her football helmet and left a note for her parents.

"Really? You need a helmet?"

"Me, not so much," she admitted. "The protective enchantments I've woven into myself and my clothes are better than any helmet, not to mention I can teleport myself clear. But I'd rather not be bothered by some cop doing his job and pulling us over. You do, though. So put yours on."

"Aw, come on, babe. It's a lot better with the wind in my hair."

"I can make you, if you want." He laughed. "You want to try me? I can't fix your death, Dave. I can turn your bike into a solid mass of pure iron." Then she grinned. "Or I can make you bald."

"All right, all right." He pulled a helmet out of the luggage compartment; it was a half-helmet. "Are you sure the football helmet is legal?"

"I don't know," she admitted. "If we get stopped, I can adjust the cop's mind to a warning and switch it out for one like yours."

They took off down the road to the coast. Despite it turning curvy quickly in the hills, Dave was driving carefully and well…at first. After they got over the first set and into a straight away, he started driving faster and faster…and drove past the guard rail into open air. Angela spoke a word in Ainu and they were back on the road, teleported to safety.

Dave hit the curve, hooted in delight, and kept going. He sped up again, taking the curves even faster except when there were other cars present on the road. He went off the road again, and again Angela teleported them back. Then they did it again.

<Dave, if you go off the road again, I'm going to teleport us back to the road and let your bike crash. This is getting completely ridiculous. If you want to go flying sometime, let me know so I can get Alex or Karen to back you up.>

He slowed the bike and parked it in a pull out. "What gives, Ange? That was great!"

"Remember how I said that if you die, you're not coming back?"

"Yeah, you said Seth's being a dick about it."

"I never said that."

"Not those precise words, no, but it's what you meant."

"Dave, I can't confirm or deny…"

"Anyone who hasn't told me him or her self. I get that. Really. But that's no reason for me not to be honest about who the other wizards are."

"Actually, yes it is. You know too much about me to risk that. A memory adjustment would leave too many holes in your mind. It's balanced very close. A few votes to wipe you. A few to bring you in. The people in the middle."

"There's something else, isn't there?"

"Death suggested that Karen break us up. Yeah, she can do that, eliminating our love is something she's capable of doing."

"Ouch. If that happens he will get permission," Dave said. "What's got your face scrunched up?"

"Never mind. Can you keep it on the road, please?"

"Sure. Where to?"

"How about Bodega Bay? Malcolm's leading a dive with Bridget, Keisha, Jasmine, Solly, and Julian. We can join them in a seafood place on the docks for dinner."

"Sounds good to me."

The sun was peeking out from behind the clouds over Bodega Bay as Bridget guided the boat. It was a state of the art, purely electric yacht with powerful solar cells supplementing the batteries…along with a little magic. Her passengers were already in their diving gear.

"You and Jasmine go down first, Malcolm. We'll make sure Julian's doing Okay and start the project," Keisha said.

"Hey—I've dived plenty," Julian protested.

"Here in Bodega Bay?" she responded.

"Well, no, mostly in Hawai'i."

"It's a bit colder. We'll let the love birds go warm each other up and pair off once we're down there," Solly said.

"We hardly need your help, Solly!" Jasmine said tartly. Malcolm nodded vigorously over her shoulder.

"Yeah, we're checking on the local fecundity. Not increasing it!" he said.

"What are you concerned about?"

"You're never going to compete for the Magic Bowl when half your team turns up pregnant every year," Bridget said with a grin.

"It's hardly half. And how is that supposed to be MY fault?" Keisha, Bridget, and Malcolm looked at him with identical expressions. Julian barely stifled a guffaw as he got it.

"What am I missing?" Jasmine asked.

"You're not cleared for it yet, darling," Malcolm answered her with a kiss and a smile. She nodded.

"You sound pretty confident she will be," Julian remarked.

"Sooner or later that little tempest will blow over one way or another. The sea is patient. That fight's about the people involved, and Jasmine hasn't pissed anyone off to the degree he has."

"Someone got proposed for membership in the Round Table who had angered a current member?" Jasmine asked, shaking her head.

"Worse. Someone got proposed who used to try bullying a current member," he answered her. "The person proposed is alive because of the current member's mercy."

"Ouch. I look forward to hearing all about it some time. For now, let us get diving." She adjusted her gear and went in.

"See you guys down there," Malcolm said.

"She won't recognize me," Bridget shrugged. "But I'll go last." She'd still made no move to strap on a tank—or put on a wetsuit. She was still wearing her bathing suit and robe. Julian cocked his head at her,

"Bridget prefers to swim au naturel," Solly chuckled. "I take it you've got that enchanted to transform with you?"

"Yeppers. No need to shock Jasmine."

"As opposed to me?" Julian asked.

Solly snorted. "Jules, you're almost as hetero as I am. You'd enjoy it if she took off her suit." Bridget chuckled.

"How do you know? It's not like we've ever discussed it. I could be gay or bi for all we've talked."

"For all we've talked, true. But every time one of the girls goes on a date she tells me to keep my powers to myself, even if I'm on call for backup. Trust me. I know."

"Especially when you're the backup on call, O Fertile One!" Keisha said. "But back to the diving. I take it you'll be kind of unmistakable?"

"Yeppers!"

"What am I missing?"

"Bridget's providing security," Keisha said with a smile.

"Look for the lone orca."

"Borrowing a page?"

She shrugged. "Humans are less likely to attack an orca than a shark. Malcolm's already got the local pods on alert, so they'll pass anything useful on. I'll interpret the sounds better as a cetacean."

"Who's she borrowing from?"

"What's the other name for an orca?"

"Killer whale…Oh. Seth takes that form in the water?"

"Yeppers. I'll go with leucistic so you can't mistake that it's me." Their eyes darted to either side. "Really. Pay attention to the vocabulary portion next time? It means white. Not quite albino, but definitely unusual so you can spot me more easily. You're not quite up to just reaching out mentally. I'd go with Physeter, but we don't need any reports of Moby Dick in the area."

The others smiled and dove down. Julian found the water cold before Solly told him how to warm himself up below the waves. After that he was perfectly comfortable, but it took a lot more out of him. Bridget swam passed him, clicking her sonar as she went. They did a lot of bottoming on the seafloor...and it was fairly easy with the suits enchanted to deal with the depths. He also noticed her having a bit of fun with Jasmine, looming over her coming up behind her. She stopped after Malcolm grabbed her pectoral fin and wagged his finger at her. She bumped him with her head in response and vanished. They stopped around noon so Jasmine could do what she needed to, had lunch, and dove back down.

Then Julian found her goosing him from behind. He took off his breather for a moment, kissed the white whale on the rostrum, put the breather back in and skritched her under her chin. She sent a mental chuckle to him and swam off to challenge a great white shark.

After several hours of diving—within the official limits of the tanks—they came back to find Bridget already on board and dry as if she'd spent the whole day on the boat. "I got a call from Ange. They rode up on his motorcycle and want to meet us for dinner."

Keisha frowned at her. "Well, I'm in favor of joining them. What do you guys think?"

"That sounds good to me," Jasmine said, which got Malcolm agreeing.

"Seafood sounds great to me," Julian added. Solly added his vote. Bridget shrugged.

Dinner was sort of tense, Julian thought. He tried to draw out what the problems were but they weren't talking...or at least, not in front of Jasmine and Dave. Keisha had advocated keeping the conversation in a language they could all understand. Jasmine questioned Solly on his choice of multiple ways of cooking shrimp…including wrapped in bacon.

"I thought you were Jewish," she said.

"I was raised that way," he replied. "I've seen no indications that the Torah is accurate, though, so I went to my bar mitzvah to make my grandmothers happy and abandoned it afterwards. So why pay attention to the silly dietary restrictions? Want a shrimp?"

"Ah, no, thank you. I still follow halal as best I can."

"Oh, sorry, I didn't realize."

She shrugged. "I don't make a big deal out of it. What strike me as ridiculous are the people expecting everyone else to follow the restrictions. It is a restriction on me, part of my religion, not yours. If you'd continued past offering me a bite, we would have had a problem."

"More bacon and more shrimp for me." She grinned.

"Was your dive successful?" Dave asked Bridget. She ignored him and continued talking to Malcolm about what their survey on the dive had shown. Angela tried shaking her head at Dave when he tapped Bridget on the shoulder.

"Remove it or lose it." Julian could barely keep from changing his expression at the menace in her voice.

"Sorry." He saw her look intently at Angela but heard nothing. Angela nodded.

Chapter

Late in April, Angela went on an early morning bike ride with Dave, Malcolm, Jasmine, Solly, and Catalina from Alpine Dam. It would take them about an hour or so from there. When Catalina wanted to race, Dave and Jasmine were game and the others bowed out with hidden smiles. They kept up easily with the racers, though. They let the other three ride on ahead to the top, while they talked telepathically.

<This was a good idea, Ange. Thanks for inviting us.> Malcolm said.

<Glad to do it. We haven't been doing much socializing this past year. We really need to do more of it.>

<Agreed,> Solly said. *<We've only really been getting together to do things to push projects forward. That means we're losing opportunities to bounce ideas off each other.>*

<Blame...>

<Ange, this is on both of you. You have completely incompatible ideas of what constitutes an acceptable resolution. You and Seth really need to sit down and talk. This thing can't go on.>

Dave screamed her name. From the raised heads by Solly and Malcolm, Jasmine and Catalina had just called to them. She stopped and concentrated on what she was seeing. A minor practitioner had stunned them and was gathering them up, the abrasions and cuts from their crashed bicycles clear on their bodies. Solly erected a barrier around the three. The practitioner started looking around, then the nitrogen around him blazed to sudden glowing heat. Through their distance senses they could smell the cooking meat. He fled…and five other practitioners struck at the three of them. That hurt, but didn't penetrate their defensive enchantments. Solly put up another defense just as powerful as he'd put up around their dates. Malcolm brought frozen spears of ice and the crushing weight of the deep to bear, and three of them couldn't withstand either of the effects at all. Angela brought more heat, best suited to bringing them down. The surviving two fled while Malcolm was still busy.

"Why didn't you finish them, Ange?"

"What? Deliberately kill them? That would be murder."

"They attacked US, Angela," Malcolm said. "They also attacked Jasmine, Catalina, and Dave. Where else were you planning on invoking lethal power?"

"Not the time, Mal. Let's get the memories altered and knock the other three out for crashing their bikes in a silly race."

"They're mostly out now." Malcolm said.

"Ange, could you call Seth? We're going to need him to get much out of the corpses. You've got the closest connection to him." She grimaced but made the call.

<Thantoris, I beseech thine aid. We were attacked on Mt. Tam by minor practitioners, three are dead. We need you to get the information out of their corpses.>

<Three of them? How many fled?>

<Three all badly injured.>

<Three? Half of them got away from you? That's not good.>

<Come in disguise.>

<What sort of disguise?>

<We came with Dave, Catalina, and Jasmine. If you're not wearing one, they will recognize you.>

<State park ranger it is.> He appeared on Orcinus as an apparent mounted ranger—who looked nothing like Seth—and started

"inspecting" the bodies with his enchanted devices. She knew it was him from the horse.

When he spoke to them, it was in Coptic. "I see you're still trying to avoid killing people."

"Yeah? And?"

"A clean, moral decision."

"That you disapprove of." She certainly felt that radiating off him.

"I didn't say that. But you could still run in to someone who doesn't give you an option."

"You may be a killer, but I'm not," she muttered. Seth teleported the corpses away.

"Are you going to check out the others? Malcolm and Solly are keeping them sleeping for a few minutes.

"Did you learn anything?"

"I'll have the information in a few days. From my initial impressions, this is something we all need to hear. I assume you want to get back to your triple date. The longer we have to keep them unconscious the greater the danger someone will come by. See you at the meeting." He teleported away.

They arrived after school on Venus to have the consultation about the practitioners who had attacked them. Seth had his tablet ready to go when Julian took his seat. "Okay," Julian said. "We've got two items on the agenda today—the people who attacked on top of Mt. Tam and something Angela would like to discuss. Whoops, sorry." The others smiled at his presumption. The conference room was plain Venusian stone with a dull carpet on the floor, a long table holding beverages and snacks, and their colorful chairs.

"Good enough, actually, Jules," Alex said. It was his turn. "We're not really that formal about it, and we tend to pass the job around. Since this is just a discussion, why not you? Shevaun's up next." There was a murmur of agreement.

"If the chair needs to DO something one of the rest of us can supply it until they're fully up to speed," Karen said. "Mostly it's just administration and keeping things going. Which first?"

"Let's handle the attackers," Angela said. "They're a little more urgent. Seth?"

He stood. "These were people recruited by Maria Binay. They wanted to come after us more alone, and after a group they considered weak…"

"Three of us? Including Ange?" Malcolm said. "That's an unusual risk for them to take!"

"Despite their ages, they consider someone weak if that person is unwilling to kill, or are involved in what they consider "pacifist" causes. Hence—Angela, Solly, Malcolm. Or at least those six did. They figured Dawn and Alex would kill them, and a surprise was the only way to get through Solly's defenses. Some of them are starting to panic at the power we're showing when we do something. It's not even a question any more; they can't match it, even the oldest and strongest of them. Their teleportation range is limited to about what ours was freshman year. Even for the best of them. They're also part of a larger coalition, so far maybe more than twenty, scared of what we might do and how they're not really fitting into what we see as the future. Most of them are far more interested in making themselves richer than anything else. I've sent out the full report."

"Was there any idea why they targeted the three in front?"

"In their minds, those three were just bait. Their divinatory abilities weren't up to identifying you three in concealment if you didn't open yourselves up, so they took a chance on targeting three of our classmates. They got some notion of power in you three, but they couldn't tell if you were random potentials or the trained and ready super heroes they were afraid of. Treating our friends as bait on the *Pelewan* worked, so it was reasonable to think it would work here, too."

"What else is in the full report?" Shevaun wanted to know.

"Details. Precisely who the practitioners who attacked us here were, the people they were in contact with, their home bases. I suggest we send a team next weekend to each of their home bases; they could only guess at the other three. I'll go with one, Bridget with the second, and Alex with the third. Good enough?"

"Someone ready and willing to kill on each," Julian remarked. Seth nodded. Julian turned to Keisha. "Can you apply divination to each location and get what you can?"

"Naturally." She put her glass back down.

"I'm not sure that word applies to any of us any more but okay, that brings us to Ange. Ange?"

"Before I start, let me finish. Every time I've brought it up, I just get shut down, and I'm tired of it." She stared pointedly around the table. Seth poured himself another root beer, leaned back, and crossed his arms, but no one said anything and most nodded in agreement to let her speak.

"Okay. I know there's some strong opposition based on the past, but Dave Cleburne—my Dave—has matured a lot over the past year. And that attack on Mt. Tam suggests that he's in danger from his association with me. So, I'd like to bring our significant others in to the level of Dani, Mike, and Carmen." Maybe if she put it that way she'd get the other people with boyfriends and girlfriends on her side.

"Carmen's not on their level," Bridget pointed out. "Yes, she knows who most of us are, although I'm not entirely sure if she knows about Julian and Shevaun. Yes, she knows Mike is alive. That doesn't mean she has a free pass to the Castle, Temple, and Shore. She got a temporary pass to set things up. And it was with everyone's agreement that she learned that much and we didn't take away her memory."

"She should be able to share everything she's doing with him, though. Keeping these sorts of secrets is very bad for a relationship. And they already broke up once. Let's give them a chance, just a chance," Karen said.

"As I understand the dispute, it's primarily about Dave. We can discuss the others individually. Let's see if you guys can come to an agreement about Dave."

Keisha spoke up. "We can give it a shot, Julian. I'm not sure I agree with Karen's point, though. Dave talks. He hangs around with his friends and gossips like there's no tomorrow. He likes to talk to people a lot and isn't very watchful about what comes out of his mouth. Before

I'd be comfortable with him knowing things, he needs to get his mouth under control."

"I don't really like the idea of someone who doesn't know how to stay silent knowing enough to betray our secrets. We're really cautious about who gets to know about us for a reason, Ange. Dave just hasn't demonstrated an ability to keep secrets," Teddy said. "Before I could even think about bringing Dani in she had to prove she could keep a secret. Dave hasn't done that.

"He's kept mine. He knows about Alex and Karen and he's kept theirs."

"Not good enough," Alex said. "You just said that he's kept the secrets of his girlfriend and two other friends. That isn't good enough. I'm friends with Dave. But to keep the secrets he needs to keep, he needs to keep the secrets of people who aren't his friends, like Seth and Bridget. And in fairness I can see why other people are very skeptical of his willingness to do that. I didn't kick him off the football team for fun, I did it because he was talking out of turn. The only alternative I can think of is pure terror. While I'm sure Seth would be willing to supply that as often as we could possibly desire, we can't rely on that. Sooner or later he'd call our bluff and we'd have to pull the trigger. Which would lead to its own problems."

"I think it is time to expand our circle a little wider," Dawn said. "A lot of us have girlfriends or boyfriends who don't particularly like us not being available or telling them what's going on."

"That's true," Malcolm said. "And I'm included in that. At the same time...I understand the concerns about betrayal. And more specifically about Dave. But what's at bottom is that without unanimous agreement, he can't come up here. I'd like to show Jasmine everything we're doing. But she understands that I'm doing things I can't share with her. She's seen my power and what I can do. While she doesn't like me keeping it secret, she understands it. I take it the rest of you are essentially in the same position?" Others nodded.

"Jenny or I could take down Seth's barrier," Solly said. Seth's face went bone white. Karen felt the sense of betrayal wash over him. That wasn't a solution. Though she hadn't read his mind, the idea that Dave would not survive any longer than the barrier was a disquieting one.

"Seth has not violated our bargain, Solly," Jennifer said reprovingly. "He has every right to say no to revealing his secrets to an outsider. He has every right to protect his secrets with his power. And I will not declare war on Seth over him exercising his clear prerogatives. He gets to make the decision about what to do with his power."

"Even if it ends up killing someone we know?"

"Yes. Even then. Dave dug this grave himself. If he wants out of it, he's got a lot of long hard work to do to get that done, and Seth is the only one who can lift the prohibition. I get that Dave is important to you, Ange. But he won't survive me trying to…"

"I have a question," Seth finally spoke up. "Did you simply want me to kill him? You didn't need all the song and dance of a meeting to make that happen."

"WHAT?"

"We have an agreement, as you should remember. I don't kill Dave out of hand, and you keep the idiot away from me. This," he gestured to the entire meeting, "is hardly what I would call keeping him away from me. It's trying to force him into my presence. It looks to me like a complete abrogation of our agreement. If that's so…why continue this mummery? Tell me you want him dead and I'll see that it happens. I'll even send the corpse to planetary recycling so you don't have to look at it."

"That was NOT what I meant, Seth!"

"It wasn't? You could have fooled me."

"Seth, will you get off your one track mind where Dave is concerned?" Karen said. "You are vastly more powerful than him."

"The status quo is an acceptable compromise between what Angela wants and what I want. So no, I see no reason to change it."

"I don't consider it acceptable at all," Ange said, scowling. It got worse from there. The argument lasted for hours before Seth ended it with one word. Veto.

Chapter

37

$\mathscr{L}$ast night's meeting had been a disaster. She wasn't surprised when Bridget sided with Seth and Teddy. But now Malcolm, who she knew wanted to bring in Jasmine, and Jenny were aligning with them too. Alex and Keisha were wavering. Her request to bring in Dave had resulted in Seth demanding a mind probe to determine if she'd already told him forbidden truths. Keeping Dave away from him might be the best she could do at the moment, even though she hated to admit that. If Karen weren't a voting member now, it would have been an even split.

Her phone rang with Karen's old tone. "What's up, Karen?"

"You busy tomorrow?"

"Why?"

"Mom says I need to practice driving, and I wanted to go into Golden Gate Park. I promised her I'd bring another wizard along just in case, to ease her mind. And I think we need to talk."

"Can you drive someone else?"

"Legally, no. But it's not like they can track my Fifty-Three anyway."

"Sure."

They talked about little things on the drive down, crossed the Golden Gate Bridge, and drove into the park. A few words in Bengali ensured they got a space. Angela looked sidelong at Karen. "Okay, what's really up? You don't normally use your power to get a specific parking space."

"You're right. Do you know where we are?"

"Um, not really."

Karen nodded at some poppies. California poppies were normally rich orange-gold. These were bright pink…with black streaks. No…a black band, with the pink more intense outside the band.

"This is where you were shot."

"This is where I died—and where you called Seth to bring me back as he had you," Karen quietly corrected her, and looked directly up into her face. "Those poppies are growing where I bled."

"I know you've got a point."

Karen switched to Cushitic. "My point is that you're getting increasingly angry and bitter over him exercising his legitimate prerogatives, especially about the meeting last night. He wouldn't have objected to me knowing about him. He hoped it might change my mind about dating him. But you kept the secret, refusing to confirm even when I put it together. And you only slipped once, right after Dave broke up with you. Even though I was in no danger. He wasn't going to hurt me, and neither was Alex. And as Bridget pointed out over Beijing, even killing me would have been pointless when the final decision on death is Seth's. At most, they would have had a talk with me."

"I'm still not sure about what your point really is."

"We all get to decide who knows about us. That was one of the first lessons you taught me about this, even before you were actually teaching me magic. You know. When first I put together that Seth had brought us back from death, and was teaching you magic. You wouldn't even admit it was Seth. But now that you want to bring Dave in, suddenly you get to decide for him?"

"If he wasn't so stubborn, he'd realize Dave should…"

"Ange. This goes back further than high school. I'm not sure just how far, but every one else told me that Seth and Dave have never gotten along. It started somewhere in elementary school at least. Maybe kindergarten. Maybe preschool. I don't think Dave realizes even now how far back it goes or just how deep Seth's hatred of him runs. He doesn't have Seth's memory, and you know what that's like. Seth regards him as an enemy, while Dave thinks all that's gone before no longer matters."

"I keep thinking he'll change his mind, come to see things my way."

"But why should he change his mind? This hostility goes really, really deep, Ange. To get him to change his mind will require some sort of major shift in his thinking. You might need an outright deal. You had to agree to keep Dave away from him to seal the bargain for him not to kill Dave out of hand. Now you're pushing—*again*—to bring him fully in, and he thinks you're breaching the agreement. You want something from him. Is there anything you can offer in exchange?"

Angela brightened. "He's seeing Rachel now. He'll want to bring her in. My vote for…what am I missing?" she asked as Karen shook her head.

"He's not dating Rachel, much as she would like otherwise. If you were talking to him you'd know that. He's helping her keep her vampirism in check. He didn't make me date him; he's not going to use his far greater power over her that way. Any other ideas?"

She sighed, then admitted, "No. Last year I could have set him up with you, but that's no longer an option. He can, after all, do just about anything he wants on his own just like we can."

"Then maybe you should change strategy, and reduce what you're asking of him. Admit that Seth's not just in a position to keep vetoing Dave but has every right to do so, and that you're losing the argument with the others. Dave doesn't have to know anything for Seth to extend basic defense to him, the sort of protections they gave you freshman year when none of them were telling you anything."

"Dani knew…"

"What Dani knew and when she knew it aren't going to impress Seth and Teddy, Ange, and you know it as well as I do. You're irritating everyone else more than you're convincing those two. One vote changes, and Dave gets mindwiped, and I haven't a clue how Shevaun and Julian will vote once they have votes. The only rules for bringing in an associate are a unanimous vote, and a yes vote means I like and trust this person enough to know my secrets." Angela bit her lip. Karen was right, after all. "And it's not like they'll agree to you doing the mind probe. They'll probably insist on Seth doing it again. Are you prepared for what he might do to Dave? Or Teddy?"

She grimaced. "I was kind of hoping for Jennifer or Keisha. Or you." Karen shook her head.

"From what you told me, Dani didn't have to satisfy someone agreeing or neutral on letting her in, she needed to satisfy someone opposed. He needs to satisfy those two. And since Teddy just opposes bringing anyone in on secrecy grounds, he'll almost certainly defer to Seth who has a personal problem with Dave."

Angela twisted her lips. "You're probably right."

"Look on the bright side. Your best path to bringing him in fully is going to be by stages. Right now Seth barely tolerates his presence at practice or if he happens to be with you when he comes up to talk to you, won't speak to him, and always speaks in one of the other languages in his presence unless he needs to be understood by someone else. Get him to the point of actually deigning to acknowledge his presence first. And in the meantime, keep your agreement with Seth. The impression that you're violating it is swinging them to his point of view."

"You think there's a bright side?"

"I think, given Dave's past, that you're going to need to make the first offer to compromise. He's willing to live with how things stand. Maybe not great news for Dave, but…Teddy went and read his mind last night. You've been skating on the edge, sweetie. Dave is really going to need to prove himself." She nodded.

Angela and Dave brought their trays into the cafeteria, and Angela saw Alex, Karen, and Seth behind a privacy shield. They were arguing lowly and intently about something, but there were a couple of spots free. She tightened her lips and indicated their table to Dave. He had some trouble figuring out where she wanted to go, so she spoke a word in Ainu to help balance her tray in one hand and held his elbow to guide him when Dani popped up. "Angela, Dave, please join me."

"Not to be rude, Dani, but Angela seems to have her heart set on a different table."

"Yeah, I can see that. But they don't want to be disturbed, so why don't you join me?"

"Sorry, Dani, I need to speak…"

"Angela. They REALLY don't want to be disturbed. So much that Alex asked me to run interference."

"They can be unhappy. This is important."

"Look more closely, please. You will be unhappier if you insist on talking to them now. Talk to them later."

"If they want to be alone…" Dave started, clearly affected by the shield.

"No, Dave. We're having lunch with…"

Dani switched to halting Nahuatl. "The God of War bid me warn you that he and the Goddess of Love have joined their powers with the God of Death to remain undisturbed, at mightiest force." She cocked her head at her, her brow furrowed in concentration for the Nahuatl and her shoulders tight with tension.

That put a different take on it! Dani was warning her that the privacy shield would kill Dave, in addition to the random weirdness that Karen used and the mind controlling enchantments Alex favored. It wouldn't just inhibit him but let him through if he was determined. She could still counter act them for herself, but not for Dave; not all three of them, and not if Seth was willing to kill to keep it private. "What'd you say?" Dave asked. She shook her head, and Angela nodded.

"Looks like we're lunching with you, then." The tension went out of Dani's shoulders as she smiled in relief.

"What are they talking about?" Dave wanted to know.

"I can't tell you," Dani told him.

"Oh, come on."

"If you want to know, ask Alex or Karen. They might tell you. I'm not going to."

Dave had another question. "If it's so hush-hush, why are they having it here?"

"Dave, that's another question for them. None of them specifically told me what was going on, but I can guess from what Alex was saying in response—in Nahuatl. Karen was speaking in Bengali and Seth was speaking in Coptic. If they took that precaution, I'm not going to speculate openly."

"All this secrecy is really too much, Dani."

"Bitching about it won't help you. There are reasons for it, and I'd like the consequences of not maintaining the secrets I know where you're concerned even less than Angela would."

"Dani…"

"How's the after school job hunt going?"

Dani smiled in relief at Angela's change of subject. "Pretty good. I wish Mom and Dad would let me get a job with the Avengers or the League offices, but they think the interviewing process is better experience for me than Alex saying 'put my girlfriend on the payroll.'"

"You guys are hiring?" Dave asked

"Most of the jobs with the Gorgons are in Vegas, not here. And Seth is still chair of the League hiring committee. I suppose I could make you my personal assistant or something like that, or a Gorgons agent at the League offices," Angela responded.

"Don't the trustees manage hiring?"

"It's…complicated. Seth, Keisha, and Malcolm are the owners' hiring committee. They sit in on the meetings of the trustees' hiring committee. That would be Solly's mom, Bridget's dad, and my Mom, now. They're not likely to make an issue or object if Seth says no, and both Keisha and Malcolm would back the notion that the personal conflict means that I should hire you rather than the League." She shrugged. "The trustees are careful to pick their battles with the owners. It's only a year or less until we turn eighteen and take over anyway, so they mostly advise us and then make the formal decision for the record rather than try to overrule us."

"Dani, how'd you move from Alex's girlfriend to the inner circle?"

"I'm not in the inner circle. I lack a certain something, but I think I know what you're asking." She paused to sip her drink in thought. "Step one was to get right with the God of Death."

Dave's eyes bugged out at that descriptor. Dani smiled. "I didn't have the best relations with him either, Dave. But I apologized to him. I stopped picking fights with him. I started being at least polite to him.

From what Alex tells me—I'm still not really hanging out with him so much as I am with Alex and Ange—he also noticed me being more of a positive influence in the school generally." She shrugged. "You've got a tougher job of getting right with him than I do."

"We are still talking about the same person?"

"Dave, I can't confirm or deny any particular person. If you're not understanding who I'm speaking of by his rightful title, it's out of my hands. The secrets aren't mine to share; I'm just trusted to know them." She took a bite, chewed and swallowed and raised an eyebrow.

"Okay, okay, what's with all the secrecy?"

"I'm not entirely sure. And I'm not really sure just how far I can go in answering that question without violating the limits they've entrusted me with. I know what Alex can do, so I'm going to err on the side of caution, especially given what I know have been bad arguments about what you can be told. You want to know more, ask someone in the inner circle."

"You've SEEN me in action, Dave, and you're still not quite believing that if I say I can do something I can. Someone who never has will have a much harder time believing it. We're hoping to present the world with an undeniable demonstration of our power, one every one can see, that will cut off those tiresome arguments without us needing to make the Holocaust look like a minor tragedy. And simultaneously get the people we need to protect somewhere out of reach of anyone who thinks to use them as hostages. You're on that list, at least."

"Undeniable?"

"I can't say what we're going to do; you're not cleared for it. But… go moon watching sometime."

"What's with the minor tragedy thing?"

"The Holocaust killed over six million people. It's possible for us to cause human extinction. Some of us have already worked out how, in different ways. Zombie apocalypse. World War III. The Final Plague. Global crop failure. Infertility."

"Okay, okay."

Chapter

38

Angela stretched after sitting at the computer all night writing her report, her espresso mug half full from her last refill. She'd lost count of how many times she'd refilled her mug. Maybe she should just enchant it to be always full unless she told it not to. The sun was coming up when her text alert chimed. What was Fred doing up at this hour?

She looked at the text. He was going to jump off the Golden Gate Bridge! She couldn't speak the word to teleport fast enough. He hadn't jumped yet. He was standing on the side facing the Bay, over the fence, looking down at the waves. A word in Ainu rendered her invisible to anyone she didn't speak to.

"What's up, Fred?"

"Don't come any closer!"

"Okay." She stood there, the early morning breeze whipping her hair. "Want to talk about it?"

"No! I'm gonna jump!"

"You can if you want to. It won't solve anything. But you can talk to me first. Don't worry. I won't let you fall."

"What's the point? I'm going to kill myself."

"I've thought I was going to die. Shit on 'thought I was going to'. I actually DID die once. Someone helped me. The least I can do is pay it forward. What's wrong, Freddie? Why do you want to jump?"

"You wouldn't understand."

"Try me." He looked out at the water. "C'mon, Fred. What would it hurt?"

"You're not going to try to stop me?"

She felt her lips try to smile. She'd already stopped him. He just didn't know it yet. He didn't notice he was standing on a wisp of fog. "I won't try to stop you. Talk to me Fred. What's going on? I had no idea things were so bad for you that you'd do this."

"My parents listened to the pastor. They kicked me out because I'm gay. I can't take anymore of that pray the gay away bullshit. I want to die."

"You're not going to. And even if you did, what kind of friend would I be if I left you that way?"

"What?"

"Fred, do you remember that bus crash I was in freshman year?"

"Yeah, I guess. You, Alex and somebody else survived, the bus driver didn't. I forget who the other survivor was."

"Not quite. Only Seth and Alex survived. I died. If someone hadn't decided to bring me back, I wouldn't be here. And it wasn't a friend. It was someone I'd been treating like shit. He still came to save my ass at White Hill. Can I do less for you?"

"What are you talking about?"

She gave him a sad smile. "Look down, Fred." He did…and saw that he was standing on air. There was nothing between him and the water below. His eyes bugged out. "You've been standing on air since I first spoke to you. Now that we've established you're not falling unless I let you and I'm not going to let you, why don't you come back over here and we'll talk about it? Figure something out for you?"

"Can you make me straight?"

She breathed in. "I…probably could, if I thought about what I'd need to do for a bit. The problem is that Gaia doesn't really like that sort of meddling, and she can overrule me. You ARE gay, but so what? It's perfectly natural; she pointed out once that even muggle scientists have documented homosexual behavior in over a thousand species. She'd probably switch you back." At his incredulous look, "Sorry. I don't have permission from her to tell you her name. So 'Gaia' it is."

"She doesn't know what it's like…"

"She's dating a girl at the moment. I know she's had some bigoted assholes harass them on dates. She handles it in her own style. I think she usually gives them some debilitating disease. And renders them sterile."

"It's just a fantasy anyway."

"If you think that's fantasy…" she stepped up onto nothing but air, and walked over the barrier, then down the other side until she was standing in front of him on empty air. "What was that?" His eyes bugged out.

"What are you?"

"I'm your friend. And I'm not giving up on you." She reached out a hand to him. "I already told you I won't let you fall, and I mean that literally. Let's get you somewhere safe and warm."

"That was impossible!"

"So is my being here talking to you. When did you send that email? I was finishing my report for history, when it came in. But you're not going anywhere unless it's with me." She put a hand out to him. "I'm here for you. Let me help you." Tremblingly, he reached out and stepped to her, letting her put her arms around him. She said several words in Ainu to make people forget and cancel the emergency calls, then took him to the Seamount.

"Welcome to my place, Fred. The others aren't awake yet. Coffee? Tea? Hot chocolate?"

"You have hot chocolate ready to serve?"

She shrugged. "It's a peculiarity of working magic. If it's drawing from us we can use a caloric boost, and cocoa is better at that than coffee or tea. I'm going to have breakfast, too. Anything you want?" she asked as her enchanted platter obediently created cornflakes and umeboshi.

"No, thanks. I'd wondered why you added coffee to your morning sugar." He sipped coffee. "What is this place?"

"My place. My hidey-hole, away from everyone else. It's called the Seamount. I originally built it just to have my own little place, somewhere I could go where no one could follow me, but now it's built to withstand and contain my fury."

"But what is it?"

"A dead volcano under the ocean. I widened out a few of the chambers and passages, but Dave and I are the only people who can come in and out."

"And Dave only as long as he's in your good graces?" He sipped and at her raised eyebrow continued, "You've got the power here, unless I'm completely missing something about Dave. This place is decorated in your style, not his." He nodded at a big, framed photo of Dave.

"He loses my good graces and he's all too likely to end up a good looking corpse without a mark on him." At his shocked eyebrows, she said, "Never mind." She ate a few bites as the platter created a stack of pancakes with strawberry syrup, Fred's favorite. She smiled as he picked up his fork.

"Angela, thanks."

"Fred, if you still really want to kill yourself, we can get you something that's completely painless and will look like natural causes to anyone else. We've got an option like that for someone. But let's see if we can keep you alive. We've got power. We've got money. We like you. And we're not giving up on you without a fight." She pointed her spoon at him. "So no running off and jumping while our backs are turned. We will bring you back." The strength and curiosity suddenly spilled out of him and he collapsed into tears. She dropped her spoon and put her arms around him, just holding him. A spell kept the food at the proper temperatures.

She sent a silent spell to the others for when they woke up. It would be a few hours on a Sunday. Teddy was awake early, of course, but none of the rest of them ever felt any reason to be awake on a Sunday morning. Teddy agreed with her handling Fred's situation, and said he'd be by in disguise later. She wrote a quick note and teleported it to her mother, since they weren't used to telepathic communication.

"Are you willing to tell me what happened?" He reddened and ducked his head. "Fred, with the exception of Dave, everyone you're going to meet here is going to be capable of pulling what they want to know directly from your brain, most of them without you even realizing it. I don't think they're going to, not without your permission, but the more we know the more we'll be able to help. Okay?"

"Okay." He looked down at his coffee. Grandma would have been scandalized at her using the old chaji tea service to serve coffee, but she hadn't brought another pot and didn't feel like making one on the spot. She sipped her cocoa and waited for him patiently. "And I guess if you can do that, then you'll know if I deliberately lie to you. So I won't.

"It started when I was about eight. That's when I knew I was gay. I mentioned it to Reverend Thorne. He told me I was a sinner and there was only one way to drive the sin out. He started raping me that day." She winced in sympathy, but the only word she spoke was in Ainu, refilling his cup. "I told my parents. They didn't believe me. He was trying to get me to bring my little brother and sister to him for "spiritual counseling sessions" since they had a gay brother. Mom wouldn't listen. He was encouraging her to throw me out of the house when I finally came out of the closet to her."

"Ouch. Fred, I'm so sorry. We'll stop him, I promise you."

"How?"

"He'll be confessing to the whole congregation. From the pulpit. It'll be better than having him fall over dead, anyway. Give me a few minutes to set it up." Alex, Teddy, and Karen were better at this, and Julian had shown a surprising strength, but she knew what she was doing and got it set up well. She returned her gaze to Fred and downed what was left in her cocoa mug. She commanded the refill and addition of marshmallows. Fred looked up pensively.

"It was Seth who brought you back?"

She shook her head regretfully. "That gets into the area of secrets I'm obliged to keep, sorry. I know who brought me back. There are other people with similar abilities. I'm not supposed to tell anyone who they are. I'm not even supposed to confirm it was one of them or someone else entirely." At his look, she raised her brows and explained what she could do with a mind, what she would do to keep other people's secrets. "I'm really sorry to be putting it like this, but Dave has been…imprudent enough to draw suggestions of memory wipes and execution if that's what it takes to keep our secrets. Since I don't want something like that to happen to you, I'm simply not going to answer the question of who brought me back. Call it a handy EMT, although that isn't accurate."

"What else can you do? You CAN read minds, for example?" She nodded. "It's not the easiest thing to do—not for me, anyway—and it's invasive. We've gotten better at it since I first learned how, but it's still something that we don't do much. Only if I need the information and can't get it normally. I don't do it on tests. That wouldn't accomplish anything."

Chapter 39

Katie nudged her as they saw someone they knew walking among the graves on Memorial Day. The late afternoon shadows fell around him. "Excuse us," she said to their parents. She nodded at the black clad boy. "Someone we know."

"You're leaving us to go talk to a boy? Isn't this kind of not the place for it?" Jimmy teased.

"That's Seth," Katie said with a bit of a quaver in her voice. She started smoothing her hair back and tugging at her clothes' imaginary wrinkles.

"Oho! The boy you've got a crush on? The one who…"

"Shut up, Jimmy, he'll hear you!" Katie hissed at him.

"He's all the way over there. He'd have to have the hearing of a dog."

"Don't bet against him, Jimmy. I could hear you from over there."

"Really?"

She wiggled her ears at him. "But he already knows about Katie's crush, so that wouldn't be news," she finished with a beatific smile.

"How could you hear me from over there?" he asked in Bengali.

"He knows that language, too," she said with a crooked smile.

"Coming, Katie?" When Jimmy tried to come along Dad stopped him. "Let it be."

"If that's the guy she has a crush on, shouldn't someone keep an eye on her? She's only thirteen."

"Karen can do that," Mom said. "He'll listen to her, where he might dismiss you. And an overbearing older brother would backfire with Katie, so we'll just let her handle keeping an eye on things."

He looked from one to the other. "This is confusing. Why are you so blasé about it? Just a few years ago you were insisting I go along with Karen."

"Don't worry about it. How are your grades at Berkeley?"

"Wait a minute. Don't change the subject."

"We know some things about him that incline us to trust him. For one thing, although Katie as a crush on him, he's been polite and restrained every time he's spoken with her."

"For one thing? That means there are others."

"That Karen and Katie don't want us discussing with you. You don't need to know and we don't have permission to share."

Angela appeared, coalescing from the air. "They've taken Dave. I want back up to go get him back." Karen quickly gathered her power to put up a privacy bubble around the four of them.

"I'm there, Ange," Karen said. Angela shook her head.

"Sorry, Karen. We should go in fast and hard and merciless, and that describes the God of Death a lot more than it describes the Goddess of Love. You're the gentlest of us. I need the most ruthless of us. I'm here to get Seth's help." Katie giggled at the titles Angela bestowed on them.

"My help? Why mine? There are nine other people who could do this, and you're more than capable yourself. It's not like you can't handle the destruction and death aspects of a rescue."

"Damn it all, Seth. They took my boyfriend. I know they're wizards. I want the most dangerous option I can get to back me up taking him back. That's you."

"Weren't you the one who pushed to build Hell so we couldn't kill everyone?" he asked.

"Fuck that. If there wasn't so much collateral damage—like Dave— I'd nuke'em. We worked well together on the ship rescuing people. You're the best choice to get him out now."

"Angela, I know he's your boyfriend. But he's no friend of mine. I'm sorry you're hurting..."

"Seth! I don't want to kill him by accident. I want your reflex precision with doom, death, and despair. I can handle the destruction part. But manipulating matter the way I do causes too many collateral effects. Even ripping apart their atoms leaves three different kinds of radiation. I may not have time to contain that without you. And if he dies I'll need to persuade you to let me resurrect him anyway." He just stared at her coldly.

Karen spoke up. "Seth, I know you have problems with Dave. And I know he's the one that caused them. And I know you've got a powerful temptation to leave him to his fate. But this isn't really about him. Are you going to turn your back on Angela when she needs—okay, asks for—your help?"

"You really need his help?" Katie asked. "Um, sorry..." she added when Angela looked at her.

"Need isn't the right word. He's right; I could handle it solo. It's the collateral effects when I have to do something fast that are the problem. It's a lot safer for a rescue operation like this to have at least two of us— watching each other's backs—but he's the most precise of us when it comes to stopping someone. When he saved me at White Hill, he killed just the guilty, but I've never killed anyone. I need to get Dave out alive, given Seth's prohibition on raising him from death..." Angela trailed off as she listened to the message coming in from Malcolm.

"Um, you guys just went blank for a moment. Telepathy coming in?"

"Attack off Santa Catalina. Fortunately the attackers there were idiots."

"What do you mean?"

"Striking at Poseidon in the middle of the ocean?" Karen said. "The great whites ate well. He's getting her to the Grotto." Then she winced. "Someone just tried the Temple. The wards held. If it wasn't for the automatic alarm she'd never have known."

"They tried the Temple? That was suicidal."

"What's the Temple?" Katie wanted to know. They ignored her. "Damn. I need to get Katie, Jimmy, and my parents to safety."

"Hey!"

"There hasn't been an attack where more than one of us was present. Here they'd have to take on three of us, and Seth and Angela are two of the three most dangerous in combat."

"They just breached Lucifer's home defenses. He's fine—they'd have had a harder time if he wasn't so reliant on illusion—but it's going to take a while to calm his family down and make them forget."

"He's got better defenses than I do. Damn. I wanted to drop them off and be free to reinforce."

Seth pulled out an old-fashioned skeleton key and spoke a word in Coptic. "Here. This will get you through the wards of the Mausoleum. I know the Chapel's defenses aren't fully up yet."

"Thanks, Seth. Are you sure?"

"They haven't even tried to breach my home defenses, and I've alerted my parents to stay behind the wards I've activated." That made a lot of sense, so she nodded; his wards would kill, while Angela's were simply ferocious. "I'm going with Angela to get Dave back. By the way, Karen, I can feel that." Angela's shoulders relaxed as she looked at him in surprised gratitude.

She blinked at him, smiling softly. "You called me 'Karen'."

"A momentary slip, I'm sure. I can still feel your attempt to influence me."

"I'm not, though. Every time I've tried I've bounced, even with the resurrection bond, even with all my power over emotions and your feelings for me. I don't bother trying to influence the Round Table anymore." Angela nodded.

All three turned their eyes to Katie. "What?" she said.

"I'll deal with it, Seth. We're going to have a talk, Katie. Pushing him like that is a bad idea, which is another reason Ange and I aren't doing it. C'mon."

"We'll stay here until you get them away." Angela said.

"I was only trying to help," Katie protested as they got about midway between the wizards and their parents.

"I know. But if you really want to influence him, talk to him. Convince him. Get him to agree. Trying to make someone with our power do what you want rather than what we do is dangerous, and unlike me his reflex is deadly. We still don't know as much as we'd like about that link you have with him. You may have noticed that he realized it was happening almost immediately, he just thought it was me doing it." They quickly reached their parents. "There's a problem. We're leaving now. They'll be covering us until we're safe, then they have somewhere to be."

"Okay, I'll see you at home."

"Get your car later, Jimmy. I'll be handling the transportation until I get you someplace safe. Link hands." Katie grabbed Jimmy's hand and Mom's as Dad put his hand on Mom's shoulder and Karen's own hand. She spoke a word in Bengali and they were in the chill of the Mausoleum. "Fiat lux." Soft pink light filled the room. Another incantation brought the temperature up to tolerable.

"What the hell?" he asked. "How'd we get here? And where the fuck are we?"

"In reverse order, this is the Mausoleum, Seth's safe house. I teleported us. Thanks to Seth, I have a pass through the wards. We've had several attacks on our loved ones today. I need to go help, but one set of defenses as already been breached, so I got you behind a better protection than the ones I've set up."

"Cool. I've always wanted to come here," Katie said. She went over to a bookshelf and pulled down something, then flopped down in an easy chair with her prize.

"Always since three months ago?"

"Well…"

"Why is everything black?"

"He likes black," she shrugged. "Do you need anything else before I go?" She looked at Jimmy trying the door. "Don't bother Jimmy. You won't be able to open it anyway, and he puts up lethal wards."

"Karen, I need to…"

"Stay alive, big brother. Standard policy is to not revive someone publicly known to be dead. Katie, if something comes up, bespeak him." She nodded.

"Why does she get to decide? I've got things to do," he demanded of them all.

"At the moment, because I have the power to do it and you can't do anything about it," Karen smiled sweetly at him as she threw his babysitting motto back at him. Katie laughed at his expression. He turned to their parents.

"Sit down and read a book. We're here until Karen or Seth comes to get us. From what we know of him, she's being entirely serious about the sort of defenses he puts up to keep out intruders."

"Good luck, sweetie. Ask Seth to keep us apprised through Katie." They hugged her.

"It'll probably be me who comes to get you. Once they get Dave clear that puts all three of our most lethal and destructive members free to focus on the bad guys." She hugged them back and vanished in a flash of pink.

"Will someone please tell me what is going on?"

"Nope," Katie smirked at him. He glared at her. Mom spoke up before Jimmy could explode.

"Karen's a real honest to goodness wizard. She was murdered in Golden Gate Park a year ago and Seth—that's the boy in the graveyard— brought her back. You've seen that charm bracelet and the bullet? That's what it's from. You know Katie's cancer went into a mysterious spontaneous remission. He cured her at Karen's birthday party. She can somehow reach him if she needs to."

"Karen mentioned that their safe houses have kitchens, and it's almost lunchtime. We're limited to what Seth has on hand, but there should be something from what Karen's told us. Anyone hungry?" Dad asked.

"If she's a wizard too, why aren't we at her safe house?"

"He's been at this longer, and he puts up defenses that strike back at someone trying to get in," Katie said looking up from the book. "Basically, the Mausoleum is a lot harder to penetrate than the Chapel, so we're safer. Go make some pizza rolls or something, Jimmy."

"Wait. Isn't Seth the boy who had a crush on Karen?"

"Still does, but he's worked past it," Katie replied.

"And you have a crush on him now? That's messed up."

"Don't say that. Karen doesn't want him, and she's been giving me pointers." Mom and Dad frowned.

"You two don't like it either."

"No, we don't. At the same time, though…his assessment of her remaining life was a week. Karen tells us the other wizards regard his senses and predictions regarding death as completely accurate. He stepped in to cure her without telling anyone he was doing it. If Karen hadn't noticed, we still wouldn't know. We know he has a crush on Karen, but he never did anything. She's keeping an eye on it."

"With their history, is that such a good idea?"

"A better idea than you doing it," Katie interrupted. "Karen's smart enough not to piss off the God of Death."

"I thought she told you not to call him that," Mom told her.

"Like that's not who he is?"

"He's a teenage wizard, not a god, Katie."

"Isn't he? He brought Karen back from being shot in the heart. From what she told us about it, he didn't do any preparation. He just did it. It was no big deal to him. That's not a wizard thing in any of the novels I've read. From what she's told me, the biggest impediment to more resurrections isn't difficulty. It's keeping it a secret." She pointed at a walk-in cage full of some green birds, with red-orange faces and yellow necks. They were squabbling over some food. "You bird watch, Mom. What are those?"

"I don't know, honey. Parakeets aren't native to California. I don't know I've ever seen these. They're not the feral red-masked conures on Telegraph Hill, I know that, or the parrots or parakeets that are feral in Southern California."

Katie flipped open a large book to a picture. "Outside this room, stuffed at a museum, or in a book, you won't." Mom looked at the picture, back at the birds, and sat down weakly.

"Mom, what is it?" Jimmy asked.

"Those are *Carolina* parakeets. I've never seen any for a good reason. They've been extinct since 1918."

"But that's impossible!"

"Not for the God of Death."

"Charles, if I tell you to get down or start speaking only in Tsalagi, just do it, okay? Don't argue with me, don't look around to see what's happening, just hit the deck and get behind something. And stay down until I tell you it's all clear. Please. I'll explain later, but for now do what I tell you to for your own safety."

"Dawn, what's happening? Why are you suddenly looking for an exit?"

"Not now, Charles. I'll get you out of this, I promise." Her eyes were darting around, then she put on her sunglasses in the dim lighting of the museum. They were the pair that shielded the corners of her eyes, too…but it looked like light was leaking out from behind them. She grabbed his hand and started pulling him towards the exit. "They might not strike in front of a crowd, but I at least care about collateral damage. Let's get away from the innocents. They're probably here for me but that doesn't mean they won't go after you."

"Dawn…"

"Charles. Not. Now. I need to get you to safety so I can reinforce the others." She was making no sense at all.

"I don't get it."

"Quick explanation? I'm a sorceress, a wizard, a magician. I'm not the only one. The bad guys have launched an attack on us, our families, and our friends. My wards will keep you safe at my place. Other people have stronger or nastier, but mine are up to the task. Once we get there, stay there till I come get you."

He looked at her, convinced his girlfriend had suddenly gone completely mad, and started backing away. He found he couldn't extricate his hand from hers. She was a lot stronger than she looked.

"Charles, please stay close to me. You'll be a lot harder to defend if we're apart. I know it sounds impossible, and I'm not really going to be able to explain for possibly several hours. We need to get out of here so I can minimize the collateral damage."

"Dawn, when did you start working out?"

"I didn't. I just enhanced my strength. Charles, please. Come with me. It's a lot easier and safer if I get you out of this now than if I have to come back and get you. And a whole lot less messy than if I have to bring you back from the dead. You'll be safe at Sunholme. And before you ask, yes I do know how to do that."

"If you're not the only one who else is a sorceress?"

"I'm bound by the promises of secrecy I gave six years ago. The others haven't cleared you to know anything about them yet. I'm going to deal with the snafu problems…. I can teleport us there from here, but the muggles would notice, so I don't want to do that if I can avoid it."

"Dawn, this is really too much…"

"Charles, I got the first warning ten minutes ago. I've already warned my parents to get behind my wards. They listened to me. Right now getting you to safety so you can go on living your life is more important than explanations." Her voice went distant for a moment, and then she pulled him through a staff door. She said something gibberish and brilliant yellow light swirled around them. It was suddenly a lot hotter, and the sky went on forever around them under the scattered clouds and beaming sunshine. Another word made carvings in the rocks around them glow as bright as the midday sun. "Stay here. Go online; there's a magical connection. Help yourself to the stuff in the fridge. I'll be back as soon as I can for you." She kissed him and vanished in a yellow flash.

Angela and Seth reappeared by Dave's house in a flash of teal. "Thanks, Seth."

He nodded. "Where are we?"

"This is Dave's home. I thought it best to start here, since I'm not really sure where he is; he got a scream off to me when they grabbed him." Seth switched to Coptic. "I understand. You have wards up here?"

"I do, but they're weak. Little more than tripwires to alert me. Dave knows about me—sort of—but his parents, brother, and sister don't. They don't know about you. Dave thinks he knows about you, though."

"Thinks he knows?" Trust Seth to focus in on that detail.

"I've never confirmed it. But, look, Seth. He doesn't have our brains. He works his ass off to score a B, even with me helping him. But he's not as stupid as you make him out to be. He's picked up on some of the anomalies that Keisha mentioned when we brought Karen in. He's figured out that the Round Table is a cover for us."

"Teddy's not going to like that much more than I do."

"I know." She brought up her divinations. "We can deal with that after he's safe from the bad guys. I already checked with Teddy."

Seth spoke a few words in Coptic and he went invisible—at least to normal eyes. At the same time he'd summoned his Death costume, complete with scythe. More words brought his horse Orcinus and the pack of bloodhounds. As he mounted, he activated the magic in their collars to make them invisible and incorporeal. A command sent the dogs looking for the traces of Dave.

She finished her first set of divinations. "Seth, I know you two aren't going to be friends. Some of the others finally clued me in on the history between you. And you're right, there's no reason for him to know your secrets. But can I at least get a defense agreement for him?"

"Defense agreement?" She felt his eyes focusing on her, even though she could only see the empty sockets.

"I'm not asking you to reveal your secrets to him. I'm not asking you to trust him, or like him, or even be polite to him. But he's a vulnerability for me. All I'm asking is that you protect him like I was being protected freshman year. Stay in the shadows if you want. I'll keep him away from you. We defend each other to the limits of our powers. Cover my ass, brother. Defend me by protecting him. Please."

The skull was as expressionless as always. Concentrating on their resurrection bond, she could feel his churning emotions. When he spoke, he was gravely quiet. "I met Dave in preschool. He was bigger than I was. He pushed me off a swing and laughed. That pretty much set the pattern. We played on opposing teams in soccer. He tripped me several times, deliberately kick me and get away with it. I remember him hitting me on the playground and being the one who got in trouble for hitting him back. All of the others helped me to the nurses' office multiple times, but the school never did anything to stop it, and Karen, Julian, and Shevaun did at least once. No evidence, they said. I had permanent teeth knocked out by your boyfriend, until I had the ability to regrow them."

She winced. She'd known Dave had picked on Seth freshman year; if you didn't know what Seth was capable of he was a nerdy Goth with an arrogant attitude and few friends, and he'd had a lot of the attitude in junior high, too. But if it went all the way back to preschool, Seth's cold refusal to want Dave anywhere near him made a lot more sense.

"I think I just had this conversation with Karen and Alex. But you're right. Friends and family are a vulnerability—and Karen made the point that they are vulnerable if they don't know what's going on or who can help them. I think she's right. We need to come a bit out of the shadows to some people."

"And…?" she said, barely daring to hope.

"That includes boyfriends and girlfriends. And those who are… special. Hello Rachel." Rachel had come up to them quietly on her bike. Like most of her clothing recently, she'd abandoned the oversized shirt and cargo pants for a tight t-shirt and designer jeans. The shirt was dark red with black letters proclaiming that Buffy had staked Edward.

"I sensed your presence, my lord. What can I do to help you?"

"My lord?" Angela asked. "Since when are you a lord? And that was an almost worshipful tone." She remained invisible, even inaudible to Rachel.

"It's how Rachel has addressed me ever since we adjusted her vampirism."

Rachel cocked her head. "You are speaking to someone else, obviously someone of power since I can't see, hear, or smell them. May I know to whom you are speaking?"

Angela dropped her invisibility for Rachel. "Hi Rachel. What's with the reverence?"

Rachel inclined her head. "He saved me. He restored me to myself. He has ultimate power over me. I am nothing without him. Why should I not treat him with utmost respect?"

"There's respect and there's talking about and to him as if he's a living god."

The vampire gestured to her crucifix. "The difference between your lord and savior and mine is that I can see and touch mine." Angela was about to open her mouth to respond when she caught the quickly quashed surge in Seth's emotions and grinned.

"You know that irritates him, right?"

Rachel gave her a saucy grin of her own. "Of course! That's the fun of it. But I reside—I don't really live anymore—just a few houses down, so I heard the dogs. What's up, and how can I help?"

Angela shook herself briefly. Rachel had been very quiet and withdrawn before her vampirism. This confident, irreverent girl was nothing like that. But Karen had described her eyes when she looked at Seth perfectly—desire and devotion, mixed with a terrible fear. She knew exactly how much control Seth had over her, and he terrified her. "We're looking for Dave. I got a message from him that he was being taken by wizards, and they're blocking my location of him."

"He's not been here for some time. If he was taken, it wasn't from home."

"You're sure?"

"His blood smells very tasty."

"Don't you dare eat him!"

"I am forbidden to feed from the living. If I want blood I need to get it from a blood bank." She pouted a bit in Seth's direction.

"I didn't make any exceptions to that rule. The modifications we made to her will let her get the sustenance she needs from ordinary food."

"The cravings are still there, but I can handle them. I just like my steak rare now." She stood and sniffed the air. "I will probably be able to find him if we're close enough."

Angela didn't bother glancing at Seth; the skull wouldn't show anything. She reached out with her mind. *<Should we bring her along? They'll be expecting me, they can't really count any of you guys out, but Rachel would be a surprise.>*

<I'm concerned about how that much activity would affect her—she'll run through the blood and need it replaced the more she draws on her supernatural abilities—but it's a good idea.>

"Come along then, Rachel.

Tracking them took a long time. The magically obscured traces were harder to pick up than they expected; it took all night. They heard incoming messages from the others all over the county and out to sea; they came together and separated as events dictated. But even with Rachel's help, finding the trail was difficult at best. But they kept looking and scanning for his brain and blood. They finally found a large old house bristling with magical defenses and they paused to observe it. They could take the house, not a problem. The difficulty was in getting Dave out alive. And they'd probably notice as the protective spells died. "Do we do this the easy way or the hard way?" Seth asked her.

"What's the difference?" Rachel wanted to know.

"The easy way is to just kill everyone inside. We can bring the innocents back to life afterwards."

"I'd really rather not do it that way. They've probably got defenses up, so you'd kill the innocents but leave them alive to fight."

"Your mission, your lead, your call. And you're worried I'll find leaving Dave dead too tempting," his deadpan said calmly.

"There is that," she replied just as calmly. "How about…"

The early morning light started coming in through the windows. Dave was blinded by the rising sun, His guards had questioned him repeatedly in the night and not let him sleep. Oddly enough, he heard the dogs barking. A knock came at the door. He couldn't tell what his captors said to each other; they were speaking French. But who the hell could that be at this hour? And at the side door to the empty garage?

"Is David here?" asked a girl's voice. It was sort of familiar…Rachel? Then the hounds began baying, Angela manifested in all her glory, and Death rode through the door to a bell tolling. The guys with guns were pinned down by the dogs or Rachel broke their necks. Their leaders or employers or whatever fell to a swing of the scythe and a sudden burst of fire. Death's gaze swung to the others and they stopped resisting the big black dogs. The fight was over and it had taken just a few seconds. Dave swallowed at just how quickly that had happened as the bells fell silent. Whatever their defenses were, they weren't good enough…and he didn't have any. The bonds holding him to the chair disintegrated under Angela's gaze.

Dave got shakily to his feet to embrace Angela. Then he slowly, painfully, fell to his knees in front of the mounted figure in black.

The big black hounds surrounded them, sitting in a precise circle. The zombies came stiffly to attention. Rachel leaned against the pale horse. "Thank you, Seth." The empty eye sockets seemed to focus intently on him.

"Before you wipe my mind or kill me or whatever it is you're going to do, please, let me say this." He waited, but the black robed skeleton made no move and said nothing. Angela nodded encouragingly at him. "I know I've been an asshole. I'm not asking you to forgive and forget. I don't know how Ange persuaded you to help rescue me. I owe you more than I'll ever be able to repay. I'm only asking…begging…for you to let us start again. Let me do what I can to help Angela. Let me have open discussions with her. Please, Seth."

"So I can't eat him?" Rachel asked plaintively.

"I know Seth's a lot scarier to you than I am, Rachel, but no, you can't eat him." Angela was, oddly enough, amused.

"Huh?" Then Rachel opened her mouth and displayed fangs. Vampire fangs. Shit, she was a vampire! Dave started back. The girls smiled. He guessed Seth did, too, but the skull made it hard to be sure.

"I think we'll need to talk once the emergencies are over," Seth said. "Rachel?" he extended a hand for her to take, pulling her up behind him on the horse, and they disappeared into swirling blackness, the hounds baying as they began the hunt. That bell began tolling again to announce Death's impending arrival. Angela grabbed Dave, pulled him in tight for a kiss, and they were in the Seamount.

"Sorry. We need to move fast. The others have been stopping one little attack after another all night, and with us rescuing you the fighting's still going on. We surprised them here; they were relying on concealment. Seth and Rachel are reinforcing Alex. Karen's helping Keisha. Solly's pinned down behind his defenses and needs my help. You'll be safe here."

"Wait a minute. Rachel's a vampire?!"

"Later. I need to go." She spoke in Ainu to appear at the Nest. She announced her presence with a burst of nitrogen plasma. The attackers melted; the animated steel and plastic was no match for that sort of heat.

"Hi Ange. Thanks." The practitioners powering the drones took one look at her angry angel appearance and fled as fast as they could. She and Solly teleported them to Hell. "Do you think we should go after them?"

"Who's we? You were sheltering behind your defenses."

He shrugged. "Defensive magic is what I'm best at. I'd have gotten them to Hell in the end."

"You sure about that? It's filling up fast. We may not have an option but to kill."

"I get you. We may need another prison, but we don't have time to build it tonight. Stick it on Pluto?"

"That works. The frigid hell."

"The FRIGID HELL!" she said back at him, laughing.

"Catalina!" He vanished. She dashed off to the Church, where Mother Elaine had just arrived…to gunmen instead of the janitors. The intense heat of the nitrogen plasma she brought to bear on the practitioner with the gunmen only slowly beat down his defenses, cracking the stone and igniting wood. But like many of the attackers he'd tired himself out on other defenses. The plasma broke through and incinerated him. The gunmen fled as Angela turned her gaze to them. She'd decide what to feel…later. She nodded to Mother Elaine and was off to protect Dani's place.

Karen arrived at Stacey's place invisible. Last night had been her big debut in costume, filmy pink silks tightly wound around her and a bow in her hands, and the day wasn't over yet. A pink halo surrounded her. They'd already gotten into the still dark house; she'd mentioned at practice her parents were out of town. Naturally, she wouldn't be awake yet.

<I'm free at the moment. Anyone need us? Shevaun, Julian, Karen?> Seth said telepathically.

<I'm fine. I'm with Dawn,> Shevaun said.

<Malcolm came to help me out. We're at his grandparents' place in the City.>

<What makes you think I need help?> she demanded.

<You've never been in one of these fights before. You're a pretty gentle person. We're available if you need us.> She dimly sensed his power gather and he was in a new location.

The practitioner attacking Stacey hadn't expected to meet the goddess of love in the darkness of the barely dawn. Stacey looked at her in astonishment as she put an arrow into him. "Are you injured, Miss O'Brien?" She was wearing only an oversized shirt that hung halfway down her shins.

"Ah, no, thank you, ah, WHO ARE YOU?" Karen winked at her. *<I've got one of them snoozing at my feet. Any ideas what to do with him?>*

<We'll handle it.> Seth said immediately. That meant he would kill the bad guy.

<Seth…>

<Karen. Hell is full. We have no place to put them that doesn't put innocents at risk. This is my task, not yours.>

<Stacey will recognize you, or Rachel if not you. She's not wearing a disguise.> She paused, appalled at herself. She'd gone from objecting that it was wrong to kill to objecting to Seth doing it because he or Rachel would be recognized in a fraction of a second. What was wrong with her?

"Thank you, whoever you are," Stacey said. "Can I help with something?"

"I'm arguing with Death over what to do with him. Tartarus isn't finished yet." The attacker's body vanished.

<I said I would do all I could to keep you from facing that. I put him in a persistent vegetative state in a highly equipped hospital. In Irkutsk.>

<Thank you.> She waved at Stacey and vanished to where Coach Nguyen lived. She got there too late. He was dead in a dozen pieces.

<Now what?>

<His body's already been seen by his neighbors. We don't help him now. Move on. The body will keep. It's almost seven.> Jenny said.

<A little help, Karen?> Teddy asked.

Angela turned the rock her enemy was standing on to lava as her phone started chiming. She ignored it, concentrating on the two wizards who'd been trying to get into Dani's home. She knew Dani herself was safe in the Temple—Alex had given her a bracelet enchanted to let her teleport—but these two had come after her parents and brother. Fortunately Alex had set up powerful defenses, but he was off protecting his own family at the zoo overnight. Her enemies' defenses were pitifully weak compared to what she or one of her friends could do, but they still managed to attenuate her attacks.

Faced with the power she had and caught up against Alex's defenses, the wizards fled. But they couldn't teleport. The minor practitioners seemed to have a much more restricted set of mastered powers, and precisely what they were varied individually as she'd battled them all morning. The wizard she'd just attacked knew enough to get herself out of the lava with little more than smoking shoes.

Nitrogen plasma erupted around the other, and her defenses simply weren't up to the temperatures plasma reached. A little boy came down the street with his backpack and lunch box. The practitioner grabbed him as a hostage. She shouted something in Swahili.

Angela shrugged. She didn't have to use plasma. The nitrogen in the woman's lungs turned solid, freezing her from the inside out. As her grip on the boy slackened, Angela said, "Run along to school. I'm not going to hurt you."

"Yes, Angel Lady!"

Angela met up with Seth and the others outside Keisha's home; it was the last place that had come under direct attack. With Julian, Shevaun, and Rachel there were fourteen of them, and they made short work of the attackers. Rachel's fangs were out and she was obviously exhausted when Seth grabbed her arm. "Let's get you some food, Rachel. Before you go looking for a snack."

"Seth, before you go, Bridget suggested talking to you…"

"Is lunch soon enough, Angela? Rachel's desperate to sink her fangs into someone, and she can't under the limits. Which means she'll kill someone with her fists or a gun and drink from the corpse if I don't get some blood in her."

"Oh, yeah. Get her stable."

Chapter

Dave had never been the only person in the Seamount for so long. He knew Angela's password on the computer and browsed online for a while. He was frustrated in not being able to find anything on what was going on; no news sites had anything. When Angela returned hours later, her hair was all over the place and sweat was making her clothes cling to her. Her shirt was bloody, and the smell of smoke—from wood, from plastic, from bodies—still rose from her. Her bra showed through tears in her shirt and her pants were charred in a few places. Soot smudged her face and arms. She looked awesome.

"Finally," she said. "Playing whack-a-mole all night. They even tried breaching Dawn's home defenses, not that that worked. But cleaning up the self-cremated took a while."

Dave got up and handed her the cold orange drink. "That bad?"

"Yeah. That bad. We left at least fifty corpses, and that doesn't even count the idiots who tried to breach the Temple or failed trying to breach some of our homes. Or the draftees. I think we got them cleaned up, but techniques Seth taught us should make it look like they died of natural causes."

"You probably won't answer this, but Dawn's part of the group? With Seth that pretty much means the Round Table."

She downed the bottle of orange soda in one long drink. "Whether she's more destructive or I am is open to debate. I manipulate elements—as in the periodic table. While a lot of what she does is chemical, her interest in astronomy means she plays with singularities. The idiots who faced Seth joined his zombie horde; he's got them stashed off world somewhere. Dave, how in do you want to be?"

"What do you mean?"

"If you want in—I'll quit talking in riddles, euphemisms, obfuscations, and prevarications, I'll actually answer your questions, you'll get to see the communal areas, know who else is involved on our end—we can do that now. I'll have to set up privacy screens if we're going to talk about things outside of the secure areas, or see if I can pass you a language. We can pass them to each other, although Dani's still not as fluent as I'd expect in Nahuatl if Alex had given her the language that way. But you'll be signing up for a fight."

"And Seth's okay with that?"

She shrugged slightly. "You're not the only person we're bringing in. Rachel, for one, will be fully on board, and yeah, she's a vampire. Safely under Seth's control, but a vampire. And yeah, I mean control. She will obey him. Those that haven't told their parents yet are telling them now, except for Teddy. This was an attack on our friends and family. They need to know who else they can call on, but his family can't handle it. If you want in, there's a meeting on Venus in… fifteen minutes. I dropped by home to check on my parents' safety to find Seth had already ridden through with bells tolling and hounds baying, and he drafted a couple more of our enemies into his zombie army. They were fine—freaked, but fine."

"Drafted…"

She shrugged. She had to get this through to Dave now that she had the chance. "He made the most corpses and left none behind. He sees no reason not to zombify our enemies once they're dead. But more important…Seth isn't just dangerous. He's lethal. He's a necromancer. His power comes from death, and he's the most deadly person on the planet. He has to deliberately pull back to not kill someone, and pulling back that way is hard to do when you're furious or desperate. He kills reflexively. If he didn't have the self-control he's got, he'd have killed most of the football team two years ago, simply out of irritation. We all know how to kill with our power. He won't hesitate. Pissing off Seth that far isn't dangerous; it's suicidal. If he decides to kill, Karen's the only person that can keep it from happening. That's what got Alex to intervene with that big speech. If Seth had started defending himself, he'd have left the people bullying him dead. When we took that ship, after the one wizard fled and the other died he killed the entire rest of the guards and crew in an instant. Almost a hundred people. You're going to be interacting with him fairly often. Even though he's dropped his veto, he still doesn't like you. He dropped it to cover you as a vulnerability for me. Be polite."

"How can Karen stop him? I thought you told me you guys were supreme in your focuses. Which would make him supreme in death. No one can resurrect those he kills, right? No one can stop him from killing?"

"That's the power of love. He'll stay his hand for her when he wouldn't for anyone else."

"I get it. How many wizards are there?"

"On the planet? A thousand or so, maybe less. After Seth got through with our attackers, I'd bet on 'less' now. And they burned through a lot of the devices they'd made over the decades."

"I'm in, baby." He held out his hand. She took it and teleported them to her room at the Temple.

The elder MacLeods looked up stiffly from the chairs they were sleeping in as she, Seth, and Rachel appeared out of mid air. "Greetings. Rachel, you're dead on your feet. Excuse us, I need to get some sustenance into her before her hunger overtakes her." He was holding her arm loosely.

"Come on everyone over here," Karen called out to them in a tired tone.

"But..."

"NOW, Katie! Seth's got her under tight control, but her vampirism is still there, and she's very, very hungry!" Her eyes widened and she dropped the book as she scampered to Karen's side. It conveniently put her next to Seth, too, but on the opposite side of him from Rachel. Jimmy was still standing there with a baffled look on his face.

"Va…"

"Before you become a tasty meat snack, Jimmy!" Karen backed her words with power this time, and he joined the circle as the pink swirled around them. Their arrival back in the den was to a seemingly normal place. Karen wiped her forehead and plucked at her sweat-soaked shirt.

"Seth will be okay alone with Rachel?" Mom asked.

"She *can't* do anything to him. Vampirism kills the host as a preliminary, and only a few people realize how accurate the "Lord of the Dead" nickname is. Which means he can do as he wishes with her and she knows it. At the same time, she's desperate for his approval. How much did you fill in for Jimmy?"

"Just the basics."

"Will she be okay with him?" Jimmy asked

"He's offered to cure her whenever she wants. I don't know if that would take away her terror of him or not; he's pretty scary as is and his necromantic emphasis only adds to that. Okay, Jimmy, I'm not going to fill in much more right now. We spent all night beating them down. You're behind my wards now; please, stay here. Call Katie in sick. We think the survivors are in full flight, but we can't be sure of that. Stay here. We've got a meeting on Venus in fifteen minutes. Katie, we'd like you to be there."

"Karen, that's…" Karen's hand went up to stop Dad's negation of the idea.

"She's already proven she can reach Seth in a way no one else can. If they figure it out, Alex is sure that she becomes a target. We need to figure out the best defense for her. And at this point, that means letting her in on who she can count on for support. Besides Seth and I. That memory stone is on Venus, and it's time to give it back to her."

"She's got me," Jimmy said, bristling.

Karen put her hands on his shoulders. "Jimmy, you're our big brother. We love you. We know you're there for us. I remember you walking us to school, helping us with homework, cheering like a lunatic at our soccer games. You don't have the power to get involved. You don't have the training to get involved. At least half of us killed people today. We didn't lose anyone, fortunately, but I don't want to look at your dead body, even if it is only temporary. I don't even want to hear that Seth took care of resurrecting you before I learned about it. Katie and I are already in this. It's my turn to protect you. And that means keeping you out of it. You can help us best if you stay on the sidelines where we don't have to worry about you. Please. I'll fill you in this afternoon."

"Death is temporary?" he looked at her skeptically.

"It is when we're around and Seth's not opposed. I've already died once. I have too much left to do to revive the cow that your belt was made out of, but I'll show you tomorrow. I'll answer your questions later, I promise, but we need to compare notes and we don't have a lot of time this morning. I'll see you later." She sighed, and as she put her hand on Katie's shoulder, she said, "We should have protective devices and panic buttons for you within a few days. Until then be careful." They vanished in a swirl of pink.

"I'm alive." Dave sounded shocked as the teal light faded

She grinned at him. "My will is a pass now. Give me a moment." With a word and a snap of her fingers, she cleaned herself up and was wearing a teal robe. Even her hair was washed like she'd just come out of the shower.

"Looks like a graduation robe."

"But a lot more comfortable," she said. It was made of silk, enchanted with warmth and softness, and her clothes were repaired and under it.

"Oh. So who else is here?"

"I think you'll recognize most of them. Oh, to prevent exclamations of surprise and shock and stuff, we're letting everyone who knows him that one of them is Mike Wu. That won't mean much to Katie and Charles, but it will to everyone else."

"He's dead."

"So were Karen and I," she reminded him. "Seth holds life and death in his hands, never forget that. Just because someone has died doesn't mean anything if Seth decides he wants them alive. He hasn't revived anyone famous, but he can. Mike's the only person he's revived who's publicly known to be dead…and he stays here on Venus unless he's with one of us and in disguise. We haven't even told his family."

"I guess that makes Keisha one of you too, or he wouldn't have bothered restoring Mike. They weren't enemies, but they weren't really friends, either."

She nodded. "You're right about us being the Wizards of the Round Table. Julian and Shevaun are still learning to control their abilities, but the full members are me, Seth, Alex, Bridget, Dawn, Teddy, Jennifer, Malcolm, Solly, Keisha, and Karen. Karen finished her training this year."

"What about Dani?" he asked as they headed towards the big council room.

"She, like Mike and anyone else here I didn't just name, is an associate. That includes you. We make the distinction on power. You can't get here on your own, and nothing you do can give you the ability to do so. Bridget and Jennifer still haven't identified whatever the condition we have is that gives us our abilities. One of us has to bring you, or give you a device that will get you here."

"Oh, right, you explained something like that before."

"While we're on the subject of devices, it's better to enchant things you'll wear every day. Like a watch. Or a neck chain." She looked at him pointedly.

"Okay, okay, I get it now. You were trying to protect me with that stuff. But why was it always metal? I mean, a shell necklace from Hawaii would have been much more my style!" She cocked her head at him. "Seth can control shells, can't he? A shell necklace would have been putting a noose around my neck?" She nodded.

"We can't actually make anyone use her power, or not use it. Enough of us can restrain someone, but that's only good as long as we're actively maintaining it. We can keep it up long enough to calm them down and talk them out of it, but if they're determined to do it anyway they will. Seth's saying he wouldn't kill you was something we couldn't actually do anything to enforce, but demanding it was a severe breach. Getting you to stay away from him was the price I had to pay to him to seal a bargain.

"While we're on the subject and I can speak freely…"

"Antagonizing any of the full members is about the dumbest thing I can do. And especially Seth. I'm not *that* stupid."

"Got it in one, baby. He's not going to kill you—he's agreed to that—but that won't stop him from making you do a striptease in front of the entire school or something else you'd find embarrassing. Although that could be really entertaining."

"If you want me to strip for you, babe, all you have to do is say so."

"I know." He grinned at her. "Not the point, sweetie."

"I know," he said. "I'll follow your lead."

"Good. Come with me."

Chapter

41

"So now we know." All thirteen of them were gathered in the Temple. Dani, Mike, Dave, Jasmine, Charles, Rachel, Carmen, and Caitlin had joined them. "The practitioners on Earth are coming together to protect their power and influence," Julian summed it up.

"They don't want to step into the public eye. Someone who knows what they're facing or can catch them by surprise can still take them," Alex said. "And modern weaponry severely taxes the defenses they can put together. I think we're still good, though."

"We don't really want to step into the public awareness just now, either," Malcolm said. "We're planning on doing it eventually, but we're not there yet. There are too many people we care about who could be targeted if we do."

"Even when we do come into the open with what we can do, we're still talking about whether to really reveal who we are. It's just about an even split, and we'd need unanimity to actually do that. We're nowhere near that, though." Bridget said.

"They've got more experience. But based on the ones we've faced we're still more powerful than they are. A LOT more powerful." Jennifer was definite. "One on one, they can overwhelm a normal person. Large groups—mobs with pitchforks—are a bit much for them, but any of us could handle that mob in seconds. One of us can overwhelm one of them as easily as they can overwhelm a normal person. Their strongest defenses would not hold—now—against Seth deciding one of them needed to die, for example."

"Have you figured out why yet?" Keisha said. She was holding hands with Mike.

"Not quite. We're operating on a different level of power from them. But… I think we can start teaching some stuff to you guys," she said, nodding at the others. "I don't think you're ever going to approach our power levels, though. It's going to be a lot more formulaic than what we do, I'm afraid."

"What do you want me to do?" Rachel asked. Her glass was full of something thick and red.

"Rachel, you're the next strongest, true. At the same time, I'd rather not expose you to too much temptation or exertion," Malcolm said. The other wizards muttered agreement. "You start to get dangerous to others if you're low, and we're not entirely sure what happens to you if you violate the restrictions Seth put on you." Jenny cocked an eyebrow.

"Alex, do you have one of those sports bottles you don't need anymore?" Jennifer asked. He pulled one out of thin air and tossed it to her. She concentrated, spoke in Cornish, and passed the heavy bottle over to Rachel. "That should give you what you need, but try not to get it confiscated. Its contents would be hard to explain."

"That's a mild way to put it, but thank you. Oh, it's warm." The heft didn't seem to bother her.

"Why?" Carmen asked. "What's in it?"

"Blood, I think," Katie answered. "I'm just glad she's gotten over the desire to drink mine."

"But back to my question?"

"We're not entirely sure, Rachel. At the moment it's more a matter of being aware of each other. We just killed several of them, and the survivors fled with the best hiding they could do. They don't want us coming after them," Alex said.

"Killed?" Carmen paled. "Blood?" Charles' eyes were wide and Jasmine was looking a little shocked.

"Killed. What is it you think I *do*, Carmen?" Seth asked.

"Be nice, Seth," Bridget said. "Some of this is coming at them fairly cold."

"Okay. A few months ago a vampire turned Rachel. Karen and I destroyed that vampire. Rachel didn't want to be entirely cured, though. Bridget and I restored her humanity enough for a maintenance level, but when she calls on the abilities her vampirism gives her she burns through the blood quickly." Seth gestured at the bottle. "That will provide her the blood she needs without her needing to feed from someone." Rachel's smile showed her fangs. Charles and Jasmine edged away from her.

"Relax," she said. "I'm not hungry. My Lord would obliterate me in a second if I started preying on others."

"That is disturbingly creepy," Jasmine said.

"Yeah, and it bugs the hell out of him at the same time," Rachel said with a grin. Then she sobered. "Although...it's also an accurate description. I continue to exist as I am on his mercy. You know what these guys can do with a word? He doesn't need the word when it comes to me."

"And you're okay with that?"

Rachel nodded. "He finishes the resurrection whenever I say so. But I kind of like the parts of it that I'm keeping. So...it's a deal. They're not going to let a magical plague carrier—what the botched transferable immortality spell made me—run around without restraint." She shrugged. "Don't worry about me. I'm fine with it. It's a lot safer for you guys than where I was. And I think he would simply finish the resurrection rather than actually obliterate me."

"I've been thinking on it. Let me get with Alex for a day or so and we should have something that will let you resurrect yourself," Seth said.

"Well, then, can we get back to the killings?"

"We don't always have the luxury of taking prisoners, Carmen," Dawn said. "We filled up Hell fairly fast today."

"Hell? Really? Come on, Hell doesn't exist..." Charles protested.

"Neither do vampires, and you're sitting right next to one," Katie pointed out.

"Hell, in this instance, refers to a prison we made a few months ago," Teddy said. "It seemed preferable to killing them, but it doesn't automatically expand in size. It's the only capital-H Hell that exists."

"We'll have to work on that," Julian said.

"What happens if someone breaches it?" Carmen wanted to know.

"The spells holding it together fail and the mantle rushes in," Teddy said. He shrugged. "I'm not sure it could be breached, but we built in a failsafe. I see that bothers you."

"That…and it's a little weird to hear you like this."

"I could babble about god if you want me to, but here I'd rather be me. Also, I'm too tired to ramble about that nonsense. Making my family forget what they saw when they came for me was a bit much."

"This all sounds really dangerous," Carmen said.

"Probably," Mike agreed cheerfully.

"I am glad you are so unconcerned about our possible deaths back on Earth, Mike," Jasmine shot at him.

"You misunderstand, Jas. You're currently sitting at a table with four people who've died, and only Rachel technically still is dead. I'm still legally dead, of course. I've even visited my own grave with Keisha."

"Death is a minor inconvenience to our friends here…" Katie put in, trailing off as Seth's gaze turned to her.

"I don't get it."

"If you're killed in this, you will be restored to life," Seth said quietly.

"Even me?" Dave asked in the tone of someone who wanted to be absolutely sure about something.

"I don't like you, Dave. And I probably wouldn't handle you personally. But I won't stand in the way of Angela or anyone else bringing you back."

"I'm still confused," Charles said.

Seth looked quizzically at Dawn. "How much have you told him?"

"Not much. He is kind of new. I was enjoying having a normal romance with him. I hadn't even told him about me before today, not until the attacks started and I needed to get him to safety. His first actual experiences with magic were me not letting go and when I teleported him to Sunholme."

"Okay. I'll give you a quick answer, Charles, and let Dawn fill you in. If a full voting member says she can do something, she can. The nicknames you may have heard us use among ourselves are actually indicative of the specialties of our power," Bridget said. "I'm Gaia or Artemis, for example."

Charles started to ask another question when Dawn laid a hand on his arm. "I'll answer all your questions a bit later, Charles, but for now let it be. If I can't answer them, we can ask one of the others." He looked rebellious. Seth looked frustrated.

"If I introduce you to the pig you just ate, will that work?"

"Oh, come on…" Seth's blackness swirled out and they watched a piece of Canadian bacon that had somehow escaped his Hawaiian pizza swell into a huge, grunting boar. Charles froze as the pig sniffed at him. It was bigger than he was.

"Um, guys, it seems to be bearing a bit of a grudge…"

"I notice you didn't castrate him," Karen said.

Seth shrugged. "Why bother? When working from a small piece, it's easier not to leave out anything."

"Wouldn't the hormones in the meat be a guide?" Karen asked

"I can work with a fossil, Karen. What makes you think the magic's using the hormones?" Her brows rose in acknowledgement of his point.

"Can somebody do something about this pig?" Charles said as the boar continued snuffling at him.

"Oh, sure," Bridget said. The boar turned away from Charles to snooze comfortably at her feet.

"Bridget, do you have a plan for him?" Keisha asked

"Not really. His genetics are too fixed for him to be anything but a domestic pig, so I wouldn't release him even if there was a place to."

"Mind if I deal with him?" Bridget shook her head, so Keisha spoke a word in Cushitic and the pig vanished.

"Where'd you send it?" Mike asked.

"There's a village I came across in South America that can use a pig like that."

"Satisfied?" Seth asked Charles pointedly.

"But that's a pig, not a person…" he said weakly.

"The distinction between animal and human exists only in the fuzzy self-important philosophizing of humans. Or do I need to bring in an australopithecine?" He still seemed to want to argue.

"Have YOU ever brought some body back from the dead, Charles?" Katie asked. "Then maybe we should listen to the person who has and knows what he's talking about." Rachel nodded agreement as she parted her lips. Charles inclined his head in acknowledgement of her point and dropped the argument.

"Any way," Dani started, "as Rachel was asking, what is it you guys are really wanting us to do?"

"Keep your eyes and ears open, mostly," Julian said. "I'm not in their league yet, but if we can get them the info on where to apply their power they can handle it."

Jennifer nodded. "We need to know where to go and what to look at. I've got an idea of what to do about them, but it's going to take a while to work out what I need to do to pull it off. Seth, Karen, Bridget, can you be on that with me? Until then it's Whack-a-Mole."

Keisha nodded. "I can get the most out of a divination, but if I don't know the right questions, or have the trip wires in the right places, it's less helpful."

"We'll get you guys devices to let you get in touch with us and provide at least some initial protection until we can get to you. And maybe beam-out of the danger. I hope you like watches," Alex said.

"Why watches?"

"They're innocuous. We might use our phones more, but no one really notices a wristwatch on anyone," Keisha said. "Whereas a lot of guys don't really do jewelry, or do a minimal amount. Alex, what's enchanted on the jewelry Dani's wearing?" Dani, as usual, was almost dripping with jewelry.

"All of it."

"It's amazing that you didn't have to examine her to say that," Rachel said.

Dani chuckled. "I've known about Alex since freshman year, and a lot of the stuff I've got he gave to me, already enchanted. Then he went through my jewelry box and enhanced everything he found. Or if I got something else he enchanted that soon after I got it. They do some sort of magic detection spell and I light up like a Christmas tree. Same with my football pads."

"What does it do?" Carmen wanted to know.

"Protection, mostly. Enhancing healing of injury. Automatic translation, though that gets inactivated during class or a test. Prevention of disease. And birth control," Alex said with a shrug. "Enchanting is what I do, Carmen."

"And you put it all on her?"

"Of course not. What I'm wearing does everything hers does, and more besides. I've got easy access to my clothes, so I enchanted those, too. I'm more likely to go into magical combat. I'd have enchanted hers, too, but her parents have a thing about an open door while I'm over."

"In the interests of providing what we can now, Bridget, Keisha?" Seth said. They began a complex, interwoven casting that settled on the others.

"What'd they just do?"

"If any of you die it will alert the three of them," Shevaun said. "If you die obviously in public, chances are you'll be revived here or on Mars," Julian said. "Mike's here because he died on camera and there was no way to cover it up. We're not ready to go public yet."

"Is it time to give me a disguise yet and let me go back to Earth?"

"Let's discuss that after Teddy, Keisha, and I have gotten some sleep," Solly said. "We don't have to get anyone back home, so we might sack out here."

"Next up are our names. Some of you know some of them. We're attuned to them, so you'll get our attention if you use them," Jennifer said.

"Anyone using the secret names gets our attention, so please be careful who hears them," Teddy said.

"So who are you?" Jasmine asked.

Julian concentrated for a moment and said something in Hawaiian. "Now you know all of us." He grimaced and shook his head. "That took more than I was expecting, but it wasn't hard."

"For you, maybe," Shevaun said. "I'd be out cold after trying that!" The associates were marveling at the information that had just poured into their minds and weren't paying attention to the apprentices.

"Oh, wow," Carmen said. "I just need to think of the person and the other name comes up too—and how to pronounce it. Wow."

Jennifer smiled. "We've almost lost that sense of wonder, we do this so much."

"One thing," Seth said. "You don't have our power. Be careful. What we'll be teaching you to do, and the protections we'll be providing you, aren't intended for you to go toe to toe with the bad guys. It's intended to keep you alive long enough for us to get help to you. Don't hesitate to get word to us."

Alex nodded in agreement. "We don't have to show up to get you help as long as we know where you are, so we may simply project the help if that's all that seems necessary."

Jennifer spoke up. "I'm not sure how much we'll be able to teach you, but that's going to primarily be my job. I'm sure the rest of us will answer any questions you may have, but since I seem to have the easiest time crossing over, we think I'm best suited to devising and teaching a general curriculum."

"Um, I have a confession. I haven't told my parents yet," Shevaun said. "Dad's still on location for that next movie and hasn't been home much."

Alex heaved a sigh. "Teddy hasn't either, but that's because they couldn't handle the truth."

"I think they could handle it. I just haven't found the time, especially with Dad doing that movie."

"Targeting a public figure like your dad might be too much exposure for them, but we'll keep an eye on him and some spells. If you can get Solly and me a set visit, we'll put up trip wires and the strongest defenses we can for him. Maybe you can just tell your mom? She's not usually on location, is she?" Keisha said.

"She's visiting the set this week with Josie and Dirk."

"Nine. Think we can get to all nine places tomorrow with protections?"

"We'll split up. I'll fine-tune everything. It won't be as tough as our homes or safe houses, but it should work, especially with built in alarms," Solly said. "We've been layering those for years. The attack here fed them to the Venusian atmosphere with Keisha and Mike barely knowing it had happened."

"Eight," Karen said. "Katie lives behind my wards."

"We should probably strengthen everybody's defenses," Alex said. Teddy nodded. "Let's get the most vulnerable first, though. No one's likely to penetrate Solly's, and only someone on a suicide mission is going to try to penetrate Seth's."

"That's a point, Karen, but until August she's not going to the same school. And while it's fairly likely she'll reach out to me again, let's not count on that. We should erect some defenses at her school, too," Seth said after considering. "Someone launching an attack at our school, with all of us there and able to respond, would be defeated quickly. After Shevaun and Julian are fully trained, that's thirteen of us."

"I've got an idea," Mike said. "How about disguising me as a middle school janitor for a few weeks? It wouldn't be as good as one of you, but I could reinforce Katie, and there'd be someone else able to get off a distress call."

"I don't need…" Katie started.

"You do need the back up, Katie. However unwilling they are to confront more than two of us at once, we all need back up at times," Karen said, and shot a quick thought to Seth. Katie would listen to him, if no one else. He nodded.

"Caitlin, sometimes the back up that's really needed is nothing more than a witness or some sort of authority figure, both of which Mike can supply in a janitor's role. It's a lot better than me projecting power to kill someone if that's not what's needed. You'll see next year that we defuse a lot of situations just by showing up. Mostly so someone can intervene before I get pissed off enough to kill, but it works for all of us. We've stopped Bridget from turning certain offensive people into various animals more than once. And just as they can't restore someone I kill, we can't switch back someone she transforms."

"Back to defenses," Dawn said. "Angela and I have defenses almost as nasty as Seth's and they still tried to penetrate mine."

"Sexist stupidity?" Malcolm asked. She looked at him. "As deadly as you are, you're also one of the nicest of us, most generous, most restrained when it comes to reaching for the rough stuff. More than anyone else, you used Hell as an option. They might not have been prepared to believe that you'd reach for dangerous magic."

Keisha and Karen looked at each other and nodded. "From someone looking outside in, they probably rate Seth as the nastiest, then Angela."

"What do you mean 'almost as nasty'?" Charles asked. "Isn't he the resurrection guy?"

"His abilities are focused on either side of the death barrier," Keisha shrugged. "His defenses kill outright. Dangerous as the rest of us are, someone trying to enter an area we protected has the opportunity to decide it's a really bad idea and stop. Seth's defenses kill without warning. Electronics, too. It's rather brutally effective. I don't recommend trying to enter one of our domains without our permission."

"Is that everything? 'Cause school starts in ten minutes."

www.ingramcontent.com/pod-product-compliance
Lightning Source LLC
Chambersburg PA
CBHW020058310726
48970CB00002B/370